"YOU'RE GOING TO BE A
TOUGH ONE TO KILL!"

After the excruciating torture, Emily was still conscious and full of fight when her husband John began trying to strangle her with his hands. She fought like a tiger, kicking her legs, squirming and pulling at the duct tape around her wrists until she finally freed herself. Then she began ripping at the strong hands gripping her throat, scratching and twisting at his fingers.

Suddenly, he released her, brutally grabbed her long hair and began dragging her through the underbrush, deeper into the woods. He stopped and threw her to the ground. Emily's eyes were taped shut and she couldn't see what was next. There was a slight pause before he started to smash her in the head with the flat end of a metal shovel.

He beat her dozens of times, but every time he knocked her down, somehow she pulled herself back up. Waves of unbearable pain washed over her from the battering, the slashes, the punctures, the burns, yet still she endured, clinging to the only thing she had left: her life.

DEADLY OBSESSIONS

CLIFFORD L. LINEDECKER and DR. FRANK M. OSANKA

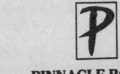

PINNACLE BOOKS
WINDSOR PUBLISHING CORP.

The names of some people in this story have been changed to protect their privacy. Fictitious names appear in italics at the time of their first appearance.

PINNACLE BOOKS are published by

Windsor Publishing Corp.
850 Third Avenue
New York, NY 10022

The P logo Reg U.S. Pat. & TM Off. Pinnacle is a trademark of Windsor Publishing Corp.

First Printing: March, 1995

Printed in the United States of America

To Carla,
And to those who love her.

Acknowledgments

The authors are indebted to many people for their kind cooperation and contributions to the preparation and accuracy of this book.

Police officers, attorneys, employees of the Price County Court Clerk's Office and the Legal Services Division of the Wisconsin State Attorney General's Office have all generously drawn from their time and talents to assist the authors with their research.

Several private citizens in Phillips shared information and anecdotes that were of invaluable help in clearing up troubling inconsistencies, while providing important background and color that greatly enhance the readability of the story.

Thanks also go to our editor at Pinnacle Books, Paul Dinas, for his support, his input, and for his patience while we were fighting a difficult deadline. Mary Jo Kewley, who reported on the case for the *Wausau Daily Herald,* is also deserving of a big thank-you for providing an insider's look at some of the events and personalities at the trial.

Special thanks, however, are due to Judith M. Hartig-Osanka. Her gracious assistance sharing her contacts and knowledge, was vital to our research and a critical factor leading to the successful preparation of the manuscript.

CONTENTS

Introduction

Wisconsin is a state of dairy farms, glacier-gouged lakes and ravines, and deep woods, whose largest city, Milwaukee, is home to fewer than one million people.

Despite its largely rural population, middle-American values, and relatively low crime rate, somehow the Badger State has been the scene in recent years of a mind-numbing number of heinous crimes involving dismemberment, necrophilia, and cannibalism.

For more than three decades Wisconsin's most notorious criminal was a tragic madman and cannibal who murdered at least two neighbor women, robbed the graves of others, and used body parts as food, sex toys, and gruesome household kitchen implements and decorations.

Edward Gein's crimes were so shocking and his psychopathology so intriguing that he became the model for Norman Bates in author Robert Bloch's famous novel, *Psycho,* and the blockbuster Alfred Hitchcock movie of the same name.

A couple of decades later, the main character in the horror movie classic *The Texas Chain Saw Massacre* and its spin-offs, exhibited much of the same macabre behavior that was practiced by Gein in real life.

Gein was a backwoods bachelor, the son of an authoritarian and fanatically religious mother who taught her two sons that God was about to destroy the world because of rage over "scarlet women" who wore lipstick and paraded in shorts and tight skirts.

His father, a tanner, died in 1940, and his brother, Henry, died suspiciously two years later while fighting a forest fire. In 1945 shortly after his mother died, Gein drove his pickup truck to a local graveyard and dug up the fresh corpse of a woman.

After reburying the empty casket, he returned to his ramshackle home on the outskirts of the rustic town of Plainfield and went to bed with the corpse. The next morning he topped off the experience by slicing a few prime cuts off the body, cooking the flesh and eating it.

Among Gein's other psychosexual hang-ups, he had flirted with the idea of undergoing a sex-change operation, since reading about trailblazing transsexual Christine Jorgensen. But the prospect of flying to Denmark to begin months of interviews and treatment sounded too complicated and expensive, so he fashioned a shirt for himself from the skin of the dead woman's upper body.

After his first foray to the graveyard, Gein began making regular nocturnal trips to the same cemetery and to two others to dig up the bodies of additional women. He scanned the obituary columns of local newspapers in order to keep up on the location of fresh corpses. On at least one occasion he was helped to rob a grave by a feeble-minded companion named Gus, who died a short time later.

Once the corpses were returned to Gein's isolated two-story house, he went to bed with them, then moved them into his woodshed where they were hung up and dressed like fresh venison. Years later sickened neighbors hesitantly recalled that Gein, who was an excellent outdoorsman and hunter, frequently surprised them during deer season with gifts of liver.

In the privacy of his ramshackle farmhouse, he continued to peel the skin from the upper bodies of the corpses he stole, and as The Bitch of Buchenwald had done, tanned and fashioned them into lampshades. He also used the leather for wastebaskets and other household items. Some nights he danced and cavorted outdoors, naked except for a skin vest, complete with sagging breasts. His head was covered with a skin mask and scalp, and human vaginas and labia were strapped over his own genitals.

At some time during the depraved celebration, Gein ran out of fresh cemetery corpses and began to kill. In early December 1954, a fifty-one-year-old woman disappeared from the tavern she managed in the nearby town of Pine Grove. When Mary Hogan vanished, few clues were left behind except for a smear of blood on the floor and one spent .32-caliber cartridge.

It was nearly three-years later, on November 16, 1957, before another woman vanished from the hardware store she managed in Plainfield, and both mysteries rapidly unraveled.

Investigators were quickly led to Gein's farm six miles west of town, where they found the hapless shopkeeper, fifty-eight-year-old Bernice Worden, hanging from a rafter in his shed. Her head was missing, and her intestines and organs had been removed as if her body was the carcass of a deer dressed by a hunter after a kill. Several human skulls, with the crowns cut off at eye level, were on the floor of the shed half-filled with feed for the chickens and cats.

Inside the cluttered and dusty house the horror was multiplied. Sheriff's officers and Wisconsin state troopers discovered a grisly collection of body parts, bones, and skin that were the partial remains of several humans. Mrs. Worden's heart was in a saucepan on the floor next to the potbellied stove.

Her dirt- and blood-smeared head was found stuffed into a feed sack between a pair of dirty matresses in the shed. A pair of ten-penny nails had been driven into both ears, then bent and linked by a length of twine so the skull could be strung up in Gein's bedroom where he could enjoy it along with other trophies. Her entrails were wrapped in a newspaper that was folded and stuffed into an old man's suit.

A box crammed with ten human skulls was pulled from under Gein's bed. Several skin shirts, bones, and other body parts were scattered throughout the house. The legs of chairs had been fashioned from human bones.

Among the most grisly discoveries were human nipples sewed together on a string, and a collection of vaginas. Most of the sexual organs were shrunken and withered, but investigators determined that two of them were from young women who could not have been among the corpses dug up from the cemeteries.

After admitting the murders of the two matrons from Plainfield and Pine Grove, in January 1958, Gein was adjudged insane and sent to the Central State Hospital in Waupun, Wisconsin. Nearly eleven years later he was finally put on trial for one of the slayings, declared innocent by reason of insanity, and shuttled back to the hospital. He remained there under close observation until 1984 when he died a natural death.

In the meantime the creepy necrophile became a sinister legend in central Wisconsin, and many children grew up on stories about the real-life bogeyman who robbed graves, defiled corpses, murdered and feasted on his neighbors. In school yards and playgrounds, they shared dark-humored jokes known as "Geiners" about the Wisconsin cannibal who was such an integral and frightening part of local lore.

Seven years after Gein's death, his degradations were publicly recalled in newspaper stories and on radio and television when a German emigrant was charged with the grisly sex murder and dismemberment of a young man who disappeared while collecting donations in rural Racine county for an environmental group.

Twenty-four-year-old James Michael Madden of Whitefish Bay disappeared on June 27, 1990, and parts of his body began showing up two days later.

Police subsequently arrested Joachim Ernst Maximilian "Joe" Dressler, an elevator serviceman and the married father of two children, and charged him with the slaying. Investigators and journalists painted a picture of Dressler as an anti-Semitic alcoholic who had an addiction to homosexual pornography, a collection of photos of autopsies, and books about mutilation. Dressler was noted for entertaining friends and visitors to his home by showing a series of graphically gruesome videos titled *Faces of Death*.

Police and prosecutors claimed Dressler stripped the hapless North suburban Milwaukee man naked, tied his wrists and ankles, hanged him upside down and tortured him. The sadistic madman slashed off his victim's genitals, stabbed him in the chest and back, shot him in the head, drained him of blood, then removed his intestines and brain, and dismembered the body with surgical precision.

In April 1991 Dressler was preparing to go on trial when the blackened remains of a couple and their three girls were found in their burned out station wagon on an isolated logging road near the tiny backwoods community of Cushing in northwest Wisconsin.

Fifteen-year-old Bruce Brenizer was taken into custody and accused of slaughtering his father, his father's live-in girlfriend, her two girls by another man, and the couple's five-year-old daughter. The bodies were chopped into small pieces and the head of one of the girls was cut off and stuffed into a duffel bag before the car was torched, according to press reports.

Brenizer was tried as an adult, convicted, and sentenced to two life prison terms for the murder of his father and the girlfriend. But he was found to be legally insane when he killed the girls, as a result of the earlier slayings, and was ordered to a mental institution for treatment.

Incredibly, when Dressler's murder trial at last got underway and moved into its fifth day, Wisconsin was rocked by disclosure of a series of ghastly sex slayings that were so monstrous and sensational the elevator serviceman's crimes dropped almost completely from the headlines outside the state.

The national press hardly noticed when Dressler was convicted and sentenced to life in prison, because world attention was focused on Jeffrey L. Dahmer's crazed blood feast in Milwaukee.

Dahmer and Dressler shared some remarkable similarities. Both were obsessed by sex with young men, and both were alcoholics. But unlike Dressler, who apparently killed only once, the thirty-one-year-old Dahmer confessed to butchering seventeen young men and boys. He dismembered most of the bodies, collected grisly trophies of his kills, and ate portions of the flesh. Dahmer was a valid criminal descendant of Edward Gein.

Unlike the darkling crimes committed by Dahmer and his psychosexual predecessor, Ed Gein, however, the story of John Ray Weber never captured the imagination of the international press.

But in the rustic communities of Phillips and Park Falls in Price County where residents are hemmed in and isolated by miles of national forests and Indian reservations, Weber's outrageous depravities were terrifying and traumatic.

Carla Lenz, 17, was murdered and her older sister Emily Ann was viciously attacked in a spasm of sexual sadism and ghoulish perversion that was so twisted and savage it seemed almost impossible to believe.

Perhaps the most shocking aspect of it all was that both the victims and the perpetrator, John Weber, grew up in Price County in houses only a few miles apart. They were neighbors who came from hardworking local families, attended school in the community, and worked as baby-sitters or in local factories.

Until the baffling disappearance of the younger woman, and a report to police almost a year later by the older sister's husband that his wife was kidnapped and brutally assaulted by strangers, it appeared to most of their neighbors that all three had led average, unremarkable lives.

Stand up, Alferd Packer, you voracious, man-eating son-of-a-bitch. There were seven Democrats in Hinsdale County, and you ate five of them. I sentence you to hang until you are dead, dead, dead as a warning against reducing the Democratic population of the state.
—District Judge Melville B. Gerry, Lake City, Colorado, 1883

Been surviving on McDonald's. Need to start eating at home more.
—Cannibal Jeffrey Dahmer, 1990 home video shown on *Dateline NBC*

I drove around with her in the back of that trunk for five days. But on the second day, Dr. Jekyll, or Mr. Hyde, rather, I got this real wild idea. . . . I took out that knife and I cut off her calf, just her muscle, and I brought it in the house and I washed it up, cleaned it up, skinned it, sliced it up, and froze it. And that night I made myself some patties and I ate Carla's leg.
—John Weber, audiotape, August 1988

Chapter One

Carla

No one, not family, friends, or police, had a clue to solving the troubling puzzle of Carla J. Lenz's disappearance. The bubbly, fun-loving, dark-haired teenager simply dropped from sight. Or so it seemed.

Almost exactly at eleven o'clock on Tuesday night, November 11, 1986, a crispy cold and windy late Autumn evening, the Phillips High School senior told her little brother, Joseph, she was going out for a few minutes. She was never seen by her family and friends again.

Carla was a bright girl who took her responsibilities seriously, and it wasn't in character for her to simply run away, leaving the nine-year-old at home by himself until her mother, her sister, Emily, and her brother Larry, returned from their swing-shift jobs at the Phillips Plastics Corporation.

Her father, Gene Lenz, Sr., was a long-haul truck driver who wasn't expected home for a few days, and the only other member of the immediate family, her brother Gene, Jr., had already moved out of the house and was living on his own.

Carla was devoted to her little brother. She played with him and helped him with his homework for school. She was a patient big sister to the boy, and a loving daughter who was dependable and quick to help her hardworking parents with whatever chores might come up around the house.

Carla talked of marrying a high-school sweetheart some day, settling down and raising a family of her own. Love, family, and responsibility were the keystones of her life.

Nevertheless, when Caroline Lenz, her son, and oldest daughter returned to their rural Worcester township home seven miles south of the quiet logging and mill town of Phillips in the heart of Wisconsin's deep woods, her youngest girl was nowhere to be found. Her homework was already completed in the room she shared with her sister and was ready for school that day.

After making a search of the house and immediate area, the Lenzes telephoned the Price County Sheriff's Department and reported Carla was missing.

Reports of missing teenagers, especially girls, are everyday occurrences for police departments in the nation's larger cities. Even in many small towns, reports of missing teenagers aren't likely to stir up major initial concern unless special circumstances exist such as evidence of an abduction, struggle, injury, or prior threat.

Teenagers run away from home because they have been physically, sexually, or emotionally abused; they have quarreled with parents; or because of boyfriend or girlfriend troubles, problems at school, and a host of other reasons.

Police and juvenile authorities have learned that most of the runaways return to their homes after a few days and families are able to begin the healing process.

But the town of Phillips and Price County weren't Milwaukee, Chicago, Minneapolis-St. Paul or any other large urban community. Carla's home county was a close-knit community of about sixteen thousand people spread over miles of deep woods, meadowland, farms, and an irregular splatter of glacial lakes. It was an area where a large portion of the residents knew each other because they had grown up together, gone to school together, worked together, or lived within easy driving distance of each other.

The air was clean and so unpolluted that residents could still look into the sky at night and see the Big Dipper, the Little Dipper, and the broad, bright splash of the Milky Way. As the trite old saying goes, Price County was a nice place to raise kids.

Price County sheriff Michael Johnson was a veteran lawman who knew the community. Working out of offices in the modern Price County Safety Building in Phillips, the sheriff had driven practically every mile of highway and backwoods logging road, and hiked along many of the forest and farm paths in his area of jurisdiction.

Strangers who happened to be passing through Phillips or who breezed into the rural county area to hunt, fish, hike, camp, or go snowmobiling stood out like sore thumbs, and if there appeared to be a chance they were up to no good they could expect a visit from the sheriff, the local chief of police or from one of their subordinates.

Carla's parents didn't have to do much convincing for Sheriff Johnson to suspect that she might not be simply another runaway who had become fed-up with the slow pace of life in the boondocks and headed for the bright lights of the big city. Teachers from the school agreed that she was one of the least likely students at Phillips High School to leave home.

The sheriff took the missing report seriously, right from the beginning, and began an immediate investigation and search for the girl. The usual signs that would indicate Carla might be a runaway weren't present. The girl was getting along well with her parents, had no serious boyfriend problems, and she was doing well in her classes at school where she was well liked by her teachers and by other students. Only a few weeks earlier, in fact, the friendly high-school student with the Dolly Parton figure and the shoulder-length brown hair that she had recently highlighted with red tint, was one of the senior-class candidates for homecoming queen. Even though she didn't win, she was one of the leaders in the balloting.

Although Carla could be serious when the occasion called for it, she was a fun-loving, vivacious seventeen-year-old with a sparkling personality and a desire to help others. Along with the usual girl talk of romance and marriage, she had confided to friends that she would like to go to college and study so she could become a counselor and help other people with their problems. She was considering joining the Army after graduation so she could take advantage of a program set up to help ex-soldiers with college tuition after they had completed their active service.

Carla was already known among her classmates and friends as a good listener who was patient and quick to offer an understanding shoulder to cry on when they had troubles with family, school, or sweethearts. She had a reputation as an achiever, and seemed to have a natural talent for getting involved and helping others work out their problems.

Among the most ominous signs that something was seriously amiss was the determination that Carla hadn't taken anything with her except the clothes she was wearing. When her parents and police examined her room, they found her dresses, skirts, blouses, and jeans still neatly arranged on clothes hangers in rows inside her closet. Underclothes and other personal items were carefully stacked in dresser drawers, and cosmetics, toiletries, and other personal grooming items were in their proper places.

The fastidious, carefully organized teenager had even left behind her billfold with driver's license and other documents, as well as a few dollars in spending money. A checkbook for her modest personal bank account was also still in her room, and she hadn't written any big checks for cash in recent days that were unexplainable. If Carla Lenz was a runaway, she didn't plan her flight very well. And lack of planning wasn't in her character.

It was especially disconcerting that she hadn't taken extra warm clothes with her. Phillips was less than one hundred miles south of the mapmaker's line on Lake Superior that marks the U. S. and Canadian border. Winter sweeps off the big lake and through the Northwoods early and stays late. Even though a hundred miles or so south, people were still waiting for the final leaf-fall of Autumn, residents of Phillips and Price County were already dealing with the season's first significant snowfalls. And a frigid, biting wind was whipping through the trees when Carla threw on a light jacket and stepped out of her house into the night—for the last time—and began walking along Storms Road.

Sheriff Johnson immediately swung into action, instituting a comprehensive search for the missing teen. He notified Wisconsin state police and passed on details of the disappearance. He had Carla's name and description fed into the U.S. Justice Department's National Crime Information Center (NCIC) computers at the FBI headquarters in Quantico, Virginia, into local and regional networks and hotlines for missing children and adults, checked police teletypes for reports of unidentified bodies matching her description, and ran off flyers with copies of a photo obtained from her parents along with other pertinent information.

The sheriff and his deputies posted the flyers at gas stations, banks, markets, and other locations throughout the geographically isolated county and into surrounding counties as well. They were even plastered on the sides of delivery trucks and more than a few pickups, competing for space with bumper stickers identifying the CB handles of the drivers. No one—residents, visiting hunters and vacationers, or mere passersby—could spend much time in Price County without seeing the poster with the smiling face and the question: "HAVE YOU SEEN THIS GIRL?"

Sheriff Johnson paid particular attention to businesses along the two main highways that bisected Price County, State Road 13 and U.S. Highway 8. If Carla had travelled out of county, either willfully or with an abductor, there was some likelihood she may have driven west along U.S. 8 toward the Minnesota state line and the sprawling urban center of Minneapolis-St. Paul, or east toward Lake Michigan then followed other routes to the bright lights of Milwaukee, Madison, or Chicago.

If she or an abductor didn't go to the big cities, they may have travelled south along S.R. 13 farther into the central or southern portions of the state. Or they could have headed north on the state road to the city of Ashland at the edge of Chequamegon Bay on Lake Superior.

Despite the massive effort and man-hours spent on the investigation and search, there were few promising tips for the law enforcement team to follow up on. Carla hadn't told her little brother, Joseph, where she was going or who she was going to meet. She hadn't confided to any of her school chums about plans to meet anyone that evening. And she hadn't slipped out to meet a boyfriend.

No one seemed to doubt that whoever Carla left to meet with, it was someone she knew. She was a small-town girl, but she wasn't so naive that she didn't know about the dangers to teenagers and younger children of putting too much trust in strangers. She was too smart to willingly have climbed into a car with someone she didn't know.

Sheriff's officers talked with boys she had dated and with some of her girlfriends, but none of the questioning shed any helpful light on the case. Despite the scores of people contacted and questioned by the sheriff, his deputies and by Carla's family members, no one turned up so much as a single person who had seen her after she walked out of her house into the frigid air of the early November night.

As Sheriff Johnson's case file on the missing high-school senior continued to grow, her family and friends joined in the heartbreaking search. They helped to distribute flyers, and talked to her school chums, shopkeepers in Phillips and nearby Park Falls, and anyone else who may have seen Carla or heard something that could help solve the distressing mystery.

Inevitably, rumors made the rounds that she was merely one more runaway and she would turn up some day when she got lonesome and homesick for her family. And officially, despite uneasy suspicions about something more ominous, that's the way the case was ultimately organized and pursued at the sheriff's department. Not even a shred of evidence had been turned up in the first few weeks of the investigation to indicate foul play was involved.

But the people who knew her best didn't believe that for a minute. One of her teachers, David Peterson, just couldn't accept the theory that she was a runaway. He was especially uneasy because she had left practically everything she owned behind, including her wallet and cash.

The men and women of Price County nevertheless continued exchanging rumors and theories about the whereabouts of the missing girl. People in Phillips, Park Falls, and other nearby towns, were nosey about their neighbors, and the winters were devastatingly cold and long. Speculating about what had happened to Carla Lenz was as good a method as any to fight cabin fever.

It was a tragic, futile guessing game that led nowhere, and the upshot was that one more small town had been robbed of its sense of safety.

* * *

Local and area newspapers, including the weekly, *The Phillips Bee,* carried stories about the perplexing disappearance and about the search for the girl. Several rewards were offered for information leading to her whereabouts. Neither the news stories nor the reward offers, however, produced a single solid tip to help police locate the teen.

One of the most seriously concerned members of her personal circle of friends and family was her brother-in-law, John Ray Weber. John was a local boy from Phillips who had married Carla's older sister, Emily, only three months before the disappearance.

Although John was six years older than Carla, and they didn't date, they developed a close relationship. He was one of the male friends of the missing girl who was interviewed as part of the search for her.

After the marriage, John formed the habit of going to Carla to talk out his insecurities and troubles when he and her older sister were having marital difficulties. Carla wasn't the type to turn him or anyone else down when they needed a shoulder to cry on, even if it was her sister's husband.

On the night Carla disappeared, in fact, Emily was living at home. She and her husband had begun to experience serious problems with their marriage almost before the rice was swept up at the church, and Emily left him. She worked as a molder with her mother and her younger brother on the eleven P.M. to seven A.M. third shift at the factory.

Now with Carla missing and everyone worried to death about her safety, John had an opportunity to return her kindnesses. He immersed himself in the community and family effort to unravel the puzzle of his sister-in-law's baffling disappearance.

Long before patching things up with his wife, he got together with her brother Larry, to reproduce and distribute flyers with his missing sister-in-law's photo and information on them. The young men stopped at St. John's Lutheran Church where John's mother was secretary and ran the flyers off on the copy machine. Even as the heartbreaking disappearance of the high-spirited and enthusiastic girl dragged on and the search effort began to wane, John couldn't manage to set the matter behind him. At times he seemed to be obsessed with the mystery.

In fact, John had been pointing his finger at various people as suspects since a few days after the disappearance. He began telling people almost immediately that he thought two distant relatives to his in-laws, *Sal* and *Paul Avilla,* had something to do with it. John's outspoken suspicions helped develop bad feelings with the Lenz family. Asked months later how her family felt about these relatives during that period when John was making the nasty accusations, Emily's reply was brief and to the point: "They didn't like 'em."

He also wasn't shy about naming names of other people as possible suspects when he was speculating to his cronies about who might be linked to the mystery.

At various times he told a friend he suspected one or more of the Avillas, or some members of a large local farm family. Carla had been associating with one or more members of the family who were close to her own age, John said.

John told Emily that it was probably his fault Carla was gone. She had a schoolgirl crush on him, and was probably so hurt or embarrassed when he tried to discourage her affection that she ran away.

Sometimes when John was alone with his wife or with her and her brothers, Gene, Jr., and Larry, he revealed a remarkably different attitude about his missing sister-in-law. "There's no sense worrying about her," he bluntly declared. "She's probably dead anyway."

* * *

By that time there was a new Price County sheriff, Wayne Wirsing, and he wasn't as eager as the missing girl's brother-in-law to give up on the chance that she was still living and could be returned to her family someday. Wirsing kept the search alive, and as his predecessor had done, he checked with missing child networks throughout Wisconsin and in nearby states for information about Carla. Wirsing was a veteran member of the Price County Sheriff's Department who had held the office before, and he was involved in the effort to find the girl from the beginning. At first he was hopeful she would telephone her mother at Christmastime to let her know she was safe. Christmas passed, however, with no phone call.

Then, after she was missing for a few months, the new sheriff built up his hopes for a while that Carla would telephone or write to her parents on her eighteenth birthday. But like the Christmas holidays, the birthday passed with no word. The twin disappointments added to the disturbing fears that Carla was not a runaway; something more dire had happened to her.

Fears for Carla's safety took another turn for the worse when a second young Phillips woman vanished. Twenty-three-year-old Marchell M. Hansen dropped from sight on November 12, 1987, one day past the first anniversary of Carla's disappearing from her family home for the last time. Like Carla, "Shelly," which was the name most of her friends called her by, was pretty, had brown hair, and she lived just a few miles north of the town.

But Shelly lived alone and she was single and pregnant. Earlier on the day she disappeared she had an ultrasound conducted, and she was so pleased with her pregnancy that she went around town showing the pictures of the fetus to her friends. She was looking forward to having the baby. A little later in the day however, she simply dropped from sight. She worked at three or four jobs, but never collected any of her paychecks for that week. Her car was found, but there was no blood and no obvious signs of a struggle.

Local gossips turned up the crank on the rumor mill one more notch, speculating about such horrid possibilities as a serial killer at work in their tiny, close-knit community. A $10,000 reward was posted for information helping to solve the mystery, but the money was never claimed.

It appeared John summed up the attitude of Carla's family and friends when he said of the enigma: "This doesn't make a lick of sense. . . . It is just amazing that something like this could happen in little places like Phillips."

John's sister, Kathy Weber, was more worried and anguished than amazed at the disappearance. As soon as she got a look at Carla's photograph in the local weekly newspaper, she was convinced her baby brother knew much more than he should about the missing girl.

". . . . Carla and I looked very similar, and as soon as I saw her picture in the paper for the missing, I knew that he had something to do with it," she said years later.

"I didn't know what, but I knew he was involved."

Chapter Two

John

John Ray Weber was the pampered baby of a family of six children. Although he was surrounded by love and attention, he began getting into one scrape after another before he was old enough to start school.

From the beginning, despite sincere efforts to help him make up for his shortcomings and build a normal life for himself, he was the family misfit.

As a child he was a chronic bed wetter who simply couldn't get through a single night without drenching himself, his sheets, and the mattress. Many nights he wet the bed more than once. His parents tried everything they could think of to cure him of his bed-wetting. They stayed up with him nights, getting him up at regular intervals to use the toilet. They even took the advice of a friend and ordered a device from a catalogue, and installed it under the first sheet of the bed. It was supposed to sound a warning and alert them if he started to urinate.

The early warning system didn't stop the bed-wetting. In fact, after they took him to the Marshfield Clinic more than one hundred miles downstate and he was treated with medication and behavioral modification techniques, it seemed to become worse. John didn't cooperate with the doctors. He didn't want to talk about possible psychological causes of his bed-wetting, he refused to avoid drinking liquids late at night, and he fought efforts to get him to urinate just before going to bed.

Nevertheless the problem seemed to have eased off a bit by the time he was discharged and returned to Phillips. Almost immediately, however, the nighttime bed-wetting started all over again. No matter what the doctors and John's parents tried, nothing permanently cured his nocturnal incontinence. One of the most humiliating experiences tied to his bed-wetting occurred after he became old enough to join the Boy Scouts and went off on an overnight camping trip. John's mother took the adult Scout leader aside before the trip and explained her son's problem. The Scout leader promised not to tell the other boys. Then he broke his promise, and the other boys taunted John so mercilessly that he quit the Scouts.

He didn't have any better luck in most other organized community activities for children. When he signed up to play baseball in the local Babe Ruth League, the coaches hardly ever called on him to take the field.

As a younger child, John was afraid of the dark. And he was an insufferable crybaby. It didn't take much to cause him to break into tears. A quarrel between his parents—just about anything could set him off. If his sister, Kathleen Ann, was around she held his hand and tried to assure him that everything was all right and he should stop crying. But the scrawny little boy bawled anyway, wiping at the tears streaming down his face with his free hand while his big sister vainly attempted to comfort him. Kathy was two years older than her baby brother.

Except for Kathy, his other siblings were half brothers and sisters from his mother's first marriage. John and Kathy were full siblings, born at a hospital in the nearby resort town of Park Falls to Lawrence and Marguerite Marcella Weber.

John entered the world on Monday, November 4, 1963. Born into a family of achievers, he never came close to matching the accomplishments of his older siblings. His oldest half brother graduated from the U.S. Military Academy at West Point where he was a long-distance running star, and one of his sisters was a straight-*A* student. With the exception of Kathy, the others were already gone from the Weber home and in college or building careers and marriages during most of John's formative years. There was six years' difference between the age of the youngest of the half siblings and Kathy, and about twenty years between John and his oldest brother.

The Webers were a well-liked, hardworking, and respected Phillips family. They traced their local roots back generations to some of the earliest Germans, Scandinavians, English, Welsh, Irish, and French Canadians who were attracted to Wisconsin's primitive North Woods during the mid- and late-nineteenth century by the inviting tall stands of timber.

By the 1960s and 1970s when John Weber was growing up in Phillips, almost forty percent of the residents of Price County were of Czechoslovakian heritage. A monument to Lidice, the Czech village razed to the ground by vengeful Germans following the assassination of Reinhard Heydrich, the universally hated General of Police during the occupation, is one of the most faithfully tended landmarks in the Northern Wisconsin town.

Growing up in the isolated and insulated small-town environment, John quickly demonstrated that he was prone to committing violent, destructive, and other emotionally disturbing acts that constantly threatened the tranquility of the other members of his family. At home and away from home his behavior was frequently bizarre and hurtful.

For a year or two while he was a preschooler, he developed an obsession with fires and arson. He was about four years old when he started a fire in a wastebasket at his house. Family members were nearby and quickly extinguished it. A few months later he set a fire in a kitchen garbage basket. His father was in another room when he heard the flames crackling, and by the time family members rushed into the kitchen, the fire had already spread to a cupboard. John was standing near the shooting flames, quietly watching.

The blaze in the kitchen wasn't the last fire John ignited however. He was with his mother visiting at her sister's house in Milwaukee one day when he set a wastebasket afire in the kitchen. Years later John told a psychiatrist he quit setting fires after his father whipped him with a leather belt. Lawrence Weber, when later asked about the incident, stated that he recalled only scolding the boy. One other apparent incident of arson reportedly occurred when John was in the eighth grade and his school desk was set afire.

Considering all his problems, it isn't surprising that John spent much of his time alone in his room while other boys from school or the neighborhood were forming groups and close friendships. He was nerdish, in a weird sort of way, as if he was somewhat off-balance and out-of-step compared with his peers. His father filled in for missing playmates, by tramping through the woods with him and teaching him to hunt squirrels, woodcock, ruffed and sharptail grouse, or to successfully stalk, bring down, and field-dress a six- or eight-point buck during the annual nine-day deer hunting season in November.

Little Johnny Weber swelled with pride one day when his father gave him an expired deer hunting license, which he took to school and displayed to the other boys. As soon as John was old enough, he bought his own license and headed for the woods to test his luck and skills alongside his father.

At other times they spent long hours sharing the intricacies of luring a careless walleye to a bait on a hook or tying a fly and landing a plump big-mouth bass on one of the local lakes. They often left the house in Phillips in early morning loaded down with an ice chest full of man-sized ham sandwiches whipped up by John's father, a couple of boxes of candy bars, green onions, radishes, a dozen or more cans of soda pop and minnows, and fished until dusk. For a while, father and son maintained a whopping twenty-five-cent bet on who would catch the first fish of the year.

Lawrence Weber taught his son to operate the three-horse-power Johnson outboard motor on their boat, and the first time the boy turned the engine up to "fast" he could hardly keep it in the canal. But his father was patient and it wasn't long before John was guiding the little craft through canals and lakes or up and down the river like a veteran.

On one of their fishing expeditions the engine of the boat caught on fire and John was certain that both he and his father were going to die. The boy tossed his jacket into the lake and was preparing to go in after it, when his father calmed him down and put out the blaze.

Often they camped out, feasting on sandwiches and hot black coffee brewed over a campfire, while Lawrence Weber spun hunting tales about himself and his father, or told ghost stories to his boy while John fought to stay awake and huddled close to the comforting presence of the firelight—and to his parent. Sometimes in the middle of a hunt or a fishing trip, they simply stretched out and napped for a while, savoring their closeness and their time together in the wilderness.

The elder Weber was a big strapping man who was an excellent woodsman and fisherman and an attentive parent. Some close family members and friends called him "Laurie," rather than the more formal, "Lawrence." Sometimes he and John simply walked together through the woods, or listened to the eerie cry of loons while they peered together across the inviting coolness of one of the lakes that bordered the town or lay a few minutes' drive away. John was his father's shadow.

Years later, Dr. Harold Fahs, a licensed clinical psychologist, would write in a report after treating John: "Father and son had continued their exaggerated relationship, father confiding in son rather than in wife, and spending weekends primarily with John."

John was less close to his mother, although she was also an attentive parent. Mrs. Weber had a fine, sweet singing voice and John especially enjoyed the hymns she often sang while the family was gathered together in their home. But the same psychologist, who reported on the father-son relationship, wrote of Marguerite: "The mother is most flighty, inconsistent, and equally as forgiving as the father."

Years later John also recalled his mother's forgiving nature where he was concerned, and observed that she even believed his most outrageous lies. Mrs. Weber suffered a nervous breakdown when her son was five or six years old, and continued to have occasional problems of the same kind after that, according to some of John's medical records.

During one of his hunting outings a shotgun misfired and the shell exploded, cutting his face and damaging one of his eyes. He had to have laser surgery to repair the damage, and for years after the mishap he complained about seeing occasional flashes or streaks before his eyes.

Other troubles also continued to plague the unhappy child. As a schoolboy he had difficulty making friends, and lagged far behind most of his classmates in studies. Other boys and girls at Phillips Elementary School or from the neighborhood seldom hung around with him, and on the rare occasions when they did they usually tormented him. He spent an inordinate amount of time in his room by himself.

Years later Kathy conceded during sworn testimony that her little brother was a boy whom others simply couldn't help pestering. Even she picked on him. "He was just the type of kid that you pick on," she said. "I don't know. I can't explain why. He was just always different."

When John tried to join in with the games neighborhood kids were playing, he inevitably wound up running home in tears. He didn't stick up for himself when he was playing near his home or when he was in school. He ran away from fights with other boys when he could, and when he couldn't he usually wound up getting beaten up. Even the girls in his neighborhood and at school made fun of him. He was an easy child to bully.

Years later, John's mother was blunt in recalling his troubled childhood. She said he considered himself to be the "dummy" of the family.

During John's childhood and early teen years up until 1977, his parents operated a mom-and-pop store called Weber's Grocery. When John's Grandfather Weber died he left the business jointly to his wife and to his son, Lawrence. The building was left to the widow. At first, operating the store was a family affair and everyone pitched in—Lawrence, his wife who took care of the books, his mother, and the children.

But according to a story John eventually recounted to a mental-health professional, cracks began to develop in the cohesiveness of the enterprise after his father's brother, Bob, moved in to live with his mother. Lawrence bought out her share of the business, but she and his brother continued to live in the quarters at the rear of the store. She still owned the building, and there were quarrels over money. The sales were too good to be bringing in so little a profit. It appeared someone was tapping the till.

The situation was made worse by the elder Mrs. Weber's reputed dislike for her daughter-in-law. Marguerite not only already had four children when she married John Weber, but she was four years older than he was and the two women didn't get along.

Despite the friction between his elders over the business and other matters, little Johnny loved hanging around the store and dogged his father's tracks, following him in and out of the big walk-in cooler, scooping minnows out of a tank for fishermen, and drinking in information. He talked excitedly about some day helping his father run the business, and eventually taking it over by himself.

One day while his father and grandmother were quarreling

over the business, she summoned her son into the bathroom. When Lawrence Weber walked inside, his mother showed him her dresses that had been hanging in the bathroom closet. They were smeared with feces.

Later someone cut the buttons off one of the uncle's shirts that was hanging in the bathroom closet. Another time John snatched his uncle's car keys out of the ignition and tossed them over a shed into tall weeds. There was no question the boy was responsible for all the perplexingly hostile stunts. But when he was confronted about the button-cutting and the feces-smearing, he denied having anything to do with either caper. He could lie and deny responsibility for his delinquency or keep a stubborn silence without a hint of guilt. Most of the time after one of his misdeeds, John was let off with a scolding or other minor punishment.

Even as an elementary-school student, he had begun keeping meticulously written records of his activities and daydreams in lined-paper notebooks. His diary-type entries were a combination of truth and disclaimers, a form of personal historical revisionism marked by excuses and denials of responsibility for the various scrapes he got himself into.

On the day of the button-cutting John wrote in his journal about watching "Fonzie" on the *Happy Days* television sitcom, and chatted about other activities. According to his account he was helping his father lock up the grocery at the end of the workday when his grandmother confronted her son about the button-cutting. Lawrence Weber defended John and claimed his brother had lost the buttons in a fight. The boy ended his account by observing: "Now they are not talking to each other."

John told his therapist nearly a decade later that his father and grandmother wound up not speaking to each other for ten years. By that time, Dr. Fahs, the same psychologist who made the observations about John's relationship with his parents, pointed his finger directly at the boy as the culprit who was raiding the cash register and creating family discord. He wrote of John's parents: "Their mutual distance, in reference to relationship, has enabled John to get away with stealing large sums from stores, stealing the family car for joyrides, projecting blame on grandmother and uncle, etc., for a long period of time."

John sometimes spent large sums of stolen money on other children, and at least once treated several of his classmates to the movies in a pitiful effort to buy friends. Even that didn't work, however. The children accepted his largess, then went off by themselves to play, leaving him behind by himself. At other times he slipped the money from the till in $5, $10 and $20 bills, then flushed it down a toilet.

The thievery and lying were bad enough, but the boy was involved in other behavior that was even more potentially destructive. The feces-smearing and button-cutting incidents were only two examples in a series of disturbing and frighteningly violent acts he committed, usually against women and girls.

When he was seven or eight years old Kathy wandered into his bedroom where she found a Sears catalogue and began paging through it. The lingerie section had been chopped to pieces. Someone, presumably her little brother, had circled the photos of the models or the garments with a pen or pencil, then scissored them out and cut ugly slashes through the bras and panties.

John also recalled chasing a little girl classmate, tackling her and running his hands over her body. She apparently didn't report him to teachers or to her parents because she was only seven and she didn't realize the sexual significance of the act.

Alone without other children to play with so much of the time, John developed several imaginary companions. Imaginary companions aren't unusual for children whose brothers

and sisters aren't close enough to their own age to be playmates, or who for other reasons are often left to their own
devices for entertainment. They usually fade away as the child
grows up and begins to interact more closely with people his
or her own age. John's inability to make friends easily with
other neighborhood children could have been a factor that
would lead him to manufacture an imaginary playmate.

But one of his companions was different than the others.
He first appeared when the boy was about ten years old, and
he showed up whenever John was in trouble—or about to get
into trouble. If John's father was angry and yelling at him, the
special companion showed up. When John got into a jam over
some escapade, one of his sexual outrages, or another misstep
of some sort, the companion was usually the one who plotted
the mischief.

According to John's later account, the playmate was devious
and a regular troublemaker. Initially John and his companion
were about the same age, but as he grew older the illusory
chum began to outstrip him in age and turned increasingly evil
and malicious. John had several accidents during his adolescence, and later blamed his "companion" for the mishaps including a nasty motorcycle crash. John's mysterious friend
didn't have a name, but they often talked, argued, or conspired
together.

Regardless of whether he was telling the truth when he told
psychiatrists about the reputed imaginary companion, he
couldn't seem to stay out of trouble for long.

A couple of years after Kathy discovered the mutilated cata-
logues, she found a one-page story in his room that he had
written. It was a sadistic fantasy about him and another boy
taking a girl into the woods, tying her to a tree, and torturing
her by sticking pins into her body and abusing her in other
sexual ways. John was left-handed, and the awkwardly slanted
yet meticulously formed letters of the script left no doubt that
he was the author. Kathy put the story back where she found

it, and didn't say anything to her parents about the frightening discovery. She didn't want to get her little brother in trouble.

He was in trouble often enough without her tattling on him. But when Johnny was yelled at or disciplined for something he had done wrong, he didn't react like most children would. He didn't show any emotion; no fear, anger, or remorse. He simply stood there without giving his parent any back talk and waited until his mother or father was through. Then he went off somewhere by himself.

As the sexually precocious boy grew up, he began to worry that his penis was too small. And he had particular trouble relating to girls. He abused them. In September 1973 on Kathy's twelfth birthday, her friends were invited to the Weber home for a party, and the girls played outside until the sun dropped behind the trees and evening shadows began cloaking the yard. At last they trooped into the house, a few blocks from the small Phillips downtown business area. When Kathy realized that one of her chums was missing, she went outside to look for her and found John and another neighborhood boy holding her down and grabbing at her crotch. The terrified girl was struggling and trying to get away when Kathy appeared and rescued her friend.

At about the same time, Kathy was having trouble keeping track of her underclothes and swimwear. One after another, her brassieres, panties, and the tops and bottoms of her swimsuits were disappearing from her room or the laundry. At first she thought her mother had lost an item or two while doing the wash, or simply hadn't yet cleaned them and returned them to her room. Eventually she realized that the clothes weren't simply misplaced. They were being pilfered by her younger brother, John. But she didn't say anything to her mother about it.

At last, however, she was running out of underclothes and told her older sister Ellen about the problem. The sisters searched John's room and discovered a treasure trove of missing lingerie. Bras and underpants were stuffed into a cardboard tube that had once held a map; others were behind stacks of books, and some were piled in boxes. The most chilling aspect of the discovery was what John had done to the underwear. The bras were cut in half, and the panties slashed with scissors. John didn't stop pilfering his sister's clothes, even after he was exposed. The clothing continued to disappear: underwear, swimwear, shorts, and T-shirts.

He was infatuated with his sister, and during his adolescence when other members of the family weren't around, he began putting on her dresses, underclothes, and shoes, and parading around the house. While he was cross-dressing, he masturbated and composed elaborate fantasies in his mind about dominating and forcing Kathy to submit to incestuous sex. Sometimes he tried to imagine what it would be like to be a woman. Eventually he decided that even though he enjoyed his ventures into transvestism, he wouldn't want to be female. Periods and pregnancy would take all the fun out of it.

He also spied on his sister, watching for unguarded moments when he could catch a peek of her without clothes on in her room or in the bathroom. One day when Kathy was fifteen years old she was cleaning her brother's room and made another shocking discovery. Scores of X-rated magazines were stacked under a dresser. She didn't look inside the books, but the covers told her more than she wanted to know. They weren't *Playboy* or *Penthouse,* not even examples of average heterosexual pornography. The pictures showed women trussed-up with ropes, chains, and gags, or being spanked or paddled. John had collected a lurid treasure trove of hard-core bondage and discipline, or "B & D" porn.

Kathy told her mother about her discovery. Marguerite Weber had never seen magazines like that in her life, and later confessed she didn't even know what "so-called bondage" was. She assured her daughter she would take care of the problem, and destroyed the magazines. But it didn't end the trouble. John simply obtained new magazines, and they continued turning up here and there on the Weber property for years. But when his father sat down with him for a man-to-man talk about the pornography, he obstinately denied the magazines were his.

John was increasingly pestered by sadistic sexual fantasies of kidnapping women, tying them up, and torturing them by attacking their sexual organs with pins, knives, and bottles. He drifted into darkly chimerical flights of fancy about mutilation and murder, and especially liked to daydream about shoving bottles and other large objects into the rectums and vaginas of females in order to cause them as much pain and humiliation as possible. Sometimes he wrote down his fantasies. The writing was meticulous and the letters carefully formed, rounded, and evenly spaced. The script stuck properly to the lines on the paper, and were within proper margins. As John grew older, he began recording some of his sadistic fantasies on audiotape in his soft-spoken, rather pleasant and soothing voice.

Dark urges crept through his mind and when the pressure of his lusts became too strong, he looked through his magazines and masturbated. As his addiction to bondage and sadistic pornography and fantasies built, his behavior became increasingly bizarre.

Kathy's personal conflicts with her brother were multiplying and becoming increasingly weird and threatening. The situation in the home became so ominous and sinister that Kathy locked her bedroom door at night before going to bed. Even then, she sometimes lay awake for hours, fearful of some new threat or outrage from her baby brother.

One day early in 1979 John approached his sister with an audio cassette tape and asked her to listen to it. She agreed and after John left to go to his room, she slipped the cassette into a tape player and pressed the button. The message was ugly and to the point: "I have to see you without your clothes on!" a voice, which was clearly her little brother's, rasped.

Kathy clicked the machine off, ripped out the tape, and marched to John's room. "What is this? What is happening here?" she demanded as she shoved the tape back at him.

Then she told him again she knew he had troubles and offered to help if he would only explain what the problem was. John said no one could help. He was being overwhelmed by problems and no one else would ever understand. Kathy gave him a prayer book to read. But she never saw him reading it. She didn't tell her parents about the tape for more than a year.

One day the Webers returned to the house and discovered John had shot up a bedroom with a .22-caliber rifle. Most of the shots appeared to have been aimed at a crucifix hanging on one of the walls. Although John denied he had anything to do with the indoor shooting spree, he was punished for firing the .22 inside the house by having his rifle shooting privileges taken away for a while. Years later he told his father about shooting a hole in a bedroom ceiling. He claimed he was aiming at a spider.

The Webers did their very best to create a normal, happy home for their children, including John. They were fond of pets, and at one time while John was growing up, the family kept four cats and three dogs, including a mother and two of her offspring. John's obsessive fantasies of inflicting pain on women didn't extend to the animals. He was fond of the family pets and especially gentle and loving with them.

But while he was preoccupied with indoor marksmanship and kinky sex, his performance at school continued to drop. He wasn't very interested in his classes and spent much of his time daydreaming, either about sadistic sexual activities and bondage, or about outer space. He didn't participate in many extracurricular activities either, and although he tried out for some of the more popular athletic teams such as the basketball squad, he was a washout. The only sports he was good at were low-prestige activities such as Ping-Pong. A poor student, who wasn't good at sports and had trouble making friends, he ran away from home several times.

He was about ten or twelve years old the first time he made a serious effort to run away. His father finally caught him stealing money from the cash register at the store, and he pedalled away on his ten-speed bicycle. He rode approximately eighteen miles north to Park Falls before he was picked up and returned home by police. John later said he took the money for his friend, the imaginary daredevil sidekick who took the place of real boyhood pals. His friend told him it was okay to take the money.

He was fifteen when he ran away from home again, this time after bringing home an *F* on his report card. He was the first one of Marguerite Weber's children to ever earn such a low grade in any subject. John forged and cashed a couple of checks for spending money, loaded his .22 rifle and a shotgun in one of his parents' cars and headed south. He got all the way to Tomah, a city of roughly seven thousand about one hundred miles downstate at the southeast edge of the giant Fort McCoy Military Reservation before he had a change of heart and returned home on his own. He told his mother he was ashamed of his grades and couldn't face his older brothers because he couldn't match their performances in college.

Trouble of all kinds seemed to stalk the baby of the Weber family. When he was fourteen he was knocked unconscious and his nose was broken in a car accident; and a couple of years later he hurt his ribs, knee, and fingers, and cut his leg when he piled up his motorcycle.

He ran away in a family car again after another nasty incident with his sister, Kathy. In the spring of the same year she was given the tape cassette, her brother's off-the-wall behavior took a frightening and violent turn. They were alone in the house one day when John walked into the room where she was and pointed a .22-caliber pistol at her head. The frightened teenager pleaded with him to point the gun away and to tell her what was troubling him so they could work things out. After a while he agreed, and handed the pistol to her. She put it back in their father's dresser drawer where it was normally kept. A decade later, she couldn't remember all the details surrounding the incident. They were simply blocked out.

But that wasn't the only time her brother threatened her with a gun. Kathy was napping on a chair in the living room in front of the television when John woke her up one day while they were alone in the house. Their parents were at work.

"Kathy, I got to show you something," he said.

He was sitting on a couch, holding a magazine, and she was still half asleep when she glanced at it. She didn't like what she saw, and told him it was disgusting. Then she drowsily slipped back into her nap. The next thing she was aware of was her brother holding a .22 rifle on her and telling her she had to get up and go with him.

The nap was over for good and Kathy was wide-awake. "I'm not going anywhere," she said.

So John threatened to kill her if she didn't do as he said. He insisted she go with him so he could show her something. Frightened and in tears, Kathy got up from the chair, then plopped down on the floor.

"I am not going anywhere with you," she sobbed.

She begged her brother to put the gun down so they could talk. She refused to negotiate while a gun was pointed at her head. "If you want to put the gun down we will talk about it and then take it from there," she coaxed.

Eventually he agreed, and laid the rifle aside somewhere. She couldn't see it from where she was sitting on the floor. But it appeared Kathy had managed to get past the most crucial stage of the confrontation, and she felt safe enough to ask what her brother wanted to show her.

"I have something in the bathroom I want you to see," he said.

Kathy agreed to go into the bathroom with him. The rifle was left behind in the front room while they walked into the bathroom and she sat down to wait for John to produce the surprise. But he wasn't ready to show the mystery object to her right away. "I want to put tape on your eyes so you can't see," he said. "So, okay?"

Kathy permitted him to tape her eyes. She also allowed him to tie her hands behind her back with a strand of rope. But he went too far when he started to tape her mouth. She was being trussed-up like some of the women in her brother's pornographic books. Kathy tore her hands free from the rope and ripped the tape away from her mouth.

"What's going on here? What is happening?" she demanded. She told him that if he had something he wanted her to see, to get the show on the road.

"Okay! Okay!" John agreed.

Kathy's eyes were still taped when he slid an object into her hand. It was small, slender, and wooden. She thought for a moment it might be a gun handle. Then she wondered if it had something to do with drugs. He wouldn't tell her what it was, and pulled it back from her hand. At last she got fed up with the game playing and ripped the tape from her eyes. The wooden object was gone.

John broke down and began blubbering. His sister had seen him in tears many times before, but as her fears for her personal safety were pushed into the background her concern for John grew. They walked into the kitchen together and she got him to sit down at the table where she asked him what was going on.

"John, please tell me what's the problem?" she coaxed. "I know you've had problems, and have problems. If you can just talk to me about it, maybe we can get some help or somebody could help you," she coaxed.

She asked him if he was abusing drugs, or if the object he placed in her hand was a gun he had obtained illegally?

He claimed some teenagers from Chicago who were in the area had given him the object, but he still wouldn't identify it. Kathy never learned what it was.

"No one can help me," her brother sniffled. Blubbering and with his cheeks wet from tears, he insisted that no one could ever understand.

When Kathy's parents returned home, she told them about her confrontation with John and the rifle.

John ran away. He climbed into an old car with bad tires the Webers owned and drove toward the Minnesota state line, then basically followed the Mississippi River south. He was headed for an older sister's home in Florida. His parents notified police that their son had run away with the vehicle, but he traveled past Iowa and Illinois, as far as St. Louis, Missouri, before he changed his mind. He was a few minutes' drive from the famous Gateway Arch that symbolizes the Mississippi River city and was running out of money when he swung the vehicle around and drove back home. Mrs. Weber was walking home from work and cutting through an alley a few nights after John left when she saw the garage door was open. The old car was inside, and her errant son was in the house.

It was obvious to his family that he was seriously disturbed, and there was considerable reason to believe that he was a threat to his sister's safety. His parents conferred with authorities at the Northern Community Mental Health Center in Phillips and it was decided to send him to St. Joseph's Hospital and the Marshfield Clinic in Marshfield. He was admitted to the Child-Adolescent Unit of the hospital.

John and three other teenagers ran away from the hospital.

When he showed up at home his parents didn't immediately take him back. Instead, his father spent the day fishing with him.

Mental-health professionals at the clinic didn't believe John was cooperating as well in his treatment as he could, and were concerned that more serious trouble was in store for him in the future. A licensed clinical psychologist who worked with him determined that John was a seriously disturbed adolescent, who was very capable of hurting females.

Dr. Fahs gloomily predicted the troubled adolescent would perform a hostile act of some kind against women by the time he was eighteen, and by the time he was twenty-one would likely be in jail for offenses tied to his aggressive sexual fantasies. The youth disliked the psychologist, whom he considered to be too blunt and sarcastic. He later complained that the man accused him of being a homosexual.

When John was officially released from the hospital on May 24, 1979, authorities wrote on his discharge report that he hadn't cooperated with his therapy, he was suspicious of others and exhibited inappropriate judgment. His therapist reported that efforts to help the boy were impeded because all three family members, John and his parents, had "sabotaged the therapy."

For a while after returning to Phillips, however, John apparently behaved himself. He wrote a letter to Dr. Fahs admitting that he had done some bad things, but said everything was under control and he and his parents were making a fresh start together. At home he talked sadly about meeting and losing a girlfriend at the clinic named Lynn, who was a bright spot in his troubled young life. He barely had time to get to know her before she died a pitiful, lingering death of anorexia nervosa, he claimed.

"It is considered that John is a seriously disturbed adolescent, quite capable of physically hurting the opposite sex and whose prognosis is considered poor. Since the family and John continue to take the entire situation quite superficially, it is recommended that he be continued in psychiatric outpatient therapy," the therapist added.

Kathy left the family home and moved in with relatives eighty miles downstate in Wausau to attend her 1979-1980 school year there. Marshfield and Wausau are about a thirty-minute drive from each other. Kathy was a senior and wouldn't be graduating with her classmates in Phillips, but she was separated from her weird little brother and wouldn't have to worry about guns being pointed at her head, her underclothes being stolen and slashed to pieces, or sleeping behind a locked bedroom door.

The pretty teenager was concerned about her parents and didn't want to contribute to their problems. She wanted the family to stay together, so after graduation she returned to Phillips for a long visit and found herself a summer job. She tried to believe that her brother could be helped and his sinister behavior would change for the better.

He had worked hard helping out when they still had the store. From the time he was in grade school, he returned home after classes, helped his mother around the house, then went to the store to help his father.

As John moved into postadolescence, when he wasn't at the store he shoveled walks and mowed the lawns of elderly neighbor ladies who couldn't do the jobs themselves. By the time he reached junior-high and high-school age, he even managed to make a few pals whom he occasionally brought home with him or roamed the woods and otherwise chummed around with. Johnny was still far from the most popular teenager in Phillips, but at least he had a few buddies who accepted his company without picking on him.

John was especially tenderhearted and caring with pets. He loved and pampered the family's animals. And although he was a hunter, as most of the boys and many of the girls his age who lived in the rugged North Woods country of Price

County were, he tried to kill the animals as humanely as possible and avoided causing unnecessary suffering. He refused to use a bow and arrows, although a couple of his friends were bow hunters, because he thought it was too painful for the animals. Sometimes John turned down a shot at a handsome white-tailed buck when he wasn't sure of making a quick, clean kill. He didn't want to see animals suffer.

The Webers owned an eighty-acre plot of heavily forested land bordered by State Road 13 and Rock Creek Road in Flambeau township about eight miles north of Phillips, which they visited often. During the colder months they regularly fed birds and squirrels there. During one of the trips Mrs. Weber and other family members found a cache of pornography she called "stinky magazines" hidden in the shed along with a roll of tape, rope, a couple of dog chains, and some *s* hooks. The magazines had photos of women who were tied and gagged, and men with whips.

John was responsible for one disturbing incident after another in what seemed to be a never-ending chain of unpleasant surprises and disappointments. It was nearly impossible to relax around him, and his behavior created an emotional roller-coaster-like atmosphere. Things would quiet down, then there would be another discovery, another shock, another threatening or violent act.

If John's story about his anorexic girlfriend was true, his mourning for her didn't prevent him from continuing to collect and hide magazines featuring bondage and discipline and scenes of torture and pain that could have excited the lusts of a Marquis de Sade.

His reputed mourning for the anorexic girl also didn't prevent him from once more beginning to pester his sister with his quirky shenanigans while she was home visiting from Wausau.

A black swimsuit disappeared after she had washed and hung it on a line inside the house to dry. She and her brother were the only ones home at the time, and she asked him if he knew where her swimsuit was. He said he hadn't seen it. The vanishing swimsuit was one more curious mystery in a long line of mysteries linked to Kathy's disappearing clothes.

About nine o'clock the next morning, Kathy was lingering lazily in bed, awake but not ready to get up. She was enjoying the fresh air from the open window and the sheer luxury of idling awhile. While she was lying there, she heard her brother's voice and it sounded like he was talking with someone. A few moments later he knocked at her door and said that one of her boyfriends from Wausau had shown up and wanted to see her.

That was exciting news, and it chased away the last of the sleepy indolence.

"Oh, really," she called back. "Which one?"

John said he didn't know, but that he was short and had dark hair. The description sounded like one of the boys Kathy had been dating, so she popped out of bed, ran a brush through her hair, climbed into her clothes, and walked out of the bedroom.

No one else was anywhere to be seen in the house except for her brother, John. "Where did he go?" Kathy asked.

John told her that she probably took so long to get dressed, the boy apparently drove away to gas up his car or to take care of some other errand. But he assured his sister that the boyfriend would be back.

That sounded reasonable. After all, the round-trip drive between Wausau and Phillips was nearly two hundred miles, much of it winding road. And it seemed that anyone willing to undertake a journey of that distance to see her was serious enough to stick around in Phillips for at least a few more minutes.

Kathy was walking around in the kitchen thinking about the mystery boy, wondering if he was who she thought it was, where he had gone, and whether or not he would return to the house to see her, when she heard what sounded like an explosion. "I thought a bomb had hit our house," she recalled more than a decade later.

Then she realized the top of her head and her hair were slick with blood and glass. Blood and razor sharp shards of glass had formed a grisly pool around her on the floor. When she turned around, her brother was standing behind her, holding half of a shattered beer bottle in his hand and staring with an almost indescribably demonic look on his face.

"It was his eyes just turned from his natural color to black," Kathy later described him during courtroom testimony. "It was an evil, dark, evil look. It was really scary, a scary look. I'll never forget it."

Staring into the bleakly chilling wasteland of her brother's eyes, the alarmed teenager realized he had busted the bottle over her head.

"What in the hell did you do?" she croaked in horror.

John's expression didn't change. He stared back with the same spaced-out malignancy on his face. It was pure wickedness and depravity.

"My God, John, what did you do here?"

Suddenly, his face contorted and he broke into tears. Then he turned and ran out of the room. Kathy lurched after him, following him through the house into the garage. He appeared to be getting ready to jump into the family's Ford Bronco.

The vehicle had been backed into the garage and the tailgate was down. A .22-caliber rifle in a case, a length of clothesline rope, dog chains, a roll of wide orange plastic tape, scissors, a shovel, and an axe were piled in the truck bed. It wasn't difficult to figure out who the sinister collection inside the truck was assembled for.

"So, I could see that everything was ready for me to be hauled away in it," Kathy shuddered when she recalled the blood-curdling experience.

Despite Kathy's frightful injury and the hellish scheme that appeared to have been concocted for her, she didn't back off. She pleaded with her brother not to leave, instead to stay and to talk. John apologized. He said he didn't understand what had happened, and that he had to leave. He couldn't cope.

Kathy knew John was dangerous and she was scared to death of him. After he smashed the bottle over her head, she told her parents about the attack as well as about the incident with the cassette tape more than a year earlier.

When she was living at home or visiting, she kept the door to her room locked after going to bed. Then she lay awake for hours, worrying and desperately hoping to make it safely through the night.

"I was extremely afraid for my life," she later said of her brother.

One night in mid-September about a month after John attacked her with the bottle, she stayed up late, afraid to go to bed until about 12:30 or 1 A.M. The house was dark and quiet when she finally decided it was probably safe to try to get some rest. But when she padded sleepily to her room, she found a letter lying in front of the door. Her name was scribbled on the envelope.

Kathy was trembling and her hands were shaking when she bent down to pick it up. She carried the letter into her own room, and as she opened it up to read she was already beginning to get dressed. She had decided she was going to leave the house and stay the rest of the night with her older sister and brother-in-law, Mark and Marilyn Farnsworth.

The letter was three pages long. It began by advising Kathy that although she would be shocked and surprised by the contents, she must read it all. She disregarded the instruction to read the entire letter. The first few paragraphs were more than enough to convince her of what she already knew: It was one more sick example of her younger brother's depraved incestuous obsession with her.

The letter was a filthy sexual extortion attempt that directed her to go into John's room wearing a T-shirt without a bra, then strip off the shirt and submit to his perverted demands. John wrote that he had been sexually excited ever since she returned home, and had come up with a plan to relieve his frustrations by convincing her to submit to him. He claimed he had secretly taken photographs of her and a girlfriend while Kathy was taking a bath and the friend was dressing. He would have the photos mailed to three different skin magazines for publication and nationwide distribution if she didn't go along with his perverted scheme, he threatened.

He warned as well that if she didn't comply with his demands or told relatives about the scheme, he would be found in the room later that morning with his head blown off. And he demanded that she call in sick at her job and continue sexually submitting to him for two weeks, including sessions at the farm where they would be assured of privacy, if she wanted the photos and negatives. He urged her not to be frightened and not to cry. "Incest goes on all the time. There's no reason a brother & sister can't discreetly use their bodies for satisfaction & blackmail is the only way I could obtain it," he concluded. "My life is in your hands."

Kathy finished dressing and pulled a housecoat on over her clothes so it would appear she was staying home. Then she padded through the post midnight shadows of the house to her brother's room and knocked at the door.

"John," she called, "have you seen Brownie? I have to let her out!" She knew the dog was sleeping in another room, but the ruse succeeded in deflecting her brother's attention and confusing him. He behaved as if he was in a daze while he perched on the edge of the bed and replied that he hadn't seen their pet.

Encouraged by the success so far, Kathy continued walking through the darkened house softly calling out the dog's name. On the way into the kitchen she ran into her mother, who had gotten up to use the bathroom. When Mrs. Weber saw her daughter fully dressed, but wearing a housecoat and wandering around the house calling the dog, she asked what was going on.

Kathy explained as calmly as she could that she was going to her sister's house to spend the rest of the night. She asked her mother to go back to bed, and promised to explain everything later in the morning. Marguerite appeared still to be half asleep, and she took her daughter's advice, returning to bed.

As soon as her mother's silhouette disappeared into the darkness behind the bedroom door, Kathy headed out of the house. There was a moment of fear and frustration when she had trouble getting the door open because it was locked from the inside. But she finally pulled it open, hurried outside, slid into her car, and drove through the quiet of the deserted streets to her sister's house as quickly as she could.

After rousing her sister and brother-in-law out of bed, Kathy showed them John's letter. It was disgusting and scary, and it clearly threatened not only Kathy's safety but John's life as well. The concerned trio decided to contact the psychiatrist who had been treating him as an outpatient since the attack on Kathy with the bottle. They telephoned the doctor at his home. According to Kathy's testimony, *Dr. Basil Marky* listened while the letter was read to him. Then he said there was nothing he could do at the time. It was the weekend, and he advised them to get in touch with him on Monday.

The psychiatrist's response was not only disappointing, but worrisome. John had threatened to kill himself, and there were no guarantees in his letter that he would wait until Monday or later to carry out the threat. The Farnsworths had a baby, so Kathy stayed with the infant while the couple drove across town to rouse Lawrence and Marguerite Weber and advise them that John was up to his old tricks again.

Mark gathered up John's guns and carried them out of his room, while other members of the family were waking him up and getting him into the kitchen for a conference. When they sat him down at the table and showed him the letter, he claimed he couldn't remember writing it. He denied he was the author even though it was pointed out to him that it was in his easily recognizable unique and meticulous handwriting. John was reacting in typical fashion; when he was confronted with some outrage he had committed, he blandly but stubbornly denied having anything to do with it.

Despite his denials, John had spent much of the past couple of months in and out of trouble. A day or two after the incident with the letter, a Social Services worker in Phillips recommended that John be temporarily admitted to the psychiatric unit of the Wausau Hospital Center in Wausau for evaluation. His behavior had turned the summer into a horror fest for the family and despite counseling and other efforts to help him he didn't appear to be getting any better. He didn't want to finish his senior year of school in Phillips, and his actions were increasingly threatening and dangerous. The Webers arranged for their son to be admitted to the hospital.

The primary objective at the hospital was to evaluate the new patient to determine what direction his treatment should ultimately take. John's chimeras continued to torment him at Wausau where he was placed under the care of Dr. Charles Albert Garvey, an experienced clinical psychiatrist who had been practicing his profession in the community since 1976. John was given psychological testing by Dr. Thomas Zentner.

As part of his evaluation John completed the Minnesota Multiphasic Personality Inventory. Generally referred to in casual conversation by mental-health professionals as the MMPI, the test is built around approximately five hundred questions that are to be answered "yes" or "no," then categorized and compared with the replies of thousands of other people who have previously completed it. Like most tests of its kind, the MMPI leaves itself open to broad interpretations that can lead to startlingly varying conclusions by different examiners. Each may be equally well trained and well-meaning, yet come up with two conclusions that are almost completely opposite. Like law, psychiatry is far from an exact science.

John was also submitted to other analyses, including a Rorschach, which is closely tied to psychiatry and psychology in the minds of many laymen who know it as "the inkblot test." Another test given to John was the "Thematic Apperception Test." The TAT involves showing photographs or other pictures to a patient, then asking him or her to develop a story to go along with the illustration.

Some of the TAT pictures are of common objects or scenes that usually elicit very similar responses from patients. Others are more ambiguous and designed to elicit more personal reflection in developing the story in order to provide more insight into the patient's thinking processes or fantasies. John didn't cooperate well with the psychologist, according to the doctor's report. He refused to answer questions about some of the pictures. The patient readily provided or confirmed information that was already known about him, but closely guarded information that was unknown to others.

Dr. Garvey nevertheless diagnosed John as suffering from a "borderline personality disorder." Psychiatrists, who are not always known for speaking in easily definable terms and phrases, still don't all agree on exactly what a borderline personality disorder is. There is no uniform definition that is accepted by everyone. The best Dr. Garvey could do in describing it a few years later was to observe in a somewhat bewildering manner:

"For John, at that time, we used that diagnosis to describe a series of maladaptive behaviors and difficulties with the law and with his family that we thought might have been driven by confused or chaotic thinking behind those behaviors."

Antipsychotic drugs were prescribed to help him sleep. The dosage was beefed up when he revealed he was having sexually sadistic dreams or daydreams about the psychiatric-ward nurses who were helping care for him.

* * *

Treating John was a challenge. He lied, withheld information, and did his best to manipulate his doctor and the staff. It was behavior that was considered by the professionals to be typical of sociopaths. In common usage, the word "sociopath" is interchangeable with "psychopath," and refers to people who are aggressively antisocial. Sociopaths lie, steal, cheat, damage, destroy, and hurt other people or animals. They may be of either sex, heterosexual, homosexual or bisexual, and of any race.

Many experts say that severe sociopaths are so lacking in what most people consider to be normal conscience that they can maim or kill as easily as they can eat a pizza.

Dr. Garvey and a colleague were also concerned by observations that indicated John was narcissistic—so self-centered he was willfully determined to get what he wanted, no matter what the consequences to anyone else. But as Garvey said later, he and his colleague concluded that "what you saw wasn't necessarily what you got with John." Both doctors were concerned that some other underlying condition, or something else, was also behind John's behavior. But they weren't able to pin it down.

The health-care professionals involved with John's evaluation and treatment agreed that at that time he should not be allowed to return to his family home in Phillips. Eventually they recommended he move into a group home where he could become involved in the structured routines and behavior-modification programs. They added that he should continue seeing a psychiatrist and described him, among other things, as being given to grandiosity. The last couple of weeks or so that John remained at Wausau, hardly any new information was learned about him. He was basically waiting for space in a group home to become available.

* * *

After a little more than five weeks of inpatient treatment, on September 19, 1980, John was discharged from the center at Wausau Hospital and driven southwest across the state to Century House, a group home in the Mississippi River town of LaCrosse on the Minnesota border. A thriving city of nearly one hundred thousand people, LaCrosse represented a big change for the troubled teenager from the security of the small North Woods community where he grew up.

John didn't drink, didn't smoke, and didn't experiment with drugs. His most alarming bad habits were all tied to kinky or sadistic sex: pornography, voyeurism, incestuous desires, and excessive masturbation.

Dealing with and changing his unacceptable sexual behavior were among the most pressing challenges John was faced with as he began his senior year at Logan High School, practically in the shadow of the Mississippi River cliffs that border the city. His poor scholastic performance was another, and he responded to that concern by producing the best grades of his scholastic career. The lowest mark he received was a *B-*. He also plunged into extracurricular activities at Logan, singing with the choir, holding down a job on the school newspaper, and at the end of his senior year winning a role in his class play.

It was a far cry from his lackluster performance at Phillips High School, where faculty members knew him as a nice boy whose grades were average or low average, but who never got into trouble. He told one of his teachers there he was thinking of writing a science-fiction novel. The supervisor of the Guidance Office at Phillips High had talked to him every once in a while when he came in complaining of headaches and "floating things" in front of his eyes that were "driving him crazy."

It was a different story at Logan High in LaCrosse. The boy, who had been recording sadistic sexual fantasies since early childhood, was signed up for a journalism class and clearly liked to write. Another of the students in the class was a pretty freshman girl *Lisa Pattos*. John was attracted to her and the teenagers soon developed a pleasant boy-girl relationship. She knew that he was living at the group home on the city's north side.

One of his Century House counselors, Kathy D. Rondestvedt, wrote in a report he was felt to be the best adjusted student from group care. It was a determination based on her personal observations and information shared with her by John's teachers and guidance counselors. Another professional who worked with him outside the group home later described his behavior at Century House as "nearly flawless."

Ms. Rondestvedt also noted in a report that John indicated hiking, jogging, music concerts, and tinkering with small engines as other areas of special interest to him. They were activities shared by many boys and young men with well-rounded and emotionally healthy lives. From his first days at Century House, John didn't behave as a morose loner. Instead he took part in a variety of activities with other teenagers and with staff members, inside and outside the community of the group home.

In various respects, it was true that John appeared to adjust rapidly and exceptionally well to the disciplined life and routine of Century House. He got along well with the staff and with other students. He even managed to stop his bed-wetting when he went to live at the group home.

Ms. Rondestvedt, who met with him at least once a week to discuss his problems and behavior, noted on her intake staffing report that he exhibited very low self-esteem and felt inferior to other members of his family. John bared his heart to her about his disappointment over his inability to match the accomplishments of his older brothers and sisters.

He also told her the pathetic story about Lynn, his anorexic girlfriend who had withered away and died of anorexia nervosa. He blamed the tragedy in part when he slumped into a period of depression. John confided to his counselor that he and his late sweetheart had a sexual relationship, and said he was upset because it was near the anniversary of her death.

Shortly before the Christmas holidays, staff members found some letters he had written and left lying around. One of them referred to the effort to force his sister into submitting to his sexual demands by threatening suicide. Another named a girl he had worked with for a while on a part-time job, and provided a detailed step-by-step imaginary account of her kidnapping, forcible rape, and other sexual abuse.

When he was confronted about the extortion and fantasy letters, he claimed at first that he didn't know if they were his or not, although he conceded that since the signatures were plainly his they probably were. Then he told Ms. Rondestvedt he had written them a long time ago, before moving into Century House. John was practicing more of the same old tiptoeing around the truth or downright lying that he habitually used when he was confronted with unpleasantries by his parents.

The counselor referred him to the Gunderson Clinic at the Lutheran Medical Center in LaCrosse for treatment of depression. He complained to Dr. Larry S. Goodlund, his psychiatrist at the clinic, that he was having agonizing nightmares about the anorexic girl. According to his description of the dreams, his girlfriend was in a car that plunged over an embankment. He watched the car burn, without making any effort to help her. John also told of earlier dreams of being at her funeral.

The teenager also told his psychiatrist he had sexual relations with the girl while they were at Marshfield. Later, he used to think about her frequently, and masturbated while he concocted fantasies about her, he admitted. John said he stopped that practice after learning she was dead. Dr. Goodlund wrote on a report that John appeared to hold her almost on a pedestal as the perfect girlfriend, and apparently felt he should honor a vow not to have anything to do with other girls until they met again.

John complained during his first meeting with the psychiatrist that he wasn't dating at that time because he was afraid to ask girls to go out. He didn't like aggressive girls, but said he had recently gone out with a girl who asked him for a date. He liked her but was upset because she had taken the initiative. John added that he didn't like for girls to drink, smoke, and use marijuana. He hadn't developed any of those bad habits himself.

During another session, John conceded that he was hesitant about dating because he was worried about his own behavior. Dr. Goodlund later observed in a report on the meeting that the teenager was apparently afraid to date because the girl he liked the best was several years younger than he was—and probably brighter. Earlier the psychiatrist observed that John felt inferior to her, and had a poor self-image.

Asked about the sex fantasy letters found in his room at Century House that led to his referral to the Gunderson Clinic, John said he didn't know why he left them lying around instead of destroying them. He insisted he would never try to act out his sex fantasies because he knew they were wrong, but he admitted he liked the thrill of danger.

John blamed his habit of writing the fantasy letters on his parents, claiming he resorted to concocting the stories because they weren't open enough about sex and didn't discuss the subject much. John described his father as strict, and said his mother permitted him to get away with more things. During one of his sessions he confided that he was writing a novel. Dr. Goodlund cautioned him to be wary of using the project as a method of withdrawing from reality.

At one point, the psychiatrist observed that his patient tended to see himself as two separate people: one good and one bad. In another report, he observed that John might be behaving so well because of a desire to prove the gloomy predictions made about his future while he was at Marshfield were wrong and to show that he could properly fit into society.

Ultimately, John was diagnosed by his psychiatrist as "an obsessive-compulsive personality." Those individuals tend to be excessively orderly, neat, and precise, so much so that it can interfere with their ability to function normally. John was considered to be of average intelligence, although some other mental-health professionals who worked with him at various times described him as being of slightly above-average I.Q.

Despite his improved performance at school, John continued to exhibit awkwardness in making friends and went out of his way to please the other residents and staff. He was so anxious to avoid trouble with the other teenagers that he gave them money, loaned them cigarettes, or did chores they wanted him to carry out. If it appeared that trouble was about to flare anyway, he backed down. He did whatever was necessary to avoid confrontations, and eventually began spending more time with the adult staff than with the boys and girls his age.

John continued to drag his feet in the degree of his cooperation with his therapists, and some of the professionals who worked with him were pessimistic about the chances of his behavior permanently improving.

Nevertheless, John was permitted to return home for the Christmas and New Year holiday period, and he brought his school records from LaCrosse with him. Kathy also traveled back to Phillips for the holidays and moved into her old room. John appeared to have taken a turn for the better, and he didn't pester his sister with sexual demands or threaten her as he had done in the past. If the doctors and counselors in Wausau and LaCrosse had indeed helped him to deal more normally with his sexuality, there was good reason to rejoice. But he had undergone periods of apparent normalcy before and his family was cautious.

During the Christmas visit, sadistic fantasies about kidnap, bondage and torture which he had composed or rewritten from pornography magazines and recorded in spiral notebooks were found in a box stored on the porch with his school records.

It appeared the carefully detailed tales of gross sexual abuse and torture had been written while he was living at Century House, where he seemed to be doing such a good job of putting his sexual life in order by forming normal romantic relationships with girls his age. Often he rewrote stories from pornographic magazines, and changed the names to those of girls and women he knew, including his sister, Kathy, and a girl from school. Another woman who turned up in one of his perverted sex fantasies was an exceptionally pretty teacher, whom John and several other high-school boys seemed to be smitten with.

The notebooks found with his school records were turned over to one of John's counselors when he returned to the group home in LaCrosse.

In April 1981, about a month before he was scheduled to graduate from Logan High School, he told Dr. Goodlund he planned to join the Army. The psychiatrist thought the structure and support would be good for him and told his patient it sounded like a good idea. John also talked over his plans to enter the military service after graduation from high school with his father.

Lawrence and Marguerite Weber discussed it and decided that a stint in the Army might help their troubled son. John's father was a military veteran and was familiar with the discipline provided by the service. With luck, the Army would provide a good avenue to help the boy mature and work out some of the problems of his chaotic childhood and adolescence. Before indicating final approval of John's plan, Lawrence Weber talked with his son to make sure he understood the seriousness of his decision. He couldn't join the Army, then decide a few days or weeks later that he didn't like military life and leave. John understood, and indicated he was making a mature, knowledgeable decision. He still wanted to enlist.

John's Army plans, relationships with girlfriends and his performance in school, dominated much of the conversation during his final three sessions with Dr. Goodlund. The youth was upset because he had broken up with his girlfriend, he worried about one of his classes that he was afraid he was going to get a failing grade in, and he discussed his relationship with his parents. He confided that he was going to appear as one of the actors in his senior-class play.

A few days after his final session with Dr. Goodlund, John graduated with the Logan High School class of 1981.

Despite his alarming history of setting fires, raiding the cash register at the store, molesting little girl schoolmates, twice threatening his sister with a gun, smashing a bottle over her head, threatening suicide, hoarding and writing pornography, and all the other missteps that marked his young life, he had never been charged with a crime nor spent a day in a jail or a reformatory for juveniles. Even his inpatient treatment at psychiatric clinics hadn't lasted for more than a few months at a time.

John passed muster for enlistment in the military and after spending a few days at home, his parents drove him back to LaCrosse for induction. He was still under eighteen and needed the permission of a parent, so his father signed his approval for the three-year enlistment. Although he told Dr. Goodlund he didn't want to go to Germany, his enlistment papers indicated he would be expected to serve eighteen months there— half his time in the Army.

Before leaving Wisconsin to begin basic training, John gave Lisa a small Timex watch. Her parents thought the gift was inappropriate. Their daughter and the young military recruit weren't even dating.

In May 1981 John raised his right hand and was sworn into the Army.

Chapter Three

In the Army

John did well in basic training. He had moved into the Army from the closely structured and disciplined environment of the halfway house and he was already familiar with rules, regulations, and the system of punishment and reward based on performance.

John had an advantage over some of his fellow recruits, as well, when they bivouacked or trained on the firing range. He grew up surrounded by wilderness and woods, and he was a camper, hiker, and hunter. Although when he began basic training he may not have been familiar with the powerful, accurate, and relatively complex nomenclature of army rifles, he knew long guns and was already a good shot with his .22. He didn't blink, flinch, and jerk his hand in anticipation of the explosion of a bullet being fired when he pressed the trigger of a weapon.

Every training platoon or company has a pitiful sad sack or two that other recruits pick on because they can't seem to get the hang of army life and cry because they're miserable and homesick. But John didn't occupy that role in basic training. Even though he was one of the youngest trainees he held his own and forged a position for himself as an equal with his peers.

His success indicated an important turnaround from his wretched childhood experiences in Phillips when other boys and girls from the neighborhood or school picked on him because he was a hopeless wimp. And army life was a far different experience from the disordered and flustered flight to St. Louis after his summer of trouble while he was harassing and attacking his sister.

This time he wasn't pushed into leaving home by fear or confusion over his atrocious behavior. He made the decision on his own, and he was handling the responsibility like a man.

After he completed basic training he was sent to an Army school to learn how to repair and maintain helicopter engines. John was a good student. He had an aptitude for tinkering with engines and felt good when he had a tool in his hands and was faced with the challenge of repairing an engine or maintaining it in good working order.

His first permanent duty assignment after completing school was at Fort Carson, Colorado, where he worked as a helicopter mechanic and was eventually promoted to flight platoon crew chief. The army base is directly across from Cheyenne Mountain, the underground White House that is built on wooden pallets that would presumably help it hold up from a nuclear blast.

John slid easily into the camaraderie of the red brick barracks, and appeared to enjoy living with other single young men his age and sharing in their talk, activities, and companionship. He had friends who enjoyed his company and didn't single him out as a weakling or misfit. Like many of his fellow GIs, at mail call he was even receiving letters addressed to him in fine, delicate, feminine handwriting. Lisa and he were exchanging chatty correspondence a couple of times a month.

The structured life of basic training and the Army helicopter school, along with the responsibility of his job as a chopper mechanic, were good for him. Just as he had seemed to respond well in many respects to the discipline of life in the group home, it appeared he was taking to the army routine and at last was maturing and keeping up socially with his peers. He complained about the discipline and regulations of the military, but most of his fellow GIs groused about army life as soldiers usually do. And he clearly enjoyed his work.

When the young GIs from Fort Carson were given off-base passes, they often headed for the bright lights of Colorado Springs, the strongly fundamentalist city of 215,000 people at the northern border of the base. At other times they drove a few miles south to sample the more exciting pleasures of Pueblo, a rowdy city of half the size that some of the soldiers who prowled the saloons and massage parlors took to pronouncing "Pee-eblo."

The Fort Carson GIs also sometimes set off on sight-seeing expeditions to Pope's Bluffs and the Pro Rodeo Hall of Fame, to the Florissant Fossil Beds National Monument or to Pikes Peak at the edge of the Pikes National Forest just outside Cripple Creek.

During the fall football season, groups of soldiers drove to the Air Force Academy about thirty minutes' north through Colorado Springs along Interstate Road 25, when the West Pointers were in town to cheer for Army's Cadets or watch the local Falcons square off against Navy's Middies and other college opponents.

Denver was only an eighty-mile or so drive north of the base along Interstate 25, a distance that was easily accessible on a weekend pass or short furlough. There they could watch the American Football Conference's Broncos play the Chiefs, Raiders, or the Seahawks at Mile High (Stadium). Or they could wait for winter and catch the National Basketball Association's Nuggets in action at McNichols Arena with visiting Western Conference teams from Minneapolis-St. Paul, Salt Lake City, Houston, San Antonio, and Dallas.

If their tastes ran to more earthy attractions, there were always hookers to be found on the stroll in the Capital Area, in massage parlors, or on the street in the free-swinging Denver suburbs of Commerce City and Aurora. And, of course, wherever the GIs looked for entertainment and good times, saloons and beer drinking were always available.

However, just as there were glaring flaws in John's performance at Century House, his performance at Camp Carson was also accompanied by a disturbing element of negativity. He began guzzling beer, smoking marijuana, and experimenting with cocaine and LSD. He quit drugs altogether after a few months and concentrated on booze, after he had an especially frightening bad trip on LSD.

He got into a nasty argument with his own reflection in a mirror that ended when he smashed the glass with his fist and slashed his hand. John blamed the episode totally on the LSD, and years later still insisted the mirror image he picked the fight with had nothing to do with the alter ego who had dogged his tracks since childhood.

At about the same time he was experimenting with drugs and booze, he also formed his first and only back-alley relationship with a married woman. *Tracy Boothe* was the wife of a young soldier who was a close friend of John's. The married couple lived off-base in Colorado Springs, and during the fall of 1982 John was first introduced to Tracy by her husband. A few days later he moved in with the couple and their Doberman pinscher, "Herr," as a boarder. Soon after that John and Tracy secretly began a romantic affair.

Committing adultery by cuckolding one of his best friends wouldn't be the worst sin John committed in his life. But even taking another man's wife into his bed wasn't sufficiently exciting to make him perform. John was not a very proficient lover. Throughout his early teenage years about the only time he could maintain an erection was when he was masturbating to sadistic pornography. Cozying up to a real-life woman who was compliant and willing, simply didn't fit in with all those titillating fantasies about females who were trussed-up, frightened, or in pain. Without the lurid appeal of the whips, chains, and bondage equipment that existed in his fantasy world, he simply couldn't perform during their stolen moments together. John was impotent.

However John told Tracy at least one story during their comfy tête-à-têtes that indicated he was more of a man in bed than he appeared to be. He told her he was the father of an illegitimate child in Wisconsin, and the mother was giving their son up for adoption. John showed Tracy a picture of a little boy who he said was his son, and another photo of two young women standing together. He pointed out one of the women and said she was his child's mother.

The curious affair limped along, and in June 1983 when John was about midway through his enlistment he went on furlough to Phillips. Along the way he dropped Tracy off at her parents' house just outside a small farming community in Minnesota.

It is a long, exhausting drive from Colorado Springs through Nebraska and South Dakota to Minnesota. And after John and his friend's wife arrived at her family home, he stayed four or five hours to rest and chat. Tracy introduced John to her mother, and they had a pleasant visit. Years later, she recalled her impression of him as a friendly young man who was nice enough to bring her daughter home for a visit.

As they continued to visit, Tracy's mother was swept by an uneasy feeling that something improper might be going on between her daughter and John. But nothing was said by either of the young people to firmly indicate they were involved in a romantic relationship.

The ill-fated dalliance came to an abrupt end a few weeks after John and Tracy returned to Fort Carson, when he mailed a letter with photographs he snapped of her in her nightgown to her husband. The reasons behind his exposure of the affair were never fully explained, and may have simply been his method of breaking up the relationship without directly confronting Tracy.

If John was merely taking a coward's way out, it was a curiously precarious way to end the liaison. Tracy's husband acted about as predictably as he could, and during a man-to-man face-off with his boarder gave John a half hour to gather up his possessions and clear out. John didn't try to explain anything or to argue, and meekly packed his things and left. He had lived with the couple eight or nine months.

Tracy and John saw each other a few more times to talk after he was kicked out of the home. She made it clear that she no longer had a desire to continue their former romantic relationship, and wanted him to leave her alone. John agreed, and there were no more meetings, no telephone conversations, and no letters exchanged between them.

Soon after the unpleasant confrontation, both John and Tracy's husband were assigned to duty in Germany. She returned to Minnesota to stay with her parents until housing and travel could be arranged so she could rejoin him at his new base.

Trouble surfaced for John in Germany when traces of THC, an element found in marijuana, reportedly showed up in his urine and that of several of his fellow soldiers after the men in his company were given a routine urinalysis. He was disciplined with restricted privileges for a while. Army authorities later learned that there were errors in the laboratory testing of the urine, and formally advised him and some of the GIs that the finding was a mistake. John's record was cleared.

He managed to stay out of any further serious trouble and in 1984 after three years of active duty he was flown back to the United States, separated from the Army under honorable conditions and entered the Reserves. He was mustered out as a Specialist Fourth Class with a good conduct medal and a certificate of achievement.

John returned to Phillips, moved into his old bedroom at his parents' house at 417 South Avon Avenue, and quickly found himself a job as a laborer at the Cayouga Wreath Factory in the hamlet of Fifield, about five miles south of Park Falls along State Road 13. His sister, Kathy, had left the family nest and gone off on her own, so he was the only one of the children at home.

As a military veteran who was nearing his twenty-first birthday, John didn't appear to be the same pitifully addled and vulnerable adolescent who practically fled into the army three years earlier. If the old saw, "He left as a boy and returned as a man," wasn't yet totally true, it nevertheless seemed that he had made giant strides in maturing and putting his emotional house in order.

John and his father resumed their treks to the woods and local lakes, and it was like their old times together. His father would slip on a hunting outfit, pick up his prize .32 special, they would load the dogs into the family Bronco and head for the woods.

John loved the blue Bronco, and reveled in the vehicle's sturdiness while it slogged through mudholes and bogs that would have hopelessly mired a less powerful vehicle. He cried when his father finally had to trade it in. He considered the old Bronco, like the dogs, Brownie, Sassy, and Tippy, almost a member of the family.

Once his Army service was behind him, John also quickly began dating. At Fort Carson he had continued to exchange letters with Lisa, and soon after returning home he made the long drive from Phillips to LaCrosse for a date with the girl who was such a faithful correspondent while he was away serving his country. There had never been anything in any of John's letters that was freaky or disturbing. The teenagers dated in LaCrosse at least twice, once taking in a concert, and another time watching a high-school basketball game and sharing a pizza.

As a casual boyfriend, John was attentive and courteous. He wrote letters to Lisa between the trips to LaCrosse. And when they were together he didn't do anything offensive that might be considered either threatening or weird. They didn't have sex with each other, and were simply two young people enjoying entertaining dates together.

Nevertheless, in February 1985, their relationship petered out. There was no quarrel or nasty breakup. John just stopped writing. Lisa figured he had become interested in another girl. But the staggering logistics of a boy from Phillips driving a round-trip of more than three hundred miles to date a girl in LaCrosse may have been just too much of a burden for the relationship to survive. An appealing dating pool of girls was available to John much closer to home in Phillips and in neighboring communities in Price County.

On March 1 John found himself a full-time job at a local factory, Winter Wood Products, as a general laborer. Winter Wood Products was not only closer to home, but the new position offered more steady work than the seasonal job of making wreaths for Christmas and other occasions. Winter Wood Products was a subsidiary of the Radio Flyer Corporation in Chicago, and employees manufactured a variety of items from wood, including tables, legs for park benches, and wheelbarrow handles.

John was a good, dependable employee who easily caught on to the various jobs in the factory, whether it was piling lumber or operating saws, lathes, and other machinery. He seldom missed work, and he quickly fell into the after-work routine, stopping in at local saloons with other young coworkers for a few cool ones, catching a couple of movies on their VCRs, tinkering with the engines on each other's cars or trucks, and tramping the woods together to hike, hunt, or target shoot. Sometimes he and his pals got together at a local range for trapshooting, or they cruised Phillips and Park Falls in their jalopies, checking out the local girls.

He even bought himself a motorcycle and began considering the possibility of someday taking time off for a ride West to see what the country was like in Idaho and Oregon. Like Northern Wisconsin, both were heavily forested and they had the additional attraction of mountains. It seemed that John Weber had evolved in the Army from crybaby to a good ole boy.

The young Army veteran was doing so well that he wrote to Dr. Fahs to let the psychologist know that his gloomy prediction of a few years earlier was off the mark. He had passed twenty-one and he hadn't seriously harmed another human being—and he wasn't in jail. The message was clear: he was controlling his behavior, staying out of trouble, and was proud of it.

John met Emily Ann Lenz in November 1984 through her mother, Caroline, and Emily's brother, Gene, Jr., while he was working with them at the wreath factory. Emily was the oldest of two daughters, and was a senior at Phillips High School. John's oldest sister graduated from Phillips High with Emily's mother. Like most of the young people who grew up in Phillips and elected to stay there, Emily loved nature. For a while after graduating from school with the class of 1985, almost exactly a year after her boyfriend's release from the Army, she worked at JJB's Floral, Inc., Greenhouse and Garden Center in town, transplanting flowers and other plants. She was eighteen, and she did some serious thinking about staking out a career for herself in horticulture or forestry.

Soon, John knew the whole Lenz family, including Emily's

sister, Carla, and two other siblings, including Joey and another older brother, Larry. Gene, Jr., and Emily were twins. They were born on November 27, 1966.

When John was chatting with his parents about his love interests, he mentioned Carla about as often as he did Emily. Mrs. Weber and her husband liked Carla, and they were pleased when their son indicated he had a serious romantic interest in her. Lawrence Weber later admitted he had hoped John would marry her. For a while it looked to the Webers like a coin toss between which of the sisters their son might marry, but John was apparently exaggerating his romance with the younger girl. She had other boyfriends closer to her own age.

The Webers were disappointed when their son indicated he had paired off for good with Emily. John decided they had too much in common to ignore. Both of them liked rock music, and they shared other interests as well. John decided he was in love with the slender 113-pound, five-foot, four-inch beauty with the long ash-blond Farrah Fawcett hairdo.

Suddenly, he didn't have much time anymore for long jaunts into the woods with his father, or for spending an entire day casting for lunkers on one of the local lakes. He didn't spend as many hours with his head and shoulders jammed under the hood of one of his jalopies. And instead of taking his mother for a spin on his motorcycle, now it was Emily who was most likely to be seated behind him and holding tightly to his waist.

Despite his head-over-heels infatuation, their relationship was spotted with occasional nastiness and spats. Emily initiated a showdown with him once over a letter scribbled in John's unique handwriting that she found lying on her sister's dresser in the room they shared. The letter was an apology to Carla for trying to kiss her, and pleaded with her not to tell

Emily about the incident. When Emily confronted him about the pass he made at her sister, he asked her how she found out about it. After she told him she read the letter, he tried to dismiss the matter by explaining that he was drunk at the time it happened.

The trouble over Carla was bad enough, but John made matters worse when he made the claim to his girlfriend that he had carried on an affair with her mother. He later admitted the story was a lie. He said he did it because he wanted to see how much she would put up with before she left him. The invention about Emily's mother was only the beginning.

Lies, ranging from innocent fibs to deliberately malicious slander, would eventually mark their entire relationship. He lied about his drinking, about where he was and who he was with when he was away from the house and off work, and about his pornography collection. John was caught in lies time after time, but it made no difference. He either stuck doggedly to his story, even though it was already proven false, or he shrugged his shoulders and walked away when he was confronted with the truth.

Following graduation, Emily rented a house owned by John's parents at 475 South Avon, across the street and about a block from their own home. But she was more welcome to them as a renter than as a daughter-in-law. When the young couple announced they were planning to get married, the Webers were even less enthusiastic. Marguerite Weber later said she didn't expect the marriage to last. Lawrence Weber had similar misgivings. He felt the marriage was a mistake. Nevertheless, both John's parents reluctantly gave their blessings to the union. He was a grown man and it was his decision to make.

On July 8, 1986, about a month before the scheduled wedding, he bought a 1977 Pontiac Sunbird from a neighbor. The deal was closed on the birthday of Emily's little brother, Joey.

But her fiancé was furious when he learned the battered old car didn't shift gears properly. On July 10, two days after John bought the Sunbird, the Fifield teenager who sold it to him was chopped to pieces on the Soo Line Railroad just outside Park Falls by a seventy-eight-car train. Witnesses indicated John Kenney, Jr. was lying between the tracks at eight o'clock in the morning and didn't respond to the train whistle before he was struck. Autopsy evidence later disclosed his alcohol level was a whopping 0.125 percent. The blood alcohol level used to establish that a person is legally drunk was 0.10 percent in Wisconsin at that time, as it was in many other states.

The teenager "got what he deserved," John said of the tragedy. Two days after the young man's burial, the cemetery caretaker discovered someone had desecrated the grave. Several holes were punched into the earth, reaching all the way to the vault.

On August 9, John and Emily were married. One of John's buddies from their high-school days stood up with him as best man. Carla was the bridesmaid, and danced with the groom at the reception. After the wedding, John carted most of his belongings across the street from his parents' home and moved in with his bride at 475 South Avon.

Chapter Four

Emily

Almost as soon as John moved in with Emily, they began battling with each other. They quarreled over things that were almost unimaginably petty, ranging from what music tape they were going to listen to or John's tinkering with the engines of his clunkers, to more serious disputes over her old flames and his drinking, or his habit of roaring away from the house by himself on the motorcycle to hang around with his friends.

In addition to the normal stresses of two young people adjusting their lives and activities to the demands of marriage, there were special problems. John had developed a neurogenic bladder that acted up when he was nervous, upset, or drinking too much.

A few months after the wedding, John began soaking the sheets, sending him and his bride scrambling out of their water bed in the middle of the night. About once every week, sometimes more often, he drenched the bedclothes and himself with urine. He explained to Emily that sometimes his bladder hurt him so much that he couldn't slip out of bed and get to the bathroom soon enough. The bladder cramps were devastatingly painful, and when he had attacks he doubled over in agony and pressed his groin with his arm until the hurt eased.

* * *

The impotence that troubled him when he was romancing Tracy Boothe continued to haunt him after his marriage to Emily. He couldn't even perform on his wedding night.

Emily later recalled that her husband "was always feeling sorry for himself." She said of his troubles performing his marital duties, "He was always whining about it." She told him not to worry because worrying would probably just make the problem worse.

John looked healthy enough, however. His body was rangy and slim, his hair sprouted in unruly wavy clumps almost to his shoulders, and a sprinkle of angry red zits caused by infected hair follicles spotted his face. But he was bothered with a host of other more serious physical or emotional problems. There were times when he breathed so fast he was almost panting. He had headaches, spells of dizziness, chest pains, feelings of numbness on his left side, blurred vision, and spells of constipation.

The young couple sought counseling for their marital problems, but Emily wound up attending the sessions more often than John. He was failing at marriage, like he had failed at just about everything else in his life: as a son, as a brother, as a lover, and now as a husband.

There was a positive side, however, that provided John and his wife with some reason for optimism about their future together. His in-laws were fond of him and appeared to warmly welcome him into the family. They remembered his twenty-third birthday, the first after his marriage to their daughter, with a practical gift for an outdoorsman, a handsome hunting knife. John loved the knife, and spent hours sharpening it.

* * *

He was a hard worker who was earning regular pay increases and steadily moving up the seniority ladder at Winter Wood Products. And despite the elder Webers' misgivings about their new daughter-in-law, once she was married to their son they backed up the young couple as best they could.

Emily had found a better paying job at Phillips Plastics with her mother and brother. Both she and John depended on the income, and when occasional layoffs or work slowdowns created a money pinch his parents were understanding about late rent payments. They didn't demand a lease, and John and his wife paid $200 rent on a month-to-month basis. But they fell behind more than once. Lawrence and Marguerite Weber gave their son and daughter-in-law plenty of room to maneuver and never served them with an eviction notice when they were late with the rent.

The couple's rocky marriage continued to limp along in roller-coaster fits and starts. They broke up, got back together, broke up again, then got back together once more. The first time they broke up after the marriage was about the middle of October 1986 when Emily moved back in with her parents and her siblings. The troubled young couple had been married almost five weeks.

Only Emily's brother Gene, Jr., was living out of the family home and on his own at that time, and with her Monte Carlo, temporary shelter provided by her parents, and her job at Phillips Plastics, Emily was able to support herself.

John went to Carla for sympathy. Often when he and her older sister were feuding, he told his troubles to Carla. She provided a good listening board, and along with sympathy she patiently offered gentle advice aimed at helping heal the domestic rifts. Although there was still plenty of time before making a final decision, Carla was seriously considering pursuing a career as a counselor. Listening and advising her brother-in-law while he unloaded his troubles was good, practical experience.

Carla was a good student who kept busy with extracurricular activities, and helped with the chores around the house. But she always made time for her sister's husband when he telephoned and said he needed to talk because he was having trouble with Emily. He usually picked her up in his beat-up 1970 Oldsmobile Cutlass at her house on the outskirts of town in Worcester township, or met her somewhere nearby.

During their quieter, less fretful times together after they reunited, John and Emily socialized with a circle of other young married couples. But he also hung around with his buddies much of the time drinking beer, listening to records, riding his bike, or working on engines. He spent so much time with his friends that it became the source of one of his problems with Emily. Then John began to talk about signing up with the local Big Brothers-Big Sisters program, which would cut even further into the time he spent with his wife. The plan eventually died on the vine.

John loved old cars and trucks and put together a motley collection of jalopies. In addition to the Cutlass and the Sunbird, the couple drove around in a 1954 Chevrolet pickup truck and Emily's old Chevrolet Monte Carlo. The clunkers in John's ragged fleet of vehicles were creased with bumps, marked with broad smears of paint primer, and advertised their noisy presence with rattles and rumbles, but he loved each one of them.

Most of his buddies also drove ancient cars and trucks that had seen better days, but could be kept running by skillful mechanics. Along with the few pals from his high-school days, he made new friends at the factory and around Phillips.

Timothy Dale Denzine was one of the employees with whom he formed a close friendship. Although Denzine and John attended Phillips High at the same time, they barely knew each other then and didn't chum around. But they hit it off when John began working at Winter Wood Products and were soon tramping through the woods, hunting birds in the fall, angling for lunkers in the cool waters of local lakes, getting together for outdoor barbecues, tipping a beer or two—or merely standing around shooting the bull. John even hauled away a truckload of gravel from behind Denzine's house one time for a project he was working on at the farm.

Occasionally when they were at work or hanging around together, John sounded off to his pal about his troubles with Emily. Denzine had undergone domestic problems of his own, and didn't allow himself to be drawn too deeply into those talks. He preferred leaving John alone to work out his own marital difficulties. John once told his friend that he saw strange flashes—in front of his eyes, and claimed it was caused by injuries from a shotgun accident when he was a boy.

John also became close to another fellow employee Kevin Richard Scharp. Like John, Scharp had returned to civilian life only a few months earlier after a hitch in the Army, when the two former GIs met on the job at Winter Wood Products. Scharp noticed that John was unusually jumpy at times and apt to become annoyed at minor occurrences, such as someone dropping a chunk of wood near him or by the machine they were working on.

But the two Army veterans quickly became chums and hunting companions, even though John's sense of what he considered to be ethical behavior when they were stalking birds or other small game was keener than most of the local men.

John also observed a stern self-imposed sportsman's code in regard to hunting wild birds. He set up strict rules for himself and refused to shoot a bird while it was sitting on the ground because that would be depriving the game of a fair chance to escape or survive. He loved guns, but he respected them and used them only for hunting or target shooting. Although he never filled his house with guns, like some of the other men around Phillips, he had his .22-caliber rifle, a shotgun, and kept a prized .25-caliber automatic stuffed safely under the mattress of the water bed.

He was fond of and attentive to his family's four cats and extraordinarily devoted to their dog, Brownie and her two grown-up pups. John took it exceptionally hard after they all died within a few months of each other when the younger dogs were fifteen years old. John cried openly in front of his friend. He personally buried the dogs at the farm a few feet off Rock Creek Road, and sobbed over their graves.

John and his father conducted a little burial ritual for their pets. They wrapped the dogs in a swath of cloth or tarp before lowering them into the graves, then tossed a shotgun shell in after them as a memento of the good times they had experienced hunting together. Occasionally they decorated the graves by sticking a wildflower or two into an empty shotgun shell casing and jamming it into the ground of the soft earth.

John got a couple of puppies, and he and Emily kept them in their little house as pets. He did his best to select dogs with markings and personalities to match those of the family pets he grew up with, but they couldn't totally replace his trusted old companions.

John and Roxanna Scharp, Richard's wife, got along well. They both loved books, and when the two couples visited, he and Roxanna often talked about books. Horror novelist Stephen King was a favorite author of theirs, and they exchanged conversation about which of his novels they had read or were reading. The couples usually got together two or three times a month to have a few beers and talk. John once told Roxanna that he had a book about torture and said he would show it and other books to her when he had a chance, but at the time they were packed up and stored at his parents' house.

John also read nonfiction books if they were sufficiently titillating and sadistic. He especially liked *The I-5 Killer*, which author Ann Rule wrote when she was still using the pen name "Andy Stack." The book traces the sordid crime spree of serial sex slayer and bandit Randall Woodfield, who roamed the Interstate 5 freeway in California, Oregon, and Washington state raping and otherwise sexually abusing or murdering dozens of helpless victims. Emily listened at times while her husband read passages aloud from some of the books. He especially relished ghastly descriptions of rape and murder.

One day Emily discovered a stack of hard-core pornographic magazines in her bedroom closet. Several were bondage magazines, filled with pictures of young models gagged, blindfolded, and trussed-up with heavy straps or ropes that cut into their breasts, choking them into obscene shapes that bulged and swelled into ugly lumps of tortured flesh. The magazines showed signs of frequent use, and most of them didn't have their covers. John explained to his wife that they were left at the house by one of his friends after a party.

On an occasion or two Emily was also puzzled by the disappearance of some of her underclothes, including a pair of black panties. The enigmatic vanishings wouldn't have been nearly so curious if she had known about John's history of stealing his sister Kathy's underwear and swimsuits, then cutting them up. But nobody told her.

John and his friend, Scharp, attended many of the same beer parties. And they tinkered with the motors on John's vehicles and with other engines he was rebuilding, until July 1986 when Scharp went back into the Army. Roxanna left Phillips with her husband.

John started to drink heavily after his marriage. It wasn't unusual on weekends for him to guzzle a twelve-pack of twelve-ounce Millers in an hour or two, then walk or drive away as if nothing was wrong. At the end of his shift during the workweek, he usually loped into one of the local saloons and put away five or six beers, or picked up a six-pack and headed for home to finish the drinks before flopping suddenly into bed. Some nights he polished off as many as eighteen cans of beer by himself.

In the winter of 1987, John learned he had multiple sclerosis. He was hunting one day when he suddenly began slurring his words, and started having difficulties controlling the left side of his body. The muscles wouldn't work. He was with one of his buddies, and soon after he got home his speech improved and he began feeling better. But something serious was clearly wrong. He had also begun to have occasional trouble talking. He stuttered.

John returned to the Marshfield Clinic, this time as an outpatient for medical tests and evaluation. The clinic maintained facilities in Phillips, Park Falls, and in other communities in Wisconsin as well as in Marshfield.

A doctor at the clinic recognized the symptoms and made the diagnosis. He reported that John had multiple sclerosis. The doctor's diagnosis may have been easier to make because he was so familiar with the symptoms. He also had the central nervous system ailment that is characterized by hardened brain or spinal tissue and loss of muscular coordination or development of speech difficulties.

John's ability to work, ride his motorcycle, and do other things he was used to doing weren't immediately affected by the debilitating disease. But he continued to stutter. It wasn't a constant problem, but from time to time when he was talking he would hesitate, stammer, and struggle to force out the words. It was a frustrating and embarrassing development for the young husband, and one more troubling situation that at times severely tried the patience of his wife.

When he was able to talk more easily, John explained that he knew what he wanted to say. He just couldn't make the words come out and flow freely at times, especially when he was drinking heavily.

* * *

Keith Newbury was a few years younger than John and was still attending Phillips High School when they met through Carla's brother Gene. Keith was a cousin to Carla, Emily, and their brothers. Phillips was a small isolated town, and many of the old families—and more recent families—had intermarried over the years. It was common for cousins and in-laws to socialize, attend church or school together, and work together.

Despite the difference in ages, John and Keith began hanging around together, hunting, listening to music, and talking. John confided in his younger friend about a lot of his problems, including his troubles with Emily. He whined that she wasn't giving him enough attention. John was frequently quiet and depressed, and it seemed to Keith he kept to himself more than he had prior to the marriage. John told his younger friend about the diagnosis of multiple sclerosis.

In February 1987 the Army called him back to Camp Carson on temporary duty for a couple of weeks to help train other soldiers as helicopter mechanics. He and Emily had just gotten back together about a month earlier, following their first breakup the previous October, and she made the long drive to Colorado Springs with him in their battered old Cutlass. It was filled with clothes and other personal items. John always kept the trunk of the car filled with a litter of boxes and bags, but he managed to make some space and squeeze in a few more things. His car trunk was his personal territory and packing for the trip to Camp Carson marked one of the rare occasions when his wife had an opportunity to peek inside.

They had sold Emily's Monte Carlo, and John permitted her to drive the Cutlass. She had a key for the ignition, but he wouldn't give her a key to the trunk. When she asked for one, pointing out she couldn't get to the spare if she had a flat tire, he put her off. "Yeah, yeah!" he stalled. "I'll get it for you later." He never followed up on his promise, and Emily never had access to the trunk.

In Colorado Springs the couple moved into a cramped apartment to wait out John's abbreviated tour of duty. He wasn't happy about his orders to Camp Carson, but he explained to Emily that he had no choice. He told her long before receiving his call back to temporary duty that he hated being in the Army.

Despite the encouraging signs they might be beginning to adjust to living together as husband and wife, John and Emily continued to have some serious misunderstandings and spats. Inevitably, it seemed their marriage began once more to sour. In May 1987, they broke up and John moved back across the street into his old room at his parents' house once more. He was devastated and blamed another man for taking Emily away from him.

When Emily and John were living together, he had the infuriating habit of refusing to talk to her when he was angry. Sullen and uncommunicative, sometimes he maintained his silence for weeks, and when they were both in the house, he would walk past his wife as if she wasn't even there. It didn't do any good to try and talk with him, or to yell at him. John didn't even bother to let her know what he was mad about, and he met all of her efforts to break the frustrating impasse with stubborn silence.

So Emily wrote letters or notes when she wanted to communicate with her husband, or simply get some of the frustration and anger out of her system. One day after enduring three weeks of John's silence, she scrawled a furiously angry three-page letter on lined notebook paper. Marked repeatedly with the same ugly expletive for sexual intercourse, Emily's letter ranted about tapes by various rock groups they were quarreling over. She accused him of trying to hog their entire tape collection for himself and demanded he return to her a stereo equalizer.

Emily was furious because he had cleaned out their bank

account of their shared earnings, and demanded that he split the money with her. Accusing him of playing dirty, she reminded her husband about an embarrassing secret their friends would be interested in hearing. Months later when the note became a matter of public record, the general inference was that she was referring to his troubles with impotence and possibly his bed-wetting as well. Emily wrote she was anxious to move out of the house, and told him that if he didn't "have the balls" to tell her what the problem was they should end the relationship. She said she hated being married to him as much as he hated being married to her.

Warning him not to even think of fouling up her life anymore, Emily wrote that she wanted to start over without him. The word "without" was underlined eight times in angry, hooked scrawls. They split up a few days later.

Ironically, it was John who started the divorce action in papers filed at the Price County Courthouse, a few blocks away from his parents' home. Wisconsin is a no-fault divorce state, and according to statutes it is not necessary to provide a reason or grounds for seeking dissolution of a marriage.

At that time and later, John blamed another man who worked with Emily for taking her away from him. A relative of Patrick Schmidt had tipped him off that her brother reputedly had something going on with Emily. Schmidt was a good-looking bachelor, and John was convinced he was romancing Emily. But jealousy and blaming other people for his problems weren't new to John.

The real reason for John and Emily's breakup was more likely an accumulation of the problems the couple had been trying to cope with since the first days of their marriage.

He was living at home when Kathy made the five-hour drive to Phillips with a girlfriend for a long weekend visiting and spending some time looking up old friends and fishing on the local lakes. She hadn't lived at her parents' home since 1979 when she moved to Wausau to finish high school, and she eventually moved in with an older brother in Mukwonago, a little Wisconsin town of about four thousand people a half-hour drive southwest of Milwaukee.

She told her friend from Mukwonago a few things about her brother's sporadically abnormal conduct. Her friend had met John a few times before and replied that she didn't believe it was anything they should worry too much about. They could handle it. But Kathy had seen John at his most erratically dangerous, and she wasn't so sure. She was uneasy about staying in the same house with him, and as she always did when he was around, she kept a vigilant eye open for trouble.

Despite John's fitfully atrocious behavior, he was still her little brother. After he returned home from the Army, she continued to try and be the best big sister that she could be to him. She often telephoned him from Mukwonago to talk and exchange chitchat about their family and activities.

Kathy and her friend visited with them and with the elder Webers in Phillips about once every two months. Once or twice the two young women from downstate went out for a night on the town with Emily and John. Kathy noticed on those occasions that her brother drank a lot of beer, but even when he obviously had too much he was never mean or insulting. On those occasions he was more likely to become depressed and sorry for himself, and he never acted as if he was looking for a fight.

During Kathy's trip home in the spring of 1987, she was sorry for John because he seemed to be taking his latest breakup and the divorce action with Emily so hard. She tried to assure him that someday he would find the right woman. She even offered to try and fix him up with some of her girlfriends. John wasn't interested in either suggestion. He responded with tears, and moaned that Emily was the only woman he loved and no one could ever take her place. He blubbered that he never wanted to be married again.

* * *

Kathy's tangled emotions took an outlandish turn from sisterly sympathy to creepy foreboding shortly after she and her friend from Mukwonago returned to the house at about eleven o'clock one night during her visit home. John was still out with his friend. Kathy sat up for a while, but by midnight, she had followed her friend to bed although she wasn't yet asleep. It wasn't the first time she had lain awake far into the night while she was in her room, and her brother was somewhere in the house.

The television and all the lights in the house except for a small nightlight in the kitchen were shut off when John walked into the living room about one A.M., and silently sat down in the darkness on a chair. Then he began talking to himself.

Kathy was jolted to attention and she strained to make out the low, whispered words. Then she realized that she was listening to a macabre conversation her brother was having with himself. She remained curled up on her side as if she were sleeping while she eavesdropped and peered through the open bedroom door. John was talking as if he were two people. His shadowy form was outlined in faint silhouette by the milky illumination of the nightlight, and Kathy could make out his hands moving about as he talked and gestured to himself. Sometimes he said his words in anger, as if he were arguing with another person.

It was one more creepy demonstration that her baby brother was still a deeply disturbed young man with a mind that was seriously garbled.

The feuding couple nevertheless got together again and began seeing a marriage counselor in an effort to patch up their differences. In January 1988, shortly before their divorce was to become final, they began living together once more as husband and wife.

On July 23, 1988, they attended the wedding of their friend and Emily's cousin, Keith Newbury. A couple of weeks later Emily stopped at the newly married couple's home to watch videos of the ceremony and reception, in addition to some other films. She left a note at the house for her husband telling him where she was so he could join the group after work. When he didn't show up she telephoned and asked him to join them. Her brother Larry and his girlfriend, Michelle, were there, and Emily thought John would enjoy the early evening get-together. He promised to drive over, but he never showed up.

John was drinking so often and so much that summer that Emily had trouble telling when he was on the sauce and when he wasn't. She had to smell his breath to be sure. It was hard to tell exactly what his normal state was. His eyes were haunted and in their sunken sockets they looked like a dead zone. It was a period when his self-control was fraying at the edges and unknown to Emily and his friends, his sanity was rapidly leaking away. He was preoccupied with his private demons and lusts, rapidly plunging into a dizzying descent into darkness.

Most of his buddies were aware that he had seriously stepped up his drinking. John dropped in at his friend Tim Denzine's house every once in a while with a couple of rental videos, and it wasn't unusual for him to polish off a twelve-pack of Millers while they watched the movies together.

Nevertheless, during that summer when Carla had been missing nearly two years, Emily began feeling that she and John were sharing some of the best times of their marriage. They rode around together on the bike, visited with other couples, and attended auto shows together. Once they drove downstate to the town of Iola near Stevens Point for a big show.

Perhaps more important, John's self-confidence was given a big boost after he found medical help for his problem with impotence. He considered different methods of treatment. But after driving 140 miles to Minneapolis to see a specialist, he eventually settled on treatment that called for taking an injection of the opium alkaloid, papaverine, directly into the base of his penis shortly before intercourse. Papaverine is a vasodilator—it widens blood vessels and has been used to treat such ailments as irregular heartbeat and reduced blood supply to the lower limbs. Patients whom papaverine is prescribed for are usually advised by their physicians to avoid alcohol because it increases the sedative effect. It was effective for John's particular problem, but it was painful.

Even John's stuttering was showing signs of easing off. There was no longer as much reason for him to feel inadequate when he was with his wife.

On August 2, he started a second job at Marquip, Inc., a factory in Phillips that manufactures machinery and other equipment for the corrugated industry. He worked four hours on the second shift from 3:30 P.M. to 7:30 P.M., Mondays through Fridays. There was just time between jobs for him to stop by at home for a few minutes, say a few words to Emily, and grab a sandwich before driving to the plant.

He told Jeff Hutchins, the production personnel manager who interviewed him and did the prehire screening, he wanted the job so his wife could quit work at the plastics factory. John didn't mention on his application or during the interview that he had MS. He stated that he was healthy and had a good back. Emily left the plastics factory to become a full-time homemaker for a while.

About the middle of the month John and Emily attended a party for Keith's older brother, Chris. He had returned to Phillips on leave from the military before being sent to the island of Guam for duty. The party at the home of the brothers' parents in Phillips started in early afternoon, and forty or fifty people drifted in and out at various times. Emily's brothers Gene, Jr., and Larry were among the crowd.

John was drinking Millers, and by ten P.M. when the party was breaking up, he was depressed and sitting by himself in his 1970 Oldsmobile listening to music. The last of the guests was leaving when Keith spotted him. Some other party goers had told him John crawled under the porch of the house earlier in the evening. Keith was concerned about his friend and he walked out to the car to see if he was okay and to chat.

John wasn't in a talkative mood, but he told his friend that Emily went home without him, and he was thinking about driving out to his parents' place north of town. He said he wanted to be there by himself for a while.

At home later that night his temper flared during a nasty confrontation with Emily in the bathroom. He grabbed her, shook her, and banged her head against the bathtub a couple of times. When she tried to get away, he refused to let her leave the house or use the telephone. Later he apologized for hurting her and promised to quit drinking. Emily also offered to support him by not drinking herself.

During the Price County Fair a few days after he roughed up Emily at the house, John announced to some of his buddies who were hanging around with him that he was going to give up drinking because it was causing too many problems for him. Sometimes when he was drinking and he and Emily were having one of their quarrels, he slapped her around, he confessed. Keith Newbury, and a few other friends and acquaintances of John were at the fairgrounds on the northeast edge of Phillips when he made the vow. He was holding a cold can of Miller in his hands.

Even the Scharps had cut down on their number of visits with him and Emily during the past few months, although Roxanna still considered John to be an easygoing, pleasant person. But he was drinking more than ever before.

On a more positive note, John and his wife were considering

taking his parents up on an offer to allow them to move into their own place on the eighty-acre spread north of town. The elder Webers were thinking of moving out there themselves, and said John and Emily were also welcome to put up a house or haul a trailer home to the property and settle down.

About mid-morning on Friday, September 2, employees at Winter Wood Products were looking forward to the long Labor Day weekend when John approached his supervisor and explained he wasn't feeling good and wanted to go home. He had a good attendance and work record, and a few minutes after obtaining permission to leave he walked through the plant.

Later that day John failed to show up for his 3:30 P.M. to 7:30 P.M. shift at Marquip. It was his fourth absence in the four weeks he was employed there. Unlike the previous absences, however, he didn't bother to telephone the second-shift supervisor to say he wouldn't be in to work that day. He simply didn't show up.

Instead, he spent part of the afternoon at the farm with his father, who was working on tombstones for Brownie and her pups. John tinkered with his pickup truck. He wasn't in a very talkative mood, but he said he wanted to get some of the preliminary work done by Sunday so he could begin taking out the motor before the end of the long weekend. The work was going slowly, however, and he tossed down a few beers while poking at the truck's innards with his wrenches and other tools. Lawrence Weber later recalled that when they parted company about 5 P.M. his son was not intoxicated.

Chapter Five

The Attack

Early Sunday evening Alan Lobermeier was holding down the fort as duty officer at the Phillips Police Department on what appeared to be shaping up as a relatively quiet three-day holiday weekend when the telephone rang.

The caller, who identified himself as John Weber, reported that his wife, Emily, had been abducted and assaulted by three men on Saturday night.

"They kidnapped her, beat her up, and left her naked in the woodlands," he blurted out. Continuing the startling account, John said she was released after the beating and returned to the house early that morning in terrible shape. After cleaning her up and tending to her wounds, he eventually telephoned his mother-in-law for advice and Mrs. Lenz and a daughter-in-law came to the house, picked up Emily, and drove her to the Flambeau Medical Center in Park Falls.

John went along to the hospital with his wife and in-laws and was telephoning from there.

Lobermeier, a part-time officer who later joined the four-man department on a full-time basis, pressed for a few more details from the caller, including the location of the abduction. John said his wife was grabbed and pulled into the car as she was walking near a structure at the edge of the downtown area in Phillips known as The Normal Building. Lobermeier asked

John to stop in at the police station when he returned to Phillips that evening for a more intensive interview to fill in additional details, and the young husband agreed to.

A moment after hanging up the telephone Lobermeier began punching in the private number for Chief of Police Craig A. Moore's home and informed him about the reported kidnapping and assault. Chief Moore listened while the officer passed on the information about John's call, then advised that he was leaving home to drive to the station. His brief holiday was over.

Moore arrived a few minutes later at the basement offices shared with the Price County Sheriff's Department and took personal charge of the investigation. The Phillips police force was small, and Chief Moore was the most experienced officer on the department. He was serving his second round of duty there and had been chief for about fifteen months. Moore began his career as a law enforcement professional in 1972 when he joined the Wisconsin State Patrol. He served four years as a trooper before leaving to accept a position as a detective in Manitowoc with the Manitowoc County Sheriff's Department a few miles south of Green Bay along the shoreline of Lake Michigan.

In 1979 he moved again, this time to Phillips and a job as a patrolman and assistant chief of police. Three years later he left to take his first law enforcement job outside the state, and accepted a position as chief of police in Greybull, Wyoming, a town of twelve hundred people at the edge of the Bighorn National Forest and the Bighorn Mountain range. Greybull was only a few miles from the Montana border and was even smaller and more isolated than Phillips. He remained in Greybull for about five years, serving part of that time as undersheriff of Bighorn county, until June 1987 when he returned to Phillips as the new chief of police.

* * *

Moore conferred with his subordinate for a few minutes, then headed for The Normal Building for a quick look around the area. There was no purse or anything easily visible in the immediate area such as cosmetics, a checkbook, or other items that looked as if it may have been spilled from a purse, and no shoes or other articles of clothing to indicate a struggle or abduction occurred there. The chief climbed back into his car and drove to the Weber house, where he knocked at the doors of the neighbors on both sides of John and Emily's home. He asked the residents if they had heard or seen anything unusual going on at the Weber house that day and the previous night. No one had anything helpful to report.

Back at headquarters, Moore talked with his colleagues at the Price County Sheriff's Department and arranged for a deputy to stop at the Flambeau Medical Center and do an initial interview with Emily. Park Falls Police patrolman Edwin Simpson was sent to the hospital to take photographs of her injuries.

At about 9:30 that evening John walked into the Price County Safety Building and met with Moore in the basement headquarters. The young husband's shoulders were slumped, the sleeves of his checkered shirt were rolled up, and his eyes had a look of worried apprehension.

Moore recognized the nervous husband. He knew almost everyone in Phillips, especially the young men John's age who caroused in the local saloons, spun their tires, and kicked up gravel when they were feeling good and showing off, got into minor scrapes over other bad driving habits, or scrapped over the local girls. Most of the trouble they got into was minor and was quickly sorted out. There was a bit more serious orneriness now and then, but it was nothing to compare with the murderous shoot-outs and other violence of the big cities.

Moments after John walked into the office, he was repeating his story, and providing important details to fill out the bare outline he had given to Lobermeier during the telephone call. Moore and his subordinate talked with him in a small interview room next to the steps leading from the ground floor to the basement a few feet down a hallway from their own offices. Although the room was carpeted, it was furnished with only the basic necessities, a long table and a couple of chairs. It wasn't designed for comfort.

Before beginning the interview, however, Moore read the obligatory Miranda warning to John advising him of his rights. Although John was not being treated as a suspect in his wife's reported abduction and beating, the chief was careful to touch all the legal bases and was "going by the book." It was a routine process, but John nevertheless bristled at any thought that Moore might believe he could have something to do with the attack on his wife.

The young man was especially shaken when the chief asked him to take off his shirt so he could be checked for marks or bruises. John's upper body was free of suspicious marks, except for a small bruise on his right bicep. His hands were also checked, and although they were cracked and dirty with grease in the creases and under his nails as if he had been working on car engines, they were free of fresh scratches or lacerations.

Moore explained that checking him for bruises and repeating the Miranda warning didn't mean he was making an accusation. They were merely formalities, and the same process was followed with everyone else he talked to in similar situations.

Despite his misgivings about being read the warning, in other respects John was the model of a concerned husband who was angry and determined to see the abusers of his wife brought to justice. He consented to the reading of the warning. While Moore read from a printed copy of the warning, he made check marks on the paper as each of the rights was explained. When he completed reading and explaining the warning, the nervous young man signed his name, "John R. Weber," to indicate he had been properly informed and understood his action in waiving his Constitutional rights under the

Fifth Amendment. Then he settled back to answer questions and to tell his story to Chief Moore and the patrolman.

Moore started the interview by asking if John had anything to do with Emily's beating. He was taken aback by the blunt question, and replied with a question of his own. "Do you feel that I have got something to do with this?"

The police chief said he didn't have an opinion either way. He was merely concerned with gathering facts.

According to John's account, he and his wife were spending a quiet evening at home watching television Friday night when at about half-past ten Emily announced she was in the mood for a snack downtown. John wasn't hungry and had no interest in going out, so she left by herself to walk the few blocks to the tiny business district. She hadn't returned by 11:30, so John turned off the television, undressed, and went to bed.

When he woke up at about seven o'clock the next morning, Emily was stretched out naked on top of the covers next to him. Still groggy with sleep, John slid out of his side of the bed without waking her and padded into the kitchen to begin brewing a pot of coffee. A few minutes later when he walked back into the bedroom and flicked on the light, he got a closer look at his wife and snapped wide-awake. She was lying on her face and her body and legs were a mass of cuts and bruises.

When he turned her over he saw that her face as well as her body was a battered, bruised, slashed, and punctured mess. Blood and dirt were smeared everywhere, and her face looked like it had been torn up by a bobcat or one of the feisty black bears that roamed the Chequamegon National Forest. Her eyes were swollen shut, her lips were cracked and twice the size they were supposed to be, and the few areas of flesh that weren't covered by blood or dirt were bruised an ugly purple. Pieces of duct tape were stuck in her hair.

John hurried to the bed and asked what had happened to her. Emily was barely conscious and had difficulty talking through her bruised and mangled lips, but haltingly, a few words at a time, she recounted a horror story.

She was just beginning the walk home after finishing her snack when a car skidded to a stop beside her, three men grabbed her, pressed a thick strip of tape over her eyes, and hustled her inside the vehicle. She was threatened with a knife while she was subdued and blindfolded. As soon as she was in the car, they drove away from Phillips and into the woods, where they stripped her naked and beat and tortured her. After they finished the dreadful assault, they pushed her out onto the road, still nude. Everything happened so fast and efficiently she had no chance to get a look either at her attackers or at their car.

Somehow Emily managed to struggle to her feet and drag herself back through the quiet streets of the town and the gray light of the freshening dawn, stumble inside the house, and drop into the bed at about 6 A.M. beside her slumbering husband.

John was shaken by the nightmare story. He said he did his best to clean her up, and clipped the chunks of duct tape from her head with scissors instead of ripping it free and tearing her hair out with it. Then he helped her into the bathroom, filled the tub with warm water, and gently eased her inside.

He dabbed at the streaks of dirt and blood with a wet wash towel, then helped her out of the tub and dried her off. John said when he began trying to treat some of the worst of the injuries with ointments and covering them with bandages from a first aid kit, Emily screamed that she didn't want him to touch her. She was in terrible agony. At last he helped her slip into a clean nightgown and put her back into bed. When he tried to leave the house to call the police or summon help from somewhere else, his wife insisted that she just wanted to be left alone. John said he was confused and didn't know what to do.

Emily remained in the bed, moaning in pain and alternately drifting off to sleep or slipping in and out of consciousness throughout the morning and most of the afternoon. Her husband managed to get her to drink a little water, but it made her sick. He was sure she was getting worse because her wounds were full of dirt and she hadn't had any professional medical attention. Nevertheless she pleaded with him not to call a doctor or notify the police, because she was so embarrassed over being stripped and beaten. She didn't want anyone to see her in that condition.

Throughout the day he checked on her condition hourly, until finally about five o'clock he realized she had to have more help than he could provide. He telephoned her mother and told her that Emily had been viciously beaten and was in bad shape. Mrs. Lenz and a daughter-in-law hurried to the house and arrived within a few minutes. The women took one look at Emily, and immediately got her out of bed. Then they slipped a blue sweater over her shoulders and helped her from the house and into their car and drove her eighteen miles to the Flambeau Medical Center.

It was quite a story for Chief Moore to digest. He had heard other stories as bad, or worse, and during his sixteen-year police career he saw more than his share of men and women who were badly beaten or savagely murdered. Living in a small town is no guarantee that someone will avoid becoming the victim of violence at sometime in their lives. If anything, it just lessens the odds a bit.

But like other lawmen, the chief didn't believe everything he was told, and it was his job to check out the dreadful account the concerned young man had just related to him. Even if Emily had begged her husband not to tell anyone about the savage attack on her, it was difficult for the chief to understand why John complied and waited almost a full day before summoning help. Moore asked him to run through the story again.

John patiently repeated the account. He added a snippet or two of information he left out the first time, but the story was basically the same. There were no glaring discrepancies or differences in the two accounts.

A mixture of sincerity and puzzlement marked John's expression while he had recounted the dreadful events of the previous evening and the morning. There was also an element of husbandly anger. He blustered that he would like to get his hands on the mystery men. He added that he had no idea who attacked his wife. They were probably maniacs, he remarked, as much to himself as to the police chief. John said he wanted the men caught and sentenced to the maximum prison terms possible for doing what they did to his wife.

He was curious about how they would be run down and captured, and what would happen to them. He was especially interested in the investigative techniques that would be used, and who else the chief was likely to talk to about the case. Like many experienced police officers, Moore had developed valuable instincts over the years that served him well, and he was getting disturbing signals from the husband.

John was visibly nervous, and the focus of his questions about the directions the investigation would take were especially suspicious. But there were other elements of the story that were difficult for the seasoned lawman to accept. It was hard to imagine a healthy young woman like Emily could have been snatched off the street so quickly and expertly, then held for three or four hours, and never at any time get a look at any of her abductors. And why was she grabbed, humiliated, and treated so roughly? Judging by her husband's story, rape wasn't the reason for the abduction. And robbery didn't appear to be the motive either.

It was especially difficult to believe that a naked woman who was half-blinded by swollen eyes, and beaten so badly she could barely move, had wandered through the streets of Phillips in a daze at five or six A.M. and had not been noticed by someone. Even at that hour of the morning there are always people who are awake, either returning home after late-night work shifts, nights out on the town, or merely because they're early risers. Yet, no one had telephoned the police department to report that a naked, bloody woman was staggering along the city streets.

The shaken husband talked and behaved as if he was sincerely concerned about his wife's well-being. But again, if that was true, why did he wait so long before summoning help? That was hard to understand. Something wasn't right about the story, and Moore was looking forward to checking it out by taking his own formal statement from Emily.

After John finished running through the account the second time, Moore asked permission to go to the house so he could gather up evidence such as the tape and chunks of hair clipped from Emily's head. There was a possibility that fingerprints of one of the abductors might be on the tape. The chief also wanted the clothes Emily was wearing the night she was attacked. When he asked where they were, John replied that he didn't know, but they might be at the house.

It was about 10:30 P.M., approximately an hour after the interview began, when John agreed to accompany Moore to the house to look for evidence. He even provided the transportation, because the Phillips Police Department's only car was in use by another officer carrying out normal patrol duties. One of Emily's brothers accompanied them.

John led the way into the kitchen through a side door, and walked immediately to the bathroom. A strip of gray duct tape with chunks of Emily's hair matted in it was one of the first bits of evidence collected. John bent over and plucked it from a wastebasket by the sink and handed it to Moore. The chief pulled another piece of tape and matted hair John had missed from the wastebasket and placed it along with the first chunk into a clear plastic evidence bag. John identified both the strips of tape and matted hair as the pieces he had clipped from his wife's head while he was cleaning her up.

When Moore noticed a door on a cabinet was off its hinges and slumping over the toilet, he asked what had happened. It looked like someone may have fallen against it with a lot of force. John replied it had been that way for a while. The bathtub was filled with dirty water and John explained it was left over after he washed Emily. He drained and filled it several times while caring for her wounds, but the water left over was still dirty. Moore drained the tub, and swabbed the sediment at the bottom with toilet paper, which he kept as evidence.

Before leaving the house he also stripped the sheets and a blanket from the couple's water bed to take back with him to his office. The bedclothing was spotted with dirt, twigs, leaves, and what appeared to be bloodstains. John supplied bags for Moore to put the linens in. The police chief asked him to stick around town and the county area so that he would be available if he was needed further to help out during the investigation. John could hardly have been more accommodating, and he quickly agreed. He expected to either be in Phillips or at the Flambeau Medical Center visiting his wife, anyway.

The clothing Emily was wearing when she was kidnapped wasn't at the house. It seemed the abductors may have kept them or thrown them out along a backroad or highway somewhere.

It was eleven P.M. and Chief Moore was back at his headquarters, when he slid the evidence bag inside another larger plastic container and filled out an evidence custody form. Then he attached the custody form to the outer container and filed the package in the Phillips Police Department evidence room. It had already been a long day for the chief, but the investigation was just getting started.

Moore decided to do his own follow-up interview with Emily. During her brief and difficult talk with the sheriff's deputy at the hospital, she briefly confirmed the same basic story her husband had told. But Moore wasn't buying the yarn about three mysterious kidnappers, either as told by John or as told by his wife. He suspected that Emily was covering up for someone such as her husband, or another relative or individual she had a close relationship with.

The chief telephoned the medical center and asked if Emily was strong enough for him to meet with her for a few minutes that evening for an interview. He was advised that she wasn't. She was in bad shape and a lengthy rest was essential to her recovery. Emily's brief earlier contact with law officers at the medical center had already exhausted her. She permitted Simpson to photograph the lacerations and bruises to her face, limbs and torso, even her punctured buttocks. Despite her weakened condition, however, she firmly resisted having pictures taken of cruel damage inflicted on her genitals. Her pelvic area was modestly draped in a sheet for the picture-taking.

Moore talked with her doctor and a nurse and set up a tentative interview for late the next morning when she was expected to be better rested and to have recovered some of her strength.

At about 11:45 Monday morning Chief Moore drove his squad car to the Flambeau Medical Center for a talk with Emily. When the chief arrived, John was already chain-smoking Salem Lights in the visitors' lounge. He was dressed in a pair of blue jeans, a brown jacket, rumpled white shirt, gray tennis shoes, and a blue baseball cap. John had a two-pack-a-day habit when he was separated from the Army, but before the day was over he would go way over his usual limit.

As Moore was ushered into the Intensive Care Unit, a single room just off the main nurses' station at the small hospital, he was confronted with a woman who had been nearly beaten to death. Even after she was cleaned up, her injuries treated by doctors and nurses, and she was given medication and put to bed, Emily still looked as if she were in great pain. Her face and head were one big purple-and-yellowish lump of damaged tissue and bone.

According to the medical professionals who treated her, she

had knife cuts over her upper body, puncture wounds on her breasts, multiple contusions and bruises of the face, ragged gashes were rudely exposed on her legs, and she had been sexually assaulted. Her most critical injuries were blunt trauma to her head. Her face and skull had been repeatedly smashed with a hard object.

Moore didn't know Emily and he mentally estimated that she was a stocky woman who weighed about two hundred pounds. But the truth was, before her beating and torture she weighed just about half that. Swelling had bloated her face and head way in excess its normal size. Her eyes were swollen completely shut and she had to depend totally on hearing or touch to determine who was in the room with her.

"If she had not received critical care within that hospital Emily probably would have died," Moore later recalled.

The chief told Emily who he was and gently inquired if she could answer a few questions. He wanted to know what happened to her and explained he needed any details she could provide about the possible identity of her attackers. He clicked on a tape recorder and placed it on the pillow next to Emily's mouth.

The injured woman could barely move her grossly puffed and broken lips. But slowly, she managed to force out enough painfully whispered words to provide a bare-bones confirmation of the same story her husband told to Moore about her abduction and beating. It was the same story she told to her mother and sister-in-law, then repeated to the sheriff's deputy.

At times Moore could hardly make out Emily's faint responses to his questions. He was patient and careful, but doggedly picked at inconsistencies or suspicious elements in her account. Despite his caution, when he pressed too hard for clarification or additional information, the intensive-care nurse who was watching the patient's vital signs warned him that Emily's blood pressure was rising.

Moore broke off the interview to give Emily a chance to compose herself and rest before trying again. John was lying down, curled up on a sofa with his back to the doorway when the chief walked by the visitors' lounge.

The next time Moore took a break from questioning Emily, John was waiting for him when he walked outside the intensive-care room. The concerned husband followed Moore outside to the parking lot, pestering him with one question after another. "What's happening? What did she say? What's going to happen to the guys when you catch them?"

John indicated he was especially concerned about the effect prolonged questioning might have on Emily's health. He was worried that Moore might be putting more pressure on her than she could handle, he said. The police chief replied he was merely providing an opportunity for her to talk about what happened and help him get to the truth. He kept his other replies as noncommittal as possible, and fended the curious husband off until he was advised that Emily's blood pressure was down and he could resume with her questioning.

But every time he turned the questioning to the possibility that someone other than three mysterious men may have been responsible for the assault, Emily's blood pressure began shooting back up again. Moore started using her blood-pressure fluctuations as an unofficial polygraph, and began consciously sorting out pertinent questions or lines of questioning that sent it soaring. The subject that caused her blood pressure to rise most often was her husband, but gradually she began dropping increasing hints that he was involved with the beating.

During another of the recesses in the questioning, Moore asked the doctor who was in charge to ban anyone else from visiting Emily until the interview was completed. He didn't want John trying to pry information out of his wife—or inserting himself into the process in a possibly more menacing manner.

Each time Moore left Emily's bedside, John tagged along after him, peppering him with questions. Moore was professionally trained as an interrogator, and during his career had questioned hundreds of criminal suspects. He recognized that John was boring in like a professional. He had the instincts of a natural interrogator, and was coming as close as he could come to giving the policeman the third degree. He was able to phrase his questions so that it was difficult for the lawman to deceive him or lead him astray without betraying some emotion or hint about the true direction the talks with Emily were beginning to take.

By that time Moore had long ago given up any idea that Emily was abducted by strangers, and although he still didn't have a motive he was virtually certain that John had beaten her up. But if that was true, the inquisitive spouse had already shown a chilling capacity for violence, and the chief or no one else, could predict how he might react if he learned that he was a definite suspect. Moore continued veiling his answers in vague ambiguities.

Chapter Six

The Truth

As a practical matter, Emily's interview by that time had basically become an interrogation, gentle though it was. Although she was beginning to budge slightly, she was still reluctant to explain some of the most troubling inconsistencies and provide a more believable story. The tale she was telling simply didn't make sense.

Moore was convinced she was holding back the truth and lying, and he was no longer faced with the fairly easy and routine job of merely gathering information. He had to expose the lies and force out the truth, and that can be an especially ticklish job for a police officer when he is dealing with a victim instead of a perpetrator.

Moore realized that one of the major roadblocks to a breakthrough was fear. Emily couldn't see, and she wasn't sure of exactly who was in the room with her or how many people were listening to their conversation. She couldn't tell whether or not her husband was standing beside the bed. Inside the little room, Moore assured her that only he and the nurse were there, and no one was lurking in the hallway. John was in the waiting room and no one else who would possibly wish to harm her was around, he said.

Then the small-town cop played one of his favorite and most effective cards. He asked Emily if she believed in a Supreme

Being and felt that she could speak with Him? For Moore, using a belief in God to get the truth from a reluctant victim, is not a slick interrogation technique hatched by a hardened hypocrite. He is a man of strong religious beliefs, and he had learned that there were times when a shared belief can be used as a bridge between himself and the individual he is questioning to break down emotional and other barriers.

It was a technique that worked for him before with other victims who were either afraid to tell the truth, or were holding back for other reasons. The same approach seldom worked with criminal suspects. But Emily wasn't a criminal suspect; she was a victim. And it worked with her. She replied that she believed in God, and she agreed when Moore asked her to pray with him. They asked God to protect her and to give her the strength to tell the truth.

Emily spilled out the story, and it was even worse than Moore had suspected. But the young woman on the bed was obviously relieved when she finally began unloading her uncomfortable secret to her patient interrogator.

There was no mysterious trio of brutal kidnappers. John tortured her and nearly beat her to death while trying to murder her after luring her to the woods at his parents' property off State Road 13 and Rock Creek Road.

Moore and his law enforcement colleagues eventually reconstructed the attack and events leading up to the crime, based on Emily's statements and other information later developed during the investigation.

According to their reconstruction, on Friday, the eve of the Labor Day holiday, Emily spent most of the morning and much of the afternoon alone in the house on South Avon catching up on housecleaning chores. About 3:30 P.M., John telephoned and asked if she was doing anything. When she indicated she wasn't busy, John told her he had been to his parents' country place and had a surprise he wanted her to see. He said it had something to do with the talk about moving out there, but refused to give her any more details.

If she wanted to know what the surprise was, she had to wait for him to pick her up at the house in about an hour so he could drive her out to the spread in Flambeau township. The surprise sounded like an exciting way to conclude a quiet, boring day, and Emily eagerly agreed with his suggestion of an early-evening drive. John had apparently gotten over his pique from the previous night when he was in the mood for romance and she wasn't.

When he arrived at the house at about five P.M., Emily was waiting. She was dressed casually in tennis shoes, a pair of acid-washed jeans, a white sweatshirt with red sleeves and an Olympic symbol with the words "Montreal 1976," and a brown jacket with yellow letters spelling out "Winter Wood Products" on one side and her name on the other side. As Emily slipped into the old Cutlass beside him, John cautioned his wife not to look in the backseat. He said it would spoil the surprise if she peeked. Emily was excited and in a good mood, and she never once peeked into the backseat to see if the same busy clutter of odds and ends John habitually piled up there had been replaced with something new.

Before they left town John drove to a local IGA store and they went inside where he paid the clerk $2.49 for a 150-sheet, lined, spiral Mead notebook. Then they returned to the car to continue their trip to the country place. John didn't explain to his wife why he wanted the notebook.

While they headed north on State Road 13 she asked him a couple of times about the surprise and speculated that he was going to point out the site of the dream house they were planning to build. But John insisted she had to wait until they got to the property and saw for herself.

At last they reached the Weber place and John pulled the car off Highway 13 and onto the driveway leading to the pole-barn. Stopping at the building, he asked Emily to wait inside for a few minutes while he left to get her surprise ready. And he cautioned her not to peek out the window if she didn't want to spoil things.

As Emily settled down inside the quiet building to wait, it had started to drizzle. She heard John drive away in the car. Although she kept her word and didn't look through the window, she could tell that he didn't drive far and was still on the property because she could still hear the engine running.

Nevertheless it was twenty or twenty-five minutes before he returned. He had an open can of Miller in his hand when he picked her up. Once she was in the car he headed back along the driveway, then cut through a field and entered the woods. After guiding the car through breaks in the trees for a while, he stopped and asked Emily to close her eyes.

She figured John was finally going to reveal the surprise. She squeezed her eyes shut, and waited.

Curiously, as soon as she closed her eyes John began fooling around with her long brown hair, lifting it up in the back and running his hands over her neck. He didn't tell her to open her eyes or say anything about why he was playing with her neck, and Emily began to get uneasy. Then she started getting scared.

"Is this going to hurt?" she asked.

She barely asked the question before she felt something long and metallic pressed to her throat. Emily snapped her eyes open.

Her husband was holding his favorite hunting knife against her skin. It was the knife her parents gave to him as a birthday present.

John snarled that he wanted to know if she was cheating on him and fooling around with some other man.

Emily wasn't cheating and she tried to convince him that he had nothing to worry about.

John advised her that he was going to blow his head off, and brought her to the woods so she could watch him kill himself.

"Was it a short little gun?" Moore broke in, hoping to get

an idea of the caliber of the weapon. Emily said she didn't know. Although she was nervously watching for a firearm, John didn't produce his pistol or one of his rifles.

Instead, he switched direction. He ordered Emily to use the new notebook to write some letters, and to address and write notes on a couple of birthday cards. One of the letters was to John and the other was to Emily's father. John had already written both letters in his own handwriting, and insisted that she copy the messages word for word. John reached into the backseat and handed her a packet with the sample letters, cards, envelopes, and some other material.

There was no way Emily could miss the ominous significance of his meticulous preparation and the menacing demand. But John made it clear she had no choice except to do as she was told. He smashed her in the mouth with his fist and threatened to cut off her breasts if she refused.

Reluctantly following her husband's directions, the frightened woman copied a letter apologizing to her father for leaving, but stating that she couldn't let her parents know where she was. She added that she didn't know when she might return home.

In the letter addressed to her husband, she said she was sorry but couldn't continue the way things were going. She wrote that she should have never returned to him, and noted that she was aware from the way people looked at her what they were thinking. They would never forget. "Neither will I. I know you will be better off without me," she added. Continuing to copy from the message prepared by John, she said she knew his parents hated her, and she was sure her own parents wished she had disappeared instead of Carla. Throughout the letter, Emily assumed all the blame for their marital troubles.

Continuing to follow the original prepared by her husband, she said she was taking a few personal items she needed with her, and had written a personal check for $250 cash needed to get started on her own. She promised to pay it back. Emily

wrote that he should not search for her and said she was determined to start over again alone "without anyone around me
that I've hurt. It is hard to live with what I've done, especially
when you treat me as good as you do."

Nervously scribbling in the rapidly fading light, Emily
asked John to tell her mother that she loved her, even though
she knew she was never the daughter her parents wanted.
"Carla was!" she wrote. After telling John she hoped he would
find someone to love who treated him better than she had, she
was allowed to conclude the note with the words:

> I am sorry
> Love, Emily.

In a PS John composed, she asked him to tell their friends
they had been right about her, and to take care of their puppies
and her plants.

The letter traced a pitiful portrayal of a renegade wife eaten
by guilt and recriminations for her failure to be a deserving
mate to a loving husband. She was depicted as a woman of
such poor character, in fact, that she not only let her husband
down but betrayed the trust and love of everyone else who
cared about her.

In another shorter note, Emily was instructed to write that
she was enclosing a $30 money order to him. She wrote that
it was all she could afford at that time, but she would continue
to send more each payday. Again she apologized for hurting
those who loved her and said she hoped everyone was well.
After signing her name, she was made to add a PS. "Remember that I'll always love you."

John had composed the original of the shorter letter on the
front of an equipment inspection and maintenance worksheet
he had kept from his army days as a helicopter mechanic and
crew chief. Emily's note was written on the lined notebook
paper.

He gave Emily manila envelopes to address for each of the

letters; two to himself and one to her parents. She was instructed to write only her first name in the spaces for the return address.

John had also filled out messages to be copied on the cards. One of the cards was to be addressed to him for his birthday on November 4. The greeting on his card began, "Because you're a wonderful husband." He made her address the other card to her father and include a note for his birthday on October 24. The greeting on the card designated for Gene Lenz, Sr., began, "For a faultless dad, a no fault insurance policy." Finally he made her address envelopes for the cards and write out a personal check to herself for $250 cash from their joint bank account. Emily was so nervous she made a mistake and ruined the first check, so John made her write another.

The trembling, terrified woman already had every reason to expect the worst when she glanced at another piece of paper included in the packet her husband handed her. It was a long list filled out in what she recognized as John's handwriting. Three items he had listed among other notes to bring along with him included a gun, a knife, and some of Emily's clothing. He was keeping her too busy and watching too closely for her to have a chance to read much farther along the list, but she had time to make out one more entry and it was the most frightening of all. He had scrawled a reminder to dig two graves.

John told his wife he was going to get rid of her—like he got rid of her sister, Carla.

The appalling words cut through the quiet forest gloom. Emily's younger sister was no runaway, and she hadn't been abducted and carried off somewhere by strangers. John had known ever since she vanished that she was dead, because he was her killer.

Now Emily was alone with her husband in the rapidly darkening woods, and she realized she was also in grave danger of being murdered. Furthermore, no one else even knew they were together. He could murder her, mail the cards and letters in a few days or weeks, and no one would ever know what really occurred on his parents' property on that Labor Day weekend. She would disappear—just like her sister, Carla.

John got out of the car, walked around to the passenger side, and ordered his wife to get out. When she hesitated, he reached inside and dragged her out. He ordered her to strip. Again she hesitated, then slowly began to comply with his command. He was pointing the blade of his hunting knife at her, and judging from what she had glimpsed on the list, she believed he also had a gun stuck somewhere. Emily began reluctantly peeling off her clothes, and continued until she was wearing only her panties and bra in the chill late-summer evening drizzle.

Emily turned and ran for her life. Her husband scrambled after her, screaming, "Stop, or I'll kill you for sure." Even if she escaped she didn't have any marks of violence on her body and no one would believe her, he yelled. Emily was barefoot and nearly naked, and the threat worked. She got only a few yards before she stopped. John gripped her underpants in his hands and dragged her back to the front of the car. While she stood there shivering and waiting, he growled that he didn't want her looking at him and pulled a roll of duct tape from the car.

Emily was too frightened to try and run again, while he roughly wrapped strips of the tape around her head until he had covered her eyes and her mouth. Then he pulled her arms behind her back and taped her wrists together. She was helpless to resist when he used the buck knife to slash off her panties and bra, leaving her completely nude.

She was John's most lurid bondage fantasy come to life: a naked, frightened young woman who was bound, blindfolded, and gagged. He had gained total physical mastery over her, and according to his own peculiar whim could inflict whatever terrible pain and gross sexual indignities on her that he wished. Or he could exact the ultimate homage, and slowly savor the agonizing snuffing out of her life by torture.

John threw her onto her back and sat on her, while he carved two bloody slashes along her left breast, one at the top and the other to the side near the middle of her chest. Emily was as defenseless as she could be when he dropped the knife, clenched his hands into fists and began slamming her in the chest as hard as he could. She couldn't even scream through the duct tape gag. But the agony was just beginning.

John flipped her over on her stomach, sat on her with his back to her head, and cut two more deep slashes in her flesh, one in her right leg and the other in the left leg. Then he began jabbing the blade of the knife into her buttocks. The brutalized woman was writhing with pain and fear when her tormentor suddenly stopped slashing and chopping at her with the knife, and lurched to his feet. A few moments later Emily heard the click of his lighter, then smelled the smoke of a cigar.

He puffed the cigar to a rosy glow, then slowly as if he was savoring every moment, he pressed the tip to her cheek, then removed it and pressed it to her right breast. Finally he forced her legs apart and pushed the fiery end against the delicate and sensitive membranes inside her vagina.

John dropped the cigar and picked up one of the wheelbarrow handles he had brought home from his job at Winter Wood Products. The handles are long and smoothly rounded on one end, and square and larger on the other end. He began raping her with the wooden shaft, first vaginally, then anally. John alternated the ends.

While he jammed at her with the brutal implement, he accompanied the abuse with hateful taunts. "You must like this, because you're coming," he snarled one moment. "That's for not being in the mood last night," he growled at another. John hadn't forgotten or forgiven the rejection after all. Blindfolded, gagged, and with her hands bound behind her, Emily could do nothing but squirm and twist her body. John couldn't see her frightened eyes or hear her screams; but the pain and fear hung over the quiet forest like a red mist.

As soon as the last of the sun slumped behind the trees,

darkness had enveloped the forest. Inside the cloaked circle of trees and underbrush, there was no twilight and the deadly struggle between the fully clothed and booted man and the naked woman was marked only by their own grunts, the dull, moist splatter of the raindrops, and the cries of the nightbirds that were beginning to stir and ready themselves for the evening's hunt.

Somehow after the excruciating torment, Emily was still conscious and full of fight when John began trying to strangle her with his hands. She fought like a tiger, kicking her legs, squirming and pulling at the tape around her wrists until she finally loosened her hands. Then she began ripping at the hands gripping her throat, scratching and twisting at his fingers, straining with every ounce of her strength to pull them free.

Suddenly John released his hands from her neck and twisted his fingers in her long hair, then began dragging her through the underbrush deeper into the woods. She stumbled along behind him, trying to stay on her feet. When he finally released his hold on her hair, he knocked her to the ground again and started kicking her in the head. Emily's eyes were still taped shut and she couldn't see, but it felt like he was wearing his steel-toe boots. The kicks slammed one after another into her face and head, while she tried to roll away, clambered onto her hands and knees, or struggled shakily to her feet.

He finally stopped kicking her. But he had only interrupted his kill-crazy frenzy to switch to an even more potentially lethal weapon. Moments after the kicking ended he began smashing her in the head and face with the metal end of a shovel. Emily later estimated that she was kicked and hit in the head a total of at least twenty times. While he batted at her with the shovel, he grunted: "You're going to be a tough one to kill."

Emily could think of only one thing during the desperate struggle. She wanted to live. She didn't want to die. And she used every ounce of strength and will she had left in her tortured body to fight back. Every time he knocked her down with the shovel, somehow she managed to get back up on her feet. He knocked her down again, and she got up again, determined to win the deadly contest with her husband.

Nobody was counting, but like the other tortures the beating also ended. John simply stopped. He was panting and exhausted.

Pain washed over Emily's body in waves from the battering, the slashes, the punctures, and burns. She had slumped back to the ground when she brushed a hand over her left breast. A safety pin was stuck into the flesh and closed. Emily didn't even know when that particular torture was inflicted, and she had just been beaten almost to death. She nevertheless managed to work quickly and quietly while forcing the inch-and-a-half-long pin open. At last she pulled it out, and slipped it under some pine needles she was lying on. She wasn't even aware of any pain from her manipulations of the safety pin. Emily hurt so severely from just about every other bit of her body that the relatively minor pain from the pin wasn't even noticeable.

If her tormentor observed what she was doing, he kept it to himself. Instead of beginning some new torture or finishing off the weakened woman, he leaned over her and began talking.

"Remember what I said about Carla earlier?" he asked. "It's not true."

Emily passed out. Occasionally she slipped back to consciousness, and John was beside her or nearby.

"I remember that night when he was talking to me," she whispered to Chief Moore in the hospital room. "He was talking in a nice voice, you know, like he was real nice. Like he really felt bad, and I know he did."

Then she added yet another eerie surprise to the already bizarre story she was recounting to the lawman.

"All of a sudden there was another voice completely different. Mad! And he kept saying the name was 'Natas,'—that's 'Satan' spelled backwards. And that voice kept saying, 'Don't let her live!' It was real mean."

Emily said the other voice, which she described as "the good voice," objected to killing her, however. "I got to let her live. I can't kill her," she quoted the good voice as arguing. He was so upset by the murder demands of the bad voice that he pounded his fist into the ground.

"It just kept going back and forth like that. I wasn't even there. Like I wasn't even there," she shuddered as she recalled the spooky quarrel. "But he kept going back and forth like that."

Moore asked if her husband's voice changed to a lower, gruffer timbre, or if it was merely louder.

"It was a completely different voice, lower, meaner," she responded.

"You never heard him speak that way (before)?" Moore persisted.

"Never that way," Emily said. "It really scares me. That really scares me."

Moore asked what would happen to her if her husband was locked up. Could she survive? Emily said she could survive.

"You've shown that already. You're quite a fighter," the police officer told her. He asked if she had a job. Emily didn't, but she knew her parents would take her in until she found work. "I can't believe I lied to them about this," she said.

Moore told her not to worry about that. "Emily, you've got to realize that you truly thought you were going to die," he pointed out. She agreed.

"For some reason, I truly think that there was all the intention in the world there," Moore observed of her narrow escape from death. But something happened to her husband to snap him back to reality.

"I can't believe that he would want to do this to me," Emily moaned.

* * *

The interview returned to the immediate aftermath of the attack when the injured woman remained stretched out on the sodden leaves and pinecones, painfully playing tag with consciousness, into the predawn hours of the next morning. At last her husband finally roused her and said he was going to look for the car so they could drive home. The mournful cry of turtle doves and the noisy morning clatter of starlings, crows, grackles, and a multitude of songbirds was crackling through the gray light of the rain-dampened forest when he slipped his jacket over her bare shoulders.

It was about five A.M., twelve hours after he picked her up at their house to show her the "surprise," when John finally helped her into the car and drove back through the woods toward the highway. He stopped at the garage to pick up a couple of cans of soda, after Emily mumbled that she was thirsty. John claimed he couldn't take her home earlier because he couldn't find his car in the dense woods, so he stayed with her and protected her through the long, torturous night.

At some time, either in the woods or during the trip home, John told his wife he had stopped beating her because he could hear her voice. He was able to hear what she was saying. It was a perplexing statement, but Emily was in no condition or mood to concern herself with the esoterics of John's thinking processes. She had been cut, battered, and defiled; there was hardly an inch of her body that wasn't either lacerated, punctured, or grossly swollen. She ached and hurt all over.

When they reached their house on South Avon, the sky had already lightened and faint streaks of pink and gold were signalling the imminent rise of the sun. John helped her out of the car, then supported her with his arm under her shoulder and around her waist while she wobbled unsteadily into the shadowy house. Inside, he lowered her into the bathtub, bathed her, and cleaned and bandaged some of her wounds. At last he helped her into their bedroom and she slumped into bed. He was the very picture of a concerned husband, caring for his badly injured wife.

Emily slept for almost ten hours until about 3:30 Saturday afternoon. Although the duct tape had been removed, her eyes were swollen shut and she couldn't see. But she knew her husband's voice when he sat on the edge of the bed and began reciting a story he wanted her to tell to explain the reason behind her dreadful condition. John sounded sincere, caring—and worried.

It was the story he later recounted to Officer Lobermeier and Chief Moore, and the same basic account that Emily provided of her ordeal during her early interviews with Moore and the Price County Sheriff's Department deputy. She was temporarily blind, had been beaten nearly to death, and she was afraid not to do as her husband told her.

When Emily painfully whispered out the last of the story to Moore about her husband's murderous attack on her in the woods, it was a few minutes before two P.M.. Monday. The determined police chief had spent nearly three hours conducting the off-and-on interview with the critically injured woman, reassuring, persuading, and praying with her while he struggled to fit together the pieces of the puzzle. But he felt that she had at last given him as truthful and complete an account as it was possible for her to do at the time. There were still loose ends to clear up, as there always are, but Emily could be reinterviewed later when she was rested and stronger. And leads could be followed up through other people and avenues.

Chapter Seven

The Arrest

One of Emily's statements that still troubled him was the reference to Carla. Moore was in Wyoming when Carla disappeared, and even after he returned to Phillips he wasn't closely involved in the search effort because it was a Price County case. He was only superficially aware of the investigation being conducted by his colleagues with the county. And he hadn't known either of the sisters before his talks with Emily, so he didn't know about the family relationship. He knew the missing girl's last name was Lenz. Emily's was Weber.

So far as Moore knew, Emily's puzzling remarks about John's boast of killing Carla, then his denial, marked the first time that anything was said or occurred that cast the young Phillips man in a role as a suspect in the teenager's possible abduction and murder. In fact there had been no previous official indication by investigators that she was anything more than a runaway.

Moore had other knotty situations to deal with before he could dig out more information about Carla, however. He realized after his interview with Emily that the attack occurred outside his legal jurisdiction. John assaulted his wife in the rural county area, not in the city of Phillips. Consequently the primary law enforcement responsibility in the case was with county sheriff Wayne Wirsing, not with the chief of police.

But other pressing considerations were also involved. Moore had been a county sheriff and a detective, and knew the importance of moving swiftly once the cat was out of the bag. John had to be arrested immediately. Moore wanted the homicidal husband in custody for Emily's protection, as well as to prevent him from fleeing, destroying evidence, or committing some other act that could conceivably interfere with the expeditious progress of an orderly investigation.

"I'm not a territorial person," he explained months later. "I don't believe in jurisdictions. I believe in getting the job done."

The first matter for him to take care of was getting John safely in custody, and he was still waiting expectantly in the lobby for news about Emily's latest round of questioning.

Moore expected to have the advantage of surprise in his favor when he put the collar on John. But at approximately 165 or 170 pounds, the lanky factory worker was heavier, as well as taller, than the police chief. He was also younger, and presumably would be frightened and desperate when he realized he was being arrested. Moore walked to the nurses' station just outside the intensive-care room, picked up the telephone, and quietly relayed a request to the Price County Sheriff's Department for a backup officer.

A few minutes later patrolman Josef Jeffrey Jeske of the Park Falls Police Department walked into the hospital. Moore explained to the young officer that he was going to make an arrest, and there was a chance the man would try to break free and escape.

Moore was a quick study, and after his talks with John, and his knowledge of the crimes he was apparently responsible for, the chief thought there was a good chance that if he got away once he wouldn't be taken alive. He also figured that if he was the only lawman John had to deal with, or there was a possible escape route that was still unblocked, John would make a run for it.

The police chief and the patrolman worked out a whispered plan of action, then Moore moved down the lobby and approached John. He told his suspect to turn around, to spread his feet and place his hands on the wall. He was under arrest. Moore's order was gruff—all business and all cop.

John's eyes darted toward an exit door. Jeske was just moving away from the door, farther into the lobby area. The Cutlass was parked a few feet away from the exit just outside in the parking lot, but there was no escape there. Moore had his eyes on John's eyes, and he saw the desperation of a cornered man who would do just about anything to bolt for freedom. But there was no place to run.

"I knew if he got to that car that, the thought that was going through my mind . . . was that if John gets to his car John is not going to stand trial. John will commit axicide or something," Moore recalled later. The chief explained that "axicide" is a term used by law enforcement and others for using a motor vehicle to commit suicide. "I figured he was going to get in the car and just whip the pedal to the metal and never arrive any place in one piece."

When John was placed under arrest and cuffed with his hands behind his back, he had no way of knowing exactly what or how much Moore knew about what he had been up to. But he knew he had beaten his wife half to death. And he knew the role he had played in the mysterious vanishing of her sister. His back was to the wall.

By an unfortunate occurrence of bad timing, just as Moore led his prisoner through the exit door, Emily's parents had just gotten out of their car and were approaching them from the parking lot. They drove to the hospital to visit with their critically ill daughter, and suddenly they were face-to-face with their son-in-law being dragged away in handcuffs by a policeman.

John immediately yelled at Mrs. Lenz: "I don't know what's going on, but they have put me under arrest for Emily."

The Lenzes had been through about as many nasty shocks recently as they could handle. Gene Lenz, Sr., demanded to know what his daughter's husband was doing being dragged away from Emily's sickbed in handcuffs. It appeared that Moore was heaping just one more indignity on the shell-shocked family, but the chief had no time just then to soothe the injured feelings of Emily's parents.

He told them that after he locked John in the cage car outside, he would talk with them for a few minutes. In the meantime, however, he ordered them to stand aside and get out of his way. The unpleasant confrontation had put together one of the puzzle pieces that Moore was left mulling over after his interview with Emily. Emily's maiden name was Lenz, and she and Carla were sisters.

The Lenzes were waiting for his explanation when he walked back into the lobby after securely locking John inside the cage car. Moore was blunt, brief, and firm. He explained that their son-in-law was going to be charged with several offenses, including aggravated battery of Emily. And there might be some evidence, as well, that John had something to do with their younger daughter, with no elaboration about a possible kidnap or murder.

In the meantime, Emily was very ill and needed them to be with her, he said. Moore broke off the uncomfortable talk, convinced the couple didn't believe a word he had said about John.

Before driving away with his prisoner, Moore advised Jeske that he was going to impound John's car and asked the Park Falls officer to guard it until a wrecker operator arrived. The chief had already frisked his prisoner, and he gave the keys to the Cutlass to Jeske. The Park Falls officer stayed in the parking lot at the rear of the hospital with the car until a local automotive repair and towing service operator showed up with a truck. The officer unlocked the driver's side door so that Herbert H. Damrow, Sr., could reach inside and make sure the steering wheel was secure. Then Jeske locked the door again, Damrow hooked the car to his wrecker, hoisted it up, and hauled it away to the garage adjacent to the Price County Public Safety Building. As the tow truck rumbled out of sight pulling the battered yellow-paint-and-primer-covered clunker behind it, Jeske turned and walked to his squad car and resumed normal patrol.

Moore had driven John as far as Rock Creek Road, where he was met by sheriff's deputies in a two-man car. While he was with Moore, John continued to pester him with questions.

At Rock Creek Road, John was transferred to the sheriff's squad car and driven straight back to the Public Safety Building by the same route the tow truck operator took a few minutes later. At the Safety Building, Moore helped the prisoner out of the cage car and led him inside to the Price County Sheriff's Department offices, where the cuffs were removed from his hands and he was turned over to the jailer, Sgt. Daniel Lee Greenwood.

The slender young man's features were contorted, and he looked like he was about to cry. John was still asking futile questions. He worried about missing work and losing his job. He worried about how his parents would handle the news when they learned of his arrest. In response to a question from Greenwood asking if he had fainted recently, he replied that he had. While helping fill in questions on a medical form, he explained to the jailer that he had MS and was taking medication for a bladder-control problem. He also confided that he had once had some trouble involving his sister and consequently was counseled by a psychiatrist. And he confided that he was a drinker.

John was frightened, worried, angry and resentful. He

couldn't understand why he was being submitted to such humiliation, because he hadn't done anything wrong, he told the jailer.

More alarming, he indicated he was thinking of killing himself, and said he had tried earlier the previous summer to commit suicide. Greenwood filled in the proper forms with information about the disturbing conversation.

The jailer also filled out the usual booking card, then ran the new prisoner through the routine. He inked and pressed John's fingers and thumbs onto the proper spaces on fingerprint cards, and stood him before a horizontally lined backdrop while a mug shot was snapped. The prisoner was also ordered to climb out of his outer clothing and put on a jail-issue jumpsuit. His trousers, shirt, and shoes were stacked in a basket that was locked, tagged with his name, and stored away with the personal effects of other inmates. The cap and the jacket—the same jacket he used to cover Emily with during the long, chill morning hours in the woods and on the ride home—were tagged with his name and hung in a linen closet.

John had run out of questions or given up on getting answers, and he was subdued and quiet when Greenwood at last led him into one of a pair of holding cells on the main floor of the building, then shut and locked the door.

He was the only prisoner in the cell and no one was locked up in the unit next to him. He slumped onto the bunk, and curled up facing the wall. There was no blanket in the receiving cell, but the failure to provide a cover was neither an oversight nor deliberately cruel treatment. It was one of the precautions taken with new inmates locked in the receiving cells to guard against suicide. John seemed oblivious to the deficiency, and a few minutes later he dropped into an exhausted slumber.

Greenwood, nevertheless, was concerned that his prisoner might commit suicide, or at least try to do away with himself. The experienced officer had taken suicide-prevention courses, and took some of the new prisoner's disturbing responses to questioning very seriously. So he telephoned the Counseling and Personal Development Center, located about ten minutes from the jail, which provided mental-health services for Price County.

The jailer told Donna L. Searle there was a new inmate at the lockup whom he suspected was a suicide risk. It was normal procedure to ask Ms. Searle or a male colleague to come to the jail and evaluate an inmate when there was concern about a possible suicide attempt.

If the evaluator is sufficiently concerned at the conclusion of the interview, jailers and the mental-health professionals arrange for an emergency commitment to a mental-health clinic or psychiatric hospital where the prisoner can remain under close watch while under treatment with counseling and medication. The professionals who use the law to commit a patient involuntarily to a psychiatric hospital refer to it as "a Chapter 51," for the heading of the Wisconsin State civil code which outlines and establishes the regulations for the procedure. The law is specifically framed to deal with patients who are considered dangerous to themselves or others.

Ms. Searle met with the suspect in the booking room, and was greeted by a denial. "I didn't do it. If I did that, I don't want to live," he said.

John was embarrassed, scared, and mentally and emotionally exhausted by the mess he had gotten himself into. This time he was in serious trouble that his family couldn't resolve for him, and a few days in a mental-health clinic, a year in a group home, even a three-year stint in the Army couldn't get him out of it.

The experienced social worker and counselor listened and observed carefully, mentally evaluating his orientation and his awareness of where he was and what was happening to him. She asked if he experienced blackouts. He said he didn't.

She was sufficiently disturbed by his emotional state and talk of suicide that she asked him to sign a brief contract with her, promising not to hurt or try to kill himself while he was in jail. She explained that if he didn't sign there was a good chance he would be sent to an institution where he could be safely cared for and protected from himself, he later recalled in sworn testimony. The Mendota Mental Health Institute at the edge of Madison was the most likely place.

John didn't like the jail, but at least it was in Phillips close to his family, and he didn't want to be sent to a mental institution miles away from home that he knew nothing about. He agreed to sign the paper.

Dated September 5, 1988, at the top and at the bottom, the statement read: "I, John Weber, give my word that I will not harm myself or attempt to kill myself. If I begin to have thoughts with the intent to do myself harm, I will notify the jailer, who will notify the counseling center."

He wrote out the statement in a curious scrawl that differed from his usual penmanship, and was part script and part printing. But the words showed his usual care with spacing and forming readable characters. He signed the statement, "John R. Weber." The social worker witnessed the statement, signing her name, "Donna Searle," absent the middle initial.

It was a written promise designed to provide social workers with an indication of whether or not inmates were really an immediate danger to themselves, rather than as some legally binding document. Presumably if John was willing to sign, that was an indication he wasn't ready to do away with himself.

Based on her training, experience, observations of the inmate, and on his agreement to sign the contract, she decided there was no evidence of delusions or paranoia. And even though he claimed to be having suicidal thoughts, there was no immediate need to invoke "a Chapter 51." She had used the contract twenty to twenty-five times before, and never had a signatory go back on her yet. Ms. Searle left with the document, and John was returned to the receiving cell where he quickly dropped off to sleep once more.

* * *

Faithfully, at least once every ten minutes throughout the dreary eight-hour shift, Greenwood nevertheless pushed the chair back from his desk, stood up, and walked downstairs to the holding cell. Quietly, he pushed back the small sliding window at the front of the metal-and-brick cubicle and peered inside. At the opposite end of the cell, John's body could be seen in the glow of the single, soft light. Most of the time he was lying on his side, face to the wall with his knees drawn up to his chest in a fetal position, apparently asleep. A few times he had shifted position and was facing the front of the cell, or he was lying on his back.

Greenwood didn't call out to John. Even when inmates were under close watch, it wasn't jail policy to needlessly disturb prisoners by waking them up to ask if they had been asleep. The jailer had to satisfy himself with visual checks, but each time he peered into the cell and took a good, long look to make sure the prisoner was breathing, moving about, or providing some other indication he was alive.

When night jailer Samuel Taylor, Sr., reported for duty at five P.M., Greenwood advised him that the inmate in the holding cell was a suspect in the attempted murder of his wife, and in the death of another woman. Greenwood cautioned his relief officer to watch the new prisoner closely and to check on him at least every ten minutes. The major concern of authorities at that point wasn't the possibility of an escape. John was on a suicide watch.

As soon as Greenwood left and Taylor began his shift, he picked up the prisoner's food tray from the cell. He didn't pay any attention to whether or not any of the meal was eaten, and he didn't feed him again during the night. Meals were served at the jail on a normal schedule, mornings, at noon, and early evenings. There was also a bubbler in the cell that John could use to drink from any time he wished.

Despite the document John signed promising to behave, Taylor didn't take any chances. As Greenwood had instructed, he checked on the new inmate every ten minutes. Taylor had only been on the job a little less than a year, and he didn't want a dead prisoner on his watch.

Taylor never spoke a word to the prisoner during the entire eight-hour shift. And nothing occurred to indicate that John had awakened at any time. There was no sound of a flushing toilet, and no requests for food, a cigarette, or an opportunity to make a telephone call. At one A.M. when Taylor went off duty, he passed on the same instructions about checking on the man in the holding cell at least every ten minutes to his relief, John Pavlek.

Moore had also undergone an exhausting night and day, but for the time being sleep was an elusive pleasure that he couldn't afford. He arranged for other officers to begin the process for obtaining warrants to permit an official search of John's car. Then he telephoned Lawrence Weber, advised him John was under arrest, and said there was good reason to believe a crime had occurred on the property along State Trunk 13 and Rock Creek Road. Moore explained he wanted to conduct a search. John's worried father agreed to meet the law officer at the farm.

Moore requested assistance from the Wisconsin State Patrol, and Trooper Bryan Floyd Vergin met him at the Weber country spread to look around. The state trooper and John's father arrived at the farm before the police chief, and they chatted for about twenty minutes before Moore finally drove onto the property. Vergin couldn't tell the older man much about what was going on because at that time he didn't have much information himself. And it wasn't his job to answer questions about investigations by his brother lawmen.

Moore asked for permission to make a consent search of
the property, and both uniformed officers made a point of reminding the elder Weber that he had the right to refuse. He
agreed to let them look wherever they wanted to, including a
pair of outbuildings—a shed and a structure that was sometimes referred to as a polebarn and at other times as a garage.
John frequently used the polebarn when he was working on
his cars, his pickup truck, or his parents' Chevette, and he had
the run of the place.

Lawrence Weber's ready cooperation was a welcome development for Moore that eliminated the time-consuming necessity
of formally applying to a judge for a search warrant. Agreeing
to a consent search of the property was only the first instance
in what would become a pattern of cooperation with investigators by John's father. Law enforcement authorities recognized
the family's willingness to help for what it was, good citizenship
and good neighborliness. While recognizing their responsibilities to the community, however, the elder Webers continued to
be loving and supportive to their son.

After Moore briefly recounted Emily's description of the
location of the attack, Lawrence Weber led the officers to a
faint trail with tracks a short distance from the buildings. A
few more squad cars pulled up and officers joined Moore and
Vergin as they followed the trail into the woods. Near the edge
of a swamp, Moore spotted a shovel lying a few inches off
the foot trail. It was lying beside a freshly dug hole, and several
long brown hairs were stuck in the metal seam.

The officers had found the site where Emily was sexually
abused, tortured, and beaten. There was an eclectic collection of
curious odds and ends that seemed to corroborate her amended
account to the chief. There was an empty gold-colored Miller
Draft beer can, a roll of silver duct tape, a tangled mat of several
strands of long brown hair, the butts of two Salem Light filtered
cigarettes, a Dutch Master cigar wrapper, a mud flap, a blue
baseball cap with a "Rumors End" logo, a Sears rechargeable
flashlight, and a hacksaw.

One of the most ominously significant items collected from the woods, however, was a wooden wheelbarrow handle. The dirty wooden implement, which was about three inches in diameter on the larger end, was stained with a rust-colored substance which had the appearance of dried blood.

Measuring one fresh hole in the ground, the officers determined that it was twenty-eight inches deep by thirty-four inches by twenty-six inches. The oblong trench was a bit small to serve as a grave for an adult woman, but there was plenty of room for it to be expanded. A second depression also discovered nearby by the officers was larger and measured roughly forty by forty inches.

Vergin sat down at his home a few hours later that night and drew three rough maps. The most detailed drawings were made of locations where Emily was assaulted; one a long view of what was believed to be the site of the original attack, and another of the area near the swamp where she was beaten with the shovel.

The drawings of the attack sites showed the location each piece of evidence was collected from in relation to the depression in the forest floor where the grass had been crushed with a heavy object or objects and matted down. Each item was designated with a number on the more detailed map, then jotted down on two lists at the left edge of the drawing. A single directional arrow with the letter "N" was drawn to designate north. The second map, showing a closer view of the hole in the ground, had no lists. Instead, Vergin sketched pictures of each item of evidence and wrote in the identification beside each item.

The third map was a view of the Front Forty of the Weber property, showing the location of the entrance road, the outbuildings, and a couple of ponds.

At the very bottom of each of the maps Vergin scribbled, "By BFV 9-5-88" and included the exact time. All three maps

were completed between five and 5:40 P.M. He also noted on
the drawings that they were "not to scale."

When Moore and the state trooper drove away from the
Weber place and returned to Phillips earlier that evening, they
were carrying a carload of incriminating physical evidence that
could be critical to backing up Emily's story. Moore completed
processing of the evidence at the Safety Building, and turned
the material over to Chief Deputy Sheriff Timothy Gould to
store in the evidence locker along with other articles collected
at the farm. Gould and Sheriff Wayne Wirsing had the only
two keys for the locker, which was in a basement room of the
Price County Safety Building. It was about as closely guarded
and secure as the vaults of any of the banks in the county.

Then Moore got together with the sheriff and some of their
colleagues and prepared to search John's cluttered old yellow
jalopy.

Chapter Eight

A Secret Revealed

Maybe I could get away with killing you. Maybe that's what I'll do. Maybe I'll cut off your legs and your arms. Yeah, that's what I think I'll do.
—John Weber, 1988

It was almost exactly eleven o'clock Monday night when Chief Moore returned to the Safety Building in Phillips from the Weber country place.

Except for a four-hour break to clean up, shovel down a quick supper, and grab a few minutes of shut-eye early that morning, he had been constantly awake and busy for nearly two full days and nights. He was running on black coffee and adrenaline, and he still had several long hours of work ahead of him before he could even begin to consider another break.

An hour after swinging back into action he was at the home of Price County circuit judge Douglas T. Fox. It was exactly 12:01 Tuesday morning when the judge signed a search warrant for the Cutlass and another for John and Emily's home at 475 South Avon.

Moore got together with his assistant chief Dennis Dosch, Sheriff Wirsing, Chief Deputy Gould, Deputy Keith Johnson, and Price County District Attorney Paul L. Barnett to execute the search warrants on John's car. A two-part search had been authorized to be conducted simultaneously on the same vehicle. One permitted the investigative team to make an inventory search of the vehicle and to make an itemized list of everything found inside. The other document was a classic search warrant that listed specific items the lawmen were looking for, and included the clothing Emily wore to the farm. Several of the items were included on the search warrant for the house, as well.

The Cutlass itself was the last specific item of evidence on the vehicle search warrant that was listed to be seized. Moore's first priority was the missing mud flap and other signs that the car had bottomed out while being driven through the field at the farm.

Working systematically and examining the car and the contents an inch at a time, the lawmen began their search and inventory. Dosch took the lead, meticulously checking on top of, underneath, and between the seats, combing the floors, examining the side upholstery, and poking through the glove compartment until it was emptied. Every item he found was handed to Moore. One at a time, Moore accepted the papers and odds and ends, and logged them in according to their identification, condition, the exact location where they were found, and the time and date. Then he tagged or packaged or sealed them in evidence bags that were also marked with the date and time.

It was a painstakingly slow process, but the professional care they were taking was absolutely vital for establishing and maintaining integrity of the process. Even a slight mistake or omission could have devastating legal repercussions during the judicial process and might lead to a ruling that a suspect piece of evidence was inadmissible.

Before the search began, Deputy Johnson photographed the car, and he continued snapping pictures at intervals while the team of lawmen moved from one space to another. It was important to make a photo record of items as they were before they were disturbed by Dosch, and in many cases after they were removed. Johnson took a couple of shots of the glove compartment before the first item was removed.

Dosch pulled a buck knife from under the driver's front seat and handed it to the chief. Moore examined it momentarily, then placed it inside a brown lunch bag, and in turn dropped the bag inside an empty cardboard Kodak film box. He marked the bag and the box. The officers repeated the same process with a brown leather sheath for the knife, and with other items.

The officers noticed that the door handle on the front seat passenger side appeared to have blood smears on it, so Johnson took photographs of it. Then it was unscrewed, bagged and marked as evidence.

The backseat area of the car was stuffed with bags of material, and other items littered the seat and the floor. Among the items retrieved from the back were a shopping bag containing an unopened package of Glad lawn bags and a new package of freezer wrap. A container for Prestone antifreeze was on the floor of the backseat, and three others were later found in the trunk. Three of the four containers were partly filled with soapy water.

The glove box presented the search team with a treasure trove of articles that were marked as possible evidence. A receipt for a .25-caliber pistol purchased from Bill's House of Guns on Highway 17 was among several papers retrieved from the box. It was dated November 9, 1984, and signed by John R. Weber. A cash register receipt and a layaway form, which indicated John purchased the weapon on installments, were clipped to the larger form.

Another, possibly even more interesting item found in the glove box was a partial roll of gray duct tape. The chunks of duct tape retrieved from the wastebasket in the bathroom of John and Emily's home, where he said he discarded them after scissoring them from his wife's hair, were also gray and appeared to share other similarities such as width and thickness. Moore placed the tape in a paper bag, then marked the sack with the vital information. After retrieving and inventorying everything from the glove box and the passenger compartment of the car, the officers moved to the exterior of the car and the trunk.

Three mud flaps hung over the tires of the Cutlass. The fourth flap behind the left front tire was missing. At first glance, the three flaps that were intact and attached appeared to be similar to the flap found at the farm. The bumper was also bent and hanging down, and bits of grass and dirt were stuck behind it as if it had bottomed out and scraped the ground somewhere. Photos were taken of the bumper, and the soil and dirt were collected and bagged as evidence.

The interior of the trunk was a mess. Before anything was touched inside, Johnson snapped the obligatory photographs. He took a sequence of shots, moving from one end of the trunk to the other in order to ensue that nothing was missed.

Inside, several articles of women's clothing were near the top of the litter. One of the items was a brown company jacket with the logo "Winter Wood Products" and the name "Emily" embroidered on the right-hand side. There was also a red-and-white sweatshirt with an Olympic symbol and the word and date "Montreal 1976," a pair of tennis shoes stamped with the words "New Balance," a single white sock with blue, green and pink trim, and a pair of acidwashed blue jeans. A beige brassiere and a pair of pink panties were also bunched up together with the rest of the clothing, and were retrieved, bagged, and marked.

Several brown grocery bags filled with empty cardboard twelve-pack cartons and empty beer bottles and cans were pulled from the intimidating clutter. Most of the empty beer containers were gold-colored cans of Miller Genuine Draft, although there were a few cans and bottles of Miller Highlife. Five empty cans of Miller had already been pulled from the passenger compartment.

Then Dosch lifted out a black nylon bag that was zipped

shut and stuffed with a curious variety of articles to be inventoried and logged. Among items found inside were a clipboard holding the original messages to be copied by Emily on the letters and birthday cards, several "to do" or "need" lists later confirmed to be in John's handwriting, which included everything from engine repairs to more ominous gatherings of materials and phrases such as "PH 1." Investigators would later decide that the mysterious letter and numeral referred to "Phase 1."

Several of the papers clipped to the board were military forms, work sheets for equipment inspection, repair, and maintenance. The government forms were blank on the back and some had large open spaces on the front, which could be handy for note making—or jotting down lists.

One of the papers on the board was filled out in John's handwriting with the title "Secure Her First," which was followed by a detailed list of items to save or acquire, including notes. After the notation "PH 1," the author had penciled in the words, "Bedroom Items Needed."

Moore didn't have time then to read through all the lists, although he would carefully study each one of them later. It wasn't a pleasant experience to look forward to. They read like something out of a horror novel.

Under the heading "Need To Buy," one of the papers listed "hair brush, paper, pen, bondage for legs, freezer paper, B-day card," the words "two," "saw," "big," and the non-word, "kife," which Moore eventually decided was probably a misspelling for "knife." The list continued with more reminders. "Move car. Pack things. Lots of plastic. Boxes. D pins. Garbage bags. Duct tape. Beer. Masking tape. Dils. Paddle. Clothespins. Needles. Cigars. X-mas cards. Two letters? Gloves, rubber/leather. Curling Iron. White bottle. Vicks. Oil for ass. Shavers. Scissors/cream/soap/bucket of water. Rag. Checkbook."

Other notations on the same document repeated the words "Secure her first," and added the reminders, "go over

story," "get purse," "take off ring," "get watch," "clothes," "trin-
kets," "write check," and "have her for cash." The words, "Have
her for cash" were enclosed in parentheses. Continuing on, the
note listed reminders to close drapes, lock doors, clean the drain.
One difficult-to-decipher notation said something about a twenty-
gauge gun before adding other less intimidating items. "Personal
hygiene items," "makeup," "rags," "shampoo," "laundry soap,"
"dress up in panties," "pantyhose." The mind-numbing litany
continued with one item or reminder after another. But even then
the author wasn't through. And the back side of the paper was
filled with others, listing everything from extra checks to items
to be saved, including bras, panties, dresses, panty hose, and
shorts.

At the top of the back page, the author had penciled the
important reminder: "Take shot in dick just before PH 2. 3cc."

The lists read like dismal roadmaps to the movements of
the evil phantoms tearing and ripping their way through John's
imagination.

In the most sinister notations of all, however, the writer
had scribbled in John's distinctive straight-up-and-down script
with rounded letters: "Burial spot. Compost heap? When
does Dad use it? Make sure compost heap is same as before
execution."

It would still be a matter to be legally determined in court,
if at all, but there appeared to be little doubt to what the notes
about the burial spot and the compost heap referred. The word
"execution" left a bit more room for debate. Was the writer
referring to putting some plan into action—or was the word
written, to indicate the deliberate snuffing out of a life?

If Moore and the other officers had been familiar at that
time with the suspect's personal and mental-health history they
would have recognized the obsessive list making. John had
been a fantasizer and recorded his sick schemes of abduction,
bondage, torture, and rape in minute step-by-step detail since

he was old enough to write. He compiled handwritten lists and fantasies as a juvenile, and as an adult. And at some point, it appeared that fantasy was no longer enough. John transformed his sadistic dreams of blood and pain into reality.

An 8.5-inch by 11-inch bound blue spiral notebook, which was stuffed in beside the rest of the material, continued the letters Emily had copied from John's originals. There was also a can of Barbasol shaving cream, and a wine bottle. The words "First Anniversary" were printed on a label on the bottle.

Other items in the bag included a pair of brown rubber gloves, a pair of bright pink panties slashed along one side, clothespins, a Copps IGA bag with a new package of masking tape inside, an unopened package containing two precision glide needles, an opened package of safety pins, a hypodermic syringe, a container for a prescription drug that may have been papaverine, a partly filled bottle of Vicks VapoRub, a cigarette lighter, a pair of mustache scissors, two wooden wheelbarrow handles—and a fresh cucumber and three carrots. What appeared to be a single hair was stuck to the cucumber. It was a curious collection indeed that John Weber stored in his black bag. Almost all the items were reflected in the lists.

Under other circumstances most of the articles retrieved from the bag would have appeared to be unexceptionally mundane personal grooming or household implements. But in the twilight world of a sadistic sex pervert whose fantasies run to bondage, discipline and pain, objects like needles, mustache scissors, clothespins, rubber gloves, shaving lotion, and phallic-shaped vegetables can take on far more sinister significance.

Even the notch carved on the side of one of the wheelbarrow handles was enough to arouse negative suggestions. Virtually everyone knows that many of the Wild West gunslingers used to carve a notch on their pistol grips for every man they killed.

So what, if anything, did a notch carved on a ten-inch-long wooden wheelbarrow handle signify?

A green duffel bag taken from the trunk yielded other items that were as darkly threatening as the contents of the black bag. Several brassieres of various sizes, a pair of soiled pink panties with flower embroidery, eight soiled pairs of size thirty-four to thirty-six men's underpants, and a vibrator were crammed inside. The brassieres were ripped and slashed.

Perhaps one of the most unsettlingly scary finds was a dirt-smeared stuffed toy rabbit. Someone had transformed the doll from innocence to obscenity by slashing an ugly hole through the rabbit's crotch.

Approximately one hundred skin and porn magazines were scattered throughout the trunk and were gathered up, sealed in plastic, marked as evidence and piled into brown paper shopping bags. Most of the magazines were of the *Playboy* and *Penthouse* variety. The cover of a six-year-old copy of *Penthouse* headlined a "Special Report: TEENAGE PROSTITUTION." A more up-to-date January 1988 issue of *Club International* featured a titillating cover story headlined *"TIME FOR SEX,"* and listed the professional names of porn movie queens Ginger Lynn, Seka, and Taja Rae. But a few of the magazines were more hard-core porn featuring scenes of anal sex and situations of bondage and discipline such as spankings, in explicit detail. At least one magazine featured a nude model who appeared to be inserting a wine bottle into the vagina of another woman. That magazine and others showed signs of being well-worn. Some of them were five years old or older, but a receipt found with some of the magazines was dated a few days earlier in August.

Another list, written on a blue sheet of paper, was stuck in among the magazines. It repeated many of the steps or items appearing on the other lists, but included a few additional items such as "three handles, one with groove," "50 pins," "super glue (sic)," "smell good," "shovel," "pillows," "change of clothes," "mousetrap," "knife (2)," "Miller/one King bottle," and "brace and bracket to hold legs open."

The most incriminating discovery during the search was made by Chief Moore. The search team was looking around in the front seat, when DA Barnett asked if anyone had played an audio cassette that was in the tape player. The plain, black cassette wasn't labelled, and Moore figured that John or Emily had probably used it to reproduce some music from one of their favorite rock groups to play on the car stereo. But he turned the ignition key to "accessory" and pushed the tape in. A moment later he heard a soft male voice he recognized as John's from their past confrontations.

"Now, if you do exactly as I tell you, when I tell you, and what I tell you, you will be all right," the monologue began. "I needed to explain something to you, and I want you to listen closely and understand. I have a lot to tell you, so you better just sit back and relax."

His voice was mellow, almost soothing, but Moore had just listened to the prelude of a message that was hardly designed to make someone relax. Moore called for a break in the search to listen to the full message on the tape. It was 2:20 A.M., and the little knot of law enforcement officers were one minute short of being exactly three hours into their search of the vehicle.

The story that unfolded from the tape as Moore and his colleagues listened in stunned silence, was even more terrifying and bloodcurdling than the details of the savage attack on Emily.

John's quietly dispassionate account was a shocking story of feral cruelty, madness, and evil; a mind-numbing recitation of betrayal, sadistic sexual abuse, agonizing torture, savage murder, necrophilia, and cannibalism that violated some of society's most fearsome taboos.

Directing the monologue at his wife, John assured her that she wouldn't be killed. Then he said he was going to tell her a story that began in about September 1986 and ran on through November. The recording was eerily similar to his speech on the tape he made years earlier and gave to his sister, Kathy. But the content was more grim and terrifying—and it apparently didn't stop with mere fantasy.

While Chief Moore listened to the tape, John told Emily that while they were going through marital problems he was talking to Carla and to another woman. "Well, the first time that I talked to Carla, I knew right away that she had a crush on me and I knew how she felt. So I would go out and I would talk to her, and we would go for rides," he said.

The situation continued into late October when he began hatching a plan, he continued. "Yes! I know what happened to Carla. I know real well. The same thing is not going to happen to you. You are going to live. However, you may be a little sore and you will definitely remember me. So I will explain what happened."

At about 10:45 or eleven P.M. on November 12, he telephoned Carla and asked her if she wanted to go for a ride, he said. She agreed. "So I grabbed the kit that I had prepared earlier, weeks earlier, and I hopped in the Sunbird and I went out on Storms Road." John said she was already walking down the road when he picked her up.

On the way into town he told her to duck her head so no one would see her, because it would make people suspicious if she was seen riding with him. Carla ducked her head until they had passed through town and were continuing on their way to the farm. They talked about different things while he drank beer, and he shared a couple of bottles with her.

John said he parked his car at the country place and they continued talking for a while about his relationship with Emily, and how much he appreciated Carla's friendship. Carla told him he could talk with her anytime. Then he told her he was

thinking of going away and was wondering if she would go
to Colorado with him, he said.

"And of course she said no, that she wanted nothing more
than to see me and you get back together." He continued that
Carla admitted she had strong feelings for him, but nothing
could be done about it.

"So I told her that I had a surprise for her, and that she
would need to close her eyes and turn away," John continued.
He said Carla objected that he didn't have to give her anything,
or do anything for her. But she kept her eyes closed, while he
reached in the backseat and pulled a .25-caliber pistol from a
red Marlboro bag he had packed with articles he expected to
use at sometime or another during the night. The bag was
John's murder kit.

". . . she still had her eyes closed, with a smile on her face,
and it took a while," he said. "I sat there for a good thirty
seconds or so, wondering whether or not to do it. And I went
ahead."

Suddenly John grabbed the startled teenager by the hair at
the back of her head and shoved the muzzle of the pistol into
her mouth. She was "kind of stunned," he said. "She gave me
a weird look, and she didn't know what to think at first. I told
her that she would do exactly as I say or she would die. And
I told her that she was gonna watch me blow my head off.
And she kept screaming, 'Why?' "

John ordered the terrified girl to shut up, but she wouldn't—
or she was so scared that she couldn't. So he wadded up a
sock and jammed it into her mouth. Carla pulled the sock out
and grabbed for the pistol. The struggle between the high-
school girl and the wiry factory worker was no contest. John
hung onto the gun, but he quieted down for a while.

He pinned her head and shoulders on his lap while they
talked and Carla tried to soothe him. John talked about girls
he used to know, and whined that he had been hurt so many
times he didn't want to live anymore. Carla finally asked what
he wanted of her.

John told her. He said before he blew his head off he wanted her to strip for him. Carla refused and asked him why.

"And I said, 'I just want to see you naked,' and she hesitated," John recalled. When she tried to talk him out of the demand, he put the gun to his head and pulled the trigger. He knew the safety was on, but Carla didn't. "No, John, don't. Please don't," she begged.

John pointed the gun away from his head, and the man and the girl sat silently for a while in the darkened car. When John at last broke the silence, it was to make another even more frightening threat to the teenager beside him.

"Well, maybe I will kill you first, then me."

Carla didn't want to die. John let her up and reluctantly she began to take off her clothes. "She started with her jacket. She had that purple jacket on, and she took that and her shirt off, and then took her shoes off and then her pants," he said. "And then she stopped."

"Oh my God," John exclaimed. Carla asked what he meant by that. "I guess you're as big as they say you are." John continued to describe Carla's breasts. "I didn't even know what I was saying, but her tits were bulging out. They were big. And she asked a question: 'How far?' And I said all the way. So she slid her panties down below her knees and took her bra off. But I really wasn't paying attention. I was so scared at the time, and I wanted to stop and I couldn't," he said. "And I wanted to go home. I just wanted to forget it, and I couldn't.

"And she had her arms across her tits and I couldn't see them very well, but I could see her muff, and it looked like it was black. But actually it was brown, and she had it trimmed up. She must have shaved it or something, because it wasn't a big bush . . . and I lost it for a while. I just spaced out, I had the gun in my hands."

When he realized what was going on Carla was talking, trying to reason and calm him down. In a desperate effort to regain her dignity and cover herself, she had also managed to climb back into her underpants and bra, and slip her T-shirt back on.

John snapped out of his daze and reached into the back of the car for a roll of duct tape. When the frightened girl asked what the tape was for, he snapped back that he was tired of hearing her. In moments, John had pressed strips of the heavy tape over her eyes and mouth. Then he pushed her upper body forward with her face against the dashboard and pulled her hands behind her back, wrapping strong coils of the tape around her wrists. The teenager was helpless. She couldn't see, couldn't talk, couldn't move her hands. She was stripped nearly naked and was alone in the woods with a madman.

Carla stopped struggling. She was like a deer caught in the headlights of John's sadistic dreams, and there was no escape.

"I knew she couldn't get out of that," he said. After securing her hands, he pulled her away from the dashboard. ". . . and I took out that knife that your parents had given me that I spent so much time sharpening, and she had her shirt on," he said. "And I started at the bottom, and I was amazed at how easily that cut," and I cut it up, and she kind of flinched. I don't know if either the knife, you know, touched her tits or if maybe she was just scared or something."

Then John backtracked in his account. While Carla was removing her clothes, she had made him promise not to touch her, he said. He agreed he would only look. At about the same time he said that after he shot himself she should take the car, but she said she would prefer to walk.

Returning again to his dark work with the knife, John said he played briefly with Carla's breasts then slashed off her bra, first cutting through the right strap, then the left, then the middle between the cups. John lit a cigarette and smoked while he resumed playing with her breasts, then moved to her genitals. He described his activities in minute detail, as the abuse became increasingly rough. Finally he pressed the lit end of his cigarette to the side of her left breast and the nipple.

"Then I hauled out a plank, similar to the one you put under your plant stand and I slapped the top of her left thigh hard. I slapped her right tit on the nipple, and then underneath it and gave her a good whack across the head just for good measure," he said. "And that was about my fill of the inside of the car."

Incredibly, as John described the barbaric assault, his voice sounded as serene and emotionally controlled as a teacher reciting from a dry history text. His recitation had the droning air of a patient pedagogue, repeating an unremarkable story he had told dozens of times before. But the very smoothness of the narrator's voice added to the ghastliness.

John then slid out of the car, walked to the passenger side, grabbed one of his captive's breasts with one hand and her hair with the other, and dragged her outside. The ground was covered with snow, temperatures were dropping to five below zero, and a biting wind was whipping through the trees as he pushed her roughly against the car, bent her over a fender, and jerked her legs apart. She forced them back together.

John reached in front and behind her, knotted her underpants in his hands, and jerked her off the ground, he continued in his account. He referred to the cruel act as giving her a "snuggie." Then he slashed through each of the legs of the panties with his buck knife and ripped them from her body. Carla was naked again.

Moore was appalled at the icy description of the almost unbelievable ferocity and the ghastly abuse of the innocent teenager that was being delivered so matter-of-factly. He had raised three daughters of his own. "As we know, young ladies have this motherly instinct, this counseling instinct, going to help people, change people," he said months later of some of the thoughts that were going through his mind while he listened to the tape. "It's sad that this is taken advantage of, and certainly was in this case," he said.

* * *

According to John's story, he picked up the plank and began beating her again. He smashed at the back of her right thigh and calf, striking her thirty times or more. Finally he inserted the board between her legs and moved the edge up the inside of her thighs and rubbed it menacingly against her crotch.

Then he grabbed her hair, pulled her upright, turned her around, and demanded oral sex. "If I feel one tooth I will cut your tits off," he warned. John described the sodomy in detail, as well as other vile acts he said he forced on her at knifepoint.

John claimed he followed up that abuse by urinating in her mouth. "I had been drinking beer the whole time," he said. Then he stuffed a pair of soiled underpants he previously masturbated on, into her mouth, spun her around by the hair, bent her over and began beating, poking, and twisting her dangling breasts. "I think that had to be about the best part of the whole evening, is when I did that," he gloated.

But he soon tired of that pleasure and moved on to a more horrid perversion. He pushed her limp body back into the car, grabbed a wheelbarrow handle, rolled it in the snow, then repeatedly plunged the end in and out of her vagina. Then he violated her anally with another handle, bringing a groan of pain from her lips. He burned her vagina with a cigarette, repeatedly pierced her flesh with a safety pin—once plunging it so deep he felt the bone. He pushed the tip of the same pin through her right nipple, then began pushing other pins from a pin cushion everywhere in her breast.

John replaced the wheelbarrow handle in her rectum with one of the beer bottles he had been drinking from. He switched the other handle with a king-size beer bottle, then he cut the blindfold from Carla's eyes with his knife. The tape ends stuck to her hair. She was face-to-face with the inevitability of her own mortality and a horrible death at the hands of a madman whom she had trusted. She was alone, isolated, dreadfully injured, and utterly helpless.

John said the bottles were still sticking out from the girl's body cavities, so he kicked them with his boot until they were all the way inside. Carla was unconscious, and he could hear her hoarse breathing. "So I stepped on her throat until she died."

It was a horrid account of a bestial murder in the cold gloom of an isolated forest, but the tape was still running and there were further outrages that were so vile and repulsive they were almost impossible to comprehend. They were still to be reviewed.

After Carla died, John reported that he policed the area, picking up everything he had left lying around the car, including her clothes. Carla was lying on some strips of plastic and canvas, and he rolled her body up in the material, then squeezed it into the trunk of his Pontiac Sunbird along with everything else that was already piled there. It was a difficult fit.

According to the appalling account, which John continued to deliver with a chilling nonchalance, he had dug a grave at the farm two days earlier. But he didn't immediately bury his victim. Instead he drove around with the body in the trunk for five days, while her family, friends, neighbors, and law enforcement agencies began their search for the missing girl. Then John sprung one more macabre surprise.

". . . on the second day, Dr. Jekyll said again, or Mr. Hyde, rather, I got this real wild idea." John said he opened the trunk, and rolled the canvas off her legs. One of the few areas on the body that wasn't bruised, pierced with pins, slashed with a knife or burned was a portion of her left leg. "I took out that knife and I cut off her calf, just her muscle, and brought it in the house and washed it up, cleaned it up, skinned it, sliced it up, and froze it," he said. "And that night I made some patties and I ate Carla's leg." Later, he recounted doing the same with Carla's breast.

John said a couple of days after cannibalizing his victim he finally buried the rest of the remains in the shallow grave he had previously dug in the frozen earth at the farm. "I went out there to check on it a while back because the sand was lying on top of the grave," he continued, "and I didn't want no one to spot that from Rock Creek Road. The grave was open. Some animal had dug her up. All I found was her leg bone and her skull.

"So now you know what happened to Carla."

The finality of the statement hung in the air like a dark cloud. If John's chilling confession was to be believed and he had tape-recorded a true account, the mystery of the high-school girl's disappearance was solved. She was lured from her home, defiled, murdered, and defiled again in a ghastly act of cannibalism by one of the people whom she trusted most—her sister's husband. The already fragile hopes that she might someday be restored alive to her family had been dashed with ugly finality.

With the mystery of Carla's fate settled to his satisfaction, John turned his narrative to what he had in store for Emily. "See, I am going to make you suffer, but I am not gonna kill you. I want you to live. Maybe you will kill yourself. But I want you to live with what I have told you I have done to your sister. And I want you to live with the fact that the only reason that I am doing this is because of what you did to me. I hate you!" he hissed. "The evil part of me hates you!"

John followed up his declaration of hate with a graphically detailed description of what he believed to have been a sexual fling she had with "*Patrick.*" Then he began a filthy, graphic review of Emily's body, complaining among other things that she was small-breasted and pointed to her long legs as her best physical asset.

"I don't care much for being treated the way I was, and I have been living with this: what I have done to Carla," he said. "So many times I get horny over you or at least you would think I was, and I was just thinking about what I had done to her—and about what I am gonna do to you."

The threats, meanness, and sexually sordid words and phrases tumbled from the tape: "I put a lot of effort into what I got away with. . . . I almost went after someone else. I almost went after your mother. . . . You see, I am insane and I know it. And it's hard to keep under wraps at times. . . . But you're dead, bitch.

"But I decided, 'nah,' it would be more fun if I just do what I want, have a few laughs and leave," he said.

"So now the tables are turned a little bit and now it's me doing whatever the hell I want to, to you," he said. "I look at you and think about all the things I would love to do to you. All the things of a sexual nature."

The monologue switched abruptly back to Carla, as John marvelled once more over her large breasts. "At one point she even tried to run. She didn't get twenty yards, hands tied behind her back, tits flopping in the breeze," he said. "I made her pay the price for that. I think I broke her toes. I stomped on her feet."

After making a nasty comparison between his wife's love-making and the forced sex with Carla, John announced his view of females:

"You know, women are nothing. They flaunt their bodies and think that they can get anything they want by being a cock tease. Well, they are wrong. I pay them back, and I am definitely paying you back." He threatened to submit Emily to loathsome sexual perversions, outlining them step-by-step.

As the lurid narrative continued, John began to observe that perhaps he should murder Emily after all. At one point he snarled that he might cut off her head. He finally mused: "Maybe I could get away with killing you. Maybe that's what I'll do. Maybe I'll cut off your legs and your arms. Yeah, that's what I think I'll do."

Ever since early childhood he had danced dangerously close to the edge of violence, and at last he had plunged headlong into a maelstrom of sadism and depravity. All the sordid sexual scenarios of bondage and sadism he had formulated in his mind, written down in spiral notebooks, recorded on cassette tapes, and savored during lonely acts of masturbation, had come to life for him.

He added the ominous prediction, "You won't be the last. There's gonna be others, many others." A bit later in the tape, he expanded on the threat, remarking: "This is going to continue until I get caught, I imagine. But when I am done with you, I am going to run. The car is packed. I am splitting, taking my rifle. I am going to rob some places, make my way that way until I get caught—have a fiery death."

John heaped on one more nasty threat after another, describing terrible sexual abuse he had planned for his wife. He talked especially about her thighs and calves, which he wanted to focus some of his torture on because they were the most attractive features of her body. He said he hoped when he was through abusing her, that whoever found her picked up where he left off.

He talked about a fantasy of forcing her into lesbian acts with one of her young female relatives, but said he abandoned that idea because the chances of being caught were too great. The only time he was stimulated by Emily, he said, was when he fantasized about torturing her.

The vulgarity and ghastly intimidation continued on and on, as he switched back and forth from comparing Carla's and Emily's breasts, to his sexual torture of Carla, to a threat to fix it so his wife could never become a mother. He outlined detailed plans to perform gross sexual indignities on Emily with wheelbarrow handles, pins and needles. "You love cigars so much, I think you will even get a few treats with them," he added.

At last, after fifty-two minutes of nonstop vileness and malevolence, it was over. Mercifully, the remainder of the ninety-minute tape was blank. John had either exhausted himself, or followed through on his remark about going to bed to be alone with his fantasies and schemes of pain, fear, and sadistic sexual perversion.

It was draining merely listening to the icy chronicle that was so gruesome and filled with hate.

Moore flipped off the machine, ejected the cartridge, and bagged it in a brown paper sandwich sack and marked it as evidence. He penned the numerals and letters "39AS" on the bag. It was the thirty-ninth item of evidence collected during the "auto search." The police chief also listed the name of the suspect and the victim in the case (Emily at that time), and the date and time of recovery. Finally he signed his name.

The careful bagging and marking was the beginning of the creation of the chain of evidence, a vitally important process designed to make it possible to trace the custody of the tape from the moment it was first seized. Everybody who handled it from the time Moore bagged it and marked it and placed his signature on the sandwich sack would be expected to sign his own name, the date, time and place it was in his custody. The signatures would make it possible to follow the tape's travels from Moore to the police evidence room, out of the evidence room to custody of Moore, the prosecutor, defense attorneys, or anyone else eventually authorized to have it in their possession, back to the evidence room.

The same process was followed with every piece of evidence collected from John's Oldsmobile, and would be followed with anything that might be gathered up in the future from other locations.

Listening to the disgusting message on the tape was as unpleasant as it was shocking, but Moore would have to listen to it more than once while carefully studying and analyzing the contents.

It took the team of law officers nearly three hours to empty the passenger compartment, the glove box and trunk, to bag and mark evidence, and complete their inch-by-inch inspection

of the inside and outside of the battered old Cutlass. Except
for the .25-caliber pistol and a blue sweater Emily was thought
to have worn back home from the farm, the search team had
found just about everything listed on the application for the
search warrant—and more.

When the officers finished picking through the disorganized
jumble inside the car, the assault case, as serious as it was,
had mushroomed into an investigation that was even more
grim and challenging. It appeared that Chief Moore, Sheriff
Wirsing, and the prosecutor, Barnett, were working a suspected
homicide that had the potential of becoming the most notorious
crime in the history of Price County.

It was nearly three A.M., and it was time for Moore to have
another talk with Emily's husband.

Chapter Nine

John's Story

At 4:25 Tuesday morning downtown Phillips was so dark, quiet, and devoid of activity that the proverbial cannonball could have been fired down the main street without hitting anybody.

The basement of the modern Price County Safety Building was ablaze with lights, and a small knot of men was consumed with activity that was both as deadly serious as it was urgent, however.

Moving into the third day of the investigation set off with John's telephone call early in the Labor Day weekend, Moore had been awake for almost seventy hours. But he knew it would be hours before he could even begin thinking about taking a break for a shower, a meal, and some badly needed rest.

During his years as a law enforcement officer, Moore had developed a philosophy about investigations that is subscribed to by most of the men and women who have found themselves digging into crimes and chasing down criminals. The faster you move, the better your chances of collecting evidence that will stand up in court, of obtaining a confession or other important statements from witnesses, and of ultimately clearing up the case.

"This is something I do, the detective side of me," Moore later explained during an interview. "I try to pass on to my people that if you receive a call on anything, you need to act now. Sometimes I see hesitation; they will wait a couple of days and I just don't like that.

"As a case goes on, the case gets colder, and people rationalize. They don't want to speak, or whatever . . . ," he said. "There have been times in my career where someone's dragging their feet may have cost me a confession and I had to go with physical evidence. Or it cost me physical evidence and I had to go on a confession."

When Moore found himself confronted with a challenging case he clung to it like a pit bull, hanging on until he chewed and ripped loose every bit of information he could. He had already been on cases where he worked thirty-six hours straight, taken a four-hour break, worked another twenty-four to thirty-six hours, taken another four-hour break, then started all over again. Now, he realized, he was faced with another one of those cases.

Moore huddled with Sheriff Wirsing and Chief Deputy Gould, and the lawmen agreed they needed to move on as quickly as they could with a formal interrogation of their murder and assault suspect.

"I felt it was imperative, Number One, that I continue with what was happening so that I didn't lose anything that I had now taken in as far as memory and hadn't put into writing at this point," Moore later explained in sworn courtroom testimony.

"In order to keep those things still in my mind and fresh in my mind it was decided that an interview should take place immediately."

According to records and statements from his jailers, John had slept almost thirteen hours since he was locked up a few minutes after two o'clock the previous afternoon. He curled up on his bunk almost as soon as the cell door clanged shut. The only interruption in his rest occurred during his brief meeting with the psychiatric social worker. Then he went back to sleep and he was still snoozing when Chief Moore and his colleagues decided it was time for a talk with him.

Confirming that John was given a chance to rest and that he exercised that opportunity could be crucial to his successful prosecution. If there was any serious suspicion that he was denied sleep or food, neglected or mistreated in any other way before the interrogation, at some time down the road in a few weeks or a few months, defense attorneys could claim his rights were violated and challenge a confession or any other statement he may have made.

It was still roughly two hours before sunrise when Pavlek unlocked John's cell door and walked inside. Moore and Gould hovered behind him just outside the cubicle.

"John," Pavlek said, "there's somebody here that wants to talk to you."

John roused himself, silently rolled over on the bunk, perched for a moment on the side with his feet on the floor, then got up, stretched and wobbled forward, still groggy and obviously not fully awake after his long rest. Moore greeted John as the jailer led the prisoner from the cell. A couple of other officers stood by in the booking room and dispatch area as added security. Suspected murderers weren't locked up in the Price County Safety Building every day, and no one wanted to take any unnecessary chances with the prisoner.

As he was handcuffed, John glanced at the clock over the booking desk and noticed it was shortly after four A.M. Then, surrounded by Pavlek, Moore, and Gould, he was walked downstairs to the same interview-interrogation room used during his previous sit down at the Safety Building. While the officers filed into the high-ceilinged nine-foot by twelve-foot room with their prisoner, Pavlek asked if they needed any other assistance from him, and when they replied that they didn't, he returned to his desk upstairs. Assistant Chief of Police Dennis Dosch joined the group inside the interview room.

John agreed to talk, and Moore once more prepared to read

him the Miranda warning from a standard advice of rights form used by the Phillips Police Department.

Before running through the warning, the police chief asked John a few routine questions to help him fill in statistical information at the top of a blank statement sheet. Working together they filled in John's full name, date of birth, address, and Social Security number. Spending the first few moments concentrating on such mundane, nonthreatening information, was a routine Moore had found to be helpful in putting a suspect at ease.

After filling in the biographical information and writing the time, date, and location of the interview in a space on the left-hand side of the page, Moore began reading off the five points of the Miranda warning. Each point was marked off after it was read and John indicated he understood the meaning. Then John signed the form indicating he was waiving his Fifth Amendment rights, and he and his interrogators were ready to get down to business.

Despite Moore's caution and businesslike approach, the situation was drastically altered from their earlier conversations, and the uneasy young man knew it. Moore was no longer trying to get an overview of what had happened to Emily. John was a hot suspect in serious crimes, and the police chief had questions to ask that wouldn't be easy to deflect with vague generalities. The questioning was going to be finely focused and designed to firmly tie him to the hideous attack on Emily—and possibly to an even more serious offense.

John was hesitant and uncomfortable. Considering the circumstances, that was understandable. He was caught in an intimidating situation, alone in the bare interview room with three experienced police officers; and they weren't there to molly-coddle him. But Moore wanted his suspect to be as relaxed as possible. He asked if he thought he might be more comfortable speaking with only one police officer. John nodded his head up and down, in the affirmative. Dosch and Gould left the room.

Unknown to the suspect, the departing lawmen could still visually witness the interrogation. One side of the interview room was outfitted with a wide two-way mirror. From inside the room the glass looked like a mirror. From another room on the other side it was a window, which police officers or witnesses could use to watch the proceedings. Unlike some such setups in larger jurisdictions, the secret room wasn't audio-equipped. It was as spartanly furnished as the interview room, and the most noticeable objects inside were some lifting bars and weights that officers sometimes used for a quick workout. The space was also utilized as a squad room for sheriff's officers at the time of change of shifts.

In its function as an observation room, it served its purpose well, nevertheless. The eavesdroppers could watch everything that was going on, even though they couldn't hear enough to make out details of the conversation. The mirror-window was an important police tool and especially useful as a safeguard for officers who might find themselves alone with a suddenly violent suspect.

John appeared to be more meek—and at times confused—than menacing or argumentative. The relative composure he had shown in the earlier interview and during his conversations with Moore at the Flambeau Medical Center had evaporated. Instead of peppering the chief with questions he slumped glumly in his chair, preparing to face what was obviously going to be an unpleasant ordeal. The muscles of his face were slumped in a glum, half-scowl. He looked worried and depressed.

His Salems were taken away from him when he was booked into the jail, and Moore gave him a cigarette from his own pack, then lit it for him while they settled down to talk. The police chief did his best to frame his questions in a nonthreatening, conversational tone. There was none of the old-time third degree in the confrontation. No sweating prisoner hunched on a straight-back chair under a bright light, while a circle of tough, cigar-chomping detectives threatened him with fists or black-jacks. This was 1988 and the real world, not a James Cagney movie from a half-century earlier. Nonetheless, it was a deadly serious contest between one man with a lot to hide, and another man determined to strip away his secrets.

John actually began the interview with his own question. He asked how his wife was doing. Moore pointed out that he wasn't a doctor, but thought she was holding her own. Then he asked what really happened to her.

John said he wasn't sure, that he was confused and didn't know exactly what had taken place. Continuing to respond to questions, he conceded that he realized Emily had been beaten. He said he didn't want to believe her, but when he saw the condition she was in Saturday morning he realized he was the person who had inflicted her injuries.

He mentioned deep slashes on her body and legs, which he referred to as "cuttings." Moore asked how he had come to slash his wife's calf. "Was she kicking at you?"

John didn't remember.

Moore asked if Emily had her clothes on. John said she didn't.

Did he mean that his wife went for a ride in the car with him while she was naked? Moore asked.

John explained that she had her clothes on when he picked her up, but that he later asked her to take them off. "Everything, including her underwear?" Moore wanted to know. John admitted he cut her underclothes off with a knife.

Moore needed to pin down information to determine if Emily had resisted, had tried to escape—or if she was definitely held against her will or bound in some way. Why didn't she run away? he asked. John said he kept her too close to him.

"Well, why wouldn't a person just break away and run out to the road?" he asked. "Was she secured in any way?"

John admitted he taped her mouth, eyes, and hands.

He also said he had been drinking heavily and early Saturday decided he wanted to get drunk. He bought a twelve-pack of Miller and began drinking it in his car.

Periodically during the interrogation, John asked for additional cigarettes, which Moore provided.

John was especially cooperative answering questions about the assault on Emily. He had a history, which went back to his interviews with psychologists and psychiatrists during his early childhood and adolescence, of talking freely about subjects he knew his interrogators were already well informed about. Historically he clammed up or was less cooperative when the conversation turned to other areas of inquiry where interrogators were attempting to gather new information rather than to confirm what they already knew.

His interrogation by Moore fit into the old pattern. He admitted his attack on his wife, and added details in response to the police chief's persistent prodding. And he cried when Moore asked him if it was true he had sexually assaulted Emily with the wheelbarrow handle. He leaned against the wall, and nodded his head up and down, while fat tears rolled down his cheeks. The tears flowed another time, as well, while the questions focused on the abuse of his wife.

John didn't refuse outright to answer the chief's questions. He appeared to be genuinely confused at points about what he had done, and there were times when it seemed he was drifting away and almost losing contact with reality. At one point he said it was difficult to talk about the things they were discussing. "I have a condition like my speech," he added. "It's haywire!" Moore said he understood.

Moore asked him if he was ever treated for personality, behavior, or psychiatric problems, other than marriage counseling, or if he was ever institutionalized. John said he was in an institution when he was fifteen.

"Did you ever know what the problem was?" Moore inquired.

"There was no hope for me to live a normal life," the suspect replied. He said his mind wasn't working properly.

"Apparently you've proved them wrong," the chief said in what was an obvious effort to butter him up and help him relax. John took the opportunity to boast about his relative success when he was in the Army. "I got an honorable discharge," he offered.

The young man had been under terrific stress and he was stuttering. Sometimes his replies were smooth and evenly articulated. At other times he had to struggle to force out the words, screwing up his face and fighting to make the words roll off his tongue somehow by force of will. Months later he said he would likely have provided more information than he did, if he hadn't had such difficulty speaking.

The police chief had conducted hundreds of interviews and interrogations and he didn't think John was putting on an act. His impression was that John knew he had been found out, but he didn't know exactly how much his interrogator knew or how far the investigation was going. And he didn't want to give away anything he didn't have to.

John leaned back on his chair, balancing it on its hind legs and tilting it against the wall while he nervously puffed on Moore's cigarettes during most of the interview. Frequently he mumbled his replies; there were often long pauses between question and answer as if he was carefully weighing what he was about to say, or his remarks were vague and evasive.

He seemed to be sincerely ashamed and sorry about the dreadful abuse of his wife. Several weeks later he disclosed to another interviewer that he had masturbated five or six times in a futile effort to fend off his invisible companion who was insisting he attack Emily. It hadn't worked and Emily wound up in the hospital, and he was in the hands of the police with his back to the wall.

Moore attempted to reassure the miserable young man.

"Sure, she doesn't want to hurt you," Moore said of Emily. "She doesn't want to get you in trouble with her words." Speaking in the fractured sentences with confusing stops and starts that even professional interrogators often use at such times, the chief continued: "I told you, I told her John doesn't want to get, I told her John doesn't want to get into trouble. John has committed crimes, but let's be honest. Because a crime is committed it doesn't end the world."

John wasn't buying his interrogator's game but obvious effort to find a bright lining on the dark clouds that were squeezing the life out of his future.

"Yes, it does," he muttered.

Moore was undeterred. "Why would it?" he demanded.

"My world is gone," John replied.

He was clearly reluctant to talk about Carla when the police chief directed the conversation toward her disappearance and away from Emily's beating.

His attitude changed after Moore wrapped up his questions about Emily, and asked if there were other problems in his life he wished to talk about. Moore said he wanted to know if the same thing that happened to Emily had happened to anyone else. John denied attacking his sister-in-law as he attacked his wife.

Moore was a firm believer in making audiotapes of interrogations, and he had placed a recorder on a table and punched in a microcassette before beginning to grill the suspect. The tape recorder was only about a foot and a half from John, but his voice was so soft and low or indistinct at times that the lawman worried about picking it up on the microcassette.

Gradually, nevertheless, Moore began to drag confirmation out of his suspect that Carla was dead and John knew something about her disappearance and how she died. But he claimed he only made the tape found in his car to frighten his wife, and the chief had to struggle to squeeze cut almost every word about the fate of her pretty teenage sister. "It was like pulling hen's teeth," he later observed.

When he switched the conversation momentarily to the disappearance of Shelly Hansen, John categorically denied that he had anything to do with the mystery. It was months later before Moore learned that John had known the young woman. They worked together at Marquip. But by the time Moore learned about that, it was too late to use his newly found information to try and pry out a different story. Once John had entered the local judicial system, and defense lawyers and prosecutors were tilting with each other over matters preliminary to the actual trial, there was no possibility of submitting him to another interrogation. He was off-limits to police and prosecution.

Moore knew he had to obtain every scrap of information he possibly could during the predawn sit down with John that Tuesday morning because he probably wouldn't have another chance. But John was balky when it came to questions about Carla. He asked what was going to happen to him. And he whined that it looked like the only thing he had to look forward to was dying. His life was over. Moore tried to respond to John's morose hand-wringing as positively as he could, while framing new questions. It was important for the police officer to keep the conversation going and to control its direction.

Regardless of how hard he tried to keep the interrogation alive, it was bogging down, so Moore tried the tactic that he had already used successfully with Emily. He asked John if he believed in a Supreme Being. The dejected, frightened young man indicated that he did.

The suspect knew Moore had listened to the tape, chronicling the abuse and murder of Carla, and Moore began talking about his desire to recover the high-school girl's remains. The police chief pulled out all the stops, probing for emotion or a sympathetic response from his morose suspect. He talked earnestly about uneasy souls of the dead trapped in a limbo because they can't find eternal rest.

"I guess what I'm looking for there is I would like to gather whatever is left of Carla and properly bury her so that the good Lord can grant her some peace. The only way to do that is with a Christian burial," he urged.

"You, yourself, couldn't bury someone and have that person ever rest in peace because it is not a Christian burial. You understand what a Christian burial is, right?"

It was time to play a trump card or to bluff. Moore didn't have a trump or an ace, so he rattled his suspect with a verbal roundhouse, then tossed a snare at him.

"Who killed her?" he demanded. "The grave was found exactly where you said it would be. You told us on the tape where it would be. How would you know where the grave was, all right?"

Moore was playing dirty pool. He didn't know where the grave was and his chances of finding it without John's help weren't very promising. But criminal detection and firmly tying murderers to their crimes so they could be charged and convicted wasn't a game for clergymen. If fudging the truth and making his suspect think he knew more than he did led to Carla's grave, it was worth the subterfuge and gamble.

But the police chief's impassioned effort didn't have the effect on his listener he had hoped for. John's reaction, in fact, was about as surprising—and shocking—as it could be. He dropped his right hand under the table and began moving his forearm up and down between his legs in hard rubbing motions.

Never in his professional career, in none of the approximately one thousand interviews and interrogations he had conducted, had Moore ever been faced with similar behavior by a suspect. It appeared to the shocked law officer that John was masturbating.

Masturbation was an act that at different times in his life the young man had admitted to resorting to in order to relieve sexual tension and stress. But the astonished lawman couldn't afford the luxury of showing disgust, and he didn't ask John what he was doing or why. It was time for a break.

"Well, I don't have anything else to talk to you about," he said. Moore suggested John might be more comfortable if he was left alone for a few minutes so he could write down some notes reviewing their conversation. He explained that a copy of the handwritten statement would be passed on to the district attorney, and said it was an opportunity for John to express his own thoughts in his own way.

He gave the glum young man a handful of pink blank City of Phillips voluntary statement forms and a pen, and left the room. After a stop in the bathroom directly across the hall, he slipped into the mirror room where he could watch his suspect. As he stepped up to the window beside Dosch and Gould, he confided to his colleagues that he thought John was masturbating during the final minutes of their interview.

The mini-lecture about theology and the afterlife hadn't produced very satisfying results for the small-town police chief. But he had other tricks up his sleeve. And giving a criminal suspect a pen, paper, and privacy so he could write out a confession or some other statement was a maneuver that had worked before for Moore.

The room was quiet and illuminated by a single overhead light, while John leaned back against the brick wall in the chair, puffing at the cigarette and staring into space. Except for the two-way mirror, there were no other windows. The young man who had spent years recording sadistic sexual fantasies on paper and on audio cassettes, didn't show much interest in Moore's suggestion that he make some notes about Carla's fate.

Finally he tipped his chair upright, leaned over the table, and scribbled down a few words. He dropped the pencil onto the table a moment later and waited. He had filled out the top of the form with his name and other biographical information.

Moore was disappointed. But he would have been even more concerned if he had realized that while he was in the secret room, the microcassette tape ran out and the recorder clicked off. From where he was standing peering into the interrogation room the police officer couldn't hear the "click," and when he rejoined John he assumed the tape was still recording. It was an unfortunate twist of fate that eventually provided a rich opportunity for defense attorneys to challenge important elements of the prosecution's case against John, and was one factor in causing Moore to rethink his philosophy about taping every interrogation.

When the police chief walked back into the interrogation room about ten minutes after leaving, John was hunched over with his head resting on his arms, which were folded on the tabletop. Moore asked if he was finished writing. John indicated he was through. He said he was getting tired. Moore took the statement form and drew a diagonal slash from the end of the last sentence John had written, jotted a couple of notes to himself at the bottom, and signed his name. John had written five lines.

His lack of cooperation was disappointing, but Moore was determined to squeeze out enough information to lead him to Carla's body. He wanted the girl's remains for humanitarian reasons; so she could at last be properly laid to rest, and so her parents and siblings could finally move through the grieving process and go on with their lives.

But recovery of the body was also crucial to charging John with her murder and following up with a successful prosecution. Convicting a suspect of murder when law enforcement authorities hadn't recovered the body of the victim wasn't completely unknown in the United States, but it was exceedingly difficult and rare. It is hard to prove corpus delicti in a homicide case unless there is a body to back it up. In the event of a homicide or manslaughter in order to prove corpus delicti it must be shown that a death had indeed occurred, and that it was due to a criminal act.

Moore couldn't recall hearing about a single case in the State of Wisconsin when investigators failed to recover a body and a defendant was convicted of murder. He wanted his suspect convicted, and he was determined to give the Price County District Attorney more to work with than a hank of hair. He was convinced that his suspect killed and buried Carla, and he wanted her remains.

Using his knowledge that John knew he had listened to the tape, Moore continued to press the suspect for the location of the grave. He pointed out John had mentioned on the tape that he went back to the grave and it was disturbed by animals. Just exactly where was it that John had returned to when he saw indications that animals had been at the grave?

John talked about the general area near Rock Creek Road at his parents' farm. Moore asked him to be more specific. The young man muttered a description of a couple of landmarks, but Moore knew he still didn't have enough information. Lawrence Weber's country spread was big. There were thousands of trees, thickets of underbrush, fields, woodland clearings, and rough trails. Limited by the sparse information he had to go on so far, a search party could take weeks to comb the property and still not find the grave.

He suggested John might enjoy leaving the grim atmosphere of the jail and local law enforcement headquarters, to get some fresh air and stretch his legs for a spell while riding out to the farm with him to look for Carla's grave. "If I took you for a ride in the car, could you show me an approximate location, how far down Rock Creek Road would you go before you think you would see that area?" he asked. What could be better, Moore surmised, than to have the suspect personally point out the grave?

But John had no desire to take up the offer. He wasn't in the mood for a ride. He said he was kind of tired and suggested that he draw a map with the location of Carla's grave instead of riding to the farm with Moore and other police officers. The police chief quickly shoved a ballpoint pen and another pink statement form at John and told him he could use the back of it to draw the map on. The suspect's offer was the next best thing to riding out to the farm and personally pointing out the grave. Moore knew that in such situations people usually draw in greater detail than they speak. John was likely to point out topographical details and landmarks on the map that he would forget or neglect during conversation.

Then John dropped a monkey wrench in the proceedings, according to Moore's later recollection during courtroom testimony. "I am getting kind of tired," he said. "I suppose I am going to have to talk to an attorney." That was the last thing Moore wanted to hear.

John had just posed a delicate legal conundrum for the small-town police chief. The suspect dragged the experienced investigator smack in the middle of the kind of potential Fifth Amendment legal shoot-out that defense and appeals lawyers salivate over.

One of the primary points in the Miranda warning is aimed at ensuring that criminal suspects know they have a Constitutional right to consult a lawyer before submitting to questioning by police or prosecutors. Moore knew that even when they consent to questioning, they can change their mind at any time during the interview or interrogation and exercise their right to counsel.

He had no choice but to back off. He jerked the paper away from the suspect, and muttered something about the interview being over or it being time to stop.

"No! No! Let me draw you a picture," John objected. Moore asked if he wanted an attorney immediately or if he wanted to draw the map first.

"I have got to draw this first."

Moore made a snap decision that wasn't surprising. Barnett and John's defense lawyers could argue fine points of the Constitution and work out the legal rights-and-wrongs of his decision in a courtroom later. The police chief was determined to recover the dead girl's remains, and it appeared he had at last gotten the breakthrough he needed. He released his grip on the sheet of paper. It was the suspect's to do with as he wished.

Instead of beginning to draw, John looked at Moore and advised: "Mister, I think I'm going to lose it."

John's face was pale, his eyes were watery, and he looked to Moore like he was about to vomit. They had been discussing a grave, and a savagely butchered girl, and John's life and future were crumbling all around him.

"Mister, I am telling you I am going to lose it," he repeated. This time Moore got the feeling that his suspect wasn't about to become sick, but that he was on the verge of making a break for it.

The tension in the room was tangible, so solid and heavy it seemed someone could almost reach out and touch it. Moore leaned over and put his hand on John's, telling him to calm down, that everything would be all right. Moore talked to the young man until he relaxed.

At last John grasped the pen in his left hand, bent over the table, and began to draw a series of crude lines and squiggles. He was no artist or cartographer, but gradually a vaguely recognizable map took form on the pink paper. Chief Moore helped out by penciling in place names according to the suspect's explanations and descriptions. As he sketched, John explained that Moore should watch for two hills about a quarter of a mile apart on Rock Creek Road, a short distance from State Trunk Highway 13. If Moore and his colleagues drove

Emily Ann Weber before her vicious attack by her husband John Ray.

Emily's younger sister Carla Lenz, 17, as she looked when she disappeared in November, 1986.

John Ray, Emily and Carla attended Phillips High School. Carla was a senior when she vanished. Emily had graduated the year before.
(*Photo by Frank M. Osanka*)

The main shopping area in the small rural town of Phillips, Wisconsin.   (*Photo by Frank M. Osanka*)

John Ray Weber as a soldier in the
U.S. Army before returning to Phillips.
(*Courtesy of Darla Rae Torres*)

John Ray during deer
hunting season in rural
Price County two weeks
after his abduction
and brutal murder of
Carla Lenz.
(*Courtesy of
Darla Rae Torres*)

The house on South Avon Street formerly
occupied by John Ray and Emily.
(*Photo by Frank M. Osanka*)

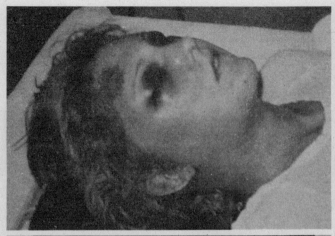

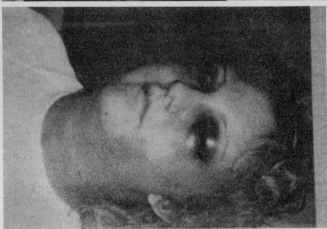

Emily Ann Weber was taken to Flambeau Medical Center in Park Falls, Wisconsin after her husband beat her brutally.

The remains of Carla Lenz as found by the police
at the edge of the forest on the Weber farm.

The final resting place of Carla Lenz.
(*Photo by Frank M. Osanka*)

Chief Craig A. Moore of the Phillips Police
Department spearheaded the investigation into
the brutal assault of Emily Ann Weber and
subsequent discovery of the torture murder
of her sister Carla.
(*Photo by Frank M. Osanka*)

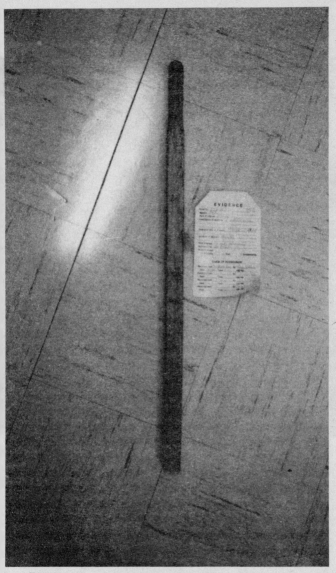

Blood-stained wheelbarrow handle used to rape
Emily Ann Weber.

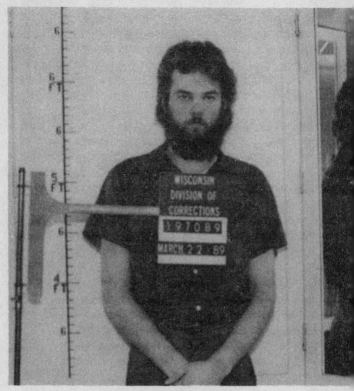

John Ray Weber being processed into the Wisconsin state prison system. (*Courtesy of the Wisconsin State Corrections Department*)

Darla Rae Torres, a native of Glidden, Wisconsin, befriended John Weber after his conviction and visited him in prison frequently. Their relationship ended in 1994. (*Courtesy of Darla Rae Torres*)

Weber photographed by a guard in the visitor's room of the Columbia Correctional Institution in Portage, Wisconsin.

as far as Rock Creek itself, they would have gone too far and would have to back up, he cautioned.

He explained that Moore should park and walk to the left onto the Lawrence Weber property after reaching the crest of one of the hills, which John designated on the map. After crossing the fence line he should bear to the right and continue on to a depression on the crest of the hill and peer to the right where he could see the grave. The grave would be marked by a jacket and a scatter of bones, he said.

For the moment, Moore had what he wanted from his suspect, and he began gathering up the papers in preparation for returning John to his cell and heading for the Weber farm to look for Carla's grave. That was when he noticed that the tape on the recorder had run out. It was a shocking discovery, with implications of big trouble a few days, a few weeks, or a few months down the line when defense attorneys began examining and picking apart statements and other evidence.

There was no way without listening to the tape that the chief could tell how long ago it had run out, at just what stage his record of the interrogation was interrupted. But he realized that he hadn't heard the tape click off while he was talking with John, either before or after taking the break.

Moore couldn't go back and retape the missing portion of the interview, so he picked up the statement form John had written on earlier while he was alone in the room, and jotted a reminder to himself at the bottom. It said: "John spoke verbally. He wanted an attorney. I asked him if he wanted an attorney before he showed us the location of Carla Lenz's body. He said, 'No. I want to draw you a map and then see an attorney.' " Then the chief signed his name, "Craig A. Moore, PPD, 6:05 A.M."

The interview was over. Moore led his prisoner back upstairs and turned him over to the jailer. John said he thought he would sleep a little while, then get himself an attorney. He was advised that a lawyer would be calling him at about eight A.M.

Outside the sky was just beginning to streak with pale pink, and sparrows, thrushes, and jays were setting up their early-morning chatter when Moore and his colleagues climbed into their squad cars to begin the drive out to the Weber place at Wisconsin State Trunk Highway 13 and Rock Creek Road.

While Dosch drove, Moore busied himself in the passenger seat writing out a more formal report based on the various notes he had taken during his interview with the suspect. The notebook the chief carried with him was as much a part of him as an arm or a leg. He depended on it, and it seemed he was always jotting down cryptic notes to himself, to jog his memory or remind him of a task that needed to be done.

While the headlights of the police cars sliced through the slate gray of the early September morning, threads of yellow, pink, and orange began lighting up the eastern horizon over the trees and swamps of the Chequamegon National Forest. Indistinct dark blobs along the sides of the highway became the mangled or flattened bodies of skunks, horseshoe rabbits, raccoons, and opossum, the past night's roadkill highlighted in the quickening light of the new day. The sun was just climbing above the tree-line when the police cars turned off State Trunk Highway 13 and drove onto Rock Creek Road bordering the Weber property.

The map drawn by John was unprofessional and provided the search team with no more than a rough idea of where the grave was, if indeed it existed at all. They knew, according to the sketch, that it should be no more than one hundred feet or so from Rock Creek Road, and probably within a few minutes' walking distance of the polebarn. John's directions eliminated most of the more rugged and primitive area of the spread, the back forty acres that were most heavily wooded or pock-marked by large stretches of swampland.

Moore, Dosch, and Gould left their vehicles near the highway and set up a rough grid search, divvying up sections of land for a close back-and-forth inspection of the sandy soil. They spread out near the fence line of the property, looking for a telltale depression in the ground, human bones, and a jacket. There were lots of bones lying here and there on the ground, but on close inspection they all appeared to be those of squirrels, rabbits, or other small forest animals. Nearly an hour after they began meandering through the trees and brush, Dosch yelled to his companions. He had found the grave. It was on a sandhill about one hundred feet off Rock Creek Road, just south of the fence line on the Weber property. Gould took a quick look, then walked back to his squad car, radioed Sheriff Wirsing, and advised that what appeared to be a grave was found on the Lawrence Weber property a few feet off Rock Creek Road.

While the sheriff and a couple of deputies pulled away from the County Safety Building for their dash to Rock Creek Road, Moore and his colleagues staked off the immediate area around the suspected grave with strips of bright yellow vinyl crime-scene tape.

Preserving evidence at grave sites is an especially sensitive and tricky job. The mere task of disinterring remains from a grave, requires the gross disturbance of a crime scene.

Carla, who was thought to be buried there, had probably been dead for almost two years, and her grave was exposed to the heat and rain of summer and the wind, snow, and ice of winter, as well as to the ravages of wild animals. Any footprints or tire marks left at the scene when the grave was being dug or she was buried would obviously have been blown away, washed away, or filled in with dust and dirt long ago. The grave was a potential treasure trove of evidence, nevertheless.

A three-man field response team of technicians from the Wisconsin Department of Justice, Division of Law Enforcement Services, and Crime Laboratory Bureau arrived from Madison and began directing the gathering, marking, and bagging of evidence. The laboratory provides teams on request, to assist law enforcement agencies throughout the state in taking photographs and collecting evidence at crime scenes.

The agency's formal title is too much of a mouthful for most people to deal with, and consequently almost everyone, including the crime-scene technicians and analysts themselves, refer to it more simply as the State Crime Laboratory, or the State Crime Lab. Sheriff Wirsing had telephoned Madison for help, and team leader Kenneth B. Olson, a chemist in the laboratory's chemistry-physics section, made the hurried drive to Price County with two other analysts.

The evidence technicians stopped at the Sheriff's Department in Phillips for a quick briefing, then continued on to the Weber farm. Wirsing arrived at the crime scene with investigator Richard J. Heitkemper and a couple of deputies. Squad cars were parked so that they blocked both ends of Rock Creek Road near the crime scene. A thick strip of crime-scene tape was stretched across the road to warn away gawkers.

All the evidence wasn't buried with the body. Several articles, including a jacket, what appeared to be human bones, a beer can, and cigarette butts, were scattered on top of or around the grave. But there were also soil samples for the field response team to take, trace evidence to seek out, and still photographs and video pictures to take.

The grave and the area immediately surrounding it were photographed from several angles before anything was touched. Olson and his colleagues measured distances and triangulated the grave site from the road and several large trees in the area. Along with the picture taking, careful measurements of the various items of evidence were made before collection to show exactly where each piece was found and its location in relation to the grave itself and to other articles.

Surrounded by sheriff's officers in brown uniforms, and Phillips Police Department officers in blue, members of the field response team began collecting, bagging, and marking articles, including beer cans, collected from the scene. Brush and debris were also cleared from the immediate area before excavation of the burial pit was ready to begin.

The early-morning sun was blazing, when the lawmen started carefully digging into the dry sand around the grave and lifting away the dirt with the tips of shovels. The grave and surrounding area had to be processed with all the care of a highly trained archaeologist or anthropologist looking for clues to early mankind. Even the configuration of the burial plot might later be determined to have importance.

The exhumation was professional and deliberate, with every effort taken to preserve evidence. The men began by digging a deep channel, or trench, around the grave until they were a few inches below what they believed to be the actual site of the remains. Then they switched to small hand tools, trowels, or similar implements, to carefully remove layers of dirt from the grave a bit at a time until they began carefully lifting out the fragile, gray bones.

As each trowel of dirt was removed from the trench, then from the grave, it was carefully shaken and sifted for chips of bones and other evidence while being deposited in neat piles alongside the rectangular hole in the ground. A purple jacket, bra, panties, and a plastic syringe with a blue protective cap still in place over the needle were uncovered during the excavation. Along with other articles later gathered up, they were placed in separate paper bags, which were folded over, stapled and sealed with white adhesive tape. Finally a hot-wax seal with Olson's fingerprint or thumbprint pressed in it was affixed to the ends of the tape to establish and maintain the chain of custody.

There was no evidence of the dangerously noxious vapors and sickeningly sweet musk that rise from fresher human graves, while the men worked. And a fresh breeze that whipped along the tree line helped blow away the slightly musty graveyard stink.

For the most part, except for grunts from their exertions, the soft crunch of the shovel and trowels as they sliced into the sandy loam, and an occasional word or two from one of their colleagues, they worked in silence. The sun quickly chased away the purple ground mist, and warmed the crime scene, baking away the last traces of dew that still clung to bushes, vines, and earth.

There was nothing left of Carla but dirt-encrusted bones, a bit of hair, and the tiniest scraps of body tissue that were in an advanced state of decomposition. Her pitiful remains were wrapped in a canvas tarp that was beginning to rot and decompose, but was still intact. A small, round metal pellet that appeared to be bird shot was spotted among the remains, picked up, and placed in an evidence bag.

The bones that hadn't already been carried away by animals or scattered along the surface of the earth, were only a few inches below the surface. The search team eventually recovered almost the entire skeleton, including the skull. Only a portion of the left leg along with the foot were missing. It appeared that the femur had been cut off with a heavy, sharp instrument of some kind. But determining if that was true, and if so, exactly how the leg was removed, would be a job for forensic pathologists.

Heitkemper radioed the Heindl Funeral Home in Phillips and asked them to send a hearse to the property and pick up a body. The mortuary was on North Avon, only a few blocks from John and Emily's home.

While they were waiting for the hearse, the officers gingerly loaded the remains pulled from the carefully excavated grave in a body bag, then zipped it closed, and crimped a lead seal with an ID tag on the outside. Heitkemper stood beside the bag until the hearse arrived, watched as it was loaded onto a cart and wheeled inside, then climbed into the vehicle beside it for the ride back to Phillips.

Olson and his crew loaded much of the evidence collected at the site into their car, then climbed inside and pulled onto State Road 13 to begin the long drive back to Madison.

The hearse, meanwhile, was driven to the Price County Sheriff's Department, where Heitkemper took temporary custody of it. The driver handed over the keys, and the investigator drove the long, black vehicle, with the body bag and the remains still loaded in the back, into the first of the wired-off cages in the garage. Then he locked the doors of the hearse, locked up the cage, stuck both sets of keys in his pocket, and left.

When he walked away from the locked garage it marked the first time the remains were out of his sight since they were removed from the grave. He wouldn't see the hearse or the body bag again until he met a driver from the funeral home at the garage so they could transport the remains to the State Crime Laboratory in Madison.

At the farm, Moore's eyes were red and gritty from lack of sleep. He desperately needed a meal and a shower, and after nearly two days without shaving he had a dark stubble of beard. But he was so psyched up and immersed in the investigation that he was hardly aware he was tired.

He had recovered what was left of Carla's body, but the investigation was far from over. There was no time for Sherlock Holmes reflection, to stop and think things over, or to batter theories back and forth with a trusted colleague. Instinct and experience told him to keep moving, to forge ahead and wrap up everything he could before taking a break in the probe of Carla's apparent murder.

Moore was troubled by suspicions that Carla and Emily may not have been John's only victims. He was aware that Marchell Hansen was missing from the Phillips area, and she was a young, attractive, brown-haired woman about the same age as Emily. Who knew how many females might be buried along the road, or in the woods or swamps along the more rugged North Forty? The police chief later elaborated on his fears, remarking:

"After listening to the tape, how many more would there have been. He had plans on others, some of them not named of course, but others. Figments of his imagination, a cheerleader for instance. Well, which one?"

Moore, Wirsing, and their colleagues decided they needed dogs to make a more wide-ranging search of the farm property for other possible bodies or grave sites. The sheriff telephoned the secretary of the Wilderness Search And Rescue Dog Units and said he had a job for the volunteer organization. Wilderness Search and Rescue is a volunteer group of handlers and animals that looks for adults or children who have become lost in the vastness of the North Woods—and for dead bodies.

Sharon Jaeger and another woman handler showed up at the farm at about dusk with a couple of the organization's best German shepherds. Ms. Jaeger drove to the Weber spread from her home in Mellen, another small town straight up State Road 13 in Ashland county, which was about the same size as Phillips and about a half-hour drive from Chequamegon Bay on Lake Superior. Like Phillips, Mellen is surrounded by national forests, lakes, and Indian land. The Bad River Indian Reservation is only a few minutes' drive to the northeast.

The last original organizing member of the search and rescue group, who had about seven years of experience and was one of the leading dog trainers, Ms. Jaeger immediately huddled with her colleague, with Heitkemper, and with other officers for a briefing. Heitkemper explained the situation and outlined the area to be covered in the initial sweep. The sun had already gone down and darkness was moving in fast, so it was agreed to concentrate the initial phase of the search along the edges of Highway 13, where it fronted on the property, and around the buildings, a nearby pond, and a gravel pit.

The handlers released the dogs from their vehicle and began combing the property for bodies or graves. The dogs are leashed only at the beginning of most searches, mostly for their own safety while they are near their transport vehicles parked along roads or highways. As soon as they enter a woods or safe area, however, the leashes are removed and they are allowed to run freely, eagerly sniffing for the scent of living or dead human beings.

Ms. Jaeger and her companion were working with air-scent dogs. The animals don't need to sniff an article of clothing or anything else associated with someone they're looking for. They're trained to pick up human scent from the air. Plumes of air, heat and moisture swarm around a body, but the sensitive nose of an air-scent dog can pick up human odor even long after a person has moved on.

As soon as the German shepherds bounded from the vehicles they sniffed the air, perked up their ears, and strained at their leashes. In the specialized lexicon of their handlers, the dogs had "alerted," indicating they were picking up a foreign human scent—or methane, the deadly gas that escapes from decomposing bodies. The dogs were also trained to alert to methane, and they attempted to join a group of law enforcement officers gathered a few yards away.

The handlers didn't know it at the time, but the lawmen were standing near the excavated grave where Carla's remains had lain for nearly two years. The women hadn't been told yet about the grave, but it wasn't difficult to figure out. Throughout the search, every time the dogs got within a few yards of the ribboned-off area they alerted and tried to get to the knot of men and the curious mound of earth.

The dogs worked in a grid, organized in a specific pattern to ensure that none of the area to be searched was inadvertently missed. And they worked to the wind. Ms. Jaeger and her dog worked to the north of the other team. As they progressed in a methodical crisscross pattern, their movements were occasionally altered to accommodate wind-direction shifts.

When John's father stopped at his country place in the early evening with a companion, the dogs were still combing the area around the outbuildings. The farm was aswarm with police officers, and squad cars were parked in the driveway in front of the polebarn and along the road. Weber talked with several of the officers. None of the information they were able to pass on to him gave him much reason for optimism. All the news was bad. Shortly after his arrival, the dog handlers loaded their animals back in their vehicle and left. They had agreed to return early the following day.

Sheriff's deputies traded off duties guarding the grave overnight. Alone with the darkness and the hunting calls of night birds, it was an eerily, solitary task that required the officer on duty to stay within sight of the ominous rent in the earth at every moment. Hemmed in by the vinyl crime-scene tape, the dreadful burial pit loomed like an open wound, illuminated in a barely distinct silhouette by the stars and a mucous-yellow moon that slumped balefully over the horizon most of the night.

Wednesday morning Sheriff Wirsing widened the search area. The handlers showed up before ten A.M. with their dogs, and again began working according to a grid pattern set up with professional care. Ms. Jaeger often rotates her animals during searches and she brought a different dog than she used the night before. Both dogs selected for the search that day, as well as the other animal used the previous evening, were six- or seven-year veterans of the program. Heitkemper brought a metal detector with him for the second day of the search, but he trailed along with the dog teams, as he had done the evening before.

Weather wise, the second day of the search was less than ideal, although it could have been much worse. The sky was clear, but a capricious breeze whipped and curled over the terrain and the direction was awkward, not the best for searching the area that had been sectioned off. Portions of the search area were also difficult to work the dogs in, especially along the edges of swamps and marshes which were lined with dense tangles of thorny shrubs, alders, and other birches.

The dogs alerted several times, including an occasion or so when they dug up bones and dirt-matted clumps of brown hair or fur. The dogs stopped, stiffened their bodies, and moved their noses around in the air until they zeroed in more fully on the scent, then cautiously approached the area or object. Once one of the dogs alerted and began pawing at a mound of soft earth before it could be called off. Heitkemper recovered some animal bones. Another time one of the dogs alerted and the sheriff's officer dug up a sliver of bone that was only about an inch and a half in diameter.

In each instance when bones were recovered, close inspection disclosed they were from one species or another of the profusion of wild animals that roamed the woods, swampland, or pastures in the area.

Whenever anything which seemed it could possibly turn out to be significant to the investigation was found, the handlers quickly pulled the dogs away and temporarily ribboned-off the area while Heitkemper or one of the other police officers was summoned. The handlers were careful not to touch any of the bones or anything else that was discovered. Heitkemper stuck close to the dogs and handlers, as he had done the first evening of the ground search and was usually the individual who made closer inspection of the finds.

Ms. Jaeger was combing an area near a swamp when her dog alerted and bounded into a heavy stand of trees. He was excited, but confused when he returned and led her through the trees to a mound of grass that had been beaten down. There was nothing else of interest to see—no clothing, no cigarette butts, no weapons, no bones, and no evidence of digging or of a grave.

While she visually inspected the grassy mound and immediate area for anything she might have missed, the excited dog continued to whimper and whine. Suddenly it alerted again and scampered a few feet away, past some more trees, then stopped and resumed whimpering and whining. He was excited and ran back and forth to the handler until she followed him to the new site. The dog had discovered a freshly dug hole in the ground.

They were one hundred yards or so southwest of the driveway leading onto the Weber property. Unknown to the handler, the German shepherd had discovered the sites where Emily spent the early Sunday morning slipping in and out of consciousness after John's savage assault and where he had dug the ominous hole. Chief Moore and Vergin had already collected evidence from the area a couple of days earlier.

About six o'clock Wednesday night, the search with the dogs was called off. The Wilderness Search and Rescue teams had put in an exhausting eight-hour day with only an occasional break to rest the dogs, and another at about noon to feed the animals and themselves. Heitkemper lunched in his squad car, dining on a can of soda pop and a sandwich. There was no time for anyone on the search team to drive into Fifield, Park Falls, or to backtrack even farther and stop at Phillips for a hot meal.

Heitkemper's squad car was parked on the north side of

Rock Creek Road across the highway from the Weber property, and the dog teams briefly wandered up a road into another wooded area to check it out. Heitkemper stayed behind to work on the metal detector, which was malfunctioning. Even then he stayed in radio communication with the handlers. But nothing significant to the investigation was found during the short foray.

Despite their dedicated efforts, no additional graves, bodies, or portions of bodies had been located at the end of the day. On Thursday, September 8, nevertheless, despite the meticulous search by men, women, and dogs, Gould was back at the grave site when he discovered another human bone. It was lying about fifty feet from the grave.

The chief deputy sheriff directed another officer to make measurements of its location in relation to the grave, then bag and seal it. Gould drove his find back to the Sheriff's Department headquarters in Phillips where it was briefly stored in the evidence locker. Then it was removed, placed in a manila envelope that in turn was securely packaged with packing to prevent breakage, and sent by certified mail to Olson at the Wisconsin State Crime Laboratory.

By the time Gould made his surprising discovery at the grave site, however, the focus of the investigation had already turned elsewhere. There was old evidence to be correlated and analyzed, and new evidence to be gathered.

Chapter Ten

Legwork

A good detective touches all the bases, and Moore and his colleagues were determined to do all the spadework necessary to wrap up the multifaceted case against John Weber for assaulting his wife and butchering his sister-in-law.

Hard-hitting professional investigative work isn't the sole province of detectives or plainclothesmen with federal or state agencies and big-city police departments.

In fact, some of the shoddiest police work can occur within some of the best equipped and trained agencies, like the shameful performance of the two Milwaukee police officers who allowed Jeffrey Dahmer to take a fleeing Laotian fourteen-year-old back to his apartment where he was murdered and mutilated.

And some of the best detection work can be turned in by some of the smallest law enforcement agencies—like the four-man Phillips Police Department and the slightly larger Price County Sheriff's Department.

From the beginning of the probe there was a refreshing lack of overt jealousy or friction over jurisdiction shown by the growing number of law enforcement agencies involved in the Weber investigation. Barely three days into the probe, the Phillips Police Department, Park Falls Police Department, Price County Sheriff's Department, Wisconsin State Patrol, Wisconsin State Crime Laboratory, and the privately operated search and rescue volunteers had all become involved.

Even the FBI played a peripheral role prior to John's arrest, becoming involved in the search for Carla and for Marchell Hansen. But the Bureau continued to take a backseat to local and state agencies throughout the twin investigations related to the assault on Emily and the murder of her sister.

Moore had taken the lead in the rapidly broadening probe, and his law enforcement colleagues joined in, divvying up responsibilities and tasks according to who was available or best trained in a particular specialty. If there was any serious bickering between agencies, it wasn't obvious to outsiders.

Price County Sheriff's Department investigator Heitkemper and a hearse driver were on their way early to deliver the skeletal remains recovered from the woodland grave to the laboratory for examination and autopsy by forensic pathologists and an anthropologist from the university. They stopped once for gas and another time for coffee, before delivering the body to the laboratories at the University of Wisconsin Hospital and Clinic at about 8:30 A.M.

Heitkemper stayed with the sealed body while it was wheeled into the X-ray department, where he met with Dr. Robert W. Huntington III. Dr. Huntington was a physician employed at the University of Wisconsin as a pathologist and teacher who had personally conducted fifteen hundred autopsies and observed at least two thousand others during his twenty-five-year career.

The police officer kept his eye on the body bag while the contents were moved through the X-ray process. Some curious small round dots showed up in the body mass when the X ray was examined. Dr. Huntington had seen similar objects before in studies of the bodies of the victims of murder or certain accidental deaths. After completing the X-ray process he and the doctor wheeled the body bag, still sealed, through the an-

tiseptic corridors to the autopsy room in the United States
Veterans Administration Hospital complex.

Heitkemper witnessed the autopsy. In addition to Dr. Huntington, the autopsy team included Dr. Kenneth A. Bennett, a
professor in the Biological Anthropology Department at the
university and an experienced forensic anthropologist; resident
physician Dr. Scott Reich III; Dr. Donald O. Simley II, a dentist and forensic odontologist who was a consultant to the State
Crime Laboratory and the Dane County Coroner's Office; and
two technicians from the State Crime Laboratory, Michael
Haas and Jerry Geurts. Along with Heitkemper, they huddled
around the remains as the seal on the body bag was broken.

The medical sleuths began the examination by opening
some of the smaller bags, and quickly eliminated a pile of
small bones from further examination because they were obviously from animals. But one of the bags contained bones
from a human forearm, small bones that appeared to be from
a human hand, and some loose fingernails.

The larger bag contained the skull, most of the skeleton,
and a bit of tissue, from a human adult or teenager. A dirty
and decaying long-sleeve, pullover T-shirt with logos that included the words "REO SPEEDWAGON" were also removed
from the bag and set aside for examination by other forensic
experts.

The skull still had much of the hair attached and was
wrapped in thick strips of a broad gauge tape. In addition to
carefully removing the tape and examining the skull, a member
of the pathology team also removed some strands of hair for
later use by laboratory analysts.

One of the first and most obvious observations the team
made was that the lower portion of the left leg was missing,
and had been removed from approximately two inches above
the knee joint. The bone appeared to have been cut with a
sharp instrument, which Dr. Bennett initially believed to have
been a saw. After careful cleaning of the leg bone, however,
the autopsy team ruled out a saw as a possible instrument used

in the amputation. There were no telltale marks of cross-scraping that are found on bones that have been sawed through. But no one on the autopsy team was able to determine exactly what kind of implement was used to remove the leg.

The pathology team had been briefed on the case and was aware of special conditions to look for that might relate to John's description on the audiotape cassette of the torture and fatal attack on Carla. Consequently they made a careful inspection of the bones of the neck for evidence to confirm his claim that at the conclusion of the assault he mashed his foot firmly on her throat until she died.

But examination of the cervical vertebra, the bone at the top of the spinal cord at the back of the neck, failed to disclose any breaks or cracks. And the hyoids, the tiny U-shaped bones that are at the base and help support the tongue, weren't retrieved from the grave site. The hyoid bones are often fractured when someone is strangled, but they are small and it is not unusual for them to be missed and left behind when human remains in as deplorable a condition as Carla's are recovered. Some apparent damage along the back of the skull at the base of the cranium was also observed and noted on the autopsy report, but it wasn't possible to determine if it was caused by strangulation.

There wasn't sufficient tissue with the remains to confirm whether or not beer bottles or other objects were forcibly inserted in the body cavities, or if one of Carla's breasts was sliced off as John claimed in the tape. The pathology team took an especially close look at the ribs, inspecting them for nicks that might have been made by a knife blade sawing through a breast, but the surfaces were smooth. The absence of identifying breaks or marks didn't mean that Carla hadn't been strangled, violated with beer bottles, or had her breast slashed off. She was big-busted, so it was entirely conceivable one of her breasts could have been slashed off without touching her rib cage. There simply wasn't enough left of her to work with to make determinations.

* * *

The identity of the small round forms picked up by the X ray was confirmed, however. They were pellets from a shotgun shell. It was a discovery that would pester other investigators throughout much of the investigation with suspicions about the possibility that Carla was blasted with a shotgun either before or after she died. Could the girl's killer have used a shotgun blast as she was dumped in the grave to add a ruthless coup de grace to the previous savagery, or simply to make sure she was dead? An expended shotgun shell was among the evidence collected at the grave site.

But the young man whom friends considered to be an especially sensitive hunter, who couldn't stand to see animals suffer, said nothing in the tape he made for Emily or in his confession about firing a load of shotgun pellets into the limp, cruelly mutilated body of the girl. Whether or not Carla was shotgunned before her killer began shovelling the sandy soil over her corpse was a question that would ultimately become a bitter point of contention at trial.

One important fact about the remains was confirmed with one hundred percent certainty before the end of the week. They definitely belonged to Carla Lenz. Dr. Simley made the final confirmation after comparing the mouth and teeth in the skull with X rays.

The day before the pathologists gathered around the remains lifted from the forest grave, Gene Lenz, Sr., carried out one of the saddest chores of his life. He visited the office of his missing daughter's dentist and asked for some of her dental records so they could be used to verify identification of the body. Dr. John Satterwhite selected pertinent X rays of Carla's mouth and teeth from her files, and directed one of his employees to deliver them to the sheriff.

In Madison, after making his initial inspection during the

autopsy, Dr. Simley carried the skull back to his office for further study. The experienced odontologist's father was the only witness as he determined the number of teeth in the skull, and used the X rays to compare their position in the mouth, anatomy of tooth structure including the shape of the roots, location and type of fillings, and the general condition of the teeth. The odontologist took his own X rays of the mouth and teeth, which he compared on a lit view box with those provided by the dentist in Phillips. Both sets of X rays, and the teeth and other configurations in the mouth of the skull matched. The remains were definitely those of the former Price County schoolgirl.

It was almost one o'clock Wednesday afternoon when Heitkemper finally walked out of the autopsy room and rejoined his driver, Steve Augustine, for the drive back to Phillips with the last pitiful remnants of the slain high-school girl. The tape removed from the skull, bits of the badly decayed soft tissue, and the black T-shirt with the logo of the Illinois-based rock group were turned over to Haas for later study.

A few days later Dr. Bennett busied himself in his personal laboratory to examine the bone fragment recovered by Gould, and determined with what he said was about "ninety percent confidence" that it was a fragment from a human tibia, a major bone in the lower portion of the leg. It had been badly gnawed by rodents, which based on the pattern of the tooth marks, he suspected were probably mice or rats.

"Normally when they do this they are going after mineral contents of bones such as salt and whatnot," he later explained. "And so the bone fragment itself was rather difficult to determine unequivocally whether or not it was human." He further explained that he made his determination that the fragment was probably human remains after comparing it with bones from other mammals including dogs and cats. But it was impossible to tell from the remnant that was available if it had come from a right leg or a left leg, the sex, or how tall the person may have been. And it couldn't be definitely matched to Carla's missing lower limb.

Earlier, while the district attorney was preparing the paperwork for the search warrants for the Cutlass and for John and Emily's home, he asked for a description of the wrap she wore on the drive home after spending the night in the woods. Chief Moore telephoned the Flambeau Medical Center to find out what Emily had worn. The hospital nursing supervisor's subsequent actions and the information the police chief said was relayed to him, later became a knotty point of contention between the prosecution and the defense.

When Moore ended the conversation, he was under the clear impression that Emily wore a blue sweater home from the woods. Consequently, the sweater was listed on three search warrants, for the car and for the house. The investigators obtained a second warrant for the house based on some of their discoveries during the search of the Cutlass. John's talk on the tape about cannibalism and the discovery of a roll of freezer paper was especially alarming. The lawmen wanted to check his freezer.

Both the confusion over the blue sweater and the specter of a Gein-like cannibalism aspect to the case were delicate problems to be dealt with in preliminary hearings. The legal complications that was developing over the sweater was one of those seemingly minor points that often sidetracks both investigators and trial lawyers, and consumes inordinate amounts of valuable time and resources. But it was vitally important because the prosecutor, acting on Moore's description of the clothing Emily had worn home from the Weber farm, listed the sweater as one of the items of evidence investigators hoped to find at the house so it could be visually examined and analyzed in a laboratory for blood stains or other trace evidence related to the attack.

Through some lapse of communication, however, the blue sweater was mixed up with John's jacket. Emily wore the jacket home from the farm, and she wore the sweater on the drive with her mother and sister-in-law to the hospital. The misstep, a relatively minor misunderstanding under normal circumstances, had the potential of assuming major importance as part of the judicial process where even the most oblique technicalities can sometimes help make the difference between winning or losing a trial.

The confusion over the blue sweater opened the door for the defense to challenge the legality of evidence collected while serving the warrants. If the warrant was defective because the information on the documents was wrong and listed the wrong article of clothing, the lawyers could ask that the evidence be thrown out.

Court and law enforcement officials were also anxious to keep references to cannibalism away from the public, especially in the preliminary hearings and early stages of the trial, in order to avoid further sensationalizing an already bizarre case and tainting or prejudicing the jury pool—and ultimately the jurors.

A twenty-four-hour police guard was set up around John and Emily's house. But when Moore, Wirsing, three technicians from the State Crime Laboratory, and other officers from the police and sheriff's departments served the warrants issued by Judge Fox for the bungalow, the interior was a mess. John and Emily's two young dogs had run rampant. Nevertheless, the officers gathered up a solid collection of material. A pair of slashed panties stained by what appeared to be blood, were found in the bathroom on top of a pile of dirty laundry. A couple more nylon bags with cigarette company logos were found in separate bedrooms, a pair of men's underpants and a brown T-shirt were collected, and a piece of felt cloth that appeared to be bloodstained was taken from a jewelry box.

Some packaged syringes were gathered from the top of a large dresser in the master bedroom, and a small bottle of prescription medicine designed for injection was retrieved from the refrigerator in the kitchen. A small plank was taken from Emily's plant stand, and a camera and some exposed film were also gathered up. The search warrant listed items related to sexual perversion, and the camera and film were collected because perverts often take photographs as mementos or trophies. The team also confiscated a shotgun with a cutoff barrel that was of illegal length. The weapon was lying in the open on the kitchen table.

But there were no human body parts stored in the freezer, and there was no blue sweater. The investigators also failed to find the .25-caliber semiautomatic pistol John was known to own, either while serving the search warrants or during a consent search authorized by Emily. During a follow-up interview at the hospital Emily told Moore the handgun was normally kept under the bladder of the water bed mattress, but it wasn't there. She was still in a tremendous amount of pain when she was reinterviewed.

During one of the searches, the police chief gathered up some shotgun shells from a cardboard box in a front bedroom used by the couple for storage.

Investigators were still piling up evidence when Barnett drew up a seventeen-page criminal complaint against the young husband, accusing him of Carla's murder and the attack on Emily. The complaint claimed he dug Carla's grave two days before killing her then drove around with her in the trunk of the Sunbird for five days before finally burying the remains. The grim document pointed out that the suspect himself revealed details of the attack in the tape recording found nearly two years later in the Cutlass. The complaint also accused him of planning a "disappearance" for Emily that was similar to her sister's and forcing her to write notes to family members saying she had gone away.

At one point, according to the document, while John was beating her with the shovel Emily screamed, "Stop it, stop it, just leave me alone. I'm not going to let you kill me. I'm not going to die."

When Barnett finished drawing up charges, John was named

on a total of eight felony offenses for the attacks on his wife and her sister; first degree murder, attempted murder, and two counts each of kidnapping, false imprisonment, and sexual assault. The State of Wisconsin has no death penalty, but conviction on even half the charges or fewer could result in John spending the rest of his life behind bars. Conviction of first degree murder alone carried a mandatory life sentence. And conviction on all counts could bring him a maximum total sentence of life, plus eighty-four years.

During his repeat talk with Emily to clarify facts and fill in or expand on details from his earlier interviews, Moore asked about the tape with John's chilling account of Carla's abduction and murder. Emily explained she never listened to it. John was rambling on about a tape and she started to play it as they were about to enter the woods at the farm, but he turned it off. She told the lawman she assumed it was linked to the surprise her husband had readied for her.

The black tape cartridge with the suspect's damning statement about the murder of Carla and his sadistic plan for Emily, was transcribed by Marilyn Kitten. Ms. Kitten wore three hats at the sheriff's department, alternately functioning as the secretary, dispatcher, and the matron who worked with female prisoners. Transcribing the tape taken from the Cutlass was an easier task than transcribing the audiotape Chief Moore had made of John's interrogation that led to the discovery of the grave.

Transcribing the interrogation was an ordeal. The first disappointment occurred when Ms. Kitten was unable to fit the cassette into her dictating machine. The situation deteriorated from there. John was naturally soft-spoken. And during his confrontation with Moore he mumbled, allowed his voice to trail off at times, and speckled the interview with "uh-uhs" and "um-huhs." Some responses were so soft and indistinct that she couldn't make out words or phrases. Although Moore had finally found time for a shower, some sleep, and a hot meal, he was still moving full tilt on the investigation, busying himself with interviews, telephone calls, and more evidence searches. But he took time out to help decipher his conversation with John on the tape. It was a tedious, frustrating task, but a job that was vital to the investigation. A couple of times after he switched the cassette player to rewind so he could back up and try to make out a word or phrase, he inadvertently pushed the record button and erased a second or two of the conversation. Before the painstaking task was completed, he had begun to seriously rethink his reliance on always taping interrogations.

"At that time I was under the old philosophy that you tape things and then dictate off of that. If anything, that case really changed my mind on doing that anymore. It's so difficult unless you have a studio with some good recording equipment. But that was a nightmare," Moore later recalled. "John mumbled a lot during that interview. You don't realize it because you're not getting instant feedback as you would in a video, and it was difficult."

Moore spent valuable hours going over the tape, filling in indistinct mumblings word by word, sometimes resorting to his memory when he simply couldn't make anything out. He eventually wrote out the entire interview in longhand, then turned it over to Ms. Kitten to type. Despite their herculean efforts, when he and the secretary finished with their exhausting task, there were still blank words that neither of them could figure out.

Of course, inadvertently allowing the tape to run out and the recorder to click off while Moore was outside the interrogation room was even more disappointing. It was a near disaster, with possible distressing implications a few weeks in the future when attorneys began seriously tilting over the admissibility of evidence.

A few days after the tape was transcribed, sheriff's deputy Todd Hintz drove to Madison with it and had three copies made at the Wisconsin State Crime Laboratory. Then he returned to Phillips with the original and two of the copies.

By that time Moore was stepping back from his position as

point man in the far-ranging investigation and passing the torch to the sheriff. The transition was smooth and painless, as Wirsing and his staff assumed a greater role for directing the investigation and huddled with the district attorney, parcelling out duties and leads to follow up.

Sheriff Wirsing knew that John owned the Pontiac Sunbird when Carla disappeared, and he began tracking it down. Wirsing and his deputies learned that when John bought his Oldsmobile, he sold the Sunbird to Keith Newbury. In the fall of 1987, Newbury sold the ten-year-old car to Kai Thomas Kelly and his wife, Jean, from the rural Flambeau township hamlet of Lugerville. The sheriff obtained a search warrant for the Sunbird, and on October 6, one day short of a month after Carla's remains were dug out of the primitive grave at the Weber place, he knocked on the door at the Kelly home.

Wirsing gave the Kellys a copy of the warrant and told them he was there to take their car. His primary interest in the vehicle was in making a search of the locked trunk, where if John's account on the tape was correct, Carla's body was left for five days between her murder and her burial. The sheriff permitted the couple to remove a few personal items from inside while he watched. Kai Kelly then showed him how to start the car, turned over the keys, and Wirsing drove away with their vehicle. It would be almost two weeks before the car was returned to the owners.

The sheriff drove the old car to the garage at his headquarters and locked it in one of the stalls. A week later, he and Chief Moore towed it to Madison and left it with Barbara A. LeMay at the State Crime Laboratories, with a request that she make a careful examination of the trunk. She gave the police officers a signed receipt, and the car was stored overnight in a locked laboratory garage.

* * *

A crime laboratory analyst specializing in forensic serology, the process of identifying blood, saliva, semen, and other body fluids, Ms. LeMay began the job of processing evidence and inspecting the car trunk early the next morning. She was especially concerned with seeking out any clothing fibers, hair and bloodstains, or other body fluids that might have been left behind by a corpse stuffed into the trunk.

Photographs were taken of the car and of the inside and outside of the trunk. Then the analyst vacuumed the interior of the trunk in order to pick up hair or fibers. The material picked up during the vacuuming process was sealed in an evidence bag for later examination.

Ms. LeMay, who trained with the Wisconsin State Department of Justice and at the FBI Academy in Quantico, Virginia, was also an expert in making forensic hair comparisons and analysis of natural fibers. She recovered six hairs when she sifted through the contents of the vacuum bag. During visual examination with the naked eye and closer inspection with a powerful microscope, she determined that the color and structure of five of the strands recovered during the vacuuming were consistent with hair samples taken from Carla's skull. No traces of blood were found in the car trunk.

Wirsing had also loaded up various items collected up to that time in the investigation, and stored in the evidence room, and delivered them to the State Crime Laboratories along with the Sunbird for inspection and analysis by technicians. They included the sand shovel, the suspiciously stained wheelbarrow handle, .20-gauge shotgun, pistol, the nylon bags found in the Cutlass, and other material.

Ms. LeMay also ultimately examined the shovel, wheelbarrow handle, the nylon duffel bags, and several items of clothing, including the jacket, the panties, and the bra taken from the grave site. A single hair recovered from the bag with the Marlboro logo was analyzed and found to be consistent with the samples taken from Carla's skull.

* * *

Ms. LeMay was unable to find bloodstains on the purple jacket or from the Marlboro duffel bag confiscated from the trunk of John's Oldsmobile. Nor did the panties, bra, and the tarp, found in and around the grave with Carla's remains, turn up any discernible blood or semen stains when they were examined.

A serology examination of the slashed black T-shirt recovered with the skeletal remains was similarly unproductive. The shirt had long cream-colored sleeves, and front and back logos, "REO SPEEDWAGON High Infidelity," and "REO SPEEDWAGON April Wine, Michael Stanley." The words "Milwaukee Stadium" and the name of another band were also part of the logo. But the lettering was so badly damaged and faded due to decomposition during the two years in the grave that the words identifying the rock group couldn't be made out.

Forensic experts at the state crime lab were careful to separate evidence from the two assaults: the murder of Carla, and the savage attack on Emily. Separate sets of case numbers were assigned for articles of evidence relating to each of the victims.

Examination of the wheelbarrow handle found at the site of the assault on Emily, and analysis of reddish brown stains on about three-quarters of the chunk of wood indicated the substance was human blood. The analyst began the examination by conducting a test with the chemical phenolphthalein, which produces a specific color change that indicates blood. The test was positive, so she ran a second test using a different method to confirm the first. The results of the second test were also positive. Unfortunately, the blood had soaked into the wood, so she was not able to recover a sufficient sample to determine the blood type.

Even if she had been able to test the substance for blood

type, the results could have been suspect. Through her training and experience, the serology expert had learned that substances in plant products, including wood from trees, can cause reactions in testing procedures that produce erroneous results. So any conclusions based on examination of the substance on the handles to determine blood type would not have been scientifically reliable.

The analyst had more luck with the sand shovel. Although she wasn't able to identify any blood on the implement, she recovered one brown hair and a portion of another from the intersection of the metal and the wood. The single hair showed the same characteristics as samples taken from Emily's head. The fragment wasn't suitable for comparisons.

A few days later Special Agent Dennis N. Miller of the Division of Criminal Investigation (DCI), for the State of Wisconsin, had a talk about the sand shovel with John's pal Timothy Denzine. Denzine told him about his friend's eagerness to get the shovel back after once forgetting it in the woods.

Miller also asked the young man if he knew anything about John's religious beliefs, especially if there was any indication he was involved in some form of Satan worship. Denzine reported that John told him if some records were played backwards certain hidden messages could be heard, the state investigator later stated. But Denzine didn't elaborate on the conversations with John about the messages.

Denzine also talked by telephone with another state investigator who asked him about John's interest in Satanism. At the time, investigator Maxine Vogt was working with John's public defenders. According to her account, Denzine told her that about once a month during lunch or while they were taking other work breaks, his friend brought up the subject of devil worship or secret Satanic messages hidden in the lyrics of rock records. The young man indicated he didn't want to be a witness at the trial.

* * *

Investigator Carl Petske, who was working with the prosecutor, talked with John's friend Kevin Scharp. The former GI said that John talked about how pretty Emily was and about getting into a fracas with another man over her. John knew who his wife was seeing and he was following his perceived rival to get the message across that it wasn't a good idea to mess around with a married woman, Scharp indicated.

John's mother was also interviewed by a state investigator. She said she believed someone may have raped Emily prior to the September attack, and her son settled matters with the rapist in his own way.

Two weeks after the arrest, Lawrence Weber was going through articles in a spare bedroom that the boys in the family used during overnight visits at home when he found the missing .25-caliber pistol and more of John's disturbing writings detailing sex and torture plans. They were stored in a box and in a file cabinet with other personal effects the young man left behind when he married and moved in with his bride across the street. The senior Weber telephoned John's public defenders and asked what he should do. They advised him to notify the sheriff.

John's father telephoned the Sheriff's Department and talked with Gould. He asked if the chief deputy was going to be in his office for a while, because he had something to bring to him. A few minutes later Weber walked into the basement headquarters and turned over a box loaded with his son's belongings, including the small-caliber handgun investigators had been looking for. Two carefully worded chronicles included with the material were typical of John's other handwritten outlines for kidnap and sexual torture of young women.

One was a seven-page document titled, "An Ode to Tracy Boothe." Neatly penned on seven pages from a tablet of ruled writing paper, it was a detailed outline for another of his sordid sex and torture schemes that appeared to have been conceived and written while he was living with the young woman and her husband in Colorado.

John's bizarrely titled work actually outlined three game plans for capturing, binding, sexually abusing, and torturing his onetime paramour. The first and the most violent of the plans called for him to ambush her in the trailer, by lurking behind a corner then smashing her on the head with a frying pan or a bottle when she walked by. He noted that she should be struck "hard enough to at least bring her down. If she's still conscious, pull out your knife & pair of panties. Shove the panties in her mouth & put the knife to her throat. Force her into the bedroom."

He carefully specified a "2 fingers tequilla (sic) bottle" should be used if a bottle was selected as the bludgeon. John's schemes were typically meticulous and precise down to the most minor details. His reference to using a bottle as a weapon was also frighteningly reminiscent of his earlier attack on his sister, Kathy.

The second plan also relied on waiting around a corner of a room and surprising her. But instead of bludgeoning her on the head it relied on threatening her with a knife at her throat. Again, he wrote that a pair of panties was to be stuffed into her mouth before dragging her into the bedroom.

In "Plan 3" the author proposed borrowing a .25-caliber pistol from a friend and threatening her with it after calling her into the bedroom to see something. John wrote that she should be gagged with panties, then ordered to strip to her underclothes. "Plan 3 is the best one," he wrote. "If at all possible use it. If Plan 3 can't work, use plan 1, then 2 is a last resort." He detailed how Tracy should be pushed onto the bed on her stomach and have her wrists tied behind her and tape pressed over the panties stuffed in her mouth.

"You don't want to look in her eyes or you'll crack," he observed in a cautionary note. "Make sure you are ready for the responsibilities involved with the plan. Don't FUCK Up!!!"

John wrote about the possibilities of drawing out the abuse if Tracy's husband was expected to be away dealing with his Army duties. If that was the case, he indicated, he would proceed "with the long version of phases 1 & 2." Otherwise he would have to be satisfied with "the short version" and be sure to begin no later than 7 o'clock and finish up no later than 10:30.

The scheme called for him to tell Tracy that if she cooperated and did everything he ordered her to do she would be freed by noon, and he would go into the mountains where he would "blow my brains out." The threat of self-destruction was a ploy he had tried before. Then John ran through his litany of planned abuse, including slashing off his victim's underclothes with a knife and forced sex.

The second chronicle delivered with the boxload of material was a frighteningly lurid scenario that focused on the kidnap, rape, sexual torture, and murder of a young local woman whom John had apparently focused on when she led cheers at Phillips High School. Some aspects of the perverted scheme were even more incredibly bizarre than other concoctions that had already come to light. And it was especially scary, because it indicated that other women who were not a part of the murder suspect's personal circle of family and friends may have been targeted as potential prey to satisfy his raging lusts. It seemed that any attractive woman in Phillips and Price County could have become the object of one of the deadly kidnap and murder scenarios hatched by the monster, who prowled the streets and forests of their community for so long.

John realized that abducting the cheerleader would be the most difficult and personally dangerous aspect of the plan. She would have to be stalked first, in the manner of a hunter pursuing a trophy kill. Early in the summary, he talked of the need to learn the girl's address, then watch her house for a minimum of three to five days to learn her daily habits.

As an alternative, he wrote down the suggestion that he simply wait until she had driven somewhere by herself, then at the first opportunity slip up behind her, and take her prisoner at gunpoint while she was outside the car. The scheme called for her to be forced into the driver's seat of either his or her own vehicle and made to drive out of town while he continued to hold the pistol on her. As she drove, he would unbutton her blouse and fondle her breasts.

Predictably by that time, John had prepared a precisely comprehensive list that itemized tangible and intangible needs ranging from the girl's address, to a jump rope, clothespins, pins, needles, six tubes of Super Glue, leather belt, battery-operated vibrators, handcuffs, ankle clamps, blindfold, pistol, knife and shovel, several other articles, and specific items of clothing that were important to the sex fantasy. He listed "10 different sexy panties & bra's (sic)," brown, black, white and regular fishnet hose and garters, and a "skimpy cheer leading (sic) uniform," as some of his needs.

The most outlandishly quirky implement listed for his operations kit was a tape recording of the University of Wisconsin's school anthem; "On Wisconsin." In keeping with his meticulous attention to detail, John specified that the tape should be an instrumental recording only, with no vocals. An audio cassette player was also listed among the needs.

John's twisted schemes for abduction and cruel domination of helpless sex slaves were monstrous and almost supernaturally evil. And at least two local women had already been lured into his clutches. The cheerleader was one of the lucky ones and didn't even know she was targeted for sex and torture in one of his depraved schemes. But Chief Moore wasn't the only lawman or resident of Phillips who had begun to wonder if there were other young women who may not have been so fortunate.

The written materials, the pistol, and the other items were separately bagged, marked, and placed in the evidence locker.

John's father had been more cooperative with police than many parents might be in similar situations, but he wanted the house at 465 South Avon back. He wanted to serve Emily with an eviction notice and get it ready for new renters. The house had been searched, and searched again, but authorities still had it closed off and he was unable to get inside.

Lawrence Weber contacted Barnett two or three times and talked with Chief Moore about getting in, but he was always put off. At first he was told the Crime Laboratory people weren't through with it. Then he was given other reasons, or the people he talked with simply passed the buck.

Emily was finally released from the hospital and moved in with her parents after spending her entire sixteen-day stay in the Intensive Care Unit. A few days after returning home, she made six or seven trips to the house to pick up clothing and other personal articles. Dosch or one of his colleagues accompanied her each time she went to the house.

She removed the last of her belongings in the middle of December, and her father-in-law was finally given the okay to reassume full possession of his house. But Emily and the district attorney still had the only keys. Weber had a screen broken so entry could be made through a window. During the three months since his son's arrest, the house had undergone major water damage. He began the cleanup.

At just about the time Heitkemper was unloading the body bag holding Carla's remains at University Hospital, back in Phillips John was having his first meeting with a defense attorney.

Early each morning, the secretary in the Public Defender's Office in Merrill, telephoned jails in a four-county area to check for people who had gotten themselves into trouble and landed behind bars the previous day or overnight. If it was determined they were eligible for representation by the public defender, she passed on the information to the lawyers. Public defense work was coordinated out of the office for Lincoln, Langlade, Taylor, and Price Counties.

The secretary Carol R. Wakely usually made the calls between eight and nine A.M., but she skipped the daily check at jails in counties where public defenders were expected to stop on business. On Tuesday morning, September 6, she skipped her call to the Price County Jail because attorney James R. Lex, Jr., of Merrill, had business in Phillips that day. He represented a client who was scheduled for a hearing in Price County Circuit Court before Judge Fox at 8:30 A.M. He was also scheduled to handle other court matters at ten A.M. that were unrelated to the earlier hearing.

The public defender from Lincoln County had a busy morning scheduled, but when he learned about John he made time to see him. Lex signed his name on the attorney log book maintained at the jail as beginning his first meeting with John at 8:35 A.M. It was the first entry of the day. He was logged out fifteen minutes later, but returned at 11:30 A.M. for a second talk. The time out was not reported.

Early Tuesday afternoon one of Lex's public defender colleagues John H. Reid, of Wausau, also met with the prisoner in two separate sessions—once for fifteen minutes and the second time for almost an hour. Except for a few dollars, his ragged fleet of old vehicles, some clothing, and a few other personal possessions, John was virtually without means to pay for his own defense. Before the day was over, his legal representation had been essentially settled. Lex and Reid would serve as his defense team. The public would foot the bills.

He made his first court appearance at a probable cause hearing, before Price County Circuit judge Douglas T. Fox. In laymen's terms the process was designed to determine if indeed there was sufficient reason to believe that a crime or crimes were committed, and if so, that consequently a criminal trial was in order.

Through his attorneys, he requested a preliminary hearing on the charges against him and asked for appointment of a different judge. The jurist granted the hearing request, although he didn't immediately set a date. He took the petition for appointment of a new judge under advisement. He also ruled that probable cause had been shown, and ordered John held on a whopping $200,000-cash bail.

Prior to the hearing, Judge Fox rejected a defense request for the chains and manacles to be removed from the defendant before he was brought into the courtroom. The veteran Price County jurist also issued an order that anyone who wasn't a member of the judiciary and law enforcement systems had to pass through an electronic device and submit to a pat-down search before entering the courtroom for John's hearings. He directed that all packages and containers were to be checked for weapons before they were permitted into the courtroom.

John Weber was already about as unpopular in Price County as he could be, and the full story of the horrors he inflicted on his wife and her sister hadn't even begun to reach the public.

Circuit Judge Gary L. Carlson of Taylor County, which adjoins Price County to the south, was named to hear the proceedings. He was a good choice. The curly-haired jurist was experienced, and possessed a keen legal mind that equipped him with the ability to control the proceedings in a complex trial such as John's prosecution promised to be, while moving it steadily along and avoiding legal miscues that might lead to later successful appeals. He also knew how to balance the personalities of prosecutors and defense attorneys. Especially important to the approaching trial, he had a ready sense of humor that, while judicially restrained, would have a positive effect providing momentary relief for shell-shocked jurors subjected to the ugly, emotionally trying testimony that lay ahead.

Judge Carlson continued bail at $200,000. John wouldn't be walking out the front door of the Safety Building as a free man before his trial.

After his initial hearing before Judge Fox, John was transferred to a regular cell, which had a small overhead window that overlooked North Avon. He could sit or lie on his bunk and hear the taunts of young men who drove by or stopped their cars outside the Safety Building and yelled, "Weber, you're sick."

A few days after moving to the cell, John listened while mourners trooped in and out of the Heindl Funeral Home for Carla's memorial service. Then he watched while the teenager's friends and family followed the casket out of the mortuary, climbed into black limousines and private cars, and began the mournful procession to the tree-lined cemetery a few miles out of town. Carla at long last was given the "Christian burial" Moore had urged for her.

Eventually an attractive oblong stone with one end carved in the shape of a huge heart was erected on the grave. A white cross was cut into the center of the heart. The inscription on the stone states simply:

Carla Lenz
1969—1986

There is nothing else to mark the grave as special, or to indicate that the young woman whose remains lie there was the victim of Price County's most notorious crime.

* * *

Despite efforts by authorities to keep a lid on information about the possibility of cannibalism figuring in the already sordid case, it was impossible to keep it from the press. Some police officers and courthouse wags had begun to refer to cannibalism, only partly in jest, as "the C word." But the possibility of cannibalism had become a factor that had to be openly dealt with. It was mentioned in court documents, including papers at the Price County Clerk's office, filed with the application for the search warrant. And it was brought up in preliminary hearings.

News of John's arrest and the accusations he murdered his sister-in-law and tried to kill his wife, hit Phillips and Price County like one of the killer blizzards that periodically swept in from Canada and Lake Superior. It was the biggest local news story to hit the North Woods community since the devastating fire of 1894 levelled the forests and towns. And it was the nastiest.

Almost half the people in Phillips, perhaps more, knew John, Emily and Carla, or some member of their families. As sordid details of the crime and John's hidden past gradually became known, shock and disbelief quickly gave way to anger, revulsion—and sorrow for the damage inflicted on the good name of the town.

The grisly account eventually even hit the supermarket tabloids, with a half-page spread in the *Weekly World News,* which carried photos of Emily and Carla, and a schoolboy picture of John. The story was presented with the shock headline, "Husband digs his wife's grave—while she watches, say cops." At last his former neighbors in Phillips knew some of his guiltiest secrets, and the sensational story was rapidly spreading around the country and crossing national borders as well.

Detective Files, a Montreal-based magazine reporting true police cases that is distributed in the United States and Canada, eventually published a story with the titillatingly lurid headline: "Did The Wisconsin Sex Cannibal Rape And Eat His Victims?" A New York-based competitor *Master Detective,* ran a story with the slightly more conservative title, "Wisconsin's Worst Woman-Hating Sadist." But like the story in *Detective Files,* it went into detail about the possibility John had violated one of society's most stringent taboos and fed on the body parts of his murder victim.

Before the arrest, most people outside of Wisconsin, and many people inside the state, had never heard of Phillips. Now John and his reluctant neighbors were national news. And the people of Phillips didn't appreciate the notoriety. They were scared to death their town would become another Plainfield in the public mind. Nevertheless, dark jokes about the newly notorious local boy that sounded suspiciously like warmed-over "Geiners," began making the rounds of taprooms, cafes, and workplaces." According to one of the sick quips, police would never be able to keep John behind bars because all he had to do was draw a picture of a girl on the wall of his cell. Then he could eat his way out.

According to a news article in the Sunday, September 18, edition of *The Milwaukee Journal,* Sheriff Wirsing alluded to the Gein case in remarks to the press. Wally Krenzke, a former Phillips police chief and security chief at Marquip where John worked his second job, also referred to the Gein case in a quote. "I think people can relate back to the way the people in Plainfield felt," he told a *Journal* reporter. Wirsing reportedly touched on the chances of a link to the Weber case and the disappearance of Marchell Hansen, according to the same story. "Mere coincidence wants you to believe it," he declared.

The Bee quoted the sheriff more extensively about the missing Hansen woman. After remarks by Wirsing that dogs were used to search for bodies on the Weber farm after Carla's grave was found, because, "We didn't know if there would be more," the article turned to other missing persons cases in the area.

Wirsing said efforts to link other missing persons investigations to the Weber case were made as part of normal procedure. The file was still open on Shelly Hansen, but there was no evidence yet that tied John to the missing woman.

Weeks later Phillips furniture store owner Tom Metnik told a news reporter the case had brought "some of the worst realities of the big city" to the quiet North Woods town. "No one can believe it happened here," he said.

Chapter Eleven

A Suicide Scare

> *If all you foresee is bad things, then you have a good chance of becoming a prophet.*
> —Anonymous quote in letter by John R. Weber

As investigators from both sides conducted interviews and reinterviews, and defense lawyers and the district attorney cranked up the wheels of the judicial system by churning out a scatter of briefs and motions, John languished uneasily in jail.

With the probable cause hearing behind him, he was permitted normal visiting privileges. But fifteen-minute interludes with his parents once every Sunday visiting day, interspersed with occasional telephone conversations, were more frustrating than comforting. John sometimes choked up or broke down in tears during the telephone calls.

A Roman Catholic priest and a Protestant clergyman also visited and counselled him at the jail. Along with his counselor from the guidance center and family members, they tried to convince him that he could still make a life for himself, even in a psychiatric hospital or in a prison.

Self-absorbed, introspective, and depressed, he moped around, while getting used to spending twenty-four hours a day in a cramped twelve-by-twelve-foot metal enclosure and in a slightly larger narrow common area just outside that was equipped with a table and a bench. He was locked up in an especially secure area of the jail that was restricted to most other inmates, so he had the spaces pretty much to himself.

He was isolated from others and surrounded by the clanging of closing doors and the astringent smell of antiseptics, and forced to accept the uncomfortable circumstance of strangers making virtually all of his decisions for him as a fact of life.

Other people decided what he ate, when he ate, when he showered, to a large part what he was allowed to read, whom he could have as visitors, and when they could visit. Even his mail was scanned by jailers. John didn't have either a radio in his cell or a television to watch. So he read lots of novels about the Old West, and began to morosely muse that it would have been better if he was born during that time period. If he was born then, he reasoned, he would already have been hanged for his crimes and his misery would be over.

He frequently watched through a small window as people he knew drove slowly past the jail as if they were hoping to catch a glimpse of him. Others screamed out taunts and insults. A few times he watched his mother's car.

For a time at least John thought his lead attorney, Lex, didn't really want to represent him and didn't believe him. It wasn't all that unusual a situation for a defense attorney and a defendant to be in. It was an important part of Lex's job to be sure he had a straight story and complete account from his client before putting the finishing touches on trial strategy and facing off with the DA in a final courtroom showdown. It was important that he knew everything the prosecutor knew about the case—and more. He couldn't afford any nasty courtroom surprises; a Perry Mason shocker tied to a client's lies or information withheld that could blow up a case and ruin a game plan.

But when the lawyer bore in, repeated some of the same

questions over again, pointed out inconsistencies, prodded his
client for clarification, or seemed hesitant to swallow John's
version of something, the young man was offended. He was
especially upset over Lex's questions about Shelly Hansen's
ominous disappearance from Phillips one year to the day after
Carla vanished. John stoutly insisted he had nothing to do with
it, although even he admitted that the timing of her disappearance was a curiously suspicious coincidence.

Like many prisoners who are not career criminals and are
shut up for the first time, during the first few weeks of John's
incarceration he was almost wholly concerned with getting out.
He was also concerned about his wife's reaction to the beating
and the obvious result that this time there would be no recon-
ciliation. Then he began to reflect on the terrible crime he had
committed, the hurt he inflicted on the people who loved him
most, and his own negative prospects.

The gloomy murder suspect was feeling sorry for himself
when he sat down on the edge of his bunk and began writing
letters. One of the letters was to Emily; another was to her
parents, Gene Lenz, Sr., and his wife, Caroline. During his
brief, tumultuous marriage to Emily, his in-laws had been good
to him.

But the most ambitious writing project was an eventual
sixty-three-page manuscript addressed to his own parents.
From early childhood, John had demonstrated a unique ability
to express himself well with pen or pencil. But his jailhouse
writings weren't the usual lurid sex and sadism fantasies of
kidnap and torture. They were apologies, laced with large
doses of self-pity, reflections on cherished moments spent with
his family, and in two of the three letters, melancholy musings
that his life was over. He blamed early addiction to pornography and he blamed booze for the predicament he was in.
Mostly, however, he blamed himself.

John spent his twenty-fifth birthday, locked up and facing

the gloomy prospect that he would never again observe another birthday as a free man.

About ten weeks after he was jailed, a psychiatric social worker from the Counseling and Personal Development Center tipped Greenwood off that the most notorious prisoner ever to be held in a Price County jail might be planning to commit suicide. It was about midmorning when Greg Arbach approached the jailer with the disturbing news. Arbach even provided the jailer a range of danger dates. He said the suicide attempt could be expected sometime in a period extending through the next five days, ending November 27.

When Greenwood was tipped off, it was less than two weeks after the second anniversary of Carla's abduction and murder. The perceived target date for the suicide was also just a few days past the conclusion of the annual deer hunting season, which was an especially agonizing time for the locked-up outdoorsman. John could peer through his cell window and watch Broncos and pickup trucks he recognized as belonging to friends and acquaintances pass by on their way to the woods or on their way back with a handsome buck loaded in the rear or strapped to a fender.

Before his arrest he scheduled one week of his annual two-week vacation at Winter Wood Products for the November deer hunting season. Now, he no longer had a job, and the deer hunting season was progressing without him. It was the first year he missed the annual hunt since returning home, and there didn't seem to be any chance at all that he would ever hunt again.

The chief jailer passed on the troubling information to the sheriff, who directed him to take appropriate action to prevent a suicide attempt. When Greenwood left his boss's office, he made a beeline for John and moved the inmate to adjoining spaces in the two-man cell which were unoccupied. At Greenwood's direction, John took off his jail uniform, stripping to his bare skin. Greenwood didn't want his troublesome charge hanging himself with his own clothes. When the jail sergeant observed that John wasn't wearing underwear, he brought him a set of underpants and a T-shirt.

Then he moved next door and began turning John's cell upside down; searching for and removing anything that might provide even the slightest opportunity for use as a tool to commit suicide. He didn't need a search warrant or any other special court approval when he barged into the cell and began rummaging through it. It was his duty to maintain security and he could legally search cells anytime he wished. He didn't need to give anyone a reason, neither inmate, lawyers, nor judges.

Printed jail policy stipulated: "Searches or inspections of prisoners or cells may be conducted at any time for health, safety or security reasons. Prisoners must cooperate during these searches or inspections. This county jail is equipped with an audio monitoring system and (sic.) used for the safety of inmates and jail staff."

Greenwood hauled away a blanket, towel, socks, underwear, pencils, and books. He also confiscated some articles from the common area outside John's cell, including a stack of magazines from the bench. John was a smoker, and Greenwood didn't want him to have anything that could be set afire and used as a torch. In later testimony, the jailer was unable to recall if he confiscated a book of matches. "If I saw 'em, I removed 'em," he remarked, however.

While the jailer gathered up the magazines he noticed the top page of one of John's letters lying in the open. It was the beginning of a three-page letter to his wife, and after the salutation and an opening sentence, he had written: "By now you know I am dead." John wrote that he couldn't live any longer with his guilt over what he did to her and to her family, and he hoped his death could partly pay his debt to them.

Greenwood had seen suicide notes before, and the opener on John's note to Emily was a classic example. He called into the cell and asked John if he was writing a suicide note, or saying goodbye to someone. The jailer was seriously concerned and he kept after the prisoner, asking if he was planning to hang himself or to hurt himself in some other manner. John didn't immediately reply, although he eventually said something about having already tried to hang himself after tying together his socks, towel, and pillowcase. But the jury-rigged noose pulled apart.

When Greenwood completed his search, his talk with John, and scanning the letters, he took the correspondence to the sheriff. Wirsing briefly studied them, then the two officers telephoned Barnett and informed him about their discovery. At last, Greenwood returned to his desk and began putting the wheels in motion for an emergency detention. He had seen enough evidence to convince him there was a good chance the prisoner was an immediate danger to himself, and he filled out the paperwork for a Chapter 51. It was November 22.

All the letters were disturbing, but the most remarkably troubling was the letter John wrote to his parents. Written over several days, he admitted at different times in the letter that he killed Carla, he admitted his attack and intention to kill Emily, and he agonized over how he had irretrievably messed up his life and broken his parents' hearts. He repeatedly whined that the only solution he saw for ending his misery was to end his life, and he said he had decided to act before his trial in order to spare his family additional heartache.

In one of several references to his planned suicide, John specified November 27 as the date he planned to do away with himself. It would be Emily's twenty-second birthday and the first anniversary of the death of his beloved dogs.

After debating how he was going to come up with the right way to end his life, he wrote that he would probably hang himself. He had tied together some socks, tested them, and they seemed to hold well enough, he said. He worried that the suicide effort might go astray, and instead of killing himself he would wind up paralyzed or in a coma.

It was John's birthday when he wrote that he hoped this time when he tried hanging himself the knot didn't slip. He apologized for the pain his suicide would cause his parents. He asked his parents to bury him at the family farm, but said he didn't want a funeral. He surmised that he didn't have any friends left who would mourn him anyway.

Even in his jail cell, John was continuing to dig a deeper hole for himself. The letter marked the fourth confession or statement in which he had reportedly admitted to Carla's slaying. He admitted the murder on the cassette tape left in his car; again in a more oblique manner during his interrogation by Moore; and Emily said he told her during her assault that he killed her sister.

Whether or not any or all of the statements could be used as evidence against him, would be a matter to be worked out in the pretrial hearings. But the incriminating statements in the letter appeared to be one more legal nail driven into his coffin, and he was the one who was doing the hammering.

He touched on one of the curiosities surrounding the case when he wrote that even when he was about to be arrested he didn't make any effort to get rid of the mounds of incriminating evidence against him. He was simply exhausted after carrying around the guilt for two years over Carla's death, he said. John boasted, however, that police were stumped by her disappearance until he virtually solved the crime for them.

Returning to the burden of carrying Carla's death around on his conscience for so long, John wrote that he sometimes drove to the farm and sat by her grave, drinking beer and crying. At times he sat at the graves of the dogs, drinking beer and crying, as well, he said.

His confession in the letter to Carla's murder, was a carefully sanitized version of the account he recorded on the audiotape. According to the letter, Carla's death was more of an accident and was apparently devoid of the horrid sexual abuse and torture he recounted earlier. He wrote that he was drinking heavily the night he drove to the farm with the girl. When she refused to agree to join him after he left Emily and cleared out of town, he lost his composure and strangled her.

". . . I lost complete control of myself and went ahead with the sick plans I'd already made," he said. He had nurtured his sick fantasies for years, but never expected to carry them out, John wrote. Rejection, or feelings of rejection, played large roles in the attacks on both sisters, he indicated.

There was no talk of carrying Carla's body around in the trunk of his Sunbird for five days, and no mention of cannibalism. John continued to claim in the letter, as he had since his arrest, that the dreadful story he told on the tape was merely a tall tale he hatched in order to frighten and disgust his wife. He even denied stomping on Carla's bare toes, and predicted that when results of the autopsy were revealed the findings would back him up.

John talked about his dark side, the evil self he hadn't even had a name for. He was almost able to call off the attack on Emily at the last moment while they were parked in the car at the farm, but the beers he drank and the pressure from this vicious alter ego were too much for him to throw off, he said. "I screamed to myself to stop." But he couldn't. By the time he managed to regain control, Emily had been beaten almost to death.

His evil side hadn't bothered him since he was locked in jail, he claimed. John pointed out that by committing suicide, he would in a sense be committing murder once more by getting rid of his evil self. His good side would die, too, of course. John wrote that his companion had been with him since he was ten years old.

His counselor told him about stories circulating around Price County about him, and people were welcome to believe whatever they wished, John wrote. It was too late to do anything about what other people thought. He moaned about his notoriety, but also noted sardonically that he had heard some new "horror stories" about himself.

"I'll bet they make a TV movie out of this," he suggested. "I always wanted to be a star."

He made frequent references to what he referred to as the sickness or craziness that led him to commit his terrible crime, and theorized that notorious criminals Charles Manson and John Wayne Gacy, Jr., were crazy or insane as well. John was lumping himself in the same category with two of the most infamous American criminals of the modern age.

He claimed in the letter that Lex didn't expect Carlson to disallow any of the evidence because judges were politicians who were elected to office. And because of the circumstances of the case, even if the search warrants were illegal, he didn't expect them to be thrown out because community outrage could cost the judge his job.

The statement was the kind of reckless accusation that prisoners sometimes make, but one that the voters of Taylor County where the judge came from were unlikely to believe even if it was brought to their attention. Judge Carlson was a highly respected jurist known for his careful attention to upholding the law, not for breaking it. And inmates like John sometimes have a way of misinterpreting or putting their own spin on statements from their attorneys during pretrial strategy sessions.

* * *

Carla and Emily were the only two people he ever physically hurt, he insisted in a statement that ignored the time he busted a bottle over his sister's head.

During a long passage reviewing his relationship with other women, he wrote that he was close to falling in love with Lisa but she was too intelligent and had impressive ambitions. He quoted his counselor as telling him he may have dropped out of the relationship because of fears he couldn't live up to the pretty LaCrosse teenager's expectations and couldn't control her.

". . . so I picked someone simple. Emily," he wrote. Then he added an observation many husbands might make about wives after they've been married a while: "She was far from simple."

One of the most curious elements of the letter was John's reaction to suspicions that he blasted Carla with a shotgun before or after her body was dumped into the sandy grave at the edge of the forest. John wrote that if she was shotgunned, it must have been by someone else.

He claimed he was surprised when his lawyer told him twenty pellets of Number Six shot were found in her body because he didn't shoot her. He admitted using his .25-caliber pistol to threaten her with so she would obey his commands, but insisted he never used a shotgun on her.

"Someone else did," he wrote. "I don't know who, what, or why." It was a statement that was difficult to believe, and John theorized she must have been shot after burial but confessed that he couldn't imagine why. He surmised at one point that someone may have shot at one of her bones under the mistaken impression it was a grouse. He later rejected that idea because her remains were recovered from under eighteen inches of soil so the bones wouldn't have been showing. And when he visited her grave, it was still intact and new grass was growing on it.

Continuing to puzzle over the mystery, he finally concluded: "I must have shot her." But if he did, he wrote, it was an act he couldn't remember committing and he couldn't provide a motive. John indicated that his insistence he didn't even take a shotgun with him on the night he killed Carla provided one more reason for Lex to suspect him of lying. It was one more enigma in the confessed killer's enigmatic life.

John said he decided to murder his wife after he stopped drinking for three weeks, then fell off the wagon because it hadn't seemed to improve their relationship. He even stopped going off by himself to work on his car except when she was with friends or her family, but he became angry because it appeared to him that he was the only one who was making a sacrifice. So he got drunk and hatched the plan for Emily's murder. She "was a hair away from death" when he stopped beating her, he wrote.

He wondered at another point if his wife was going to divorce him or seek an annulment. He said he wanted to go to his grave still married to her, and if she served him with divorce papers before his suicide he wouldn't sign them.

Much of the prisoner's narrative was devoted to twenty-five years of melancholy memories about good times he shared with his father, and to a lesser extent with his mother and Kathy. John wrote about a fine, ten-point buck he and his father spotted but didn't shoot, about coyote pups, a whippoor-will, their fishing and hunting expeditions, and about Brownie and her puppies.

Talking about the guilt he felt for letting his parents down, he said he knew they still loved him as a son and supported him. "Dad has said, 'You don't throw away a boy because he's sick,'" he wrote at one point.

A couple of times he recorded strange, surrealistic or frightening, dreams he had while sleeping in his cell. In one he told about seeing a mushroom cloud that was the beginning of an atomic war. Another was a more personally chilling dream within a dream. It began with John, Emily, and her parents at the house with the young couple's two dogs. When Emily rejected him, he was racing away to get drunk and kill himself by crashing his bike in a creek, when he saw Carla waving to him from the window of the former Weber family store. Moments later he awakened in jail and Carla was telling him he had murdered his wife and had to pay the penalty.

Then he woke up again. He was still in jail, but this time it wasn't a dream.

In his letter to his wife, John assured her of his love for her, and said since being in jail he had written to her before. He threw out some of the letters, and his lawyer got rid of others in order to protect him, John said.

He told his wife that sometimes when he got angry during their marriage and went off by himself to drink it was because he was having trouble dealing with the knowledge of what he had done to her sister. He also talked of the dark side that sometimes took over his thoughts and controlled his actions. He also insisted to her, as he had to his lawyer and would do to his parents, that he had nothing to do with Shelly Hansen's disappearance. Emily and her sister were the only two women he had attacked, he wrote.

John told Emily he still didn't know why he attacked her, and believed his love for her made him stop. It saved her life. He talked about the life they might have shared together, but lamented that he couldn't control his other half.

Again, he denied sexually torturing and murdering Carla in the manner described on the tape. He said he had wanted to frighten Emily, and that he killed her sister when she started to struggle and he got scared she would get him in trouble. Instead of carrying her body around in the car trunk for five days, he buried her the day after smothering her with a T-shirt. Carla almost fought him off and got away, but he caught up to her when she stumbled and fell, he said.

John said he knew that by committing suicide he was condemning himself to hell where he would burn forever. But the punishment was something he deserved for the terrible things he had done to her and the Lenz family. He apologized for accusing her during the attack of cheating on him. He blamed the accusation on "Natas." It was not John Weber he said, but his dark side who had wanted to hurt her.

The letters confiscated during the search of his quarters at the jail were eventually submitted as evidence at his trial, including the one-and-one-half-page note to his in-laws. The note read:

Gene & Caroline,
  To begin this letter, I offer my apology for all the pain and suffering I have caused your family. By now you know of my death. I have tried to write to you before but it was turned down by the attorneys.
  I have no right to even write this letter, but I want you to understand my side of this. I offer my life a (indecipherable) payment for what I have done to your family. You have loved me like one of your own and I have taken it all for granted.
  Emily loved me very much and only now can I see that to be true. I knew I had serious problems for a long time, 10 years. Everyone, including my parents thought my problems were all in the past, that I had finally got a good start in life. Only I knew of the problems and I never had the courage to speak up to anyone about them. I tried several times to talk to either of my parents about it and on a few occasions tried to bring it up to Emily. Fear of them not understanding kept me quiet. I didn't want to lose the ones I loved.
  What happened with Carla and Emily was in truth out of my control. I literally became someone else. I refer to it as my 'dark side'. Drinking heavily didn't help matters

any and by no means is that an excuse. There aren't any excuses as we both know.

All I can say is I am truly sorry. I did love Emily very much and that is the one thing in my life that wasn't or isn't a lie. I know all of this is a shock to you. It was to me also. When I was arrested, I gave the police all the information they wanted. I wanted it over. It was a large burden to carry, but it wasn't as large as yours worrying about Carla.

Even now, I can't find ways to tell you how sorry I am, but saying I am sorry won't help. I can only try and pay back part of the debt I owe to you through my own death. Eternal punishment in hell through suicide is about the best offer I can make to you.

Yes, I believe in God. Father Dismas has asked me to ask forgiveness from God and at first I did. Later I asked for it back because I am not worthy of his forgiveness or anyone's. Things could have been a lot different for us if I would have been honest with myself and Emily, but like all of my life, I continued living a lie. I never loved myself or had any self-respect and only when all is gone do I realize just what I had.

It has "hit home" just what has happened. Through nightmares and dreams, I see things I never saw before. I recognize my sickness as a cancer of the mind. I could not control myself at times and only by the grace of God was Emily spared. I thank God for that everyday. I hope she can continue with her life and meet her goals head-on. She is a wonderful woman, capable of a lot of love if given the chance. I never gave her or myself that chance.

The letter was unsigned.

John was transferred downstate to the Winnebago Mental Health Institute on the shores of Lake Winnebago in Oshkosh.

The initial evaluation of the state of his mental health at the time of admission wasn't especially enlightening. It was determined that he was possibly depressed, and that his threats of suicide were more an act of desperation than an indication of mental illness. Slurred speech, slowness of gait, and other problems noted during his medical examination, were believed to be signs of his affliction with multiple sclerosis. He was found to be mentally competent.

There was a bonus advantage of the move to the institute. John would be closer to a trio of psychiatrists appointed by the court to examine him. Judge Carlson appointed Dr. Ralph Baker as the court's own expert to examine John and determine if he had a mental disease and whether or not he could conform his conduct to the requirements of the law at the time Carla and Emily were attacked. Dr. Baker was a teacher at the institute, maintained a private practice in psychiatry in Oshkosh, and served as medical director of the Green Lake County Mental Health Clinic. Forensic psychiatry, dealing with psychiatry and the law, was one of his subspecialties. For ten years, beginning in 1970, he was in charge of the sex crimes treatment program at the Winnebago Mental Health Institute until the state legislature dumped the project in 1980.

A Madison-based psychiatrist, Dr. Robert David Miller, who was training director at the forensic center of the Mendota Mental Health Institute, was named to make a similar examination for the prosecution. The center is in the building that houses patients being evaluated for the courts and those also newly committed by the courts. One of Dr. Miller's many professional accomplishments and credits with particular significance to the Weber case was membership in the International Society for the Study of Multiple Personality and Other Dissociative Disorders.

Dr. William J. Crowley, a consultant for Behavioral Consultants, Inc., in Milwaukee, was appointed to examine John for the defense. The psychiatrist, who was also assistant clinical professor of psychiatry at the Medical College of Wisconsin, also examined Ed Gein, and court officers agreed that he would not be allowed to bring up the Gein case during testimony at John's trial. Everyone directly involved in the case was still making their best efforts to avoid references and comparisons to the "Mad Butcher of Plainfield."

The eventual conclusions of the trio of psychiatrists, reached after examinations and study that extended into the new year, were very much alike in the more important respects. Each of them made a primary diagnosis identifying the defendant as a sexual sadist. Another unanimous conclusion that was especially significant indicated John was aware of the wrongfulness of his acts. The psychiatrists also agreed in a determination concurred with by doctors at the Winnebago Mental Health Institute, that he was not psychotic. He was in touch with reality.

Dr. Baker met with the defendant for a total of five-and-a-half hours, including sessions on December 2, December 4, and on Christmas Eve. He also examined material provided by the defense and the prosecution including copies of past medical reports, the complaint report, police reports, some of John's writings, the audiotape taken from his car, and transcripts of interviews with some of his family members.

The court's psychiatrist put together a history of John's life up to the time of the crimes he was charged with, as well as conducting a mental-status examination. The purpose of the examination was to check out his mental functions at that time and to attempt to determine their status at other times in his life. Finally, he listened to the defendant's version of what happened during the attacks.

Dr. Baker also went through the criminal complaint with the defendant, point by point, asking what information he agreed with and what he claimed was untrue or mistaken.

John heaped much of the blame for the attack on Emily on his other self, the "Mr. Hyde" side of his personality. He also blamed his boozing. "I could have kept control if I wasn't drinking," he declared. But he blamed Carla's murder on her attempt to run away and the struggle which he claimed led to her death when he locked a stranglehold on her. He denied torturing her or performing any sexual acts except for making her strip.

"He sees the problem as his sadistic sexual fantasies being ignited by alcohol and his losing control of these fantasies so that he actually began to do what he's fantasized about for some time," the psychiatrist wrote in his report.

Basing an opinion on definitions outlined in the Wisconsin State Jury Instructions, Dr. Baker determined the defendant was not suffering from mental disease at the time of the interview or at the time Emily was attacked. He was not a multiple personality, and he was not psychotic.

"It is my opinion . . . that Mr. Weber at the time of the alleged criminal activity in 1986 and 1988 was not suffering from a psychotic disorder," he wrote. "Thus it is my opinion that at the time of this alleged activity he was not suffering from a mental disease in which he was unable to appreciate the wrongfulness of his conduct or conform his conduct to the requirements of (the) law."

The doctor also concluded, however, that John suffered from sexual sadism, alcohol abuse, and dysthymic disorder—a tongue-twisting psychiatric term for long-term chronic depression. John had a long-term personality disorder that created difficulties in his relationship with other people, and on the physical side of his overall health, he had multiple sclerosis.

Dr. Miller, the prosecution psychiatrist, also interviewed the defendant for several hours, and reviewed his writings, police reports, the tapes, and other material previously worked up by mental-health professionals. Although he initially determined that from a clinical standpoint, John suffered from several mental diseases, his final conclusion—based strictly on the legal definition—was that he did not suffer from a mental disease.

It was the psychiatrist's belief that the defendant's mental problems did not substantially affect his ability to think, understand or appreciate what was going on around him. "Nor do I believe that it substantially affected his emotional processes in the sense that he was unable to understand what he was feeling or that he was unable to control his behavior because of such a degree of emotion," Dr. Miller later testified in court.

He also concluded that John was aware of the wrongfulness of his conduct and had the ability to conform to the law when each of the sisters was attacked. In his testimony, he indicated John received the wrong "behavioral message" from his parents when they learned that his sexual fantasies involved kidnapping, voyeurism, and torture. "They became aware of it, and yet again, nothing significant happened to Mr. Weber," he explained. "The message he got consistently from all the people who were close to him was that this is acceptable behavior. That it's okay to have these kinds of thoughts. It's okay even to hit your sister on the head with a beer bottle. It's okay to point a .22 at your sister. You know nothing much is going to happen to you."

Along with his primary diagnosis of sexual sadism, the prosecution psychiatrist identified other disorders John was afflicted with, including fetishism, transvestic fetishism, and voyeurism. Certain objects turned him on; he enjoyed dressing in the clothes of the opposite sex, and he was a peeper who was stimulated by sneaking peeks at females during various stages of undress.

Other diagnoses included John's difficulty achieving erections during normal circumstances, and what the doctor characterized as "an adjustment disorder of adult life with depressed mood." The latter condition was severe at the time of the interview, and was considered in good part to reflect the situation he was in. Anyone in as much trouble as he was in would be depressed and could be expected to have difficulty adjusting to the situation.

John denied to the psychiatrist that anyone or anything, including his imaginary companion, had directly attempted to control his mind or to interfere with his thinking. The doctor concluded John was not a multiple personality.

After briefly reviewing the defendant's history, the defense psychiatrist, Dr. Crowley, described him in a preliminary report prepared on December 20, 1988, as being of high average intelligence, but impulsive. Although John reported no "frankly delusional thinking," the doctor said he described something that was "akin" to auditory hallucinations. John heard things that weren't there.

Dr. Crowley noted that although imaginary friends usually disappear as children grow up, John's chimeric sidekick went on to become an increasingly stronger force in his life and remained with him except for the period when he was in the Army. "He is, on the one hand, inclined to view this as his alter ego, or view himself as a Jekyll and Hyde." On the other hand, the psychiatrist said, John talked about his alter ego as if it had a separate existence. "When I needed him, he was there. He could get me in trouble. He lived more dangerously than me," and ". . . the whole thing was to see how much he could get away with without being caught," were some of the statements John made about his illusory pal.

As he grew older, John had begun to suspect there was something seriously wrong with his impish friend. And after separation from the Army he started showing up when he wasn't wanted. John argued with him, usually during drinking bouts, but especially after Carla's murder.

"There seemed to be ways I could shake him. On two occasions it didn't work," he was quoted. Dr. Crowley asked what occasions he was referring to. "Carla's death and my attack on my wife," he explained.

John didn't know what the imaginary companion was and initially it was just someone he could talk to when his father yelled at him, he reported. He blamed the friend for leading him to commit the thefts at the store. And he said the playmate came up with things to think about, ideas like the attack on Kathy.

According to John, his roguish companion apparently didn't like jail any better than he liked the Army, however, and hadn't been around since the arrest. John didn't feel the illusory troublemaker had any power over him any longer. "His whole game was not to get caught, to keep things secret," the patient explained. "I feel the same way. I thought I could live with Carla's death. I couldn't. Now I don't care."

John told the psychiatrist he drank at least twelve cans of beer before killing Carla, and he was also drinking heavily when he attacked his wife. Curiously, at another point in the examination, he described his beer drinking as a safety valve. When his urges became too strong for him, he guzzled lots of beer, went off somewhere by himself, looked at pornography, and masturbated. It relieved his tension.

He also insisted again that many or most of the claims he made in the tape about the torture and murder of Carla were not true.

Dr. Crowley diagnosed the defendant as suffering from sexual sadism, alcohol abuse, and borderline personality disorder. Based on data available at that time, he added, there were no indications John suffered from any of the major mental diseases such as schizophrenia that usually provide the basis for pleas of mental nonresponsibility. "On the other hand, he is clearly a seriously disturbed individual and the diagnoses listed above only begin to reflect the degree of psychopathology which is present," the doctor wrote.

Significantly, however, Dr. Crowley stated there was no reasonable doubt in his mind that the defendant was aware of the wrongfulness of his conduct. But on the issue of John's ability to conform his behavior to the requirements of the law, the psychiatrist observed that he had a history of struggling with his most violent and homicidal impulses. "This behavior has the quality of a compulsion, and thus may actually represent impulses which are irresistible and simply not resisted."

It appeared that although John knew what he was doing was wrong and against the law, his evil compulsions may have been so overwhelming that he was powerless to resist them.

A couple of months later after reviewing additional information supplied by the defense including prior treatment records, more testing elsewhere, and samples of some of John's handwritten fantasies about kidnap, sex, torture, mutilation, and murder, Dr. Crowley submitted a follow-up report to the defense attorneys expanding on his initial observations.

Judging by the concept of what was accepted in medical circles as mental disease, he said he did not believe their client was psychotic.

Referring to a telephone conversation with Lex during which the attorney pointed out he needed a diagnosis based on the legal definition, rather than a medical definition of psychosis, Dr. Crowley reported a totally different conclusion however.

"If I use the definition of mental disease contained in the Wisconsin Jury Instructions, specifically 'mental disease is an abnormal condition of the mind which substantially affects mental or emotional processes and can impair the behavior controls,' then it is my opinion . . . that the defendant did have such a condition," he wrote.

During later testimony at the trial, Dr. Crowley also stated that it was his conclusion "to a reasonable degree of medical certainty" that the defendant was unable to conform his conduct to the requirements of the law at the time of the attack against Carla. His conclusion was the same in regard to the assault on Emily, he said. The psychiatrist explained further that he really didn't know if the inability to conform on those two occasions was due to John's drinking or to his mental disease.

Nevertheless, the John Weber homicide case was full to the brim with unique questions and problems that begged the heavy involvement of psychiatrists and psychologists. His crimes were so inexplicably atrocious, sexually warped, and firmly tied to the personal demons fighting for control of his mind that a united effort by shrinks and lawyers to unravel the puzzle was a necessity that was unavoidable.

John's attorneys were mapping out an insanity defense around their client's pleas of not guilty, and of not guilty by reason of mental disease, or NGI as it was commonly referred to—and the findings and testimony of psychiatrists could be crucial to the outcome. Their professional opinions presumably could go a long way in making the difference between whether or not he spent the rest of his life in a prison or in a mental hospital.

By that time the charges against him had mushroomed, and in an amended complaint he was accused of seventeen felonies and one misdemeanor. Conviction on all charges and sentencing to the maximum penalty would add lifetimes to the mandatory life sentence for murder.

No one, especially the defendant himself, believed that he would ever roam Phillips and the Wisconsin North Woods as a free man again.

Chapter Twelve

Preparations

Serious pretrial sparring opened on Monday morning, October 10, when John appeared in Price County Circuit Court before Judge Carlson for a preliminary hearing to determine if sufficient probable cause existed to continue his detention.

Before turning to the main business at hand, Judge Carlson first dealt with a defense motion to ban the media from photographing their client during the trial and other proceedings. The attorneys asked that if the judge ruled against that motion, that as an alternative the court direct that John could be photographed only after he was seated at the counsel table.

The defense claimed that filming John outside the courtroom or entering the courtroom in leg restraints, belly chains, or wristcuffs could jeopardize his Constitutional right to a fair trial.

Barnett was joined in opposing the motion by an attorney and an executive from a Wausau television station. Barnett argued that the public's right to know was a foundation of the judicial system, and that the media should be allowed to record the proceedings on film or by audiotape.

Lawyer Lorraine Peterson argued against the defense motion, declaring that if it was granted it would give the public a false impression that would result in a form of censorship. "I don't see how letting the public be aware of what the public that's here can see is going to prevent a fair trial," she declared. "I don't see how this is going to taint any possible jury that can be found to try this defendant."

Judge Carlson denied the motion, including the alternative request that the press be restricted from photographing John in the hallway or in the courtroom when his handcuffs and other manacles were visible.

The judge considered a related motion, aimed at restricting the setup of cameras in the courtroom to general spectator areas and to ban them from the jury box and some other areas especially advantageous for recording the proceedings. Judge Carlson determined that cameras could be set up in a specific area of the jury box where they would be a fair distance from witnesses. Two television stations from Wausau and one from Rhinelander sent film crews to record spots on the story.

The defense also asked the court for a gag order restricting authorities involved in investigation of the case and in the trial from giving interviews to the press.

Lex exhibited the front-page article from the Sunday *Milwaukee Journal* quoting Sheriff Wirsing and former police chief Krenzke and pointed out the newspaper is circulated throughout the state. He said the article could be damaging because it was made available to the public at large prior to selection and sequestration of a jury.

Barnett responded by pointing out that sincere efforts were made by authorities to control and monitor information disseminated to the press. He said that both he and Sheriff Wirsing went over statements and even gave Lex an opportunity to review and approve them before they were released.

The prosecutor added that he regretted prior comments made about the Gein case, but also pointed out that Krenzke was a private citizen and the media could quote his opinions if they wished to. Attorney Peterson added her opposition to the gag order.

"Well, this runs right to freedom of the press and freedom of speech," she declared. The attorney also pointed out that the trial involved a story that was of great public interest, and that would be reported by the press whether or not the people most closely involved and best informed were allowed to talk with the media.

Judge Carlson denied the gag order. He said he was satisfied that the court would be able to pick a jury that would be fair and impartial.

At last John was led shuffling into the courtroom wearing his loose-fitting jailhouse clothes, and with his hands and legs in manacles. His prison pallor and obvious dejection made him look skinny and forlorn. The courtroom was filled with spectators, including courthouse employees, who stole a few minutes from their chores to peek in on the proceedings.

Without question, the most mysterious and eye-catching spectator was a long-legged blonde who showed up for the hearing wearing sunglasses and a trench coat. Darla Rae Torres worked as a secretary for a public service organization in another office of the courthouse. She wasn't able to attend every minute of every hearing, but the slender beauty arranged her schedule to spend as much time as she could in the courtroom when John's case was on the calendar. A former straight-*A* psychology student at Missouri State College in Springfield, Missouri, she was fascinated by the bizarre crime and by the complexities of the defendant's mind.

One of five witnesses called by DA Barnett to testify, Emily was the star of the tragic drama that unfolded in the quiet courtroom. Before she was called, Judge Carlson granted a request by Barnett that her parents and her brothers, Gene, Jr., and Larry, who were not expected to be called to testify, be allowed into the courtroom during her appearance. He noted, however, that they were subject to the same special security restrictions established for other spectators.

Emily kept her eyes looking straight forward as she walked past the defendant and took her seat in the witness chair. It was the first time she had seen her husband or been in the same room with him since his arrest.

After the slender, frail woman was sworn in as a witness a few moments later, spectators listened in stunned silence while she recounted the dreadful attack from beginning to end. She was so soft-spoken that at times people near the back of the courtroom strained forward to hear. But she continued the account, although at times she seemed on the verge of breaking into tears, and included all the grisly details from the sexual abuse to the story that was concocted to explain her injuries after returning home.

For the first time she raised her voice and stared directly at her husband when she testified about her injuries and her long stay in intensive care.

"I was in there for sixteen days. I was in a great deal of pain," she testified.

Emily told about her husband ordering her at knifepoint to write the letters and birthday cards to explain her absence. "He said if I didn't write it he would cut my boobs off," she said.

Barnett asked what John did with the knife after he stopped punching her during one stage of the attack.

"He rolled me over on my stomach and he was sitting on my back. He made some puncture wounds on my butt and he cut my legs," she replied softly.

"How deeply did he cut your legs?" the DA persisted.

"I don't know how deep it was, but it's still open," she said. It was more than a month after the attack.

During cross-examination by Lex, Emily said she didn't smell alcohol on her husband's breath the night of the attack and didn't know if he was drinking. Lex then asked if there were any empty beer cans in the car. "I wouldn't know," Emily replied. "I wasn't allowed to look in the backseat." John sat expressionless with his eyes downcast during most of his wife's testimony.

Also called to the witness stand were Chief Moore, sheriff's investigator Heitkemper, Dr. Satterwhite, and Dr. Simley. Each of the witnesses testified about their personal role in the investigation.

At the conclusion of the hearing Judge Carlson found there was probable cause to believe the defendant had committed a felony in Price County and ordered John held for arraignment. He continued the $200,000 bond.

In another matter, Judge Carlson also granted a request by John's lawyers and ordered yet another psychiatric examination, this time to determine if John was mentally competent to assist in his defense. In accordance with defense recommendations, he appointed Dr. Richard Hurlburt of Stevens Point to conduct the examination and directed the sheriff to make arrangements for John's transportation. He also ordered that a report should be submitted to the court within fifteen days.

The appointment was made over the objections of Barnett, who asked the defense attorneys to cite their reasons for requesting the examination. Lex cited his discussions with the defendant, but declined to go into detail. The content of his discussions with his client was privileged information, he said.

Judge Carlson pointed out that Barnett could request a similar examination by experts of his own choosing if he wasn't satisfied with the results of the initial examination.

On John's twenty-fifth birthday, his attorneys entered pleas on his behalf of not guilty and of not guilty by reason of mental disease and defect. Although many rank-and-file citizens tend to look askance at insanity pleas as cop-outs commonly used by criminals to escape punishment for their crimes, they are not used nearly as often as generally believed. Insanity pleas are used in fewer than one hundred thousand criminal cases a year, but are successful only about two hundred times. That averages out to about four successful insanity pleas annually for each state.

Because John was accused of committing crimes in Wisconsin, an insanity plea was one of his options. But judging by statistics alone, the odds against successfully carrying it off were heavily stacked against him.

Early in December the state withdrew its Chapter 51 petition filed after John's troubling letters were found in his cell. Two court-appointed doctors had examined him, and one of the medical experts stated that he did not believe treatment in a psychiatric institution was necessary at that time. Both doctors agreed however that the defendant should be closely monitored because he was still a possible danger to himself.

The day after the Chapter 51 was withdrawn by the prosecution, the defense dropped its request for a hearing on John's competency. While John appeared personally in court, his defense attorney told the judge by telephone that he had discussed the matter at length with his client and no longer had concerns about his ability to help in his own defense. After asking John if he agreed with the move and understood what was going on, and obtaining a positive response, Judge Carlson granted the request. Dr. Hurlburt's report had already been filed.

Despite the surprisingly rapid settlement of the question over John's competency, the decisions didn't mean that he was through being interviewed and studied by psychiatrists. At that time he still had Dr. Baker, Dr. Miller, and Dr. Crowley to deal with. Two of the examinations were to be made at the Dane County Jail in Madison.

And late in November Judge Carlson ordered a reevaluation

of the defendant to determine "his present competency" to assist in his own defense. A few weeks later, after examination by various mental-health professionals, it was determined that he was capable of understanding the charges against him and assisting in his own defense.

In a psychological evaluation report on a series of tests conducted in order to measure and understand the defendant's mental processes, Dr. Donald B. Derozier, PhD, reported John was of above-average intelligence but was prone to paranoid and aggressive fantasies. There were periods of time, however, when he was merely aggressive, without the paranoia, and/or was nominally compliant.

The clinical psychologist, who was associated with the Nicolet Clinic in Neenah, Wisconsin, further summarized that John had a history of conflicts and uncertainty about his identity during his developmental years complicated by feelings of fear, anger, rejection, and a need for approval. Dr. Derozier reported that the structure and clear-cut role requirements of military service helped the defendant stabilize his life, although after release from the Army he had considerable difficulty in establishing meaningful relationships with both men and women.

In another of the several tests, he was asked to draw a picture of himself. He drew a badly constructed head, that wasn't consistent with his intellectual level, and suggested again to the experts that he had a poor self-image. "Secondary features on the drawing would indicate a rather blank, somewhat apathetic posture. This could imply a person who avoids facing himself," Dr. Derozier wrote.

John's performance on the Thematic Apperception Test, or TAT, however, disclosed some of the most troubling results. After peering at the photographs provided by the examiner, a disturbing number of the stories John concocted involved themes indicating persecution. Usually the stories ended with both the aggressor and the victim hurt in some way. Stories with females as the main characters were free of aggressive conflict, but the endings were still negative. One woman character died of a drug overdose, another was murdered, and another was ignored. Other stories indicated dissatisfaction by the son in relationships with the father. Stories dealing with mother-son relationships showed passive compliance and what the psychologist termed "reverse rejection" of the mother.

Results of the evaluation were forwarded to the psychiatrist, and the report was eventually used as evidence at John's trial.

As the January 3 trial date and an alternate date set for January 23 loomed ever nearer, attorneys for both sides became increasingly concerned about wrapping up their preparation in time for the beginning of the scheduled proceedings. By the middle of December, the psychiatric evaluations hadn't yet been completed, the State Crime Laboratory hadn't completed analysis on all the evidence, and there were myriad other details to complete. Even the motion for change of venue was still to be decided.

John had provided voice, saliva, blood, and hair samples to be used as exemplars, or comparisons, in tests by the state laboratory but they hadn't yet been analyzed. And when authorities attempted to obtain fresh handwriting samples from him, he began to write, then balked. After conferring with his attorneys he agreed to provide the samples, but they were still to be completed. He couldn't just start over from where he left off. Handwriting exemplars must be taken at a single sitting to be useful.

And the prosecution was still tilting with Judge Fox, who among his other duties was Price County Juvenile Court Judge, over access to psychological, psychiatric, and other records compiled for John during his childhood and teenage years.

Judge Fox issued an order releasing a limited portion of John's juvenile records, but Barnett wanted access to more documents.

Barnett and the defense attorneys agreed in a hearing before Judge Carlson that they both needed more time. Asked by the jurist to suggest a realistic date to begin the trial, Lex suggested sometime in April 1989.

Barnett worried that a trial in April, especially during the latter part of the month, would cause other problems. It was the beginning of the walleye spear fishing season and would be extremely bad for area law enforcement officers. ". . . we are going to be housing dozens of law enforcement officers from other counties, plus our own. And needless to say . . . we are going to need access to our own officers at a minimum for security purposes, and in addition as witnesses at trial," he pointed out.

Judge Carlson asked the sheriff for more information about the spear fishing season, and Wirsing said it depended on what the weather would be the next spring. "But we anticipate the last three weeks in April," he said. "Our officers, along with probably all the other officers in the northern half of the state, will be tied up."

Judge Carlson reluctantly yielded to the time-demanding complexities of the case and to local custom in the hunting and fishing mecca. He rescheduled the trial to begin March 6. In anticipation of the trial extending two weeks or slightly more, he blocked out his calendar to March 23.

Prior to getting down to the serious business of setting a new trial date, Lex asked the judge for an order to free his client's hands during the proceedings so John could assist the attorneys with note taking. Barnett objected to the proposal, citing security reasons. Judge Carlson asked the sheriff what he thought of the proposal.

"I would like to see the defendant remain in the custody

that he is in right now as far as the leg irons and restraints, due to the fact that I primarily don't have three of my uniformed officers in court at the present time," the sheriff replied.

Lex suggested a compromise. Pointing out that his client was wearing leg irons, a belly chain, and both his hands were manacled, he suggested freeing John's left hand so he could write. Judge Carlson agreed to the compromise and directed the sheriff to free the defendant's hand. But the matter was only settled temporarily, and would be brought up repeatedly during the exhaustive rounds of preliminary hearings.

Two of the most important matters scheduled for consideration were the long-pending defense motion for change of venue and argument over efforts by John's lawyers to win a court order suppressing evidence.

Before moving to the subject of a change of venue and the suppression motion, Lex raised a preliminary matter. He wanted Gene Lenz, Sr., and his son Gene Lenz, Jr., barred from the courtroom and the courthouse. John had advised him that one of the men had made threatening comments while they were sitting near him during a previous hearing, Lex declared.

The attorney said sheriff's deputies had also indicated they were especially concerned about security while hearings involving the Weber case were going on. Neither Gene Lenz, Sr., nor his sons were present in the courtroom when Lex asked to have them kept out of the building.

Barnett objected to the proposal, pointing out that relatives of victims are part of the public and have a right to attend the proceedings. Lex's request was too extreme. And certainly, no order should be made barring the Lenzes until the father and son, as well as anyone who claimed to have overheard a threat, were given opportunities to testify under oath, he said.

Lex responded that most of the law enforcement officers,

as well as the metal detectors, were there or in place, because of "the danger, or addressing the risk that arises from Mr. Lenz's presence."

The lawyer offered to put his client on the stand to testify about a remark he reputedly heard while sitting at the counsel table during one of the breaks. He claimed John heard one of the men say something "to the effect, that 'we can strangle you before any of the cops could get back here.' "

Carlson asked the DA what his response would be if the defendant offered the testimony referred to by his attorney, and the Lenzes didn't dispute the accusation. Barnett began to talk about his conversations with people outside the courtroom, when the judge cut him off. "You are missing the point," he said. "Perhaps I am," the bespectacled and balding young prosecutor conceded.

Barnett started over, and said if the scenario posed by the judge turned out to be true, the state would still maintain that adequate security measures were in place. He pointed out that the presence of the metal detectors and the pat-downs would prevent bringing any weapons into the courtroom. And officers could be seated in strategic positions in the courtroom in order to thwart any attacks such as the defense attorney had referred to.

"Officers can be seated in the same row as . . . those two individuals, in between those two individuals and the defendant," he stated. "And in fact that is what occurred at the second day of the motions hearing on December 20. Those arrangements were made."

Carlson understood the hurt and the anger that relatives of the two sisters might feel toward the defendant, but like any other judge, he was committed to preventing violence in his courtroom.

He pointed out that if the statements were made, as it was alleged, they could "be viewed as being a natural consequence of being in the position that Mr. Lenz and his son are in. That is the father and the twin brother to Carla Lenz, the decedent, and to Emily Weber, the second victim. And so it's not surprising they would vent any anger that they feel in that fashion. The question is what is the relative risk of them carrying out any such threats?"

No one appeared to notice that he had referred to Carla as the twin of Gene, Jr., instead of his real twin, Emily. The question he posed was more important than correcting sibling relationships, and he turned to the job of digging up his own answers. He asked who was in charge of security, and was told it was Chief Deputy Gould.

Before the judge had an opportunity to question the sheriff's officer, Lex interrupted to beef up his accusations of threats against his client. He said while John was being brought into the courtroom for the last previous hearing his investigator also overheard threatening remarks in the hallway. One of the Lenzes said words to the effect of, "Push us back all the way. We can send a bullet down the hall just as easily. . . ."

Lex added that the threat reputedly overheard by his client wouldn't have required a weapon to carry out. "All the frisking in the world is not going to stop a strangulation hold," he observed.

The attorney recommended that if the judge denied his request, a stopgap alternative could require the Lenzes to be frisked and checked with metal detectors before entering the courthouse, instead of waiting until they were about to enter the courtroom.

Carlson asked Gould if he believed he was able or prepared to provide adequate protection in the courtroom if the threats cited by Lex were true.

"My department will make provisions for whatever decision you make in the matter," Gould replied. Responding to further questions from the judge, the sheriff's officer agreed that people were moved to the ends of the hallways when the defendant was brought to the courtroom. The courtroom was also searched each time and people were subjected to metal detection, frisking, and bag searches, he said.

Gould explained that deputies met prior to each hearing in the case for a skull session to talk over potential or specific risks and security needs. He said he didn't know if anyone from the Sheriff's Department had talked with the Lenzes about the matter of threats or reputed threats, but confirmed that he was satisfied he and his officers could adequately safeguard the defendant.

If family members of the sisters showed up in the courtroom, they would be directed to sit on the opposite side from whatever table John is seated at, he said. "And I will have an officer on the end of whatever bench, in order that anybody going to Mr. Weber would have to go through that officer," he promised. Gould vowed to provide all the law officers both inside and outside the courtroom that were necessary to provide safety.

Judge Carlson denied the motion. "The court does not take the allegations of the threat lightly," he said. And he pointed out that in light of the nature of the particular crime, he felt it was quite possible the type of emotions existed that might lead to threatening statements. He made it clear, however, that he wasn't accepting the accusations as fact.

But the judge also noted that he was satisfied the Sheriff's Department would provide adequate security. And he added that he didn't see any advantage to singling out the Lenz father and son for special searches before they entered the courthouse.

He pointed out that Price County was fortunate to have a good secure method for moving prisoners from the jail to the courthouse. The only time a defendant was exposed to the public outside the courtroom was during the walk of a few yards from the entryway.

A few minutes later Carlson rejected another defense motion aimed at getting Barnett removed as prosecutor on the case because he was present during the search of the Cutlass.

John's attorneys claimed that because the DA was a witness to the search, the defense might wish to call him as a witness during one of the hearings.

Barnett pointed out that he was only an observer during the search and didn't participate, but several other law enforcement officers were present. Any one or more of them could be called to witness to anything he might testify about relating to what he observed during the search.

In making his ruling, Carlson noted that historically, district attorneys in large and small population counties have participated as observers early on in the criminal process.

When attention turned to the longtime question of change of venue, the defense cited case law (former precedent setting rulings in similar cases), and referred to newspaper articles to support the argument that the trial should be heard outside Price County. An affidavit that was among other documents supporting the motion, listed various publications that printed articles and the dates they appeared, along with a description of the incident in the cafe. Lex and Reid referred to the remarks they overheard as "derogatory comments of several individuals. . . ." They summed up by observing, "The nature of the comments made led your affiants to the conclusion that public sentiment is such that a fair trial is not possible in Price County for John Weber."

Arguing the motion, Lex specifically asked the judge to pass over Sheboygan County as a trial site if the venue request was granted. He cited a front-page news article in the Sheboygan *Daily Press* detailing the disappearance of Marchell Hansen, who was a native of the city of fifty thousand along the Lake Michigan shore.

Barnett argued that local media coverage had been factual, responsible, and in fact was fairly restrained and had passed over some information available through public records that "would have caused quite a furor." He also noted that coverage of the case was statewide, so there was no reason to believe it would be easier to obtain an impartial jury somewhere else besides Price County.

Responding to the prosecutor, Lex declared there had never been a more sensationalized case in Price County than the one they were concerned with at the time. Then he began to talk about some of the newspaper articles, pointing out they made several references to Ed Gein. "I don't know of any other case which has been equated with the Ed Gein case in memory," he said.

Then he added of Phillips, that ". . . rumors of possible cannibalism are rampant in the community."

The dreadful *"C* word" had been mentioned in open court.

Judge Carlson granted the motion for change of venue, although he withheld a final decision on exactly where the case would be sent for trial.

"I am satisfied you could probably go to any ten people in Price County and ask them if they know about the John Weber case, and I would guess it would be a rare hermit indeed . . . who would say they don't know about the John Weber case," he observed.

"Unfortunately the John Weber case, because of its uniqueness, its sensationalism, the mixture of I guess all of those things that heighten passion, from torture, sadism, murder to sexual crimes, you have it all bound up here in this particular case," he added. "The publicity, familiarity, the passion is all there."

The judge also patiently sorted out a flap over the serving of warrants at the Lenz home. Emily's father notified the prosecutor that any subpoenas served on his family should be handled by the Sheriff's Department because members of the defense attorneys' staff weren't welcome on his property.

Barnett passed on the message to Lex and Reid in a letter advising them that any entry by process servers working for the defense would be considered as trespassing and would be prosecuted. The DA pointed out that any documents the defense wished served by the defense could be handled by sheriff's officers.

Lex complained about the restriction and said the decision to subpoena Emily was a last-minute decision. He sent his own employee out to deliver the document because the manpower at the Sheriff's Department was already severely strained by the demands of providing courtroom security and carrying out other duties related to the Weber case.

Carlson was concerned, as he had been from the beginning of the judicial process, about the dreadful emotional assault on the sensibilities of the Lenz family and of the tension between them and the Webers. And he remarked that he saw no reason to do things that would make the tensions worse.

Property owners have the right to designate who is welcome on their property and who isn't, he observed. But he pointed out that if the defense wanted to do their own process serving to a member of the family, they could carry out the chore at some other location, such as the courthouse.

"I think I can perhaps see the Lenzes' viewpoint, and why they probably don't want anybody there," he said.

During the suppression portion of the hearing the defense pressed efforts to have evidence gathered from the searches of the Cutlass, the letters taken during the search of John's jail cell, and other evidence ruled inadmissible by the court. If the decision favored the defense and a major portion of the evidence was thrown out, it would gut the state's case and make it virtually impossible to obtain convictions.

The suppression hearings eventually extended four days into what the court officers wryly observed developed into a minitrial. And that wasn't too much of an exaggeration. Even the defendant was called to testify, and it was one of the most dramatic moments of the procedure. But John wasn't allowed to shuffle to the witness stand in his cumbersome chains and manacles until after strict ground rules were pounded out over future use of his testimony. It was eventually agreed that the prosecutor would be limited to purposes of rebuttal or impeachment in referring to anything said during John's appearance on the witness stand.

Even after that was settled, the defense attorneys made a spirited effort to have the courtroom cleared of the media and of other spectators. The only spectator, other than members of the media, was Emily and Carla's father. Even Ms. Torres, one of the most faithful observers, missed the important hearing.

The defense cited concerns about publicity, photos of their client and stories about his testimony, affecting his right to a fair trial. In a sense, if he had to testify in view of the public eye it would amount to requiring him to testify against himself, it was argued. Carlson denied the motion, observing that the courts are sometimes far too paranoid about the media. He also rejected motions asking that photographers be prohibited from taking pictures of John moving across the floor in his shackles and during his testimony.

On the witness stand during questioning by Lex, John briefly recounted his arrest and being taken to jail. He said he was depressed and feeling suicidal. He claimed he hadn't slept, or been given food or cigarettes before he was interrogated by Chief Moore early Tuesday morning. John testified he was normally a pack-and-a-half-a-day smoker, but puffed up to two packs when he was nervous. He asked Greenwood for cigarettes but was ignored, he said.

John's testimony about his behavior and treatment while he was in the holding cell collided head-on with the account of jailers and others who had contact with him at that time. John was served regular meals just like any other inmate, and it appeared he slept for twelve to fourteen hours, they said. He claimed, however, that most of the time he was locked in the receiving cell he was lying in a fetal position facing the wall because he didn't want to see anyone.

"I kept my eyes closed a lot of the time, but I was not sleeping," he said. "I was just arrested for the attempted murder of my wife, and I was under too much stress to sleep." Only his testimony about not smoking seemed to fit in with the recollections of the jailers, and even then they said nothing about the prisoner asking for a cigarette.

Asked about Greenwood's instructions and other remarks to him during booking, John said the jailer told him he would be checked every ten minutes and warned that if he beat the walls he would be restrained. "One comment was that he'd check my hands every once in a while."

John said he was also asked during booking if he had an attorney and replied that he formerly had a local lawyer on retainer but didn't anymore. The jailer responded by saying something about getting the paperwork started, he added.

Moving to the interrogation, Lex asked what his thoughts were when Moore disclosed the tape for the first time. "I believed it was all over with, that he knew everything," John replied.

The witness explained away the police chief's suspicion that he was masturbating by saying he was merely trying to relieve one of his periodic bladder cramps. "I was not handcuffed and I placed my right hand underneath my left thigh and put my elbow into my bladder to push down to relieve the cramp," he testified.

When the defense attorney turned to the final minutes of the interrogation after Moore asked John to ride out to the farm with him and help locate Carla's grave, testimony differed sharply from some of the recollections of law enforcement officers called earlier as witnesses. John claimed he twice asked for a lawyer. ". . . it was becoming obvious that he (Moore) didn't know everything that he said he did."

John said after he requested a lawyer the first time, the

chief asked him to at least help out by drawing a map. "I said, 'I really think I should see an attorney.' "

According to his story the police chief responded by promising that if he cooperated it would show on his record and that if the DA knew he was helpful it might go easier on him. John added that the tape player was six feet from him at one end of the table and he was at the other end. Moore had testified he placed the device about eighteen inches from the suspect.

Lex asked who brought up the idea of the map, and when. "That was—Chief Moore asked me if I would help him draw the map." Lex asked if he was saying that Moore's earlier testimony about the incident was incorrect.

"That's right," John agreed.

The witness also described the search of his cell by Greenwood. He said the jailer was very thorough and took away anything that could be used to harm himself with, including socks and pencils. Then Greenwood found the letters under a *Time* magazine on the bench in the common area. The jailer asked if he could read the writings, and John told him he would rather he didn't.

John said he admitted attempting to hang himself earlier. ". . . and that I was, you know, apparently planning it again. I didn't want to live." The jailer scooped the letters up and walked away with them. Greenwood returned later and talked with the prisoner about his emotions and feelings.

During cross-examination, Barnett led the witness through his first meeting with Moore at the Price County Safety Building, and the advisement of rights that he was informed of by the police chief. John agreed that he understood his Miranda rights, and also told about his arrest at the Flambeau Medical Center in front of the entrance to the emergency ward.

"We were just talking and when another officer came up, he said, 'At this time I am placing you under arrest for aggravated assault,' " John testified he was told by Moore.

"For aggravated assault?" Barnett asked. John nodded his head up and down in assent.

Returning to the Sunday night before John's arrest when he was lying down in the extra bedroom of his parents' home, the DA asked why he couldn't get to sleep. The witness replied it was because he had attacked his wife. Barnett asked what was going on in his mind while he was lying awake.

"Basically that my wife was in the hospital with severe injuries that I had caused, and I couldn't figure out why," John replied. He said he was still awake when his parents got up about seven A.M., drank some coffee with them, then drove to the hospital.

Barnett also grilled the witness about his interrogation by Chief Moore, his request to talk with an attorney, and the drawing of the map. John stuck to his earlier story.

"So you are saying that your raising the desire to have an attorney was actually an attempt to indicate to the chief that you did not want to speak with him anymore?" the DA asked.

"It was self-preservation was the reason for it," John replied.

"Self-preservation?"

"Yes," the witness responded. "I was under arrest and I just believed that I needed an attorney."

John said he continued to cooperate because Moore was very persuasive. "When you are questioned by him he can put things into terms to make it sound like I could get all the help that I needed; that he understood how I felt," he testified. "He even talked about God. And the effect that my belief in God, or whatever, could have on this."

Barnett drew an admission from the witness that he knew before he was called downstairs for the interrogation that the time would probably come when he would have to undergo questioning. And he knew his Fifth Amendment rights because the Miranda warning was read to him a couple of days earlier, so he was aware he could refuse to talk if he wished to. But he talked anyway.

When he got upset and said he needed help, Moore held his hand and reassured him that he would get all the help he needed, the witness said.

Emily followed John to the witness stand. During testimony that was much briefer than her husband's, she was questioned about the mix-up over the blue sweater that figured so importantly in some of the search warrants. Emily said she told her nurse she was wearing a nightgown with a blue sweater over it when she was driven to the hospital.

The DA also used her testimony to confirm she gave Moore permission to search her home for the missing .25-caliber pistol, while she was still in the hospital. Before she was excused, Emily answered a few more questions about her visits to the house after leaving the hospital, and about John's medical conditions and stuttering.

The hearings were exhausting but vitally important to the impending trial, and both sides in the contest left with something to mark up in the plus column. But the DA came away with the most to cheer about. He won the flap over the suppression of evidence.

Judge Carlson ruled that John's statements to police, the map he drew leading them to Carla's grave, articles and materials taken from his house, the letters found in the cell block, the tape recording retrieved from the Cutlass and other evidence collected during the investigation, were legally obtained by investigators.

The judge strongly defended Moore's credibility in respect to his story about the tape player clicking off and his account of the verbal exchange with the suspect immediately afterward in regard to a desire to talk with an attorney and drawing the map. ". . . to suggest that Chief Moore would fabricate what he testified to, knowing that the other two officers were within hearing distance is not common sense," the judge declared.

He also settled the blue sweater controversy, remarking that the reference to the article of clothing wasn't deliberately false. "I don't believe the officer had anything to gain by making up some kind of reference to a blue sweater. It is ridiculous to assume that there would have been," he said.

The mistake was the result of miscommunication somewhere between Emily, the nurse, and Chief Moore, he remarked. It was clear that what Moore really wanted to search for was the jacket Emily wore home from the fields, so it could be checked for traces of blood or other evidence. The judge also didn't buy the defendant's story that he had no sleep in the holding cell after he was booked.

Dealing with other motions, Carlson denied a move to sever the charges related to Carla from those involving Emily, remarking that they were "inextricably bound together." The evidence relating to both attacks would be heard at the same trial. He also rejected a motion to drop eleven of the eighteen charges against the defendant.

Although John's defense attorneys won their effort to have the trial moved to another location, as it turned out even that wasn't without certain cost in additional publicity that referred to "the *C* word." A few days after the hearing, Lex was quoted in a news story bylined by James B. Nelson in *The Milwaukee Sentinel,* as declaring at the hearing that: "Rumors of possible cannibalism are rampant in the community." His remarks about Gein were also included.

Additionally, Nelson reported John's statements on the tape that he "consumed human flesh." The story pointed out that John told police he recorded the tape to frighten Emily, and quoted Chief Moore as saying only the suspect knew whether the statement was "fact or fantasy." If the idea that John not only sexually tortured and murdered his teenage victim, but also may have feasted on her body had ever been much of a secret anywhere in the state, it wasn't anymore.

Moving the trial wouldn't ease public interest in the story, or lessen revulsion at the ugly possibility that a young man from a quiet little North Woods community had committed these hideous crimes.

John's trial was only a few weeks away when Judge Carlson selected Marathon County as the new location for the proceeding. John would go on trial in the downstate city of Wausau, where his sister Kathy completed high school, and where he was sent for psychiatric evaluation when he was a boy.

Marathon County had various advantages that impressed the judge, including a brand-new courtroom with special security features. It was also only a couple of hours' drive from Phillips.

At the district attorney's request, on Friday afternoon, March 3, the eve of the trial scheduled to begin early the following Monday morning, investigator Miller sat down to leaf through the stack of pornographic magazines taken from John's car trunk. He found three pages of letters corresponding to the notes John forced Emily to copy a few minutes before the assault at the farm. They were stuck between a couple of magazines.

Chapter Thirteen

Due Process

In the spring of 1989 when John's trial finally got underway in the modern three-block-long Marathon County Courthouse and Jail Building, Wausau was such a typically middle-class Midwestern community that it proudly advertised that fact on a big sign erected next to one of the main thoroughfares leading to the downtown business district.

"All-American City," the sign boasted.

The community of 38,000 people is the seat of local government for the Number One milk-producing county in the nation, and is just a little north of the geographical center of what many people refer to as "The Dairy State."

But one of the first things motorists visiting the bustling, friendly community notice as they drive past the dairy farms into the city is the water. Wausau is touched by three rivers, the Eau Claire, the Rib, and by the largest and most impressive of the three, the Wisconsin. The Wisconsin River, in fact, bisects the center of town, and residents, wishing to get from one side to the other, must drive over bridges.

At the south end of the city, there is more water, Lake Wausau. The town is a great place for anyone who enjoys fishing, swimming, or boating. And it is only an hour or two drive away from the Wisconsin North Woods and communities like

Rheinlander, Prentice, Park Falls, and Phillips, which offer even more opportunities for outdoor recreation.

Until the late 1970s most of the residents of Wausau were descendants of hardy settlers from Germany and Poland, with a good-sized mix of adventurers who pulled up stakes in New England and headed west looking for new opportunities. Then, after the Communist victories in Southeast Asia, local churches and other agencies began settling newcomers in Wausau from Laos, Cambodia, Thailand, and other Asian nations. Half or more of the newcomers were Hmong, the rugged mountain tribesmen from Laos and neighboring nations who were such fierce warriors and dedicated allies of the U.S. forces during the war.

Wausau residents were occupied with their own problems, including getting the newcomers settled into homes, schools, and jobs in factories producing paper products, concrete, and snowplows and in the dairy industry when attorneys and the judge gathered in Circuit Courtroom Number Five early Monday morning, March 6, to determine exactly how and where John would spend the rest of his life.

A tight security net was thrown around the courtroom, and three sheriff's deputies from Marathon County and two from Price County were assigned to the trial. They were all armed. Even though Wausau was more than fifty miles from Phillips, the safety of the notorious, defendant was still a major concern of authorities.

Deputies and a corrections officer from the Marathon County Jail carefully searched the courtroom before anyone else was permitted to enter. Spectators, including the press, were required to walk through a metal detector, then checked again by hand detectors before entering. Briefcases and purses were individually inspected. Signs were posted advising that no one would be allowed to leave except during recesses.

* * *

More than fifty prospective jurors were already assembled and waiting in a separate room, but before they were called for the voir dire, or questioning, during the selection process there were more motions to consider. Reid asked for another change of venue, citing an extensive story the previous day in the *Sunday Daily Herald* about the upcoming trial. The defense attorney said he also heard radio reports about the trial on his way to the courthouse.

Judge Carlson rejected the motion, pointing out that it wouldn't have mattered if the trial was venued to Fond du Lac, Sheboygan, or to Hudson near the Minnesota state line, the local or area press could have been expected to cover the story.

The attorneys also bickered again over some of the evidence and anticipated testimony, differing over whether or not it would be presented to the jury. The judge banned use of information about Emily's emotional reaction to her sister's death. He withheld a ruling on a defense argument against showing color photographs of Emily after the attack, other pictures of Carla's grave at the farm, and of a videotape of her remains being unearthed until he had an opportunity to review them.

The defense did not oppose use of black-and-white photos illustrating Emily's injuries, only those in color. "There is no need for color except to inflame the jury's passions against Mr. Weber," Reid told the court. "They're highly inflammatory. They're disgusting."

Before moving to the job of selecting a jury, Carlson ruled on a move by Lex and Reid to waive their client's right to a jury trial during the first phase of the proceeding. When Barnett rejected the proposal for a waiver, the defense attorneys asked the judge to declare the state law that provided for the waiver to be unconstitutional.

"The defendant alone does not have the right to decide to have a trial to the jury or a trial to the judge," he declared. The request was denied.

* * *

Carlson also made rulings about whether or not various articles and types of evidence would be admissible at the trial, and directed that some would be banned from the guilt phase but permitted during the sanity phase of the proceeding.

It wasn't much of a surprise to the professionals who had followed the case from the early hearings, when he ruled that the jury would not be permitted to hear references to cannibalism on the tape during the first stage of the trial. Portions of the tape referring to the defendant's boast of dining on Carla's leg and breast would be edited out on a copy and transcripts made especially for the jury.

Before the matter was even argued, Reid asked the judge to clear the courtroom of the media because of fears the information would be too prejudicial to potential jurors. Carlson said he didn't think a press ban was necessary. And Barnett promised not to "mention the magic *C* word." The ruling still left open the strong possibility that the full, unsanitized tape could be played to the jury during the insanity phase of the trial.

No evidence would be permitted during the guilt phase about John's possible interest in Satanism, including references to "Natas." It would be admissible during the second phase, however. Although Carlson initially ruled against allowing testimony about Emily's statement that her husband spoke in two voices at the attack site he later backtracked and withheld a formal ruling. "It doesn't make any difference how many people were inside John Weber's body," he observed. "It's whether the body committed the acts."

Carlson approved use of character evidence about Carla's desire to become a counselor, hospital records demonstrating the extent of Emily's injuries, and mention of John's affliction with multiple sclerosis.

Turning to John's confiscated jailhouse letter to his wife, Reid asked the court to delete the sentence, "Carla and you are the only two I ever attacked," before the rest of the document was submitted to the jury. He claimed the statement would imply to the jury that the defendant was a suspect in other disappearances. Carlson granted the motion as well as a related motion on another paragraph in the letter suggesting John was involved in other similar crimes.

". . . I think he refers to, in all the things I had done, not once was I caught. And he goes on to say the problems did not seem severe enough to risk losing everything until after Carla's death . . ." Carlson remarked.

The court granted a defense motion, which was also agreeable to the state, that no references were to be made about the Ed Gein case in either phase of the trial. The last-minute pretrial jockeying for advantages droned on and on while the prospective jurors continued to cool their heels in the jury room, waiting to be called for the voir dire.

When the motions hearing was at last concluded, John sprung a surprise. Speaking through his attorneys, he said he wished to plead guilty to nine of the counts against him, including the most serious charge of the first degree murder of Carla and of her kidnapping. The plea also included all the charges levelled against him for the attack on his wife, including attempted first degree murder, kidnapping, sexual intercourse by threat of force with a dangerous weapon, two counts of sexual contact by way of force in a sexually degrading manner, false imprisonment, and a misdemeanor count of battery—causing bodily harm to his wife without her consent.

The admission of guilt applied to the first phase of the trial, and the attorneys stated their client wished to continue his plea of not guilty by reason of mental disease or defect during the second phase. Judge Carlson and the attorneys were careful to refer to the second phase as "the legal responsibility" portion. But news reporters and other spectators were less meticulous about strict legal definitions: to them it was "the sanity phase."

John maintained his first-phase trial pleas of not guilty to the remaining nine charges, all tied to the attack on his sister-in-law, of three counts of forced sexual intercourse, four counts of sexual contact, and one each of false imprisonment and sexual disfigurement (mayhem). So regardless of his partial change of plea, the first part of the two-phase trial would continue as planned on the nine remaining charges.

To most people outside the legal justice system, the pleas were typically confusing. It appeared the defendant had pleaded both guilty and at the same time not guilty to the same charges. But basically, he was saying that "yes" he attacked and abused his wife and he kidnapped and murdered his sister-in-law. Yet, he was reserving his right to claim at the second phase of the trial, when the twin issues of mental responsibility and punishment were to be considerations, that he couldn't really help himself because he was insane or mentally impaired at the time the crimes occurred.

The chains and manacles John wore during previous appearances, while attorneys battered out pretrial differences, were gone. According to judicial reasoning, a defendant who shows up for trial in a jail uniform, with his hands cuffed, legs hobbled, and belly chains around his waist, would look so guilty the jury would likely be prejudiced against him.

Consequently, like other defendants facing a jury, John wore civilian clothes. However, unlike most other felony defendants, he wasn't spruced up in a spanking new business suit complete with shirt and tie bought especially for the proceedings so that he looked like another lawyer. Facing one or two of the most critical weeks in his life, John dressed casually. He wore blue jeans with a plaid shirt, and he had grown a full beard while in jail to go with his mustache. His wavy brown hair was shoulder-length and looked as if he had shaped it into place after waking up that morning by running his fingers through it instead of a comb. Under the artificial lights of the courtroom and after six months behind bars and locked doors, his face was pasty with the yellowish pallor of longtime prisoners. The sleeves of his shirt were rolled up a couple of inches above his elbows.

Judge Carlson looked down at the defendant seated between his attorneys at the defense table and asked if he killed Carla Lenz.

"Yes," he replied. John's voice was soft but audible.

He responded with the same one-word reply when the judge asked if he tortured his wife by burning her with a cigar, sticking a safety pin in her breast, beating her head with a shovel, and raping her with a wheelbarrow handle. He also said he understood each of the charges and the significance of his guilty pleas.

Judge Carlson accepted the pleas and rendered an official finding of guilty to all nine charges. Sentencing was withheld until later. But going into the trial on the remaining charges, John was already facing a possible maximum penalty on the first nine counts he pleaded guilty to of life imprisonment, plus 122 years and nine months. And a $20,000 fine could be tacked onto that, although considering the obvious lack of earning potential of a man serving life in prison, there wasn't much likelihood of the state ever collecting.

At last the court officers turned to selection of a jury. Judge Carlson preceded the actual voir dire by explaining the process and stressing its importance to the men and women in the jury pool. He also cautioned them to expect an occasional joke or humorous remark from the bench, but stressed that it wasn't because he didn't take the case seriously. "It is simply because I apparently have a genetic defect, and sometimes it gets out before I can slap my hand over my mouth, as my wife says," he explained. The jurist was respected by his colleagues and by attorneys who appeared before him for his intelligence and his quick wit, and his self-described "genetic defect" would come in handy more than once during the grim days ahead.

The jury selection process continued into the second day as prospects were quizzed about their knowledge of the case and asked if they or any of their close relatives had worked in the law enforcement business, had careers with the courts, knew anyone involved in the trial, or been victims of crimes. Several jurors said they were crime victims. One man had a bait and tackle box stolen, another reported a burglary, and a woman related she was beaten up by a boyfriend, but none of the reports resulted in disqualifications as jurors.

A variety of other questions was also asked. Most were posed with the same purpose—weeding out anyone with obvious biases that might affect their judgment of the defendant. Because of the peculiar nature of the case, prospective jurors were also questioned about their reaction to listening to grisly testimony, or looking at gruesome photos and lurid pornographic magazines that were expected to be presented as evidence.

One woman was excused after she admitted she didn't think she could deal with testimony that was too graphic. Another woman whose mother organized a statewide organization called "Citizens For Decency," was given a pass after she conceded she wouldn't be able to set aside her conviction that there is a link in some cases between pornographic magazines and sex crimes. A man was excused because his wife was sexually assaulted years earlier by a family member.

Both the defense and the prosecution were also given the privilege of eliminating twelve prospects with "peremptory strikes." When an attorney uses a peremptory strike, he doesn't have to give a reason. Peremptory strikes provide lawyers an opportunity to get rid of someone they suspect may be likely to vote against their side when it's time for deliberations. The strikes may be made based on experience, good horse sense, body language, a hunch, or simply because the attorney doesn't like someone's facial expressions, virtually anything at all.

A panel of nine women and five men, including two alternates, was seated by mid-afternoon Tuesday. They represented a mixed group of professions including a full-time housewife, nurse, computer specialist, and the operator of a foster home.

The new jury was sworn in, then advised by the judge that they would be sequestered, along with three bailiffs. Their isolation began immediately, and included telephone calls home to notify family members that they were selected for jury duty and needed clothing and other personal articles delivered to them. The bailiffs were instructed to make the calls and do the talking. Television viewing in the motel rooms would be monitored with local newscasts put off-limits and newspapers censored by the bailiffs, who were instructed to clip out any stories related to the trial before turning over the leftovers to jurors. Arrangements were made to show movies to help make up for the loss of other reading and viewing material.

"Now we have made arrangements for you. We have got some cots set up in a Quonset hut on the west end of town," Carlson explained, as he soberly peered over the tops of his glasses at the momentarily stunned jury members. "I am sorry it is not heated but it is supposed to get up to the '60s by the end of the week, so it shouldn't be too much of a problem."

The talk of an unheated Quonset hut was a joke, of course. But it wouldn't be the only time during the trial that the jury was treated to examples of the judge's off-the-wall sense of humor. As the trial progressed it would become a welcome relief valve that helped ease the steadily building sense of horror and revulsion elicited by the gruesome testimony. The jury was bussed to a local Howard Johnson motel.

After the jury left, Carlson ruled on the photographs. Emily's torture could be described in testimony but photos could not be shown to the jury during the guilt phase of the trial for the assault, sexual abuse, and murder of her sister. They were not relevant to the attack on Carla, but could be introduced at the sanity phase of the trial when Emily's abuse would also be a factor, he decided.

"The state has convinced me that testimony as to the Emily Weber incident should be introduced," he said. "But the photographs are not relevant in the guilt phase."

He also ruled the prosecution could use crime lab photographs of the autopsy, including pictures of the skull, and others showing that the lower portion of Carla's left leg was missing, but only if they were submitted in relationship to the testimony of the pathologists.

Significantly, he also permitted large blowup photos of each of the sisters prior to the attacks to be shown to the jury. "She has a right to be present in this courtroom," Carlson said of Carla. "The state has a right to show a representation of what she was." He later ruled however that the large studio photo could only be displayed during the prosecutor's opening statement, remarking that it would be unduly prejudicial to the defendant to have the murder victim staring out at the jurors throughout the entire trial. He was also concerned about the possibility that the presence of the photo might lead to an emotional outburst during testimony by members of Carla's family.

The attorneys agreed among themselves that pictures of Carla's skeletal remains at the grave, and the grave itself, would not be submitted to the jury. But the defense agreed to stipulate, or admit, that the partial remains pulled from the grave were hers.

A full transcript of the unedited tape became part of the official court records Tuesday, with the result that the press had its first opportunity to obtain copies of the nine-page document.

The lurid details of John's frightening account of his sex and torture murder of Carla, and his plans for his wife, were revealed in all their ugliness. It wasn't normal reading fare for the citizens of Wausau, and top editors at the *Daily Herald* huddled together for a conference to determine what should be run in their newspaper, and what, if anything, should be withheld because it was simply too shocking or sexually repugnant.

There was considerable discussion about whether or not John actually did all the things he claimed credit for in the tape, especially the acts of cannibalism—or if he was simply concocting the most repulsive account he could think of in order to scare his wife. Even if the tape was totally truthful, there was still a question about whether or not it was the kind of information that should be passed on to readers. The assaults and slaying, after all, didn't even occur in their circulation area.

They wound up running the next day's story along with a sidebar feature on the revelations in the tape pretty much as their reporter, Mary Jo Kewley, originally submitted it. An editor's note at the top of the sidebar cautioned that the story contained material that might be considered offensive to some readers.

The article repeated John's statements about the inner contest between the Jekyll and Hyde personalities, the "evil part" of him that planned and carried out the torture killing—and the boast of cannibalism. Everyone in Marathon county, except the jury, had an opportunity to learn whatever they may have wanted to know about the hitherto hidden *C* word.

Angry letters to the editor from readers who didn't agree with the decision, began arriving at the newspaper the next day. One disgusted woman writer sarcastically observed that thanks to the *Daily Herald* readers now knew what other newspapers were referring to when they talked about "heinous crimes." In a PS she suggested that the newspaper should be displayed on the top shelves of drugstores and kept out of libraries.

* * *

Not everyone, of course, agreed with the critics. And although the courtroom wasn't completely filled, a majority of the seats were occupied when the trial moved to the testimony stage. The onlookers whispered among themselves about the reports of cannibalism, peered over the heads of their neighbors to catch a glimpse of the defendant, and anxiously awaited the beginning of opening statements.

Many of the spectators were retired residents who preferred the real-life drama of trials to the packaged pablum of television soap operas, game shows, and situation comedies. News reporters usually arrived early to find choice seats near the front of the courtroom, while television camera crews set up and filmed from the back or other vantage spots near the edge of the action.

Ms. Kewley slid into a seat on a bench just to the left of the defense table where John was seated between his attorneys. She was facing the jury box and had a bird's-eye view of the action. Darla Rae Torres was seated a few seats behind her, with her own notebook and pen, and whenever she had a chance she attempted to catch the defendant's eye. John's defenders had already heard the rumors going around that she had more than a casual interest in him. She was talking seriously to friends about putting together a book on John's story, and was staying in a Wausau motel while attending the trial. She dressed casually for most of the trial, in slacks or blue jeans and a casual blouse.

The district attorney shared the prosecution's table with investigators Miller and Carl Petske of the Wisconsin Department of Justice, Division of Criminal Investigation. Bulging accordion files were heaped on top of the table, and at various times during the trial others were stuck underneath at the feet of the DA and his investigators.

* * *

Before permitting attorneys to begin opening statements, Judge Carlson outlined each of the charges against the defendant in explicit detail, defining specific acts of sexual abuse and mutilation. Some jurors and several spectators responded with audible gasps at the vivid description of savagery and depravity. John sat quietly, with his head down while he shuffled through a stack of photographs of family members and of the three dogs buried at the farm.

Carlson also explained the judicial reasoning behind opening statements. Testimony and evidence are presented piecemeal, a bit at a time, jumping here and there with little consideration for chronology. Presented in that manner it can be difficult for jurors to assimilate and put together in an understandably coherent package in their minds. So at the beginning of a trial they are given a reasonably chronological peek at what is to come.

"The opening statements are to give you the picture so that as the evidence comes in you recognize its importance," the judge explained. "You realize where it fits in the general picture of this case." He cautioned the jury however that opening statements are not evidence.

"And if the attorneys in an opening statement make any statements as to what they think the evidence is going to be, which is not proven out, you are not to consider anything that they said as being evidence in any way," he admonished.

Barnett's opening statement was brief. After setting up Carla's photo blowup on an easel about fifteen to twenty feet from the jury, he reviewed the charges once more, repeating much of the same information gone over moments earlier by the judge. He talked of the lack of medical evidence to back up portions of John's statement on the tape about individual acts of sexual abuse of Carla such as inserting various objects into her vagina and rectum. Because of the decomposition process, the fleshy parts of a body eventually vanish, he pointed out. Consequently, the prosecution intended to use circumstantial evidence to prove the defendant's guilt.

While the prosecutor described John's statement about burning Carla's vagina, and sticking pins in her breasts, he turned and looked at the large picture of the victim. When he talked about John slashing off her nipple, then her other breast, he peered at the photograph of the pretty teenager again. At another time he pointed at it.

The district attorney knew exactly what he was doing. There was none of the flamboyance of some prosecutors and trial attorneys in his delivery, and his recitation of facts was dry and nearly emotionless. He dressed neatly but conservatively in dark suits and had the crisp, efficient look of an accountant. His courtroom style throughout the trial would be that of a cautious technician who at times appeared to be paying almost agonizing attention to detail.

But each time he turned to look at the photo, the eyes of every one of the jurors followed him. The contrast between the fresh-faced innocence of the victim, smiling out of the photo at the panel, and the verbal description of her ghastly abuse was devastating. The presence of the dead girl was palpable and hung over the courtroom like a shroud.

Referring to the puzzling shotgun shell found with Carla's remains, Barnett revealed it was the state's theory that when John unloaded Carla's body from the trunk the empty hard cardboard casing somehow got mixed in with the tarpaulin-covered body. "Nobody is contending that John Weber shot Carla Lenz," he declared. The DA claimed, however, that testimony would show the shell was fired by a shotgun owned by John, and establish yet another link between the defendant and the murder victim. When the district attorney concluded his opening statements a short time later, he had spoken exactly thirty-two minutes.

Based on some of his remarks, it appeared reasonably certain that when John insisted to his lawyer and in the letter to

his parents that he couldn't remember shooting Carla, he was
telling the truth.

Before beginning the opening statement for the defense, Lex
asked for a bench conference out of hearing of the jury. The
attorneys and the judge huddled briefly, then Lex began his
presentation. The defense attorney's delivery was also fairly
low-key. Patiently, Lex laid out the facts of the case and the
story as he wished the jury to see it. And he began the job
by reminding the panel again that the defendant had committed
some loathsome acts.

"On November twelfth, 1986, our client, John Weber, kidnapped and murdered his sister-in-law, Carla Lenz," he said.

"On September third, 1988, Mr. Weber kidnapped, sexually
assaulted, and physically assaulted his wife, Emily Weber."

That wasn't exactly astonishing news, but it was important
to demonstrate to the jury that no one was attempting to paint
the young man seated beside Reid at the defense table as an
angel. John scratched idly on a yellow legal pad with a pencil,
while the lawyer opened his defense.

Lex recounted the guilty pleas to nine of the charges, and
indicated that it was part of a search for truth. The district
attorney already admitted he had nothing "aside from the tape
made by John Weber to scare his wife, Emily Weber," the
lawyer declared. "He has no physical evidence directly proving
John Weber is guilty with respect to the remaining charges
against him."

The public defender retraced John's early-morning interrogation by Chief Moore, the drawing of the map that led
authorities to Carla's forest grave, and the seizure of the letters
from John's jail cell. "The documents that have been taken,
together with the tape recording, are riddled with admissions,"
he conceded. "Mr. Weber has admitted to everything in those
documents, except for the charges that remain against him."

He asked the jury to pay particular attention to the admissions in the letters, because they "purport to be suicide documents." He also cautioned that all circumstantial evidence is inferential; it calls for conclusions based on logic.

"John Weber is guilty of what he has done," the attorney declared. "It does not necessarily follow that he is guilty of what he has been charged with," Lex added of his client.

A few minutes later following the conclusion of the defense statement and after the jury left the room for the noon lunch break, Judge Carlson returned to the subject of the earlier bench conference. Lex had asked for a mistrial, citing three separate sets of grounds.

He objected to the manner in which the district attorney utilized Carla's photo; complained that Barnett wrongly claimed the missing leg from Carla's remains fit in with John's statement on the tape; and said he shouldn't have told the jury he was going to bring as much of the cassette tape into evidence as possible.

"I think that's an obvious reference to the fact that the defense has been successful in pretrial motions . . . in excluding certain portions of that tape," he said about the final point.

Lex claimed he was caught in a dilemma when his opponent kept Carla's photo before the jury for the duration of the presentation and repeatedly pointed to it. "We could object and inflame the jury against us for Mr. Barnett placing it up there, or we could face what had been done and try to deal with the problem later," he said.

After listening to rebuttal argument by Barnett, Carlson denied the motions.

Emily was the first witness of the trial. Her family turned out in force for her testimony. Her parents and her two older brothers along with other adult family members were seated together in a group, providing moral support for her during the approaching ordeal. Emily wore slacks and a crisply attractive blouse for her appearance on the witness stand.

During direct examination by the district attorney, she filled in a brief amount of biographical information and said she was currently living with her parents. She told of meeting John when he worked with her mother and brother at the wreath factory in Fifield, of dating him for about eighteen months and then marrying. He smoked Salem Lights and drank Miller beer, sometimes from king-size bottles, she said.

As the DA gently led her through the testimony her voice was soft but audible. She kept her eyes on Barnett, without glancing at the jury or at her husband. John fiddled with a pencil and scratched occasionally at the legal pad in front of him, while he listened to his wife's testimony. He assiduously avoided making eye contact with her.

Emily said her husband was a hunter who had several firearms, including a twelve-gauge shotgun, a .410-gauge shotgun, a .22-caliber rifle, and a .25-caliber pistol. He also had a twenty-gauge shotgun, which she thought may have belonged to his father but was kept at their house. And he had a hunting knife, which was a birthday gift from her parents. Emily identified the .25-caliber pistol, which Barnett removed from a box and showed to her.

The witness described the two nylon athletic bags with the cigarette logos, and confirmed that John had a Cutlass when they married and later purchased a Sunbird. And she testified that throughout their marriage he worked at Winter Wood Products helping manufacture park benches, tables, and wheelbarrow handles.

Barnett led her through the separation when she moved back in with her parents, to her job at Phillips Plastic, and at last to the night her sister disappeared. The DA asked if John knew about the work schedules of herself, her brother Larry, and her parents, and that Carla and Joe were home alone that night. He would have known, she said.

"Would it have been unusual for your sister, Carla, to have

left that home at that time of night after the three of you had gone to work?" he asked.

"Yes," she replied.

"And why was that?"

"She didn't want to leave Joe at home alone."

Emily's replies throughout her testimony, especially the early stages, were short and to the point, generally composed of the adverbs, "yes," "no," or "yeah." She trembled the entire time she was on the witness stand and was clearly looking forward to the time when the ordeal would be over. Barnett provided more information with his questions than she did with her answers.

"Since your brother, Joe, would have been nine years old at the time this occurred, do you have an opinion as to whether Carla under those circumstances, that is, after the rest of that house, rest of the household members have left for work, would have voluntarily stayed out of the home for a period of time other than a short period of time?" Barnett asked.

"You mean do I have an opinion on that?" Emily asked in return.

"Yes," Barnett agreed.

"Yes, I do," she said. "She would have never left the house unless it would have been for a very short time," the witness replied.

At last, after filling in more details about the summer of 1988, Barnett led his witness to the evening of the assault. Emily recounted how John lured her to the farm, had her wait for a while in the polebarn, then picked her up in the car, drove into the woods, and told her to close her eyes.

Emily said he had lifted her hair up and was feeling around the back of her neck when she became frightened.

"Is this going to hurt?" she asked.

She said she felt something, opened her eyes, and saw that John was holding a knife to her throat.

"He asked me if I was seeing anybody," she said, adding that she denied she was fooling around.

"Was that the truth?" Barnett asked.

"Yes," she said.

Emily told about writing the letters and her belief that her husband had a gun with him.

"Now, what if any threats did Mr. Weber make to you to get you to write the letters and complete the checks and fill out the birthday cards?" Barnett asked.

"He said if I didn't, he said if I didn't do it, he would cut my boob off," Emily replied.

While spectators listened in shocked silence and Mary Jo Kewley and other reporters furiously scribbled on notepads, the witness recounted how she was forced at knifepoint to strip to her underclothes. She testified about momentarily breaking away, being dragged back to the front of the car where duct tape was wrapped around her head, her hands were taped behind her back, John sliced off her remaining clothing with a knife, and slashed her breasts, punctured her buttocks, and cut her legs. Barnett asked how deep the wounds on her legs were.

"The one on my right leg closed in about a week and a half. The one on my left leg took about a month and a half to close up," she said. She still had the scars. Then the witness told about John burning her on the right cheek, right breast, and inside her vagina with a lit cigar, and sticking and closing the safety pin in her left breast. Finally she told about the vaginal and anal rape with the wheelbarrow handle.

Emily's testimony was delivered matter-of-factly but her words, which drew a picture of the horror she endured alone in the woods with a bloodthirsty, sex-crazed madman, were as graphic and chilling as any Hollywood slasher movie. It was worse, in fact, because everyone in the courtroom knew that it was more than a simple work of fiction.

It left horrified spectators gasping and rocking back and

forth in their hard pew-like seats. The jurors were also visibly affected, especially the women. Tears rolled down the cheeks of a juror in the front row, and another in the back dabbed at the corners of her eyes with a handkerchief.

Judge Carlson called a short recess and had the jury led from the room. Then he admonished the spectators about their reaction to the testimony.

"I realize this testimony is difficult, certainly for Emily, and probably for other people here. But I would ask that the people in the gallery not make any noises or sounds," he said. "There were a number of audible gasps and sighs and things like that."

He pointed out that he had already asked the jury and others who were involved with the trial to control their emotions, and he expected the same from the spectators. He asked them to remain silent and not draw undue attention "to the already difficult nature of the testimony." If they were unable to comply, or wouldn't, he had the option of ordering them from the courtroom, he noted.

Even though John had already pleaded guilty to all the charges related to Emily's assault, her testimony was devastatingly effective. It was also important to the successful prosecution of the remaining charges against the defendant because the details of the incident, beginning from the time she was lured to the farm, to the time she was bound and attacked, demonstrated a similarity to his account on the tape of Carla's sexual torture and murder. Most of the basic elements, up to Carla's murder, were similar in both incidents.

• John stated on the tape that he lured his sister-in-law to the isolated farm by subterfuge. He lured his wife to the farm with the promise of a surprise that she had reason to believe was tied to their talk of a dream home.

• He boasted that he cut off one of Carla's nipples, then slashed off her other breast with a knife. He told Emily if she didn't do as he ordered her to do he would cut her breast off. Then he carved a couple of slashes around one of her breasts.

• He forced Carla to take off her clothes, then after she slipped her underclothes back on he cut them off with his knife. He slashed Emily's underclothes off with a knife.

• He dug Carla's grave before taking her to the farm and attacking her. He dug another hole, apparently while Emily was waiting for him in the polebarn, before beginning the second assault.

• Comparing the two assaults, it would seem reasonable that if he committed one, he committed the other. They followed the same general pattern.

When court resumed, Barnett turned the narrative to John's attempt to strangle Emily when she pulled her wrists free and struggled to rip his hands from her throat. The DA asked how much she weighed at that time, and Emily said about 113 pounds. She estimated her husband's weight at about 165 or 170.

Barnett asked if John had persisted could he have strangled her despite her struggles, and why she thought he stopped. But Emily was prevented by defense objections from answering either question. However she was permitted to describe how John dragged her through the woods by her hair, then began kicking her and beating her on the head with a shovel.

John kept his head down, fiddling with his stack of pictures, during the nastiest portions of his wife's testimony. Sometimes he studied a particular photo for a moment or two. At other times he betrayed his unease by rapidly flipping through them almost like he was shuffling a deck of cards. Throughout most of the trial, whenever the testimony turned to torture or suffering of the victims, he pulled out his pictures.

Changing directions a few minutes later, Barnett asked his witness if she had an opportunity to listen to part of a certain tape recording. She said she did, and that Sheriff Wirsing had brought it to her.

"Did you recognize the voice on that tape?" the prosecutor inquired.

"Yes."

"In your opinion whose voice was on that tape?"

"John's," she said.

Responding to further questioning a few minutes later, Emily said the defendant brought up her sister's name a couple of times while they were in the woods. The first time he told her he was going to get rid of her like he got rid of her sister. The second time, after he broke off his attack, he claimed he lied when he told her about getting rid of Carla.

Barnett asked about her earlier testimony that every time John knocked her down with the shovel she got back up. "And what do you remember John saying as you are being struck, knocked to the ground, and getting back up each time. What did he say?" the prosecutor inquired.

"He said," she replied, " 'You're going to be a tough one to kill!' "

The prosecutor's direct examination of his star witness was concluded, and Emily was permitted to leave the stand. Defense attorneys withheld their opportunity to cross-examine her until the following morning, so the DA could call on a trio of other witnesses who wished to get their testimony over with and return to Price County instead of staying over in Wausau or driving back to the city for an extra day.

* * *

Park Falls patrolman Josef Jeske was the next witness, and he was quizzed about his part in John's arrest at the Flambeau Medical Center and his guarding of the Cutlass until it was taken away. The other witnesses were Herbert Damrow, the wrecker operator who hauled the car to the Price County Sheriff's Department in Phillips; and Kai Kelly, who bought the Sunbird from Keith Newbury. The court was adjourned at 5:30 P.M.

Barnett also noted that analysts from the State Crime Laboratory had arrived in Wausau the previous night and he asked for permission to reopen his direct examination of Emily to cover some items of evidence they brought with them. In addition he wished to question her about the removal of a few strands of her hair while she was at the medical center in Park Falls to be used in laboratory comparisons. Carlson granted the request.

But the judge rejected an effort by the state to block testimony from Chief Moore about portions of the defendant's early-morning interrogation indicating he was hospitalized for psychiatric treatment when he was fifteen. The allowable testimony included John's understanding of the nature of his illness. The information constituted part of the evidence related to the "free, voluntary, and intelligent nature of the alleged confession made by Mr. Weber," the judge declared. The jury was entitled to know.

When the trial resumed and Emily returned to the stand she identified John's hunting knife as the weapon he held at her throat and later cut and punctured her body with. She also identified the Marlboro and the Winston athletic bags. All three items were placed into evidence.

Turning to her treatment and care at the Flambeau Medical Center, Barnett asked if the attending physician, Dr. James Sergeant, had removed some bodily fluids and other items from her.

"Yes," she replied.

He asked if some of those items were snippets of hair. She said Dr. Sergeant clipped some hair from the back of her head, cutting as close to the roots as possible.

At that point, as Barnett concluded his questioning, Carlson had the jury escorted from the courtroom so Lex could briefly question her out of their hearing before beginning formal cross-examination.

The defense attorney opened his questions by promising the witness he would try to make the process as free of trauma as possible. Then he quickly moved to statements she gave to authorities and asked if she recalled John making references to "Natas" on the night of the attack. There was no response, so he tried again.

"Or a reference to Natas?"

"Yes," she said.

Continuing to respond to his questions, she explained that John was sitting next to her at the farm when he mentioned the entity or being and it was after he stopped beating her. She couldn't say exactly how long after her beating or other abuse that he made the statement because she was lapsing in and out of consciousness.

"Do you recall there came a time when John began to pound his fist into the ground?" Lex asked.

"No," she replied.

After some prodding, Emily said she recalled after the beating that John was talking in two voices while he was referring to Natas. The shaking witness was passed to the DA a few minutes later.

Emily said when they left the farm, her husband told her it

was about 5:30 in the morning. But she couldn't see if daylight was breaking because her eyes were swollen shut.

Lex had one more opportunity to question her before the jury was called back into the courtroom, and he asked how many references John made to Natas and what the substance of the conversation was. Emily recounted the eerie argument that John and the evil alter ego had over her fate.

When the lawyers ran out of questions, Lex reiterated a previous motion to permit Emily to testify to the jury during the guilt phase of the trial about John's quarrel with himself, or with "Natas," before leaving the woods and driving his wife home. The judge stuck by his previous ruling on the matter, however. The testimony would not be allowed during the guilt phase of the trial.

Emily was still seated and waiting patiently when the jury filed back into the courtroom. Her parents and other family members were watching from the gallery, as they had done the day before.

Lex opened his cross-examination by repeating again, in front of the jury, that he wanted to make things as untraumatic as possible. Then he asked if she recalled being questioned at the medical center by Chief Moore on September 5 and September 7 and if both interviews were tape recorded.

Emily said she recalled the interviews and both were taped. The process continued for a while with questions about the pistol she initially believed John had with him at the farm. Emily said she told Moore she believed her husband had the gun because he said he was going to kill himself. Later she learned he didn't have the gun.

Lex inquired if she told Moore at one point, "I thought he had a gun but he didn't have one at all. I don't think he intended killing me." Emily didn't answer. "Do you recall saying that?" Lex persisted.

"No," she said.

Lex questioned her about the trunk key for the Cutlass which she drove after her Monte Carlo was sold, and about the trip she and her husband took to Colorado in February 1987 when he was called back into the Army for temporary duty. Emily agreed they took a large amount of clothing with them on the trip, but said John packed the car trunk. She added that she may "have thrown a couple of things in," but the trunk was already open.

After Judge Carlson upheld an objection from the prosecutor to the line of questioning, Lex turned again to the night of the attack and led the witness through the experience from the time John picked her up at home to the episode inside the car when she was made to write the letters and notes.

The defense attorney asked if she saw a wheelbarrow handle or if John mentioned a wheelbarrow handle at any time during the evening of the attack. She didn't see it because her eyes were taped, and he didn't mention it by name.

"So it was only subsequent to those incidents that you might have found out there might have been a wheelbarrow handle, or wheelbarrow handles, involved? Is that correct?" he asked.

"I don't understand," the witness replied.

"It was only later on that you found out that there were, in fact, wheelbarrow handles involved?"

Emily silently stared back at the defense attorney. There was no reply, and he withdrew the question.

Shifting gears slightly, Lex altered the line of questioning. "Emily, is it a fair statement to say that prior to August of 1988, John never physically assaulted you?" he asked.

"He almost did once," she said.

"When was that?"

She said it was earlier that year, about springtime.

"When you say 'almost did,' he never actually touched you, though, did he?" the lawyer persisted.

"No, because somebody came over then," she replied.

Lex returned the line of questioning to her interview with Moore and the beating. He asked if she saw John wearing steel-toe work boots, or if she saw him wearing sneakers the night of the assault. She conceded she didn't notice or couldn't remember seeing what he was wearing on his feet. He asked if there was a time when John tore out clumps of her hair. She said she believed he tore the hair out with his hands.

"It's a fair statement, is it not, that you were terrified during the course of these incidents on September third?" the lawyer inquired.

"Of course!" she said.

The testimony moved on through other aspects of the assault until the defense finally concluded direct examination and the witness was passed to Barnett. The District Attorney opened redirect examination by turning to the question of John's boozing. Emily agreed that she previously testified her husband didn't appear to be drunk the evening of the attack.

"Have you in the past made any statements to John Weber concerning the extent to which he's been drinking?" Barnett asked.

"I told him once," she replied. "I got mad at him for drinking and I told him he drank so much I couldn't even tell if he was drinking or not."

Through several questions, Barnett established that Emily saw John drinking one beer and heard him popping open another can while they were at the farm.

Barnett then turned to her hospitalization. "Would you please tell the jury the amount of pain that you were suffering on September fifth of last year?" he asked.

"Well, I couldn't move by myself, because everything had hurt so bad," she said. "I had to have the nurses help me move." A few questions about her interview by Chief Moore followed before the DA concluded and Emily was at last permitted to leave the witness stand.

Chapter Fourteen

Guilt

Moore was the next witness and he recounted the high points of his investigation from the defendant's initial report of an abduction and assault on his wife. He was testifying about the early-morning interrogation following John's arrest when the judge called a recess for lunch.

During the panel's absence, the lawyers and the judge sanitized the transcript and the tape Moore made of the interrogation so that it could be presented to the jurors when they returned.

While the defendant stood by as an observer, the judge and the attorneys worked into the lunch break, quibbling over whether or not references to John's accusations to his wife about a romantic interlude with *Patrick Schmidt* should remain in the transcript. The DA wanted them stricken from the guilt phase of the trial, arguing that the information was "immaterial, irrelevant, and highly prejudicial." Reid argued with classic legal hyperbole that it should remain in.

"We believe that the reference to [Schmidt] bolsters our position, or our hypothesis of innocence as to the remaining charges in this case, which is that the allegations raised in the tape recording purportedly made by John Weber for the benefit of Emily Weber were highly exaggerated, to cause Emily Weber much distress," he declared.

Barnett responded that the jury would hear references to a

perceived rival on the other cassette tape that was found in the Cutlass, anyway. John explained his thoughts about Schmidt and Emily in the monologue and said something about refusing to tolerate it. The DA reminded the judge that when John held the knife to his wife's throat and asked if she was being unfaithful to him, she replied that she wasn't.

"And that is true, that she was not at that time being unfaithful to him," Barnett added. "The parties were separated in 1987, over a year prior to the incident, and there was a relationship with another fellow." He argued that if the phrases were left in it would "cast a misleading pallor" over her testimony. She testified truthfully and there was no evidence she had a relationship with anyone other than her husband from the time they reunited in 1987 to the time of the attack, he insisted.

Reid responded by pointing out that the defense wasn't setting out to attack Emily's character. But the disputed phrases were important to show the defendant's state of mind before and at the time of Emily's beating because, as the DA already indicated, it was an issue linked to the attack on her sister.

Carlson ruled for the defense. The disputed lines were permitted to remain in. By agreement of both sides, however, portions of the interrogation dealing with Shelly Hansen, and information about the fact that both she and John had worked at Marquip, were dropped.

When court was called back in session, Moore answered further questions retracing portions of his investigation. His testimony was used to introduce many of the state's exhibits into evidence. By agreement of attorneys for both sides, the police chief's testimony was interrupted briefly so one of the crime laboratory analysts, whose father was seriously ill, could testify out of order.

Michael A. Haas explained he was a team leader with a field response team and a nineteen-and-a-half-year veteran with the agency. It was his job to analyze hard physical trace evidence such as paint, glass, soil accelerants, and explosives. He was present at Carla's autopsy to collect evidence and see to it that photos were taken.

Haas said he carried toxicology samples of Carla's kidney, liver, and brain, along with the black T-shirt, tape unwrapped from the skull, the green tarp, and some small metallic objects from the autopsy room at the VA hospital, and distributed them to the proper parties at the crime laboratory for further study and analysis. Before the T-shirt and the tape could be analyzed, they were placed in dryers to dry out.

A few minutes after taking the witness stand, the crime laboratory analyst was excused and left the courthouse for the drive back to Madison.

When Moore was recalled, he resumed his testimony about evidence collected from the Cutlass and during other periods of the investigation. He said he and his colleagues found about one hundred magazines in the car trunk.

"And how would you characterize the general nature of those magazine contents?" Barnett inquired.

"I would say that those magazines were pornographic in nature. Some of the magazines pictorially spoke of bondage, I believe one was of spankings. And overall, the majority of the magazines dealt with some type of sexual gratification," he responded.

"Okay," Barnett continued. "Sexual gratification from what kind of acts?"

"It would be involving sexual intercourse and oral sex."

"Did there appear to be any depictions of anal insertions?"

"Yes, there was."

Gradually, Barnett's questions were approaching the possibilities of a link between acts depicted in the magazines and statements that John committed anal rape with inanimate objects—the wheelbarrow handles and a beer bottle. Barnett asked if some of the pictures showed objects other than penises being inserted in anuses.

"Not that I recall," Moore replied.

After a few more questions, court was recessed for the day and the jury excused. At Barnett's request, the judge also agreed to eliminate a few more lines from the record of John's interrogation from use at the first phase of the trial. Barnett contended that the lines, "You see, I am insane, and I know it. And it's hard to keep under wraps at times . . ." were more appropriate for the second phase.

The next morning when Moore returned to the witness stand, the district attorney resumed where he had left off, introducing various items of evidence collected during searches at the house on Avon and at the farm. Less than an hour into the testimony, the jury was provided with transcripts of John's interrogation and the tape was played for them. The tape continued for approximately an hour. Following a few more questions by Barnett and brief cross-examination by Reid, the police chief's testimony was concluded for the time being.

Among other points made by the defense attorney, he established that approximately a day and a half lapsed between the time of the attack on Emily and the time Moore took custody of the car. There was plenty of time prior to the arrest for John to have gotten rid of incriminating evidence from the vehicle, at his house and at the farm if he had wished to.

The next witness, Dr. Bennett, was quizzed about the postmortem, with much of the questioning focusing on Carla's missing left leg. He testified it was severed about two inches above the knee and said he couldn't identify exactly what kind of instrument was used to remove the limb. But it was not a saw.

The forensic anthropologist also testified there was a small fracture of the skull at the base of the cranium. A couple of days after the autopsy he also inspected the small bone fragment found near the grave site by Gould. Based on his examination he was about ninety percent confident the particle was human, and was a piece of a tibia—one of the major bones in the lower leg. Because of the poor condition due to the gnawing of rodents, it was impossible to tell if it was from a right or a left leg. The witness said he was unable to establish that the fragment was part of Carla's remains.

During cross-examination Lex asked the witness if he was able to determine if the cranial damage occurred before or after death. Dr. Bennett replied that he had no opinion. "So, in other words, it's safe to say that it could have been some sort of fracture that took place after death?" the attorney inquired. "That's right. Could have been," the witness replied.

In response to further questions about the damaged skull, Bennett suggested that the injury could have been caused in numerous ways, including falling down or being struck with something.

Turning his attention to the missing leg, Lex asked how certain the witness was that it was severed by a sharp object. About one hundred percent, Bennett indicated.

"Is it possible that this could have been caused by, say, the activity of a large animal like a bear?" the defense attorney inquired.

"No," Bennett replied.

Lex passed the witness to the prosecutor for redirect examination. Barnett asked, based on the witness's observations at the autopsy, if the condition of the bones of the neck indicated Carla was strangled.

"There is no evidence of that whatsoever," Bennett responded.

Lex had one more opportunity to question the witness on recross-examination. He asked the forensic anthropologist if when he testified there was no evidence of strangulation, he meant he was able to form an opinion, and his opinion was that Carla wasn't strangled.

"No," Dr. Bennett replied. He explained there were no broken cervicle vertebrae (neck bones), but they wouldn't necessarily be broken during strangulation. The hyoid, the small bone just above the Adam's apple, might be broken, or the ring-shaped cricoid cartilage at the lower part of the larynx could be fractured. But the cartilage was destroyed by decomposition and the hyoid was not recovered from the grave. So they couldn't be examined for evidence of strangulation.

Barnett then established that strangulation could have occurred, but the condition of the remains was so poor that an exact judgment to determine if Carla was strangled simply couldn't be made. It was nearly one P.M. when Bennett was excused as a witness and the jury was given a lunch break.

Dr. Huntington was the first witness when court resumed for the afternoon session. The forensic pathologist was an experienced witness who appeared to be completely relaxed as he rattled off an impressive *curriculum vitae,* listing his education and professional credits.

Unlike many of his professional colleagues who have difficulty speaking in plain English that's comprehensible to people outside the medical and academic communities, Dr. Huntington's testimony was refreshingly understandable and sprinkled with down-home colloquialisms. He had the rare ability to testify about complicated subjects, while using a minimum of esoteric medical or legal terms. Early in his testimony he pointed out the court reporter had asked him "to be very careful with my two-dollar terminology," and he said he was attempting to oblige.

Moving through the autopsy process a step at a time, Dr. Huntington said the basic portions of the skeleton were present, except for the Adam's apple cartilage, the hyoid bone, and the left leg below where it was cut from two different sides on the forward surface and broken off the rest of the way. Barnett asked if he knew if the leg "was artificially removed."

The witness rephrased the question for himself, basically

asking if the leg was severed by any natural process. "Lord, no," he said. It was partially chopped off. But like his predecessor, the forensic pathologist conceded he couldn't identify the tool used to remove the leg, although there were no cross-scraping marks on the bone to indicate use of a saw. When Barnett asked for an opinion about the possible tool, Dr. Huntington suggested an axe or a hatchet—even a knife with a blade large enough so that someone could step on both sides and force it down and through the flesh and bone.

Turning to the injury at the back base of the skull, the witness explained that instead of a fracture, the line where two bones came together was fanned slightly apart. Barnett asked if he had a scientific opinion about what may have caused the fanning.

"Basically, the way you would explain this is a side-to-side pressure effect," he said. The fanning could not have been caused by a punch from a fist, he added in reply to a follow-up query.

There was nothing about the remains to indicate that beer bottles could not have been inserted into the vagina and anus, he stated. But he noted there were no bottles with the remains, and again pointed to the meagerness of soft tissue that would make a determination possible. The same problem with the absence of tissue existed in attempting to determine if the victim's breast was sliced off. There were no marks on the ribs indicating they were nicked or damaged with a knife. But a female breast could be removed by running the knife parallel to the rib cage without touching the ribs, the witness observed.

The prosecutor returned to the question of strangulation. He asked if John had stepped on Carla's throat to stop her breathing while she was going into spasms after her breast was sliced off, would evidence of strangulation necessarily show up in the skeletal remains studied at the autopsy.

"No. There is nothing that would have to show," the doctor said.

Despite the negative reply, it appeared the prosecutor had tied the witness's earlier testimony about the possible cause of the fanning at the back of the skull, to the remark about Carla being held down with a foot on her neck until she died. The jury was left with a dreadfully graphic mind's-eye view of the defendant grinding or twisting his foot from side to side on the dying teenager's neck as she spasmed on the ground.

Barnett asked a few more questions, then turned the witness over to Lex. The first hint of bad chemistry between the two occurred when Huntington asked the lawyer to speak toward him when asking questions. The older he became the more difficult it was to hear, Dr. Huntington said.

Lex quickly established that the tape wound around the skull extended from about the forehead and over the nose. But when the attorney asked if it extended below the mouth, the best he could elicit from the witness was a remark that it "would be reasonable."

Dr. Huntington said he was unable to determine the cause of death, including strangulation or damage to the cranium. When Lex asked about the metal pellets found with the remains, the witness said they were found among some fatty-like material that had settled along the muscle area of the back. But there "was nowhere near a full bird-shot load," so it was an open question if the pellets were fired into her body or if they were already at the burial site and were simply gathered up with the remains.

Lex asked if it was possible the injuries to Carla's cranium could have been caused by dropping from a height of three or four feet and landing on a hard object. Dr. Huntington said he would prefer considering a height of much more than four feet.

"But is it possible?" the defense attorney persisted.

"Counsel, it is possible that a hula girl on an elephant will enter the courtroom within the next five minutes. One should not depend on it," the witness replied. "So the answer is, I believe it to be unreasonable that a height of that, would produce that fanning. Okay, possible, given some structure. But again, unreasonable."

A few eyebrows were raised in the jury box at the unexpected reply. And there was some tittering among the spectators. But Lex appeared unfazed by the witness's analogy.

He asked if during study of the body mass any safety pins or straight pins were found. None were found.

Returning his attention to the skull, the public defender reestablished there were no visible fractures on the outside and that it was possible the fanning on the inside of the skull could have resulted naturally from decomposition.

"Or as a result of the way it's in a grave site, pressing on that skull," the witness replied.

"So, in other words it is possible there was no trauma at all?" Lex asked.

"Exactly what I've said, sir. I am sorry it took you so long to catch on."

Ignoring the final sarcastic jibe, Lex announced that he had concluded with his questions.

Barnett used his redirect examination to again explore the possibility that Carla was shot. Dr. Huntington explained that close-range shotgun blasts leave a single large hole and the wadding is usually deposited into the wound along with the bulk of the pellet load. Injuries inflicted from farther away spread pellets through a larger area of tissue without the wadding. No wadding was found with Carla's remains, and there was much less than a full load of shot.

After some additional discussion of shotgun injuries, the witness testified it was "unlikely to the point of being unreasonable" that Carla died as the result of a shotgun blast.

When Lex approached the witness to ask a few more questions, he was advised: "Strengthen thy voice and proceed." Speaking up in a Bill Clinton rasp, the defense attorney established that Carla could have been struck with the edge of a shot pattern, accounting for finding less than a full load of pellets with the remains. But when he posed a follow-up question asking if Carla could have been lying on the ground, he was greeted with an objection from the prosecutor. Barnett was overruled. When the doctor was allowed to answer, his reply was typically chafing.

"Counsel, the question is fogbound," he protested. While conceding that Carla could have been struck by the edge of a pattern, he repeated his previous statement that it was not reasonable to believe she was killed by a shotgun blast.

The irascible pathologist was followed to the witness stand by a trio of state crime laboratory analysts. Kenneth Olson was the first and he traced his part in the investigation both collecting evidence at the site and examining it in Madison.

Allen E. Wilimovsky, a firearms identification expert, was the next witness. He had examined the fired twenty-gauge shotgun shell found at the grave site, and the Ithaca twenty-gauge pump-action shotgun seized from inside John and Emily's home. Based on a test firing of another shell with the twenty-gauge, and microscopic comparisons, Wilimovsky testified the empty shell found at the grave site was fired with the same weapon.

Barbara LeMay was the final witness from the crime laboratory, and she recounted her work analyzing and comparing the hair, and the examination and inspection of various pieces of clothing, the wheelbarrow handle, and other articles for traces of blood or other body fluids.

When Judge Carlson dismissed the jury for the evening, he advised them they would be returning the next morning for a Saturday session.

Emily's physician at Flambeau Medical Center, Dr. James Sergeant, was the first of nine weekend witnesses and it was quickly obvious he didn't share Dr. Huntington's casual ability to break down tongue-twisting technical medical jargon into easily understandable layman's language. Nevertheless, his testimony drew a ghastly picture of the horrendous physical damage inflicted on Emily.

Dr. Sergeant said he first saw Emily in the emergency room and it was immediately obvious she had multiple injuries. His initial observations disclosed her legs were lacerated, her neck, upper chest, and groin were black-and-blue, and there was redness above the right breast. Her eyes were swollen so tightly closed it was difficult to pry them open so he could perform his examination.

When Barnett asked if he was able to formulate a principal diagnosis based on his initial observation, the witness asked to refer to his records. "She had so many diagnoses I am not sure what we settled on for principal diagnosis," he explained.

After briefly inspecting his records, he reported she had contusions, facial swelling with blood clots under the skin, lower abdomen and of the labia, abdominal pain of uncertain cause, lacerations of the legs including an especially deep slash in the lower left leg that was gaping open—"and a physical condition compatible with a history of being beaten."

Records of the final diagnosis at discharge showed much of the same conditions noted during the initial examination, as well as puncture wounds of the buttocks, lacerations and abrasions in the vaginal area, and swelling due to internal blood loss. She also had contusions, "probably to the liver and pancreas, based on the abdominal pain and the elevated enzyme activities," the physician concluded.

Barnett asked if the injuries to Emily's breasts could have been inflicted with a sharp knife. "I think they are consistent with that," Dr. Sergeant replied. Asked about the injuries inside her vagina, the doctor testified there were abrasions and breaks in the surface of the mucous membrane. "Either forceful rubbing against it with something that was not perfectly smooth would be the common way to get those kinds of abrasions, like deep scrapes," he explained. "Like road burns if you fell and scraped your knee."

The prosecutor asked if the injuries could have been caused

by abuse with a wheelbarrow handle, and the doctor agreed they could have been. He said there were also contusions inside the anus, but although some blood was observed during examination there was no gross amount of bleeding. He agreed again the damage could have been inflicted by the insertion of a wheelbarrow handle.

Reid's cross-examination was brief. He asked only three questions related to the victim's pelvic injuries. There was no advantage for the defense in unnecessarily continuing to dwell on the savage injuries inflicted by their client on his wife.

Heitkemper followed the doctor to the witness stand, and much of his testimony was taken up recounting how he maintained a tight chain of custody while transporting the remains from the shallow grave at the farm to the Sheriff's Department, then on to Madison for the autopsy. The investigator's boss, Sheriff Wirsing, was next on the stand and most of his testimony focused on his part in the handling of evidence, including the Sunbird, the shovel, and John's fright tape.

At midmorning, Lawrence Weber was called as a prosecution witness and told about finding the .25-caliber pistol among his son's belongings and turning it over to a sheriff's deputy along with some other articles. He also explained that after his son hauled a load of sawdust to the farm in his pickup truck, he (Lawrence) sorted out a large number of wooden legs for park benches from the pile and stacked it in a corner of the polebarn to be used later as kindling or firewood. Weber said he had planned to obtain a woodstove for the building. Barnett asked later during redirect examination if part of his son's job at the factory was producing wheelbarrow handles. The witness said that was true.

A Phillips police officer and Chief Deputy Gould testified about their roles handling evidence and chain of possession in the case. Sheriff's secretary and dispatcher Marilyn Kitten and Sergeant Greenwood followed them to the stand.

* * *

Following a lunch break the meticulously censored tape discovered during the search of John's Oldsmobile was scheduled to be played for the jury. As he did when the tape was played during preliminary hearings, the defendant waived his right to be in the courtroom. It was a decision he made against the advice of his legal counsel.

Before the jury was brought back into Court Room Number 5, the judge cautioned the gallery that the tape was graphically explicit and disturbing. He admonished the onlookers against making any kind of emotional displays while it was playing. There were to be "no sharp intakes of breath, no crying or sobbing, no noises, no nothing," he asserted. "If there is, the deputies will immediately remove that person from the courtroom."

Carlson suggested that anyone who was particularly squeamish should leave. "I don't mean to unnecessarily titillate everybody, because I don't believe anybody will find the tape particularly titillating," he said. "But I think you will find it extremely disturbing, and I don't want any adverse reactions from anybody in the courtroom." Then the judge asked the clerk about ventilation in the courtroom and said he didn't want the temperature too warm.

When the jurors resumed their seats in the jury box, Deputy Sheriff Todd Hintz, the final witness establishing the chain of custody for the tape, was called to testify. Minutes later, Barnett announced that he was ready to play the tape. John got up from the defense table and quietly was escorted from the room.

Carlson explained the defendant was exercising his right to absent himself from the courtroom, and advised the panelists the decision should not be considered when they deliberated his guilt or innocence. Then he turned to the matter of the gruesome content of the tape the jury was about to hear. Although he planned to have the tape played from beginning to end without interruption, he promised that if any juror felt they couldn't continue listening without taking a break they should simply raise their hand and he would order a recess.

"The playing of the tape is not going to be a comfortable

experience for anybody, and if any of you at all feel uncomfortable, please don't hesitate to let me know. Or let the bailiffs know. They will be watching to make sure," he said. He suggested that anyone who wanted water should get it before the tape was turned on. A box of tissues was also available, he pointed out. Hintz was instructed to activate the recorder.

As John's voice began recounting the gross sexual and other physical abuse inflicted on the helpless teenager, who was stripped naked and alone in the woods with a sadist, a sense of horror settled over the courtroom.

Despite Carlson's precautions and even with the loathsome portions related to cannibalism, along with references to a dual personality edited out, listening to the defendant's calm recitation of sexual torture and murderous savagery was an ordeal that quickly had several of the female jurors in tears. The tears rolled down the cheeks of some, while their shoulders silently shook. Other jurors choked and sobbed audibly, horrified at the ugly account they were listening to. A few jurors seemed to be trying to shut out the foulness by unconsciously placing their hands over their mouths.

Whenever a woman juror broke down and cried, one of her neighbors handed her a tissue and put an arm around her shoulder to reassure her. Tears also trickled down the cheeks of some of the spectators, but the crying in the gallery was silent.

The judge called a couple of breaks to give shaken jurors an opportunity to collect themselves and get their emotions under control in the jury room before the playing of the fifty-two-minute tape was resumed. During the recesses he cracked a few of his trademark witticisms to relieve the stress. But his jokes were never related to the case and they were never morbid. He was careful to frame them around mundane, everyday affairs, as gentle reminders that life would go on as before. The judge's efforts provided a welcome release from the ugliness.

New horror built on old, as the ferocity described in the narrator's matter-of-fact account increased. Jurors continued to dab at their eyes with tissues and to sob while John turned to his crude insults and threats toward his wife. "You know, women are nothing. They flaunt their bodies and think that they can get anything they want by being a cock tease. Well, they are wrong," he snarled. "I pay them back, and I am definitely paying you back."

The first side of the tape was completed a few minutes later, and Deputy Hintz flipped the cartridge over, reloaded it, and turned on the recorder once more. It was more of the same. When the recorder at last flicked off, the jurors were white-faced and exhausted. For a moment there was absolute quiet in the courtroom. Judge Carlson called a recess and the jury filed outside, walking rapidly as if they couldn't wait to escape.

During the break, John was returned to the courtroom; Barnett advised Judge Carlson that he was ready to rest the state's case; and the defense asked for dismissal of the remaining charges against their client. The defense lawyers contended the state had not proven its case. Carlson denied the motion to dismiss.

The judge also responded with a firm thumbs-down when Reid said he and his colleague planned to recall Emily to the stand as a defense witness for questioning related to "Natas" and the possibility of a dual personality at work within their client's psyche. Barnett also opposed the proposal, pointing out the judge had already rejected earlier requests to go into the same subjects, and noting the hardship that would be inflicted on Emily. She had to make a two-hour drive each way between Phillips and Wausau. The DA obtained permission from the judge to leave the courtroom long enough to advise the Lenzes, who were waiting outside, that they were free to leave and return to their home.

The jurors were recalled long enough to dismiss them for the remainder of the weekend, with instructions to return at nine o'clock Monday morning to begin the second week of the trial. They had listened to the tape, and it appeared the worst was over.

Monday morning, John's lawyers formally advised the court they would not be presenting a defense for their client.

Before proceeding immediately to closing arguments, however, the judge and the lawyers had some details to work out about exactly what portions of the letters John wrote in his cell could be mentioned in the statements and what would be banned. In general, the portions that were eventually excised referred to "sickness," "Natas," and other possible aspects of a dual personality and an uncontrollable dark side to John's personality.

After the jury was seated, members were advised that the defense would not be presenting witnesses, and closing arguments would begin.

Barnett talked again during his summation about the quality of circumstantial evidence, and cautioned the jury that during their deliberations they should disregard any consideration of the second phase of the trial. "We don't have Carla Lenz here to testify of her own first-hand personal knowledge regarding what occurred on the night of November 11 and 12, 1986," he noted. "But we believe, ladies and gentlemen, that through the introduction of circumstantial evidence, coupled with the defendant's own description of what occurred on that night, that we have established proof beyond a reasonable doubt."

He pointed to the passage of time as being responsible for the lack of physical evidence, and cited Dr. Huntington's testimony about the difficulties making conclusive findings at the autopsy. Reviewing other testimony, he noted that John said on the tape he threatened to blow his head off when he first confronted Carla in the car.

"That's the same thing he said he was going to do when he had Emily out there," Barnett declared. "She was going to watch him blow his head off. That's a pattern, ladies and gentlemen. It's part of the plan, part of the preparation the defendant undertook in respect to his assault on Carla Lenz. He further made Carla strip. All at the threat of killing her.

"You remember he said, 'Maybe I will kill you first and then myself,' if she didn't strip? He made the same threats to his wife, ladies and gentlemen. He forced Emily Weber to strip at knifepoint, his own wife."

He talked about Carla slipping her underpants and T-shirt back on after John drifted away into his own reveries, and about the defendant snapping back to reality and slashing off her remaining clothes with a knife. Emily's underclothes were cut in the same fashion. He recounted other similarities in the attacks on each of the sisters, backing up the state's contention that the acts were part of a pattern.

Barnett reviewed physical evidence gathered up by investigators, and the work of the crime laboratory analysts that helped link the material to the victims and the defendant. He held up the pistol used to threaten Carla, and he showed the jury the bloody wheelbarrow handle Emily was raped with. He pointed to a notch cut in the wood, which he said "represented the same thing that the gunslingers from the Old West used to suggest—a victim."

Five of the six hairs removed from the trunk of the Sunbird were consistent with the hairs taken from Carla's skull, according to Ms. LeMay's testimony, he also pointed out.

"That, ladies and gentlemen, is very strong corroborating and circumstantial evidence that Carla Lenz was in that (car) trunk for a period of time," he said.

Turning to John's statement on the tape that he stomped on Carla's toes and broke them after she ran, he noted that none of the toes on her right foot were broken. But the left foot was never found, and he said the defendant's own statement that he thought he broke her toes should be taken as a good indication of the force with which he stomped on her.

Barnett reminded the jury that the defendant said in the tape he put a lot of effort into what he got away with. "And ladies and gentlemen, the defendant is attempting to put a lot of effort into trying to get away with these other sexual assault, false imprisonment, and mutilation charges."

The prosecutor talked about the admissions John made in his jailhouse letters, and about the things he didn't admit, and about some of the crimes he already pleaded guilty to. He scoffed at defense contentions that the suicide letter to John's parents should be considered an indication of remorse.

"Remorse, huh?" he snorted. "The defendant is so calloused as to suggest in that letter, and I will quote: 'I'll bet they make a TV movie out of this. I always wanted to be a star.' "

Turning to the question of motive for the attack on Emily, Barnett said it was, "jealousy, anger, because he felt that she had done him wrong, had abused him in some respects." The prosecutor contended there were similarities in the defendant's motivation for the attack on Carla; that he was tired of being rejected by women. Barnett concluded his statement by asking the jury to return guilty verdicts on each of the remaining charges.

Lex began his summation by admitting his client was no angel.

"Ladies and gentlemen, John Weber is guilty of some vile and disgusting acts. No question about that. We have never asked you to believe or to decide otherwise."

But the lawyer strongly contended that a significant portion of claims his client made on the fright tape were fabrications. There were three reasons for the defense position, he explained. John wanted to scare his wife; he found sexual gratification and fulfilled fantasies by narrating the tape; and physical evidence didn't support many of the claims made.

Lex said John indicated he stomped on both of Carla's feet and thought he broke her toes, but there was no indication of fractures on the right foot, which was intact. No pins, needles, beer bottle or wheelbarrow handles were found with the remains. The lawyer also reminded the jury that Dr. Huntington indicated tape was still wrapped around Carla's skull from the top of her head to below her mouth. If that was so, he asked, how did Carla manage to make the dying statement attributed to her by the defendant: "God damn you, John"?

Lex picked at other evidence, and pointed to the inability of crime laboratory analyst, Barbara LeMay, to find blood on anything she examined, including the inside of the trunk of the Sunbird. "You would think . . . that if John Weber had cut the breast off of a living person that would have generated a lot of blood," he remarked.

He pointed to John's denials in his suicide letters; that most of his claims on the tape were tall-tale telling, fashioned to hurt Emily. Quotes from the letters were stacked, one after another, to buttress the contention that the tape was an unreliable blend of fact and fiction.

"Carla didn't die the death I described on the tape. We fought and she almost won, except when she fell. I caught up to her and I strangled her. . . . She wasn't buried five days after, either. The day after, she was buried . . . the things people read in the paper and see on TV about me can only make matters worse. For the most part these things never happened. Believe it or not, the truth is I killed a girl and almost killed Emily . . . Carla did not go through all of the tortures described on the tape. However she did die. I got scared, we fought, and I ended up strangling her." The letters were riddled with denials that John carried out the torture, Lex observed.

The defense attorney conceded that the natural temptation was to take the attitude, "Who cares what happens to John Weber?"

But he reminded the jury its sworn duty was to vote for

acquittal if it believed the state didn't prove the charges against the defendant. He asked them to vote their conscience.

Since the burden of proof in a criminal trial is on the state, the prosecution is permitted to speak in rebuttal.

Barnett used his opportunity to tell the jury the defense attorney had asked them to speculate, to accept a guess that John's motives for making the tape were satisfying his own fantasy and scaring his wife. "There is no evidence that that was what was intended," he declared. He said they could not speculate, could not guess, and insisted that judging from all the evidence they heard the only conclusion they could arrive at was that the defendant was guilty of the charges. "And you know it. You know it," he concluded.

Judge Carlson advised the jury that they were expected to begin deliberations immediately after he outlined his instructions. Instead of being taken out to eat, box lunches would be ordered for them, he said. Following the lengthy instructions, the names of two jurors were selected by tumbler so the panel could be trimmed to twelve. Two women, Violet Kraft and Dorothy Pabst, were subsequently excused from the deliberations. But that still didn't mean they were free to go. They remained sequestered, although separated from the remainder of the panel, so they would be available in case one of the jurors became ill during the second phase of the trial.

The jury filed out of the courtroom at 12:53 P.M. to begin deliberations. Only unanimous verdicts could be accepted for the first phase of the trial.

Less than two-and-a-half hours later, at 3:15 P.M., Judge Carlson was informed the jury had reached verdicts. When the panel returned to the courtroom, the judge asked jury foreman Terry Peters if verdicts were reached on all nine counts and if they were unanimous. Peters replied that they were.

Judge Carlson read the verdicts aloud from the bench:

"With respect to count two, charging the defendant with sexual contact with Carla Lenz, we the jury lawfully impaneled in this matter, find the defendant John R. Weber, guilty.

"With respect to count three, charging sexual contact with Carla Lenz, we the jury find the defendant guilty.

"With respect to count four, sexual intercourse with Carla Lenz, we the jury find the defendant guilty.

"With respect to count five, sexual intercourse with Carla Lenz, we the jury find the defendant guilty.

"With respect to count six, sexual contact with Carla Lenz, we the jury find the defendant guilty.

"With respect to count seven, sexual contact with Carla Lenz, we the jury find the defendant guilty.

"With respect to count eight, sexual intercourse with Carla Lenz, we the jury find the defendant guilty.

"With respect to count nine, mayhem, as charged in count nine, we the jury find the defendant guilty.

"With respect to count eleven, false imprisonment, we the jury find the defendant guilty."

John kept his eyes closed and his hands pressed to his head as each of the verdicts was read. He slowly shook his head side to side after the last pronouncement of "guilty."

The prosecution had scored a clean sweep: Nine guilty pleas and nine convictions.

Carlson advised the jury that the two alternates would be rejoining them and the sanity phase of the trial would begin the following morning. He cautioned the jurors not to discuss their deliberations on the guilt phase with the alternates. After the jury was dismissed, the DA left the courtroom to telephone the news of the verdicts to the Lenz family. When Barnett returned, the judge granted a defense move to ban the DA from displaying the blowup photo of Carla during the second phase of the trial.

Chapter Fifteen

Sane or Insane?

The job of the public defenders was difficult enough during the first phase of the trial, and it wouldn't be any easier during the second phase.

John Weber had already been found guilty of all eighteen charges against him, either through his own plea or by the jury's decision. Now his attorneys somehow had to convince the panel that he wasn't mentally responsible for his actions at the time the crimes were committed and wasn't able to conform his behavior to the requirements of the law.

But they would be working with the same jury that had heard days of testimony spelling out his meticulous planning of the crimes: the lists, the murder kits, the yarns he made up to lure his victims to the farm, and the elaborate cover story he concocted to explain away Emily's terrible injuries. Perhaps most significant of all, he managed to cover up and get away with Carla's murder for almost two years.

It was damning evidence of premeditation; that with willful deliberation and intent, John had set out to do harm to the sisters. It wasn't an accident that happened on the spur of the moment. It was carefully conceived, and carried out with cold precision.

* * *

There were also some important changes in the rules during the sanity phase of the trial. The responsibility for proof, which was on the shoulders of the state during the guilt phase, passed to the defense in stage two. The public defenders had to prove their client was not mentally responsible—the prosecutor didn't have to prove that he was. It was an important distinction.

The change in the burden of proof also meant that the defense would present its witnesses first, instead of the other way around with the prosecution leading off, as was done during the guilt phase. Finally, in summations, the defense—not the prosecution—would get two trips to the plate. During the guilt phase Barnett spoke first, then after the defense's turn, was given another turn in the batter's box for rebuttal.

Also, this time all eighteen of the original charges, including the nine John pleaded guilty to and the nine he was convicted of after the first segment of the trial, would be considered by the jury.

Tuesday morning the alternate jurors were dismissed for good. A unanimous verdict of twelve jurors was not necessary during the second stage of the trial, as it was at the guilt phase. If one of the jurors became ill during the trial or deliberations, the remainder of the panel could reach a legal verdict that complied with Wisconsin state criminal statutes.

The jury was called in and after brief instructions from the judge, Reid began his opening statement. He explained that it was the defense's contention the defendant suffered from a mental disorder during the time of the attacks against his sister-in-law and wife. The attorney described his client as a sexual sadist, a man who derived sexual pleasure from other people's pain.

"John Weber, since a very young age, has built up an elaborate mechanism, an internal device to deal with his illness, and to hide the extent of that illness from other people, whether it's his family, or whether it's his friends, his very close friends, his wife, the doctors who have attended him.

"Since age eleven, at least that we know and we expect to prove, John has covered, concealed, lied and distorted to keep his secret hidden. This camouflage of his true mental makeup continues to this day. And as we present our case, we want to show you how far that camouflage, that mechanism, has intruded into John's life as he tries to be, maintain the outward appearance of being normal . . . it's clear that . . . struggle failed."

Reid promised the defense would show that since the defendant was a preschool student, people have been aware that he was different, in varying ways. John committed his first known overt act against women when he was five years old and smeared feces on his grandmother's dress. John was a bed wetter, who had trouble making friends when he was a child, and he was picked on by other youngsters.

The defense lawyer recalled John's attack on his sister, Kathy, his diagnosis at the Marshfield clinic as a "disturbed adolescent," other troubles as a teenager, life as a young married man, Carla's murder, and Emily's assault. He said Dr. Crowley would testify that John was a sexual sadist who had a borderline personality disorder and abused alcohol.

If the jury decided John was led to commit the crimes against the sisters by his alcohol abuse, by law he was responsible for the acts, the lawyer pointed out. But if mental disease was the cause, the defendant could not be held responsible.

Barnett opened his statement by pointing out, as the judge noted earlier, that the burden of proof was changed during the second phase of the trial.

The DA said he would prove John was drunk during each of the attacks and that his motives were jealousy and hatred. He added that the definition of mental disease excludes jealousy and hatred. And as the public defender earlier pointed out, intoxication does *not* excuse someone from responsibility for their acts. It was John's own choice to get drunk before each of the attacks.

The question over the effect alcohol had, or may not have had, on the defendant's criminal behavior was critical. If it could be shown that John's mental health was so diseased, fragile, and warped that he was compelled to behave as he did, that would provide strong support for a jury finding that he was not mentally responsible. But if alcohol made him do it, or was a key factor in lowering his inhibitions in order for him to be able to go through with the bestial acts, it was no excuse.

The same issue was central to settling the question of sanity, or mental responsibility, in the trial of Milwaukee cannibal, Jeffrey Dahmer. He was an alcoholic who murdered and dismembered most of his victims, and ate portions of some of their bodies while he was drunk. Largely due to the expert testimony of Dr. Park Elliott Dietz, who is probably the nation's most famous forensic psychiatrist, the jury returned a finding that Dahmer was sane when he committed his crimes. The crux of the message that led to the finding was that the killer cannibal knew his acts were so disgusting that he had to get drunk in order to carry them through.

Getting the same message across was precisely the task that was facing Barnett. Pointing to John's excellent work record and normal-appearing day-to-day behavior as observed by his friends, the prosecutor said he didn't believe the defense could prove their client didn't have the ability to behave lawfully. The defense was in the position of proving John wasn't responsible on the two occasions when he attacked Carla and Emily, despite the fact he planned both crimes weeks ahead. John showed his ability to control his actions when he backed off his threats or broke off his attack on his sister, Kathy, the prosecutor noted. "It was a choice that was within his control."

Barnett said he expected the jury to find the defendant was legally responsible for the criminal acts he was convicted of.

"Did John Weber lack the capacity to conform his conduct to law?" he asked rhetorically. "We believe the evidence won't show that."

Emily was the first defense witness. She testified about her marriage to John, his health problems, his work performance, and their stormy domestic relationship. Lex asked if she remembered her husband doing anything that was sexually abnormal, but before she could reply, Barnett objected that the question was vague. Lex asked if she saw him do anything she considered to be perverse.

"No," she replied.

The lawyer asked if she ever found that some of her undergarments were missing, while she was living with her husband. "Once or twice," she said. Once she realized a pair of black panties was missing, she added in response to a follow-up query.

The attorney asked about John's trouble with impotency and about the boastful lie that he had sex with Emily's mother. Emily said she caught her husband in lies too many times to count.

Lex led his witness through the period of the attack and John's conversation with "Natas." After a few more questions he turned the witness over to the prosecutor. For the first time, however, the jury had heard about the defendant's reputed invisible companion, or evil alter ego.

After a few preliminary questions, Barnett asked Emily if there were any appreciable periods of time when her husband missed work. In September and in November 1987, she said. John was hurt in a motorcycle accident in September, and in November he was injured at work.

"And, of course, that would include the period surrounding your sister's murder, is that right?" the prosecutor asked.

"Yes," the witness replied.

Asked about John's accusations that Emily's relatives, Sal and Paul Avilla, had something to do with Carla's disappearance, the witness agreed the claim led to bad feeling in the family.

Skipping past areas already covered during earlier portions of the two-stage trial, Barnett asked about the cover story John concocted to explain her condition after the assault in the woods. She explained her eyes were swollen shut and she was afraid of being attacked again and killed if she didn't go along with the cock-and-bull tale he manufactured. So she repeated the story to her mother and sister-in-law, to the nurses in the emergency room and to Chief Moore.

After a lunch break, Barnett asked a few more questions, then turned the witness back over to the defense. During his brief redirect examination, Lex asked Emily about the angry letter she wrote early in their marriage when John was refusing to talk to her. Did the threat to reveal a secret that other people would like to know, refer to her husband's inability to perform sexually? he inquired. She confirmed that it was.

"Why wasn't he talking to you?" the defense attorney asked.

Emily was still puzzled by her husband's motivations at the time. "That's what I'd like to know," she replied.

Moore was the next witness, and retraced much of the same area he covered earlier, especially in regard to material involving searches and the collection of evidence. The police chief's testimony was also used to introduce more evidence, including some curious material related to Tracy Boothe.

But some of the most dramatic moments of the trial occurred when the original unedited tape taken from the Cutlass was played for the jury. The judge advised that some portions of the tape dealing with John's mental state and other matters were deleted from the earlier version and explained why they were cut. He also warned the spectators again that the information they were about to hear was disturbingly graphic. Anyone who suspected they might not be able to deal with it should leave because no emotional outbursts would be tolerated, he advised.

Moore clicked on the tape and it barely began to play before Reid approached the bench, and the judge directed it be turned off again. After the jury was ushered outside, the defense lawyer advised that his client wished to leave the courtroom. He explained that initially John thought he could deal with listening to the tape, but after hearing the beginning, before any of the abuse of Carla was mentioned, he realized that if he remained in the courtroom he would create a scene. When Carlson turned to the defendant to question him, John indicated he needed a recess to compose himself.

When the trial resumed several minutes later, Moore had left Wausau in an attempt to reach home before he was caught on the highway by a late winter sleet-and-snow storm that was blowing in off Lake Superior. Investigator Miller filled in for him as operator of the tape recorder. John was again seated uneasily between his attorneys at the defense table, steeling himself for the ordeal ahead.

It was horrible. While the tape played, John covered his ears with his hands. He moaned, his shoulders shook with sobs, and tears streamed down his face into his beard and dripped onto the table in front of him. Some jurors were unable to keep the tears from their own eyes, and despite the judge's warnings, muffled sobs were also heard here and there in the gallery. While some jurors cried, others stared at the defendant, as if they couldn't believe the voice narrating such a cold, matter-of-fact account of sexual abuse, torture, and murder could belong to the young man. One male juror kept his head down, scribbling furiously in his notepad.

Twice, Carlson was forced to call recesses so John could

be helped out of the courtroom and given an opportunity to compose himself. He stumbled and lurched between his attorneys like he was drunk. The second time he broke down, during the account of Carla's abuse, he gasped to his attorneys: "I can't take it. Stop!" His legs were shaking so uncontrollably when he stood to leave that the lawyers had to support him and help him out.

Another time a recess was called so one of the jurors could get herself together emotionally after she broke down at some of the references to cannibalism. The voice on the tape had just stated, ". . . I made myself some patties, and I ate Carla's leg." When the shaken woman returned, two other jurors patted her comfortingly on the shoulders and attempting to assure her by their actions that everything was going to be all right.

Judge Carlson was sympathetic and considerate, and played big brother to the jurors, doing his best to help them through the traumatic experience. Everyone—judge, lawyers, jury, spectators, and especially the defendant—was relieved when the approximate hour-long tape finally ended. John's face was zombie-white and he looked exhausted. At 5:06 P.M., the ashen-faced jurors were dismissed for the day.

Moore returned to the witness box at the beginning of the ninth day of the trial for continued cross-examination by Lex, and provided testimony leading to the introduction of additional articles of evidence, including the contents of the black bag found in the car trunk, girlie and porno magazines, and the dirt-soiled toy rabbit with the hole cut in the crotch. The stuffed rabbit was Emily's. Moore also read aloud from two of the lists, written in the defendant's handwriting. One was taken from the clipboard, and the other found stuffed between the pages of some of the girlie magazines.

On the back of the paper found on the clipboard, one of the notations read: "Take shot in dick just before PH 2. 3cc." But the most chilling reminder advised: "Burial spot. Compost heap? When does Dad use it? Make sure compost heap is same as before execution." When the witness finished reading the first list aloud, he was handed the list Investigator Miller found during inspection of the magazines, which he read as well. A bit later in the questioning, he read from a third list—a note found on the kitchen floor of John and Emily's house that was written on the back of the army equipment maintenance inspection work sheet.

Moore was handed four of the magazines taken from the car trunk and agreed with the defense attorney that they depicted a form of deviant sexuality. Lex asked for a closer description. "These four magazines deal with anal intercourse," Moore responded. One of the magazines also depicted spanking photos.

By that time jurors had heard so much deviant sexual material and chilling references to murder plans, there was no longer any outward reaction. There were no gasps, no tears, no need for recesses in order to repair emotional damage.

Questioning of the police chief droned on and on, until the witness was finally passed to the prosecutor. Barnett handed another pornographic magazine taken from the car trunk to the witness and asked him to describe the photograph on the back cover. Moore said it showed a model inserting a wine bottle into her vagina. Handed another magazine, he described photos including a picture of a leather-garbed woman with whips, and of another woman in bondage.

Social worker Donna Searle followed Moore to the stand and testified about her meetings with the defendant at the jail. Then John's friend Tim Denzine was called as a witness. Reid asked if he and John ever talked about devil worship. Denzine said they hadn't.

The public defender asked if he recalled talking to a woman investigator by telephone on the previous December 14. Denzine remembered talking to someone then. Did he also recall discussing devil worship with the investigator? the lawyer asked. Denzine conceded that she may have asked him about it.

"You don't recall telling her that John discussed devil worship about once a month?" Reid persisted.

"No."

"You didn't tell her that John always brought it up, talking about things like spinning records backwards?"

The witness began to waffle a bit. "If he had, if he'd have mentioned it, it was only once, and it was no once-a-month deal or anything like that."

"All right. So he did mention devil worship?" the lawyer persisted.

Denzine moved further back into his former position. "If it had come up, but not that I can remember," he said. The young North Woods native was stubborn and wasn't going to be pushed into saying anything he didn't want to say. He was guarded and seemed to have a natural ability to play his testimony close to the vest. But Reid wanted more, and he wasn't giving up easily. He asked the witness if he recalled telling the investigator that John had advised him that if the records of certain rock groups were played backwards, Satanic words could be heard. Again Denzine said he didn't recall his friend telling him that. "I just knew that from people saying it. I've heard that . . . ," he began.

Reid cut off the answer before he could finish, asking if he was saying he couldn't recall John specifically saying that. Denzine agreed that was the case. In reply to another question, Denzine said he didn't remember people teasing the defendant about his ideas of cult worship. Reid asked if he remembered telling the investigator that a foreman at Winter Wood Products sometimes teased John. Denzine conceded the foreman had mentioned it, but pointed out he teased people about a lot of things. He didn't think the foreman meant anything by it.

Reid continued pushing for a more definitive statement link-ing the defendant to devil worship or belief in Satanism, but without significant success.

"You don't particularly want to be here today, do you?" he finally asked.

"No, I don't," Denzine agreed.

Reid briefly changed directions, but after a few more questions he turned again to the matter of John's reputed link to some Satanic beliefs. He asked Denzine if he recalled telling Agent Miller in October 1988 that John claimed he could spin certain records backwards and hear Satanic messages. He said he couldn't remember making statements of that kind to either of the investigators.

John's mother was the next witness, and before she was called to the stand, Judge Carlson rejected a defense motion to bar the press from photographing her. He said he understood the motivations behind the request, but there wasn't any legal authority to approve a ban. The sixty-seven-year-old woman turned to her son before taking the stand and told him, "I love you."

Questioned by Reid, she traced John's early problems with bed-wetting and his difficult childhood. She had barely begun to answer questions and was talking about John's feeling that he was the dummy of the family, before she broke down in tears. She sobbed throughout her appearance as a witness.

Despite the difficulty, she continued her testimony while the public defender led her into other painful areas of the inquiry. He asked if when her son was about ten or eleven years old she found something unusual in his bedroom.

"Nasty magazines," she replied.

Reid asked if the magazines were more explicit than *Playboy* or *Penthouse.*

"Very," she said. "I only had to read about three lines, and I could——I destroyed 'em." She added that some of them dealt with bondage. "I didn't even know what it was." But secret caches of the magazines continued to turn up from time to time after the initial discovery, she indicated. "It was something that kept happening."

The brokenhearted mother's testimony was agonizing, and sometimes she spoke so low that observers in the courtroom could hardly make out her words. But gradually the lawyer moved her through John's attack on his sister with the beer bottle and his treatment at the Marshfield Clinic, his threat to Kathy by putting a gun to her head, his running away from home, and finally to the completing of his final year of high school in LaCrosse while he was living in the group home there.

Reid backtracked, returning to the defendant's youthful habit of stashing dirty magazines here and there. Reid asked if anything unusual was found in the shed at the farm in 1980 before Kathy was hit on the head with the bottle.

"We found some more stinky magazines. And some rope, some tape, and the magazines," she replied.

"Again, it may be clear to everyone, but I want to make sure. When you say 'stinking magazines,' do you mean something that's . . . ," the public defender began. The witness replied before he could complete the question.

"It's something I hate. Despise. Terrible magazines. They were no Playboy. They were worse," she said.

Mrs. Weber told about checking her son's room with Kathy and another daughter, and discovering dirty books. She didn't read the stories, but her daughters did. Kathy's name was substituted for a character in one of the books, and a girl who was one of John's schoolmates was substituted for another. Referring to her son as "Johnny," the witness said he wrote his own stories from the publications and substituted real people in place of the fictional characters.

She agreed with the attorney that the stories described sexually violent acts and meticulously detailed plans. One of her son's tales involved a teacher who was "very pretty and very nice," and was admired by her son and other boys in the school.

* * *

Shortly after telling about finding some writings in her son's bedroom at the family home after the attorneys asked she and her husband to look through his things, Reid called for a break. During the recess, Mrs. Weber and her boy smiled and waved at each other. Then each of them broke into tears.

After court resumed, Reid used Mrs. Weber's testimony to enter some curious Tracy Boothe notes and a map to her parents' home into evidence. The witness confirmed the seven-page letter was in her son's handwriting. She explained he was lefthanded and sometimes he wrote in script, and sometimes he printed.

Reid asked if she recalled telling a state law enforcement investigator who talked with her after her son's arrest that the person who did those things to Carla and Emily wasn't the John she knew.

"That's the way I feel," she said. "John is sick."

When the district attorney took over the questioning, he explained that although he knew cross-examination would be difficult for her it was a job he had to do, and said if she wanted to take a break at any time just to let him know. While replying to queries about her son's work at the store when he was a youngster, Mrs. Weber's pride in his performance was obvious. The boy was a devoted worker. She also talked proudly about his scholastic performance in LaCrosse.

When the questions turned to the Lenz sisters, Mrs. Weber said she liked Carla. She was less enthusiastic about Emily. When the district attorney asked what her feelings were in respect to the marriage between her son and Emily, she replied: "That's a hard one to answer. If they wanted to be married, we gave them the permission and everything. But I didn't think that it would last. Two weeks after they were married she was going with someone else."

"In your mind, do you consider Emily to be at least partly the reason why John finds himself in the predicament he's in?" Barnett inquired.

"I do," she said.

"And why is that?"

"Because they fought forever-and-ever-and-ever over everything."

Barnett asked if she believed her son attacked Emily because they quarreled so much that he was driven to the act by anger. She replied with a "yes," before the DA finished with the question. The judge sustained a defense objection to the question, but it had already been asked and answered.

The jury appeared unimpressed by the preposterous thesis that it was Emily's own fault she was so brutally attacked and beaten. It was difficult to conceive of anything Emily could have possibly done that was so deceitful or mean it justified such savage abuse.

Kenneth Kjer, an investigator for the state public defender, followed John's mother to the witness stand. At Reid's request, he read more of the defendant's lists, then launched into a detailed reading of a scheme hatched by the defendant for stalking, kidnapping, raping and otherwise sexually abusing a woman named Brenda. The most ominous phrase in the account occurred at the very end of the reading, just after a description of anal rape, when the witness read: "Then begin close down."

It was left up to the jurors, who had such difficulty dealing emotionally with the defendant's own finely detailed narrative of Carla's abuse and murder, to imagine what he meant by "close down." Barnett had no cross-examination, and Carlson called a brief recess.

Lawrence Weber was the first witness called after the jury returned to the courtroom, and like his wife, he retraced his son's troubles during his early years and his service in the Army. While Weber testified about the death of Brownie and her pups, John cried. Reid introduced three of his client's personal snapshots of the dogs as evidence.

During cross-examination, Barnett asked the witness if he had expected his son to eventually marry the younger sister.

"I had hoped he would," the senior Weber replied. He agreed it was true that he believed a marriage between John and Carla would have been good for his son and had a good chance of succeeding.

"Were you surprised when he decided to marry Emily?" Barnett inquired.

Weber said it was up to his son to marry whoever he wished, but he didn't believe John considered the matter carefully enough ahead of time. He thought his son had made a mistake.

During redirect examination, the witness testified his son told him about drinking and about a girlfriend in Colorado from his Army days that he thought he might marry someday. John also told him he killed Tracy Boothe's big guard dog with his bare hands.

Barnett asked John's father on recross examination if John told him that the girl he was talking about marrying already had a husband. "He said she had left her husband," Weber replied. When the witness left the stand he held his son's hand for a moment and patted him on the back.

The final witnesses of the day were state investigators Miller and Vogt, who testified about their interviews with Tim Denzine.

The lengthy trial was rapidly winding down, and the jury, the press, and a small but devoted band of spectators still didn't know for sure if they would hear directly from the young man convicted of the terrible crimes. Judging from his shaky reaction when he listened to the tape, however, it appeared highly unlikely his attorneys would permit him to testify and subject himself to Barnett's cross-examination.

More friends and acquaintances of the defendant, along with a couple of mental-health professionals and Wisconsin state trooper Bryan Vergin, testified during the Thursday session. Dr. Garvey, the psychiatrist who treated John in Wausau in 1980, testified about the patient's behavior in holding back information and attempting to manipulate his therapists. He and a colleague concluded that "what you saw wasn't necessarily what you got with John," the psychiatrist stated.

Prior to beginning of testimony, however, Barnett renewed a motion to exclude testimony "concerning any romantic relationship Patrick Schmidt may have had with Emily Weber in 1987" while she and her husband were separated. Testimony about a reputed affair would have the effect of putting Emily on trial, he claimed.

Judge Carlson explained that questioning would be permitted in order to show John's state of mind, what he believed to be true. But he wouldn't permit attorneys to ask Schmidt directly if he indeed had an affair with Emily.

Late in the day, following testimony by the defendant's former girlfriend from LaCrosse, Tracy Boothe's mother was called as a defense witness. Lex showed her some letters referring to the reputed suicide of her daughter, and asked if she had a son named "Tim." She said she had four boys, in addition to her daughter, but none by that name. She denied writing either of the letters and said the only time she saw them before was when they were shown to her by an investigator. She didn't recognize the handwriting.

"Those letters, in fact, refer to the death of your daughter, do they not?" Lex asked.

"Yes," she said.

"And she's still alive?"

"Yes."

During cross-examination by Barnett, the witness revealed that her daughter had a brother-in-law named Tim. He was married to the sister of Tracy's husband.

Tracy was the next witness and was asked by Lex to point out John Weber. "He's sitting there, in the checkered shirt," she said, pointing to the defendant. Lex asked if they had a sexual relationship.

"Yeah," she conceded.

"Did you ever notice anything unusual about John's ability to perform sexually?" the lawyer asked.

"He was unable to maintain an erection," she responded. But in response to another question, she said there wasn't anything unusual about the type of sexual activities he liked. Tracy related that she was still married and hadn't continued any type of relationship with the defendant. She was the mother of a boy born in 1983. Lex showed his witness the "An Ode To Tracy Boothe."

She replied "yeah" to a query a few moments later asking if she recalled a girl being killed at the Army base while she and her husband were in Colorado. When Lex followed up by asking when that was, however, the line of questioning was abruptly shut off by an objection from Barnett. Lex withdrew his last question, but the mind's-eye picture of John as a possible multiple killer hung over the courtroom. It was a question, along with its predecessor, that would never have been asked by the defense during the guilt phase of the trial. But if jurors suspected the defendant was a multiple killer, they might also believe that he was insane or otherwise so mentally disturbed that he was unable to control his actions.

Lex handed the witness a small white envelope and asked her to open it up and identify the contents. Tracy said it was her old military ID card, which she was issued as the dependent of an active-duty soldier.

"Are you responsible for ripping it in half?" the public defender asked.

"No, I am not," she replied.

Lex asked her to look at the face in the portrait on the ID and asked if she was responsible for punching the hole through it. She wasn't. Tracy said the last time she saw the card was just before her purse was stolen in Colorado Springs. The thief was never caught.

During cross-examination, Tracy admitted she posed for the revealing photographs, and said she had no idea why John mailed them to her husband. He was suspicious that something was going on between her and their boarder but he didn't have any proof until he saw the pictures. She also said, during recross-examination, that her husband did not have a weapon when he confronted John and told him to get out of the house.

Sal Avilla was called a few minutes later as the last witness of the day. He testified about his confrontations with John over Emily and the $50. Lex asked if he ever paid the $50 back to Emily. He said he didn't.

A fierce blizzard was raging outside, whipping a slick cover of snow on streets and sidewalks, when John's sister Kathleen appeared as the first witness Friday morning. She testified about her brother's childhood and his increasingly frightening behavior, including the attack on her with the beer bottle. The twenty-seven-year-old witness, who moved to New Hampshire shortly after her brother's arrest, said it was difficult putting everything together after so many years of blocking it out.

"I was always wary and well aware of what was going on when John was around," she declared. "I was extremely afraid of him for my life."

Despite her admitted fear while her brother was growing up, like her parents, Kathy's continued love for him was obvious. "You couldn't find a person with a bigger heart than he had," she said. But as her recollections flickered back and forth between fear and love, she broke into tears and the testimony was momentarily interrupted while Reid handed her a box of tissues. She wanted to finish telling the court some of the good things she remembered about her brother, however.

"With the type of person he was, he would do anything for anybody that needed help; anybody who had a problem," she said, struggling to keep from breaking down again. "He was always there for me if I had a problem. He would do anything, especially with animals, or the family, or even the neighbors. He shovelled all the neighbors' walks and mowed their lawns, the elderly women who couldn't do it themselves. He'd go and do it, you know. He was so good-hearted."

The contrast between the good little brother who helped people and was kind to others, with the evil brother who at other times committed monstrous acts was startling—and sad. It also demonstrated the two facets of the defendant's personality the public defenders were determined to illustrate.

"I imagine that's what made the other side hard to understand?" Reid said, posing his observation as a question.

"Definitely," the witness agreed.

When questioning turned to Carla, Reid asked the witness what she thought when she learned in 1986 that the teenager had vanished.

"My heart sunk," the witness replied. She and one of her sisters and a brother all came to the same conclusions at various times. ". . . Carla and I looked very similar, and as soon as I saw her picture in the paper for the missing, I knew that he had something to do with it," she said. "I didn't know what, but I knew he was involved."

Kathy never went to the police with her suspicions. "I just felt that it was sick of me to think that way, that how can I . . . put the blame on somebody who's trying to do better and . . . help himself," she explained. "I just felt guilty for even thinking those thoughts."

Barnett asked on cross-examination if she would have been

surprised if her brother had elected to marry Carla instead of Emily. Kathy said she would have been surprised because she had no idea what was going on between her brother and the sisters.

"Okay, but you were aware that your brother had feelings toward Carla?" Barnett persisted.

"No, what I was aware of was whatever was written in Carla's diary as to she had feelings for him," the witness responded. "That's all I knew. I had no idea that he liked her." Kathy hadn't known her brother was in the habit of confiding in Carla about his marital difficulties. She said he also confided in her.

During redirect examination, Reid showed her three bras and asked if she was the owner. After looking them over and checking the size, she confirmed they were hers. The lawyer asked if she would be surprised to learn the bras were found in her brother's car during the search. She wasn't surprised.

Barnett observed during recross-examination that a large number of bras were found among her brother's belongings during the car search and the sizes ranged from thirty-two to thirty-six. "Knowing that, you're not suggesting that all of those bras were yours?" he inquired.

"Maybe not all of 'em. My sister, her bras were missing. More of mine were missing," the witness stated.

"Okay, but you didn't wear different size bras did you?" the prosecutor persevered.

"No, so they could have belonged to my sister."

"Okay. They could have belonged to other women, too?" he asked.

Kathy conceded the point. "Sure," she said.

Dr. Crowley was the next witness, and after exhausting and sometimes difficult to follow testimony, a recess was called and the jury was sent out of the courtroom.

As soon as the jurors were gone, Barnett asked for a directed verdict from the court in favor of the state on the issue of legal responsibility. The defense had failed to prove that John suffered a mental disease and that as a result of that affliction he was substantially incapable of conforming his behavior to the law, he contended.

In response, Reid argued that evidence showed it was "the mental disease, sexual sadism, John's dark side" that made him unable to conform his conduct to the law. As an example, he pointed to Emily's testimony that immediately after the attack her husband spoke in a different voice, referred to as "Natas," and the two voices held a debate over her life or death.

Judge Carlson took the motion under advisement. In the meantime the trial would resume. The jury was ushered back into the courtroom, and Barnett called the last witness of the day.

Twenty-two-year-old Patrick Schmidt testified about some frightening confrontations with the defendant. The young man was not asked, either by the prosecutor or by the defense, if he indeed had an affair with Emily.

When Schmidt's testimony was concluded, the jurors were excused and sent back through the snowstorm to their rooms at the motel.

It had been a long day.

The next morning, the second Saturday and the twelfth day of the trial, Barnett called executives representing the defendant's former employers as his lead-off witnesses. They described John as a productive, responsible employee, and the prosecutor showed through their brief testimony that the defendant was able to function normally.

Dr. Miller was the final witness of the proceeding, and at 3:10 P.M., after the state rested its case, Judge Carlson ordered a twenty-minute recess so he could discuss jury instructions with the attorneys prior to beginning of summations. A total of 203 pieces of evidence were presented during the lengthy two-phase proceedings, far more than any of the attorneys had ever had to deal with before in a trial.

Following a five-minute break, Reid began his summation for the defense. He argued that long before Carla was murdered and Emily was attacked, his client's behavior had shown he wasn't responsible for his actions.

Taking a swipe at prosecution's contention that John's alcohol abuse created the condition and state of mind leading to the attacks, Reid labeled the drinking theory an easy excuse. It was an excuse John had used himself, and it was true he was a heavy drinker, he pointed out. "But we have adduced testimony, and we have shown you from the witness stand, that when John Weber drank, and he drank to excess often, he didn't get violent. He didn't lose control. He didn't go out and hurt people."

Reid cited testimony by John's father and by Emily that he said showed his client wasn't drunk when she was attacked. And he wasn't drunk when Kathy was attacked in 1979 and 1980, he added.

"There are only a couple of times where he said it was the alcohol that made me do it. Other times he said, 'Well, I took alcohol, but I took it to keep from doing it.' "

Barnett opened his closing argument by providing the jury with a vivid description to sum up what must have already been among their conclusions about the skinny bearded murderer and sexual sadist sitting quietly at the defense table.

"John Weber is a fraud. He is a liar. He is a manipulator. He is self-centered. He is a person who will disclose only that which he believes places him in the best light, and no more. He is someone who consciously, willfully, intentionally, and deliberately kept to himself the person that he really and truly is."

The DA said the tragedy of the case was pointed out earlier

in testimony by Dr. Miller. "That he (John) was unwittingly aided in those efforts by his well-intentioned parents and siblings. But there can be, ladies and gentlemen, no doubt, there can be no doubt but that John Weber is legally responsible, legally culpable for his acts."

Barnett talked about the defendant's careful preparation for the assaults on Carla and Emily, and years earlier, on Kathy. Why was Kathy able psychologically to disarm her brother? the DA asked. If John truly wished to follow through on his acts, he could have. Except for the brother and sister, the house was empty. And in one instance, the pickup truck was loaded and ready to go. "And there would have been nothing Kathy Weber could have done to have prevented the defendant from carrying out his plan, if in fact, he was not in control."

Then Barnett pointed out the critical difference between the attacks. John wasn't drinking when he went after his sister, but he guzzled can after can of beer before the attacks on Carla and Emily. "The evidence is clear, crystal-clear . . . the alcohol brought about the state of mind necessary to do those acts," he declared. Judge Carlson pointed out in the jury instructions that voluntary intoxication by drugs or alcohol did not constitute a mental disease, the prosecutor reminded the panel.

Barnett cited statements in John's suicide letter to his parents putting the blame for the attacks on his drinking and his decision to drink. "Alcohol played a very big role in my life. It's a depressant, and that's what it did. It depressed me, allowing my potential to slip away and bringing up my sickness to full power. I can't blame the alcohol, for it was me who drank it and me who felt I needed it. I know without alcohol this would never have happened. . . . The beer took away my freedom and left me with that sickness to deal with."

Claims that John drank to control his criminal impulses were also attacked by the prosecutor. He cited testimony by Dr. Miller that his studies showed alcohol decreases or eliminates inhibitions. It doesn't help people control their impulses.

Barnett also pointed out the conflict in the testimony of the defense psychiatrist, Dr. Crowley, and the typewritten report he submitted after his examination of John. The psychiatrist's testimony in court that he concluded "to a reasonable degree of medical certainty" that John lacked substantial capacity to conform his conduct to the law wasn't reflected in the report. Pointing out that Dr. Crowley had testified in more than five hundred criminal cases, the prosecutor said he didn't believe the doctor's testimony that he must have made an oversight. "It doesn't appear in his report because it's not what he, in fact, concluded," Barnett declared. To support his statement, he read a paragraph to the jury from a supplementary report:

"With regard to his capacity to conform his conduct to the requirements of the law, my opinion also remains the same. It is simply not possible for me to quantify the effect of the alcohol consumption on his acts. In other words, I do not have an opinion to a reasonable degree of medical certainty whether he acted because of the mental disease as defined above or because of his intoxication."

Expert testimony from the psychiatrists indicated John was aware of the wrongfulness of his acts, and the steps he took to conceal his behavior "were evidence of his recognition that what he had done was wrong," the prosecutor contended.

In rebuttal, Reid reminded the jury that even if they found his client was not mentally responsible they wouldn't be doing him a big favor. Instead of going to prison he would be sent to a mental institution, and could not be released until a court found that he was no longer a danger to the community. "I think you know what that means," he added, in what was apparently an inference that John would never again be free. The lawyer also pointed to the suicide letter John wrote to his parents declaring that he couldn't stand living in a mental institution.

The public defender asked the jury not to forget during deliberations to consider John's eerie conversations with "Natas" that were first overheard by his sister, and later by Emily, before deciding if he could have suffered a temporary psychosis.

After explaining his jury instructions, Judge Carlson ordered the panel to begin their deliberations. It was 5:28 P.M.

At 6:52 P.M., Jury Foreman Terry Peters notified the bailiff that verdicts had been reached. At 7:01 the jury of seven women and five men filed back into the courtroom and Carlson asked for the verdicts. John's mother was in the courtroom on one side of the aisle; Emily was seated with her family on the other side, awaiting the verdicts.

The judge read the verdicts after they were passed to him by a bailiff. The jury voted eleven to one that the defendant was not suffering from a mental disease when Carla was attacked and murdered, he announced. Barbara Fear was the lone dissenting juror.

The jury reached the same finding in regard to the attack on Emily, again by an eleven-to-one margin, with Ms. Fear casting the lone dissenting vote.

Emily permitted herself a faint smile as she listened to the verdicts, but showed no other emotion.

John also failed to show any major display of emotion. He remained quietly seated with his elbows resting on the defense table, his fingers tightly locked and his chin resting on his knuckles. He no longer had to worry about spending the rest of his life in a psychiatric hospital ward. Rejection of the insanity plea eliminated the mystery of what would happen to the North Woods sadist. The penalty for first degree murder was a mandatory life sentence in prison. If the judge chose to do so, he could also stack up 289 years on top of the life term for the other crimes, and add on a $20,000 fine for the lone misdemeanor.

After the jury was polled and confirmed their individual votes, Carlson thanked them for their service and released them to be driven to the motel, pick up their belongings, and return to their homes.

The judge announced he would schedule sentencing later in Price County, where the crimes occurred. John was led from the courtroom and returned to his cell at the Marathon County Jail.

The jury unanimously agreed not to discuss their verdict with the media. But Reid said he planned to appeal the verdicts from both phases of the trial. And Sheriff Wirsing told reporters that the verdict had lifted "a very big weight off our shoulders." After John's transfer back to the Price County Jail, he would be put on a suicide watch, Wirsing said.

Emily and her family walked to a Burger King next door to the courthouse.

Epilogue

After evaluation at the Dodge Reception Center, John was transferred to the Columbia Correctional Institution at Portage. Emily obtained a divorce shortly after his transfer there.

At the edge of the scenic Wisconsin Dells recreation area, CCI is the state's newest maximum-security prison, and it is the institution where some of the most dangerous convicts are kept under lock and key. One of John's fellow prisoners was Jeffrey Dahmer before his murder by another inmate.

Soon after John's arrival at CCI, he received a written invitation to explore the Bible with a sincere would-be pen pal. Others have also written, suggesting correspondences for various reasons. But his closest new relationship was formed with the attractive blonde divorcee from Price County who had so faithfully attended his pretrial hearings and trial.

Darla Rae Torres began writing to him at the Dodge Reception Center five months after his conviction, and they eventually agreed to collaborate on a book project. After almost a year of correspondence and sending him photographs of herself, she visited with him for the first time at CCI. The first day they visited, John hugged his guest and told her her hair smelled like springtime. Another nine months of correspondence followed before she visited again; and after moving to Eau Claire, which was an easier drive, she began piloting her late model Cougar straight down I-94 for visits every other week.

Leaving her car in the parking lot, she walked between two tall guard towers and into the administration building where the visiting room is located. Personal body searches are not conducted on visitors as part of the normal routine, but each guest is required to pass through an electronic metal detector. John's friend quickly learned not to wear jeans with rivets or underwire bras which could set off the alarm bells.

CCI permits "contact visits," meaning that John and his guest were permitted to kiss once in greeting as they met in the large, noisy visiting room, and again at the end of the meeting. In between times they sat at opposite sides of a heavy table that was bolted to the floor, talking and holding hands. Like many of the prisoners with women visitors, John has fretted about the regulations and once complained to his friend about a guard's admonition against "illegal body contact." It sounded like the guard was talking about a football game, he groused.

Curiously, Weber and Torres realized they shared the same middle name, although his was the masculine spelling, "Ray," and hers was the feminine "Rae."

It wasn't long before John lifted the title of a favorite song "Angel Eyes," and bestowed it as a pet name on the leggy green-eyed blonde from Price County. At times she called him by the pet name "Johnny Cat." And, according to Darla, as their chats drifted from book talk to more personal matters, he confessed, "I would have killed for a relationship like ours." It was a strange remark that from someone else could be airily passed off as a harmless figure of speech. Coming from John, it was likely to be interpreted as a malevolent double entendre.

Although Darla wasn't a native of Price County, she grew up not far from there in the little North Woods community of

Glidden, a town of about five hundred people a few miles north of Park Falls.

Visiting hours at the modern prison are generous. Guests may visit inmates for three hours at a time, then after a break, a second three-hour visit is allowed on the same day. The visiting room, filled with other inmates and their guests, is carefully watched over by a mix of male and female guards. Nevertheless, the atmosphere is fairly relaxed. Like other inmates, John is always dressed for visits in the dark green prison uniform trousers and shirt open at the neck with a white undershirt showing. But his hands and legs are free of cuffs and chains. Couples and families can buy soft drinks and snacks from vending machines in the room, and for a small fee to cover costs, guards will snap keepsake pictures with Polaroid cameras.

John obtained a prison job soon after arriving at CCI and earned thirty-three cents an hour. That was already considerably less than the $7.95 per hour he was earning at Winter Wood Products before his arrest. But even after he was assigned to a new job with a few-cents-an-hour pay cut, it was still enough to pay for tobacco, writing paper, and other incidentals.

Writing paper is as important to him as it has been throughout most of his life. Although his physical body could be placed behind bars, no one could lock up his mind, and he has continued to let his imagination run rampant, penning new sexual fantasies and filling his letters with lurid prose. One of his letters to his pen pal, apologizing for a falling-out, concluded with the words, "I love you babe!! Kiss me?? John." The message was scrawled in a smear of blood at the bottom of the page.

True to form, his verbal and written storytelling continues to make it difficult to determine when he is concocting whoppers and when he's telling the truth. Among the stories he recounted to his friend, is a claim that he drove Emily to work once or twice in the Sunbird while the dead body of her sister was still folded up in the trunk. He and Emily were separated and she was living with her parents at the time. Furthermore, Darla says, he told her he killed a man in a barroom brawl while he was in Germany. According to the story the victim was getting the best of one of the GIs, when John speared him with a knife throw.

He also frequently talked during their visits and in his letters about his evil alter ego, usually referring to the demonic hell spawn as "him," "he," or "his."

Eventually after a series of spats John and Darla called it quits, and at least for the time being their ambitious book project was put on hold. During one of their quarrels, in an effort to get under John's skin, Darla wrote a letter to Dahmer. She says that although he never replied, he later acknowledged during a brief meeting in the visiting room that he recognized her from her letter as John's friend. CCI has two inmates among the prison's population who have acknowledged at one time or another having indulged in cannibalism, and Darla went out of her way to develop a pen-pal friendship with both.

Although Darla and John apparently ended their on-again-off-again friendship for good in early 1994, his family support remains strong, and visitors have included his sister, Kathy. As a lifelong manipulator, it didn't take him long to adjust to prison. He still composes and writes short stories, maintains spirited correspondences with family members and other pen pals, plays softball, takes advantage of other recreational activities, and reads Stephen King novels.

He even quoted from a song a soldier sang in King's "The Eyes Of The Dragon, about a girl named "Darchy, Darchy Darla," who had a sister who was a redhead named Carla—and pointed out the eerie parallel to his pen pal. Her name is Darla, and Carla Lenz rinsed her hair with red tint shortly before she was killed. He noted other curious bits of coincidences and serendipity, as well. Prison inmates have a lot of time on their hands to ponder over such things.

For a while he attended group therapy sessions with other inmates, led by a trained social worker, but he didn't remain long before he dropped out. According to his friend he didn't like it because when he talked of his other self they insisted that he wasn't crazy, just bad. His secret companion didn't desert him for long and showed up again a couple of months after the arrest, his former pen pal disclosed.

Experts from the Behavioral Science Unit at the FBI Academy in Quantico, Virginia, interviewed John at the prison as part of their program of criminal profiling. The blockbuster novel and movie *Silence of the Lambs,* provided a fictional account of the work of the FBI's "Mind Hunters" who used criminal profiling to track a serial killer.

The Wisconsin Department of Criminal Investigation also reportedly made a study of the Weber case, including Moore's investigation techniques, and is using the information as part of its training program.

Nevertheless, many unanswered questions continue to puzzle authorities and residents of Price County. One of the most intriguing is the suspicion in some circles that John may have killed others. Shelly Hansen has never been found, and a local lawman indicated it's unlikely she ever will be. Where in Price County, with all its lakes and isolated forests, should you begin to look? he asked. The investigation of the case is still open, and the status is: "Missing. Foul play suspected."

And what really happened to John Kenney, Jr., before he was run over by the train? Did John Ray Weber have anything to do with the young man's death? A couple of years after conviction for the murderous attacks on Carla and Emily, evidence in the civil trial of a damage suit filed against the railroad by the teenager's parents indicated John may have knocked the boy out and placed him unconscious on the tracks. After the trial, however, all the evidence involving John was ordered stricken from the record. The mystery of young John Kenney's death, like the puzzle surrounding Shelly Hansen's disappearance, may never be solved.

There is also the story of the stabbing in Germany. Another young woman was mysteriously murdered at Fort Carson while John was stationed there. Still another is said to have been murdered in LaCrosse while he was living at the group home. But thousands of men and women were stationed at Fort Carson, and LaCrosse is a city of fifty thousand people with nearly as many more in suburbs and the rural county area. And John has never been named as a suspect in either case, or linked by military or civilian authorities to a murder in Germany.

It seems, however, that an uncommonly large number of people either vanished, were murdered, or otherwise died violently and suspiciously while John Ray Weber was around.

Chief Moore, for one, believes Carla was not John's only murder victim. "In my opinion, this wasn't John's first attempt. As far as we know this was his first killing, and Emily would have ultimately been his second," the chief said. But he added that considering the amount of preparation, "It's my personal opinion John has probably killed others." He conceded, however, there was no proof of that.

"After listening to the tape, how many more would there have been?" he asks. "He had plans on others, some of them not named of course, but others."

The other unanswered question that many people close to the strange case consider to be the most perplexing is the possibility of cannibalism—the dreaded *C* word that was so carefully excised from the guilt phase of the trial.

Chief Moore admits that he has had trouble getting a firm handle on it. "My mind has bounced back and forth on that," he says. "There've been times that I've thought or read through the transcript, and I thought he absolutely did those things." At one time he doubted it and believed the tape was merely an avenue for another of John's sexually sadistic fantasies. "But then, there're things he talked about on the tape that bring me back to believing," he says. "I guess it's anyone's guess."

Former *Daily Herald* reporter Mary Jo Kewley doesn't believe John is a cannibal. After covering the trial from start to finish and studying all the grisly details, she concluded that part of the tape was sexual fantasy. "I think he probably did a lot of the brutality," she says. "I have a hard time thinking he did any of the cannibalism. I think he was trying to freak out his wife."

But the tape is not the only disturbing factor that might lead one to believe John did, indeed, consume some of the flesh of his victim. What happened to Carla's leg? John said he sliced off a portion of her calf to make meat patties, and it seems significant that the leg from just about two inches above her knee was never recovered with the other remains. Of course it wouldn't be necessary to remove the leg to get to the calf. But could he have decided to keep it as a grisly trophy to satisfy one of his fetishes; or as a handy meat supply for further flesh eating? The idea seems almost too gross to contemplate—but that's typical of John's crimes.

There are other questions that beg to be answered, as well. What effect did John's addiction to pornography really have on his crimes? He was already cutting up lingerie in catalogue ads and slashing his sister's underwear and swimsuits long before he was old enough to begin collecting his own pornography. And he was only five-years-old when he smeared the feces on his grandmother's dress, an act that was certainly hostile and threatening to a female.

Moore believes pornography can become addictive, although he is careful to point out he doesn't think everyone who looks at it or reads it will necessarily be "hooked." But if there is already an attraction there, it may come to require a continual feeding with new material or new information, he says. "You need compulsive, obsessive behavior at first, but then one book isn't enough.

"In John's case, I think there may have been somewhat more of a direct relationship," he says. "The pornography induced the fantasy, and the fantasy was played out. He did that to the max."

The John Weber case is filled with questions that even the police who investigated, and the people who know him best, will never be able to answer fully. But most people the authors talked to in Phillips and Price County are satisfied merely to know that he will never roar down the streets and roads on his motorcycle or roam the local forests again.

Residents of the community were upset for a while after a three-judge interim Wisconsin State Appellate Court panel in Wausau unanimously overturned his convictions for the murder of Carla and the other offenses committed against her. The appeals court ruled on July 3, 1990, that playing the incriminating audiotape found in the Cutlass constituted an illegal search.

Judge Gordon Myse wrote in the opinion: "We reach this decision because we are compelled to do so by law. We, as a nation, must honor the Constitution sufficiently to apply its protections to everyone." The law does not apply only to those people who are deserving," he added.

The judge further wrote that the warrant police used for the search of the car did not cover the search of the tape. The court ruling went on to state: "While the discovery of the plastic cassette was the result of a plain-view search of the interior of the vehicle to which the officer had gained lawful entry as a result of the search warrant, this doctrine does not authorize search of the contents of the audiotape.

"The police are not entitled to seize an object that is in plain view unless it is immediately apparent that there is a connection between the object viewed and a crime." A bit further on in the opinion, Judge Myse conceded that the results of the case were "very disturbing." He added: "The fact that Weber must still serve sixty-three-years confinement does not mitigate the tragedy that an individual who engaged in such loathsome conduct must have his conviction for murder reversed.

"Some will say that the result in this case means that the system has failed. They will argue that so modest an infringement of the defendant's Constitutional rights should not have such severe consequences," he added of the legal nit-picking.

Others, however, would respond that there was "no such thing as a modest infringement of Constitutional rights," he continued. "They will contend that extending the rights guaranteed by our Constitution to one so despicable assures all citizens the protection by the Bill of Rights."

Lex predicted the decision would probably lead to a new trial related to the charges involving Carla. "We'd maintained all along that there were some Constitutional issues that had to be addressed," he was quoted in *The Milwaukee Sentinel* as saying.

If the ruling survived other higher steps in the appeals process, it appeared conceivable the notorious Price County criminal might someday during his lifetime become eligible for parole. And the judge's statements about protecting the rights of everyone, including a John Weber, had the air of an apology for a dreadfully troubling decision. No one took a poll, but there seemed to be little doubt that most of the convict's former neighbors in Price County would have indicated they were dead set against anything that might ever release him in their midst again.

At various times, with his own words, John had pinned the label on himself of murderer, sexual sadist, and cannibal. Now it appeared the appellate court had decided he was the victim of a legal misjustice who was practically forced to plead guilty to the kidnap and murder of Carla because of Judge Carlson's decision to allow the incriminating audiotape into evidence.

But John was never released, and it wasn't necessary to put him on trial again. The state appealed the ruling by the three-judge panel, and the Wisconsin State Supreme Court reversed the lower appellate court decision by a firm six-to-one margin. The justices ruled in the majority opinion that the seizure of the tape was valid.

Chief Justice Nathan S. Heffernan wrote that the issue before the court was the Constitutionality of the search and seizure. It was not "separate arguments that could be made defending or attacking the Constitutionality of the search and seizure."

Months later the Supreme Court upheld its earlier decision by the same six-to-one margin. The only dissent in both rulings was from the same jurist, Justice Shirley Abrahamson. Attorneys with the Appeals Division of the Wisconsin State Public Defender's Office, who handled the appeal, claimed the Supreme Court's earlier decision violated their client's rights because the justices decided the case on grounds that were never requested. There are no more pending appeals.

In Phillips, five years after John's convictions, Moore was still keeping the peace and looking out for the safety of his fellow citizens as chief of police. Investigator Heitkemper twice ran unsuccessfully against his boss for election to a two-year term as Price County sheriff. Although he had to obtain a court order to enable him to hang onto his job, there was talk in Price County that he would probably run against Wirsing again. Wirsing wouldn't consent to an interview for the book.

Barnett left the county district attorney's office and accepted a job with the Wisconsin State Attorney General's Office in Madison. Reid was still working out of the Wausau branch of the Public Defender's Office, and Lex continued to work out of the branch office in Merrill.

Many people in Phillips, who were willing to talk about John Weber and the lurid crimes he committed and left as his terrible legacy to the community where he grew up, preferred to speak anonymously. It's a small town, and people are trying to heal and to put the tragedy out of their minds.

Efforts were also made to contact Emily through her parents for an interview for the book, but she never responded. According to one source in Phillips she finally found herself a job in a flower shop or a hothouse. Another source indicated she was working at a sawmill in southern Price County. Whatever she may be doing today, the authors wish her well.

**ORDINARY LIVES DESTROYED BY EXTRAORDINARY HORROR.
FACTS MORE DANGEROUS THAN FICTION.
CAPTURE A PINNACLE TRUE CRIME . . . IF YOU DARE.**

LITTLE GIRL LOST (593, $4.99)
By Joan Merriam
When Anna Brackett, an elderly woman living alone, allowed two teenage girls into her home, she never realized that a brutal death awaited her. Within an hour, Mrs. Brackett would be savagely stabbed twenty-eight times. Her executioners were Shirley Katherine Wolf, 14, and Cindy Lee Collier, 15. *Little Girl Lost* examines how two adolescents were driven through neglect and sexual abuse to commit the ultimate crime.

HUSH, LITTLE BABY (541, $4.99)
By Jim Carrier
Darci Kayleen Pierce seemed to be the kind of woman you stand next to in the grocery store. However, Darci was obsessed with the need to be a mother. She desperately wanted a baby — any baby. On a summer day, Darci kidnapped a nine-month pregnant woman, strangled her, and performed a makeshift Cesarean section with a car key. In this arresting account, readers will learn how Pierce's tortured fantasy of motherhood spiralled into a bloody reality.

IN A FATHER'S RAGE (547, $4.99)
By Raymond Van Over
Dr. Kenneth Z. Taylor promised his third wife Teresa that he would mend his drug-addictive, violent ways. His vow didn't last. He nearly beat his bride to death on their honeymoon. This nuptial nightmare worsened until Taylor killed Teresa after allegedly catching her sexually abusing their infant son. Claiming to have been driven beyond a father's rage, Taylor was still found guilty of first degree murder. This gripping page-turner reveals how a marriage made in heaven can become a living hell.

I KNOW MY FIRST NAME IS STEVEN (563, $4.99)
By Mike Echols
A TV movie was based on this terrifying tale of abduction, child molesting, and brainwashing. Yet, a ray of hope shines through this evil swamp for Steven Stayner escaped from his captor and testified against the socially disturbed Kenneth Eugene Parnell. For seven years, Steven was shuttled across California under the assumed name of "Dennis Parnell." Despite the humiliations and degradations, Steven never lost sight of his origins or his courage.

RITES OF BURIAL (611, $4.99)
By Tom Jackman and Troy Cole
Many pundits believe that the atrocious murders and dismemberments performed by Robert Berdella may have inspired Jeffrey Dahmer. Berdella stalked and savagely tortured young men; sadistically photographing their suffering and ritualistically preserving totems from their deaths. Upon his arrest, police uncovered human skulls, envelopes of teeth, and a partially decomposed human head. This shocking expose is written by two men who worked daily on this case.

Available wherever paperbacks are sold, or order direct from the Publisher. Send cover price plus 50¢ per copy for mailing and handling to Penguin USA, P.O. Box 999, c/o Dept. 17109, Bergenfield, NJ 07621.Residents of New York and Tennessee must include sales tax. DO NOT SEND CASH.